WINTER'S

CHOSEN

Ash Parker

ISBN: 978-1-0687541-1-1 (paperback)

ISBN: 978-1-0687541-0-4 (e-book)

Cover art and book design by Ash Parker.

For my beautiful wife, who I miss very much

(who was mad about the ending of this book).

IFRY MARHEART

They travelled on the newest state line, which was hardly the luxury that its novelty might have suggested. Trains through the mountains weren't well-known for their efficiency.

"I expected better service," Townsend muttered. "Can they not provide a single refreshment?" He gazed at the carriage door as if the conductor might return with a decanter of whisky on a silver tray. He examined the arms of his seat, tracing a hole in the fabric with his forefinger.

"I don't think they have a dining car, sir," Ifry said. He thought that this might have been evident, as the train possessed only three carriages.

"Could you not ask them for refreshments? I'd accept some bread and butter."

Ifry fought the urge to tell his employer that he should have packed some food for the journey. However, Thomas Townsend had never been noted for his forethought. Townsend could not plan for love nor money, which was why he had Ifry as his personal employee. But when he was presented with a crisis, Townsend could not be matched.

"Don't make him do that. You know how he hates walking in between the carriages," said Oriana, who was curled up next to the frosted window.

"Aren't you peckish, Ori?" Townsend asked. Oriana frowned and reached into her pocket to produce a brown paper bag. Townsend took it and sniffed its contents.

"Liquorice. Again?"

Oriana had a sweet tooth that many found endearing, but that Townsend did not reciprocate. Oriana offered the bag to Ifry instead. He smiled discreetly and took one.

He and Oriana sat next to the window that overlooked the valley as they whistled past. They had been in the mountains all winter and not gotten tired of looking at them. "Do they know how long we will be?" Townsend asked of the carriage at large.

"I suppose it will be most of the day. There aren't many trains that go this way. It might depend on the conditions," said Ifry.

"Then why are we slowing down?"

Ifry glanced out the window and saw that he was right.

"I don't know," Ifry mumbled. Their destination, Racken, wasn't visible yet. Only woodland and a silver river threaded the valley below them.

"Marheart, go find out what the delay is."

"Thomas," Oriana began, but he interrupted her.

"Do you want to sit here like puppies waiting for a new owner? Marheart, go ask the conductor."

Ifry pulled himself upright without complaint. He braced himself as he approached the carriage door. The train was indeed moving more slowly, so he hoped that the crossing would not be as dizzying as it usually was. The real concern was the cold. It was far from pleasant to be hit by it, along with the high-speed winds and the knowledge that if the train lurched he could be sent tumbling to a very chilly death. He shivered, feeling for a moment as if he might throw up, and threw open the carriage door.

He fought the temptation to grab the railing to steady himself; from experience, he knew that it was fringed in sharp frost. He leapt across the gap in an ungainly fashion, stumbling as he landed. He clung onto the carriage door, trying not to look at the mountains that raced past, even as he felt the train slow its pace. He fumbled for the brass handle and ducked inside. As he crossed the length of the second empty carriage, the train lost the speed that remained.

As much as Townsend might complain about the lack of dining carriage and the threadbare seats, the carriage was downright tolerable compared to the engine. The carriage might have a musty smell that no amount of airing could shift, but Ifry choked on the coal-laden air as he crossed to the engine. He was greeted there by the conductor, whose worn station uniform now looked very smart against the overalls worn by the driving crew.

"What are you doing up here?" the conductor barked, in the heavy accent that indicated that he was from the mountains.

"I meant to inquire as to the reason for the delay," Ifry replied.

"Something on the line."

"An avalanche?" Ifry was concerned about avalanches. Back home in Darrity, Ifry had thought that avalanches were rare, but this high in the mountains, folk thought they were as normal as rain storms. The conductor tutted at him.

"Aren't we still on the tracks, boy?" He gestured at the mountainside window, which was free and clear of snow.

"Oh. What else then?"

"A janros."

"What is a janros?"

The conductor grunted and gestured to an open door, through which the wind whistled.

"Go look for yourself, tyenes," he said, using a mountain dialect word for 'townie'. Ifry knew it was not meant kindly, but approached the door without dispute.

He had not changed into his boots, so he hovered on the threshold of the engine and craned his neck to look at the tracks. The train crew had already cut furrows into the snow as they inspected the obstacle. Ifry had seen livestock on the train tracks before; his journey back into the city from a holiday had been interrupted by a poor cow who had died on the tracks. Ifry later learned that moving the creature had only taken a matter of minutes. Most of the delay was owed to the search for the cow's owner so they could pay a fine to the train company.

The janros was a great deal larger than a cow. Even slumped over the tracks, its shoulders were taller than the roof of the engine. Ifry had heard tell of creatures in the mountains, and seen the odd illustration of them in a scientific journal, but nothing had really conjured an accurate image. None of the other towns they had passed through received frequent visits from the monsters. The townsfolk knew of their existence and spoke of them with sincere tones, but had teams of hunters who kept their population in check. In the last town they'd visited, there was only one cross on the map that indicated a monster nest, and it had been well out of the way of any of the pistes.

Ifry was not prepared to see the janros laid in their way. He might have described it as a polar bear, but that would be like comparing a kitten to a lion. A polar bear would look petty against this creature. Its paws were larger than cartwheels. Each toe boasted a hooked claw that Ifry would have struggled to wrap his fist around. Even its head was larger than a bear's, with a wider jaw and teeth to match the claws. It was slumped with its head resting on a half-buried sleeper. Ifry stared. He had a fascination with looking at dead things that he always regretted. There was a rushing sound, like a busy wind down the tunnel of an underground station. It was a few moments longer before he saw that the creature's chest continued to rise and fall.

"It's alive," he gasped, even as the train crew with their tall boots approached it with grappling hooks. He whipped around to look at the conductor, who was chuckling.

"A janros never goes quickly."

"Should we not help it?"

"Foolish tyenes," the conductor muttered. "Even injured, it will take your arm off if you get close. What would be the point of helping it, only for it to steal livestock next summer, or maul another child to death? It's well that something got it."

Ifry gasped at his proclamation. Once, they had been driving in Townsend's new town car. They were going a little too fast, it had to be admitted, but the roads were emptying as dusk crept in. Ifry recalled the sickening clunk as the car went over the dog with a level of detail he would rather relinquish. Townsend had called for the chauffeur to stop right in the middle of the road and leapt out. The animal had been in a sorry state, to be sure, and Townsend thought its jaw had been cracked. He'd bundled it into his arms, not caring that the blood stained his shirt, and told the chauffeur to step on it. They'd delivered the dog to the nearest shelter, where it was declared to have a fighting chance at recovery. Townsend and Ifry had still been tipsy after a long business dinner and they'd filled the reception room with raucous cheers and cackles.

Ifry turned his nose up as he saw the train crew edge along the tracks.

They stopped short of their destination, and their eyes became trained on the rise and fall of the creature's chest.

Ifry pulled back from the doorway. He adjusted his suit jacket and shook his head, as if that would free his mind from the image. He turned to the conductor.

"How long will the delay be?"

"That depends."

"On what?"

"How much blood the creature has already lost."

Ifry grimaced and with a sharp nod to the conductor, departed the engine.

They were five hours behind schedule by the time they rolled into Racken station, which was scarcely worthy of the name, boasting only a shelter akin to a bus stop. The snow was coming down in such a frenzy that Ifry couldn't see the mountains that lined the valley. The conductor hurried them out of their carriage with their trunks and hopped back aboard without a second glance.

"He couldn't wait for the car to arrive, could he?" Townsend complained as the train rattled away. He turned up his collar and shuffled into the shelter. Oriana and Ifry tried to pull their trunks in alongside them, but quickly realised that they would have no room.

"There is a car coming for us, then?" Ifry asked.

"There had better be." Townsend stamped his feet and rubbed his arms to warm up.

"In this place, there's no telling," Ifry muttered to Oriana. He peered around but found that it was useless; even the roofs were hidden in the snowstorm. He could not hear the rumble of a motor car coming their way. He was sure that the town was small enough that a motor car could make it from end to end in ten minutes.

"Do you know the address?" Ifry asked Townsend. He was already shaking from the cold. He was not numb yet, though he knew he would be. His mind was caught, like a record on a gramophone, on the thought of being next to a roaring fire. Townsend grunted and reached into his jacket for his pocket book. Ifry found the page where Townsend had scribbled a list of lodgings for their trip. He ran his thumb down the list until he found the last entry.

"There's no one to ask for directions," Oriana pointed out.

"They have to have street signs, even this deep in the mountains." Ifry buttoned up his coat, though he suspected it would not do a great deal of good. "Better that I go and look. There can't be much point in waiting around here."

"I was told someone would meet us," Townsend muttered.

"I suspect the blizzard has made them forget themselves, sir."

"That doesn't bode well. If people in the mountains cannot deal with a blizzard, one must assume they are not equipped to live here."

"There could be any number of reasons, Thomas," said Oriana. "We were late, after all."

"The conductor should have radioed ahead," he huffed. Ifry ignored him and stepped out into the storm. He regretted the decision right away, as snow hit his face faster than if he had been going down a piste. He was not dressed for snow. He had worn a tweed suit for the train, and a wool pea coat he was rather fond of.

It was the very last place they were due. Townsend had brought his sister and his clerk with him to travel through the mountains looking for new places to build skiing resorts. He had several profitable locations already, but wanted to expand his franchise.

There had to be pistes. There would be one or two hand crank chair lifts, or perhaps even a gondola. Besides that, Townsend would need find suitable buildings for hotels and shops, or at least plots for them, and he would need contracts with their former owners.

At that minute, Ifry could not see anywhere that might be suitable for a hotel. There was a main street, thought it could scarcely be called that. There was one hand-painted sign that led him to Rosalind Street, and he praised the gods when he saw that the houses were numbered with red paint on their door frames. Now shivering violently, he approached the end and saw that it was occupied by a building that was larger than the rest. A turret with a bell indicated that it was a place of worship. There were grand columns over the door.

Townsend's address book had listed their residence as number fourteen, which was nestled against the temple fence. He did not knock. All politeness had been chased away by cold, so he turned the doorknob and stumbled inside. It was such a relief to be out of the driving snow that he did not quite register where he was. The warmth that overtook him made him sigh and close his eyes to bask in it.

"What are you doing here?" said a female voice. He opened his eyes to see a young woman, perhaps in her early twenties, with dark hair and a red scarf tied about her head. She was stood next to a blackened hearth, with an equally sooty cloth clutched in one hand. The room was a kitchen and living space all in one. There was a kitchen table with deep scratches on the legs; next to the hearth there was a bench and a couple of sagging armchairs. An iron pot was hung low over the fire. It looked like the parlour from a farmhouse from twenty years ago. Even as he knew that Townsend would disapprove, Ifry melted in the warmth of the scene.

"I am so sorry to barge in like this, but it is simply frightful out there." He smiled at the young woman and brushed snow out of his hair. "My name is Ifry Marheart, assistant to Mr Thomas Townsend. I believe he has booked lodging here."

"That city fellow?"

"Well, he certainly is that," Ifry said.

"Where is he then?"

"Huddled at the train station. He was expecting a car to pick him up."

"He won't find any motor cars in Racken."

"You know, I should have guessed that. Could I request some assistance in transporting our luggage then?"

She frowned and with some reluctance, replied, "I'll send Jos out with you."

She ducked through a low door, leaving Ifry to realise how damp his clothes were. The cold still bit at him. She returned with a tall man whose head almost brushed the ceiling beams. He was broad and wore a yellow coat that was stained at the sleeves and elbows, which offset brown skin and hair that was only a shade or two darker. His most prominent attribute was the scowl upon his face.

"This is the tyenes then?" He nodded at Ifry, who could not help but feel affronted, despite the neutrality of the statement.

"I would be him, yes." He had been taught to be polite even when others could not muster the energy to do so. He tore off his glove and held his right hand out.

"Ifry Marheart, sir."

"Jos Nothernine," he replied. He met Ifry's eye and grasped his hand. Ifry could feel the blisters on his palm, but his hand was so cold he might have held on just to warm up.

"And what do I call you, miss?"

"Eldersie Toft. This is my house. Jos boards here over winter."

"Just like us, then."

Jos Nothernine scowled at that. Ifry pulled his glove back on and winced at how wet it was.

"I'll fetch the cart." Nothernine tied a scarf over his face and departed; Ifry braced himself and followed.

The blizzard was much worse after being inside. He dug his hands into his pockets in a vain attempt to keep them warm in his wet gloves. Nothernine ploughed ahead as if there was naught amiss about walking through driving snow. He did not wait for Ifry, who lost sight of him not long after they had left Eldersie's house. Ifry only realised that it was because he had turned off the road as Nothernine crept up behind him, hauling a handcart.

"I hope you packed light, tyenes."

Ifry snorted. "My employer might disappoint you."

Nothernine was indeed disappointed as they arrived at the platform and he saw the trunks that were gathering snow.

"Hold this," he said to Ifry, and indicated that he meant for Ifry to keep the two-wheeled cart flat. He began to load luggage without acknowledging Townsend and Oriana, who were peering at him.

"It's not far," Ifry called to them. Even through the snow he could see Townsend sneer. Oriana lifted the end of one trunk and gestured for her brother to join her. Knowing that he was being shown up by his sister, Townsend helped lift the trunk into the cart.

In the end, Nothernine had to take two trips to transport their belongings to Eldersie's house. Ifry knew he should have offered his own assistance, but after two trips of his own outside, his grey coat had turned white with the snow that clung to it. His teeth were not chattering, but he thought they may as well be. He could not convince himself to step outdoors again. Still, there was work to be done. He had to brush off the snow from the lids of the trunks and towel them down with a cloth lent by Eldersie.

Oriana came to check on him when, after half an hour, he was still shaking. Despite his protests that nothing was amiss, she made him sit in front of Eldersie's hearth while she unpacked the trunks. It was not long before he had to take over, however. Oriana never folded her own clothing at home.

Eldersie's house was not large. It was narrow, like a townhouse in the city. The ground floor had the kitchen-cum-living space and, Ifry was perturbed to learn, lacked indoor plumbing. There was an outhouse and chamber pots under the bed in lieu of a bathroom. On the first floor, there were two box-like rooms for Townsend and Oriana opposite Eldersie's own; the attic housed Nothernine and Ifry, as well as Eldersie's elderly father, whom she informed Ifry that he was to ignore. The eaves were so low that Ifry could not walk without stooping. He could not imagine that

Nothernine, standing almost a foot taller than Ifry, could find any comfort in their quarters.

Ifry hung all of Townsend's shirts in his wardrobe while Townsend convinced Eldersie to warm him water for a bath, then sorted Oriana's clothes as Eldersie carried up pails of water to be heated over the hearth. Townsend complained about the time it would take for the water to heat, but quietened when he was safely ensconced in the bath.

Ifry climbed up to the attic. He had a trunk of his own, but the staircase was so skinny that it could barely fit through. He could only lift it by one end, bumping it on every step. He got stuck, the sides of the trunk scraping against the walls of the stairwell, ruining the paintwork.

He heard footsteps and dread seeped into his bones, expecting Eldersie to reprimand him for scraping his trunk along her stairs. It was Nothernine instead, filling the doorway and brushing his head on the ceiling. Ifry almost dropped the trunk onto him. Nothernine put his hands up to catch it.

"You ought to travel lighter," he said, giving the trunk a push that made Ifry stumble.

"You mean I should travel less. We have been in the mountains for months."

"You missing tyenes life?"

Ifry could not mistake the tone of his voice. There was no cheer to the way he said tyenes.

"Why, yes. You would miss your home too if you had been gone for as long as I have."

"I wouldn't know." He grasped the end of the trunk and lifted it up. "Can we move this, or will you block the stairs forever?" Ifry frowned, but lifted the trunk as best he could, while Nothernine seemed not to notice the weight of it at all. They carried it to Ifry's room, though it became clear that putting the trunk in the room would remove all of the available floor space.

"Stick it in the hallway," said Nothernine. "Empty it, then take the trunk down to Eldersie's cellar."

"Probably wise," Ifry agreed, stepping over the trunk, as the corridor was not wide.

"Thank you, sir, for your help." Ifry began to root around in his pockets for a coin to give him. Nothernine sneered and opened the door to his room. Ifry caught a sight of it. There was a shotgun leaning against the wall, with a case of ammunition next to it. The door shut before Ifry could take another measure of Jos Nothernine.

ORIANA TOWNSEND

Oriana thought that Racken could win an award for being the dullest town in the country. Thomas had spent the whole journey singing praises for the resort he had planned. Racken was to be a place where young attractive people went for the season to take in the mountain air, play on risky slopes and drink at lounges in furs and pearls. The idea appealed to Oriana. She had had enough of amateurs on the slopes, of children who skied all in a line, and every other tourist with poor technique. Thomas' other resorts were fine enough, but the families were too well-to-do. There was not nearly enough debauchery.

Thomas had promised that in Racken, there would be plenty of space for lounges right off the slopes, so you could finish a day on skis by walking right up to the bar.

But there was no hotel, and the boarding house they had come to was poky and musty, and staffed only by its owner. She had half-admired Eldersie until she opened her mouth. She was pretty, though far from fashionable, but ruined her first impression by ignoring her new guests.

Oriana's first need in every town was to find a companion of some kind, even if it was just a servant. She loathed drinking alone, but in Racken, she considered her prospects to be poor.

She tossed her coat onto the one rickety chair her room possessed. There was no coat rack to be found, and Ifry had needed to use all the space in the wardrobe for her clothes. As she lay back on the bed, she could not imagine that she'd get a wink of sleep. The sheets were a dusty colour that Oriana suspected had once been white, and there were scratches on the legs of the bed that she had to assume came from a cat, though she had seen no sign of one inside the house. There was one minuscule window that was shuttered against the snow; the walls were panelled in the same orangey wood that covered the floor. It was monotonous, and it was tasteless.

"I am going to lose my mind here," she said. There was no one around to comment on it.

Thomas was in the bath and he was always a bore, anyway. Still, there was the option she had always come to rely on.

She retrieved thick socks and the sheepskin slippers that she had had made up after their last trip to the mountains. The stairs up to the attic were steep, and Oriana could only be grateful that she hadn't yet been drinking from the flask she kept in her pocket. Thomas had watched her too closely on the train. He would only judge, she knew. It was so dark in the attic that she needed to feel her way through. She collided with the banister and cursed that no one had thought to put a candle out. She ran her hand along the wall and felt the surface of a door, so she knocked thrice and waited. The door opened and Oriana saw the face of an old man with watery eyes. He held a candle that had burned down to a stub.

"What're you?" he asked, looking Oriana up and down. Oriana hoped for one foolish moment that she might not notice if she vanished back into the dark. She had no desire to interact with her landlady's shut-in father.

"My apologies," she said. "I seem to have the wrong room."

"You need the door over there. On the right, lass. That's where your boy's sleeping."

"He is my brother's clerk," she replied, affronted that he had referred to Ifry so, as if she were his mother. The old man made no response but to shut his door and she was left in the dark again. She tried to step across the corridor, but felt her legs smack into an object.

"Shit." She hopped up and down, cursing Eldersie for having such a mismanaged house.

"Oriana?" She heard a whisper, and a door opened. Ifry stood there in his shirt sleeves, the faint glow of a candle behind him. Looking down, Oriana saw that she had walked right into his trunk.

"Why did you leave this in the way?" she asked.

"There's nowhere else. I'll move it to the cellar in the morning."

Oriana sneered at the trunk. "This place is hardly adequate."

"I have seen a lot worse, Ori." He smiled. She could not imagine that he actually had. Ifry was just a humble sort. She walked past him, pushing his shoulder back ever so slightly, just because she could. She shook her jacket so that her flask sloshed loudly enough for him to hear.

"Drink?" She smiled at him.

"You've had that in your pocket all the way here?"

"Yes. It took some courage not to down that thing while we had that delay."

"Forgive me for not being prouder of you. I managed the delay myself without temptation." He hovered by the door, which was still wide open, and spoke in whispers. Oriana reached across him and pulled the door closed.

"Ori, I am not in the mood."

"Just a tipple," she said. "This is pretty poor." She gestured around Ifry's room, which was even more paltry than Oriana's. She could not stand up straight without brushing her head on the ceiling.

"It's about what I expected. We knew that no one in Racken was wealthy." He shrugged as Oriana lounged on his bed.

"It's only brandy. Warming stuff." She offered it to him. He relented and took it, taking a small sip before he passed it back. He did not sit down next to her, preferring to lean his back against the wall. Oriana could feel the edges of a sulky mood. "What am I to do in this place?" she said-.

"Just what you've been doing in other towns," he said.

"The other towns had more *people.*"

"Sure, there isn't a lot of infrastructure here–"

"There isn't even a station," she groaned.

"You could help with the accounts. I know that you're better with numbers than you say you are."

She puffed her cheeks to show her disapproval.

"I am going to die of boredom. You simply have to entertain me, or I will perish."

"Would that I could, Ori. If a resort in Racken is really possible, then there will be a veritable mountain of work to comb through."

"Ifry, you are boring me *more*."

"Ori, I should sleep."

"When I lose my mind in this place, I'll have you personally take me to the asylum."

"I will have a couple of good ones on stand by." He held out his hand. Oriana did not take it. There had been a time when her dull days in the mountains were saved by Ifry's chatter. She slid off the bed and screwed the cap of the flask back on.

"Night then, Ifry." She pushed past him and back into the dark hall.

She could not sleep. She was agitated. Her mother used to be the same; she would call it having bees on her brain. She did not return to her bedroom, but descended to the ground floor.

Downstairs was smokey; Oriana assumed that the chimney was ineffective. Of course, this forsaken place lacked chimney sweeps, as it lacked in everything else. She coughed as she came down the last few steps, grateful that, at the very least, the house did not lack for banisters.

"Father?" called a voice. There were footsteps and she saw Eldersie's round face appear. "What are you looking for?" asked Eldersie.

Oriana thought that her rude tone was inappropriate for guests, but had to assume that it was another provincial failing.

"I was looking for tea," she lied, supposing that rude company was better than none. Eldersie huffed but lifted a hefty black kettle over the fire. She had drawn a threadbare little armchair up to the hearth. A silver tray was laid in front of it, the only thing of luxury that Oriana had seen in the whole house. Eldersie fussed about, retrieving cups and saucers, while Oriana lifted one of the dining chairs in place alongside the armchair. She saw that the tray was loaded with biscuits that were cut in the shape of sunbursts. She reached for one.

Eldersie crossed the room faster than a motor car to slap Oriana's hand away. The biscuit fell to the tray and snapped in half.

"Those are not for you," she said.

Oriana frowned. The other residents had gone to bed. Was Eldersie expecting a horde of midnight guests?

Eldersie slammed the tea set down on the hearth stones. Oriana noted that the cups did not match the saucers and all were chipped. She picked up the broken pieces of Oriana's biscuit and tossed them into the fire.

"What was that for?"

Eldersie ignored her question as she settled back into her armchair. The kettle whistled. Oriana stared at her, wondering if she was deaf. She had to be able to hear the kettle singing. Was she going to get the kettle, or did she not know how to boil water? Eldersie turned and met Oriana's eye.

"The kettle," said Eldersie. If she wasn't deaf, she certainly had to be stupid. The kettle whistled louder, and Eldersie continued to stare at Oriana as if she had no idea how tea was made.

"For pity's sake," Oriana said. She stood and took a tea towel from a stack on a sideboard. Wrapping it around her hand, she hefted the kettle off the fire and poured it into the teapot. She slammed it back down onto one of the hearth stones and slumped into her chair. "Now, wasn't that easy?"

"Yes," Eldersie replied. "It was."

"Will you let me have a biscuit, or are all the imperfect ones condemned to the flames?"

Eldersie drew the silver tray away from Oriana.

"They're all for the flames."

"Why make biscuits for fire? What monster are you feeding in there?"

Eldersie frowned and threw another biscuit. It crackled in the fire, releasing puffs of steam.

"Have you not made offerings before?" Eldersie asked.

Oriana shrugged. She had not been inside any temple since she still sat on her mother's knee. She could not say what offerings were usually made in the city. She suspected that it was money, and it was not burned, but collected in a red lacquered tin.

"Do you not worship in Darrity?"

"Oh, I am sure some people do. There's all sorts of gods to choose from, all brought from different places, you know. My brother and I have never been frequent visitors."

"I suppose it is different in the city." Eldersie turned a biscuit over in her hand then flicked it into the hearth.

"Who are these for? The god of baked goods?"

Eldersie scoffed.

"You are out of touch," she said. "I knew people in the city were bad, but I did not think it was that dire."

Oriana laughed at this. "Tell me what I don't know."

"These are for mighty Solyon," Eldersie said, holding up the sun biscuit for Oriana to examine. Oriana reached out to take it, but Eldersie slapped her hand away.

"Who - in all that is good and proper - is Solyon? And does he have a belly big enough for all these biscuits?"

Eldersie laughed. "What would you know? You owe more to Solyon than you imagine."

"Do I now?"

"Solyon is the god of summer. Without him, it would always be winter."

"Would it now?" Oriana took her turn to laugh.

"I would not laugh at things that you do not understand. You tyenes are ignorant as you are lavish. Solyon is real, and the folk of Racken would know."

"How's that? Are you the chosen few?"

"It isn't a matter of being chosen. It's a matter of proximity."

"Proximity?" Oriana raised her eyebrows. "If that's the case, why aren't you popping by with a basket of these? You can put a piece of gingham over them, ring the doorbell to see if Solyon's in–"

"I would not prattle on, if I were you." Eldersie began to pour herself tea, but her expression was as cool as the frost on her windowpanes.

"Is Solyon listening at the door?"

"No. He's far up."

"Up?"

Eldersie's eyes drifted towards the ceiling. Oriana opened her mouth to ask if Solyon was renting one of the upstairs rooms, but she saw that Eldersie's eyes rested on the shuttered window on the back wall. She was thinking of the mountain.

"Solyon does not reveal himself to just anyone. But we make offerings all the same. It is good faith."

"Who are the chosen few?" Oriana asked, thinking to press the subject until the seams of her belief were laid bare.

"The what?"

"You said he does not speak to just anyone. But he speaks to someone."

Eldersie smiled wide enough to show teeth. "Not a few. Just one."

"Who's the special person?"

"The elect."

"Is that not a fancier way of saying a special person?" Oriana was beginning to doubt whether it had been worth alleviating her boredom with religious talk. That was almost the worst kind of talk, just after the way new parents spoke about their babies.

"The elect is a special person. Every year, as midwinter closes in, Solyon chooses a champion from the people of Racken."

"Is there a ceremony? With fire? And funny hats?"

Eldersie rolled her eyes. "Religion in the city must be extravagant.

Solyon reveals himself to the elect alone. Solyon has a counterpart. The goddess of winter. She chooses her own elect. It's quite simple. No funny hats."

"You need to work on your rituals, perhaps. Too simple, and a religion has nothing going for it. You might even make it to the city if you had some funny hats."

Eldersie laughed, but said nothing more of the matter. She had noticed something just beyond Oriana's shoulder. For a mad moment, Oriana feared that godliness had come to pester them.

"Stay still," Eldersie commanded, as she drew herself up. She had the air of a creature caught by a predator. Oriana, startled by her change in tone, could only think to obey.

Eldersie reached for the worn handle of a broomstick. Oriana held her breath. Eldersie, faster than a whip, grasped the broom and raised it. It whooshed over Oriana's head, so fast that she felt the air move, and cracked against the stones. Oriana spun in her seat. She saw Eldersie holding the broom against the flagstones. A small, black creature was trapped by it, squealing and thrashing. It was too small to be a rat, but far too large to be a mouse. It was blacker than soot, too, while most rodents were a dull and varied brown. Its nose was long in a manner that Oriana thought unnatural, as if it needed to sniff in crannies that were untouched by other creatures. Even stranger was its lack of eyes. Where the sockets would have been on a mouse, there was only fur, without even a dent where they would have existed.

"Damned trits," said Eldersie. She turned the broomstick and it bit into the creature. It stopped thrashing; something rich and dark leaked onto the flagstones. "You see one of these, kill it while you can. They won't see you coming."

"I think it's high time I get to bed." Oriana placed her teacup back on the hearth side.

"I thought you might have a stronger stomach than that." Eldersie chuckled and picked up the trit's body with her bare hand. She tossed it into the fire. "You must have seen those in the mountains before."

"A strong stomach, yes. But an empty one, and I can't stand seeing good food wasted." She gestured to the empty biscuit tray.

"Just because something is not used on you, does not mean that it was wasted," Eldersie said. The flames wrapped around the trit like a blanket, mercifully covering it from view.

JOS NOTHERNINE

Dawn had not broken when he woke. This was not irregular; Jos was a hunter by trade. Hunters did not get to lie in.

He longed for the thaw. Then he would go back to his own house. It was too far up the slopes to be a practical home during the deepest snows.

He was grateful that Eldersie put him up year on year. It was habit. He stayed with her because he always had done, though he would rather be elsewhere. They were used to one another. The tyenes were another thing altogether.

People like them breezed through Racken. They didn't stay long. The railway men had done that, rolling through the town and leaving their mess behind them. They had brought more people than Jos had seen in his life. They'd filled up the drinking house and bought up all the rooms in Eldersie's house. Every able-bodied person in Racken had been drafted in to shovel dirt. When it was done, the workers and the businessmen and architects carried on down the line, and when they were gone, the dirt was piled high in the streets, the broken barrows and handleless shovels abandoned along the line. Racken's land had been turned over and ruined by tramping feet or hungry hands. Jos did not care to have more mess to clean.

The snows were fresh and clean as new down pillows as he climbed the mountain. Eldersie's house backed onto the southern slopes of the valley. He lived on the northern side, where the slopes were less treacherous. While there was decent pasture at the foot of the nearest slope, it rose sharply. There was a brook, a pencil line drawn across the slope. Jos knew to avoid it. The surface of the brook froze thinly, while water flowed underneath. As the night shifted and chilled, the stream thawed and froze in turn. In the past, he had stepped on the unseen edges and felt cold water fill his boots.

Jos leapt over a particular patch with practiced ease. To the untrained eye, it would have been just another step on the path, but Jos knew that a cattle grate was hidden under a crust of snow. Once he was past this, it was not tough going. Sure, the snows became as tall as his thighs, but there were no further obstacles. He was out of Racken proper. There weren't any paths out here, even in the summer. No one had cause to climb this slope. It was too steep and too wooded.

Jos followed the brook up to where it tumbled over the rock face. This winter had been particularly harsh, and the fall was frozen through. Jos did not understand why some people - tyenes mostly - found it beautiful. Water didn't freeze in the graceful lines that it flowed in, it stuck in place in yellowish spikes like the bones of a jagged creature. The waterfall was not wide like the cascades he saw illustrated on postcards. It was a measly thing, with ice bunched over rocks like joints.

The path up the cascade was even uglier. At points the slope was sheer and he was forced to haul himself up the rock with his arms.

There was a ledge halfway up that he knew to be comfortable seat. Perched there, he had a vantage point that overlooked all of Racken. The temple spire caught his eye. The sun emblem on its peak glittered in the growing dawn light. Elsewhere, the wide roofs boasted fresh layers of snow, and the roads were glistening and unblemished. He stared across the valley in the hopes of seeing his house. It was useless. The snows were most likely piled up to the eaves.

The railway cut through the town like a blade. No roads in Racken were straight; just like the river, they bent and wandered. But the railway men had had all sorts of instruments to make the line exact. He couldn't imagine how they did that, all the way across the country. One of them - he'd worn a top hat all day, even in the mountain air - told Jos that the line was almost a straight shot to Darrity. A long shot, to be sure, but a straight one.

Jos shook his head. What good was there in dwelling on thoughts of a far away city when there was a job to be done? He pulled himself the rest of the way up the falls. From there, it was another walk to his destination. Once, he would have not made it without rest, but the years hunting alone had made him strong.

Solyon had chosen well; for years he had been growing stronger. He had lifted wood and hay bales and kid goats. The idea had blistered in the back of his mind that if he got strong enough, he might draw Solyon's eye. It had evidently worked.

Solyon had told Jos where to go in the first dream he had sent him. It had been simple. He had been walking, then climbing the slope next to the waterfall. In the dream it had been bubbling away and the grasses swayed in the wind. The sun warmed him. What else for the god of summer? It was damned inconvenient though. Jos had spent hours wandering, looking for where the path was hidden under the snow. It had gotten dark and he'd wasted his first chance to meet Solyon. He had wished that Solyon was more conveniently placed.

Even now, Solyon's grove was like summer captured on film. As he walked through the trees, Jos felt snowmelt dripping from branches above him. The mud was soft enough to show his footprints. The wind died.

He still saw the snow-capped peaks beyond the clearing, but the grove was anything but cold. Deciduous trees reached their leafy arms down to the ground and brushed against the buttered heads of dandelions. It was an impossible place.

Solyon sat at the centre of the grove, on a fallen log with Flowers growing through the cracks in its bark. Jos tugged off his hood and gloves, already feeling uncomfortable under his layers.

"Sir?" Jos never knew how to address him. He had no title. It felt too wordy to call him 'Mighty Solyon' as Eldersie would have. Jos had settled on 'sir', even if Solyon laughed every time he used it.

Indeed, Solyon chuckled then, and turned to face Jos. He seemed middle-aged, with crinkles around his eyes, and he sat cross-legged even when it did not look comfortable. His clothes were golden, but Jos could not recognise the fabric. His skin was a darker brown than Jos's own, and Jos was already one of the brownest people in Racken.

Most strikingly of all, Solyon had an authority to him. Perhaps it was the grey threaded through his temples, or his voice, which boomed even when it wasn't raised.

"You're late," he said.

"Am I? You said dawn. I came as quickly as I could."

"That's fair enough." Solyon plucked a dandelion clock and blew on it, spinning the seeds into the air. They fell like snow.

"What news have you for me, sir?" Jos asked. He had come to learn that Solyon did not summon him for light talk.

"Volana is tricksy still."

"Has her elect not revealed themselves?" They had a stubborn one that year, it seemed.

"You would know if they had. No, I suspect that Volana has not yet chosen her elect."

"Not chosen?"

"Yes, did you not hear me?"

"I did. I just did not understand."

"It's not your business to understand the whim's of winter's goddess."

"I did not know she could delay choosing her elect."

"She does as she will. She always has." Solyon stared past Jos and at something he could not see. "She has always been awkward. She lives only to torment me with her actions. Bloody woman."

"I cannot do my task as the elect if Volana hasn't picked anyone," Jos said. It was rather obvious, but he often found that Solyon had to be led to information. If he had been ordinary, Jos would have said he was a flighty sort.

"Is that not obvious, Nothernine? It may be some time yet. Who are the candidates in your life?"

"No one," Jos said, trying not to feel saddened by the statement.

"What about the girl?" Solyon sneered.

"Eldersie? It wouldn't be her."

"Volana knows how to manipulate you all. Is she not your intended?"

Jos snorted, then remembered that he was in the presence of a god.

"Oh. No. Not at all."

"Wise. Marriage is a foolish preoccupation."

Jos nodded. Solyon always cast his judgements on mortal ways.

"I will keep alert," Jos said. "And I have been keeping myself separate. For all Volana knows, Eldersie is only my landlady."

Solyon tutted.

"She sees more than you think."

As Jos left the clearing, the wind attacked him once more. He glanced back and could not see where it had been. It might as well not have been there at all.

IFRY MARHEART

"How long have you been awake?" Townsend asked Ifry. The tiniest flame danced in the kitchen's hearth. Eldersie busied herself carrying a pail of water in through her front door. "And what's that taking so long for?" Townsend asked her. He had a coffee pot waiting in front of him.

"You should try drawing water from a frozen pump." She thumped the pail down in front of him. A little of the water slopped over the rim. "Build the fire, maybe, and this would go faster."

She left to fetch another pail. Townsend looked at the fire, but made no attempt to follow her instructions. Ifry walked over instead, adding a log from the pile that had been stacked alongside the hearth. He decided not to inform Townsend that he had only just woken. The cold was bothering him. It made him think of the past, when he was a child who played in the snow and cried when snow melted inside his boot. An old nightmare lurked at the edges of his mind, but he drowned it out with concentration upon his task.

The log crackled and Ifry hovered by it, knowing that shivers were building in him. Townsend opened his journal and flicked through the pages.

"I suspect that I won't be scouting for buildings here as I did elsewhere," he mused. "I have not yet investigated, but from reports there is no real infrastructure. Plenty of land however, which is where we should focus our efforts. We need a plot next to the railway line for our hotel; perhaps we could buy right next to the platform. That would be a fine thing. Guests could walk right off the train and up to the hotel door."

"Do you need me to make inquiries?" Ifry asked.

"No, no. I think I'll start with that myself." Townsend tapped the end of his pen on the pad of paper. Eldersie clattered back through the door, sloshing ice water over the toes of her boots.

"Do you need me to accompany you, sir? I can have the contracts drawn up before we speak to the landowners," said Ifry.

"I am sure that they won't be any different from the ones you have written before. No, no. I need you to investigate the slopes."

Eldersie shuffled past the hearth and Ifry leapt out of her way. She dumped the pail. Droplets slipped down the sides and pooled on the floor.

"But sir–" Ifry was interrupted as Eldersie reached over him to pick a clay cup off a shelf. She dipped it into the pail and used it to siphon water into the kettle.

"What was that, Marheart?"

"Sir - in every other town there has been - well - a structure to the pistes. Either there were pistes marked prior to our arrival, or I had an experienced guide to show me where to look."

"Should you not count yourself as experienced by now?"

"Not in the matter of Racken, sir."

Ifry was startled as something icy was pressed into his hand. His fingers closed around the cup, which was slimy with water. He had not felt Eldersie's fingers, they were so cold. She paid him no mind, as she moved to fussing around in her pantry. Ifry looked down at the half-empty kettle and realised that she had meant for him to finish the task.

"You're perfectly capable, Marheart." Townsend made another note, not looking at Ifry. He was interrupted as Eldersie returned, slamming a board with day-old bread onto the table in front of him. Crumbs spilled across his journal. Eldersie clicked her fingers at Ifry, who panicked and dipped his whole hand into the pail. He winced as the water crept up his sleeve. The chill, while isolated to his hand, made his limbs seize with an imagined cold.

Eldersie opened her jar, revealing porridge oats, which she began to siphon into a bowl, all while staring at the unboiled kettle. Ifry sloshed water over his front in his hurry to get the pot filled. He turned his back slightly so Townsend would not see his clumsiness.

"Sir, I don't think I should be going alone," he said between cupfuls of water.

"You can manage, Marheart." Townsend shuffled to one side as Eldersie set the table around him, shuffling mismatched knives and forks into place.

"But sir–"

"Marheart, where's that coffee?"

Ifry let the cup slip from his fingers and sink into the dark water. He reached for the kettle and fumbled around looking for the lid. Eldersie appeared at his side, producing the lid from her apron pocket. She put it in place and vanished again.

Ifry grasped the handle of the kettle and heaved. He stumbled, the water sloshing around inside, nearly putting him off balance. He tried again, knowing that he was screwing his face up in an unflattering expression. He stifled a groan and pulled his arms towards his chest, lifting the kettle up, feeling the heat from the fire on his cold fingers. He failed, missing the fire by a narrow margin and dropped the kettle onto the hearth stones. The lid rattled in place and he let out a trapped breath.

"What's the matter?" Townsend asked. Eldersie clattered back into the room, carrying a tray with dirty plates and a tin mug that wobbled on the tray. She saw Ifry, hands clutched around the kettle and breathless. She slammed the tray down, marched to the hearth side and heaved the kettle onto its hook herself. She muttered something that Ifry could not hear, but he would have bet it was 'tyenes'.

"Coffee should be on the way now, sir."

Townsend smirked, seeing Eldersie stoke the fire.

"I'm glad to hear it, Marheart. Now, about those slopes–"

"I simply cannot do it, sir."

"You will have to, or you will have to stay here all summer supervising the installation of chair lifts in unsafe locations."

"If summer ever comes," said Eldersie, as she hacked at the bread with a blunt knife. Townsend gave her a quizzical look.

"Well, if all goes to plan, we shall be back in the city before summer."

He should have known. Words meant nothing in the face of

Townsend's schedule.

Ifry changed into his warmest coat and trousers. He almost tripped on his empty trunk as he left his room. Jos's door swung open, and Ifry saw that the shotgun was missing.

Armed with his skis and poles, Ifry set out for the slopes.

He did not know where to begin. They had acquired no maps of Racken, as none seemed to exist. He supposed that he did not yet need to venture too far from Eldersie's house. There was a slope rising behind the house that looked promising. Ifry strapped his skis to his feet and set to work side-stepping up the mountainside.

It transpired that the slope was steeper than Ifry had imagined; the sunlight on the snow made everything look flat. Townsend wanted to find difficult slopes, so what use would there be in abandoning the first one he found? No, he needed to find the top, or a ledge where they might set a chair lift.

He pressed forward, stepping over some bumps that lay in his path—moguls, he remembered Townsend calling them. He would have to make a note of that. If there were boulders underneath the snow, they would have to mark the edge of the piste further in, so no one would break their skis on their way home. That sort of thing would be hell for insurance.

He climbed, cutting the edges of his skis into the snow, standing perpendicular to the slope. Below, he could see Racken unfolding along the valley. He stopped for a moment to examine it, having seen almost nothing of the place in the blizzard of the night before.

It was a quaint little place, with two rows of squat townhouses along the main road. Ifry could spot the belching chimney of Eldersie's house at the end of one row and noticed that there were tiles missing from her roof. Next door was the temple; someone had swept the path to the front door clear of snow, despite the early hour. Beyond the main street, there were the wide-roofed dwellings Ifry had come to expect in the mountains. They were wherever the land would allow, rather than where it was convenient. They always had stone ground floors, where the animals might live, then, as if the builders had run out of bricks, the upper floors were erected with lacquered timber. Such buildings would have long since burned down in the city, though Ifry supposed the eaves were too laden with snow for them to burn entirely.

The timber was pleasant, Ifry supposed. In every mountain town, as in Racken, there were carved window boxes and painted lintels and roof trims. In Townsend's resorts, guests could purchase postcards with the houses daubed in watercolour.

Most of Racken was devoted to its livestock; Ifry could tell, even though the animals were shut away for the winter. The snow was marked by the lines of fences. Every house boasted a trough outside and a post to bridle horses to.

Ifry knew little and less about keeping livestock, but it did not matter. In all of Townsend's resorts the industry changed; They could not house guests in buildings where the livestock also slumbered.

He pulled his feet up the slope. He skirted the moguls, noting that they were in fact much larger than he had imagined. Foiled by shadows over snow again.

As he climbed, he thought that he could hear a rumbling. His gaze snapped up to the peak, fearing an avalanche was about to catch him. But he saw none of the signs: no trees fell, and there were no creaks and aches as they were pushed aside. He could see none of the snow thrown up like smoke. Perhaps a train was about to pass through Racken? But the sound did not quite match that, and he could not see engine smoke approaching down the seam of the valley. Ifry also knew that there was no one in town with a motor car. It was something else, and as he moved it only became louder. He continued climbing, and the rumbling persisted. The noise appeared to follow him.

He stopped and peered behind him, feeling mighty silly. What was he thinking? That a monster from under the bed was stalking him? It was most likely a trick of the wind. He needed to press on, or he would be drawing up all the piste maps by candlelight.

He took another step up the mountain, but when he moved to lift his lower foot, he found that he could not. There was a weight pressing on the back of his ski. He turned as much as he could without moving his feet. It looked as if Ifry had skied into a snow drift backwards, but that could not be so; he had traversed the same section only a minute past and the way had been free and clear. Looking downhill, he saw that he appeared to be no further from the moguls than when he thought he had passed them. In fact, looking at the nearest one, he saw a dent in the snow behind it, like it had dragged itself a yard uphill.

The rumbling grew louder. Snow vibrated on the top of the mound that held him, and the three others nearby. Drifts of snow slid off their backs–as now Ifry could see that they had backs, and spines, and heads that they raised towards Ifry.

He could not have named them, though he had encountered one of their kind before. In one of Townsend's other resorts, they had closed one piste when a beast was spotted lurking under the powder. Ifry wouldn't have connected the beast he saw that day to the ones that tailed him now; two workmen had dispatched it by scooping it into a sack. The thing had only been the length of Ifry's forearm, and the workmen beat the sack against a rock until it turned red and called the job done.

The beasts that leered at him now were the size of the dogs that guarded city banks. They couldn't be stuffed in a sack and dispensed with in one sharp swing.

He had not gotten a good enough look at the beast last time. He had only gone along because Townsend had heard Oriana was skiing down that slope. She had been passed out in one of the bars instead.

He was having rather a good look now. They had pinched faces and six black eyes, like a fly. They didn't have jaws and teeth, but pincers, much as spiders had. Long-taloned paws grasped the end of Ifry's ski. White fur on their backs gave way to pale skin, with veins that pulsed blue through bat-like wings.

The creature nearest to Ifry roared, though not in the deep, throaty way Ifry had heard lions roar in moving pictures. It was more like a squeal, so shrill it made Ifry wince. It lunged, trying to pin Ifry with its talons. Ifry, who still had a few wits left about him, leapt aside.

Unfortunately, the side to which he leapt was downhill, and the damned thing still had one ski under its paw. Ifry crashed face first into the snow and rolled, cracking his elbows on the ice. He threw out one hand to stop himself. He would have loved a moment to find his feet, but the creatures were above him and growling. He tried to get up and found that he had lost the ski the creature had pinned, scuppering any plans of skiing to safety.

He did not have long to dwell on this discovery. He did not even have time to roll onto his back before he was pinned by a creature. He coughed, struggling to fill his lungs. He felt its claws dig into the skin in between his shoulder blades. The creature's breath was hot against his scalp. Spittle dropped from its pincers and landed, scalding, on Ifry's ear.

He struggled and kicked, but his limbs found nothing but snow. He could only crane his head to one side, where he could see the edge of the slope and the rocks that decorated a sheer cliff. He had the unwelcome thought that this might be the last view he would ever see.

He felt a sharp nick on his back and cried out. He was sure that the creature's claws had cut through his coat, jumper, shirt and through his skin. He flailed again, for all the good that it did, and felt something dragging on his arm; he feared that another creature had got him, before he understood that the strap of his ski pole still weighed on his wrist. He folded the loop into his hand until he found the handle. Grasping it, he jerked it upwards towards the creature. He was lying face down, so it was hardly surprising that he missed. He tried again, and the point of the pole glanced off the creature, which shrieked.

Any victory was dampened when a clawed foot landed on Ifry's hand. His wrist bent backward as a second creature leered over him. He cringed away from its rank breath, and looked back at the crag.

There was a woman stood there. She was pale, with light hair and a blue cloak thrown about her shoulders.

"Help," he yelled. "Help me!"

She did not seem concerned. She held up her hand as if to wave at him. She did not move towards him, but appeared to vanish behind the rocks, although he knew there was only a drop beyond. He cried out again, rather uselessly, as she had no doubt fallen to her own demise. He screwed up his eyes, not knowing what else he might do.

Someone shouted from the slope above him. Ifry opened his eyes but could not see who had spoken.

There was a sharp bang and Ifry winced. The creature that had stood on his hand keeled over. There was another bang, and the air was knocked out of Ifry as the creature on his back fell onto him. The other two squealed and he heard flapping as they fled.

"You daft sod," said the voice.

Ifry groaned in reply. He felt the weight lift off of him as the creature was shoved aside, then felt a hand on his back. Compared to the creature, it felt like the touch of a butterfly's wing.

The hands turned him over. He blinked in the light and saw the face of Jos Nothernine peering over him, shotgun hanging on his shoulder.

"What possessed you to come up here alone?" Jos asked.

"Idiocy, like you said."

Jos smirked a little, much like he was trying not to but failing. Ifry sat up and it felt like his back was bursting open.

"Can you walk?" Jos asked.

"I suppose we'll see."

Jos held out his arm and Ifry grasped it. As he gathered his feet under him, he slipped, and his knees buckled. He caught himself on Jos' outstretched arms.

"Oh, my apologies." He tried to step back, but slipped again.

"Let's not go falling again, shall we?" Jos looked at Ifry's feet. "You've still got one ski on, look."

"Ah, so I do." Ifry bent to unfasten the buckle, but Jos' hands were there first. He freed Ifry's foot, then picked up the ski and stood it upright in the snow.

"What are you doing that for?" Ifry asked. He needed that ski.

Jos looked at him oddly.

"I'll pick them up later. You're in no state."

"What if those things come back?" Ifry pointed up the slope in the direction the gargoyles had flown.

Jos shrugged, as if the creatures were no worse than cows or sheep. "I've got my gun. It's my job to keep gargin and their ilk back from the town."

"Do you go everywhere with that?"

"Wouldn't be able to do my work without it."

Ifry filed that thought away to warn Townsend later.

"You've got to hold tight." Jos patted his own back.

"That's – that can't be dignified."

"Neither is rolling down the mountain while bleeding out. Now stand on the back of my skis."

The pain in his back was only becoming sharper. His second ski had slid away and was already at the bottom of the slope. There was naught else to be done.

Ifry put his arms around Jos' waist, and stood on the back of his skis. His bleeding hand was pulsing, yet even through his layers, Jos felt warmer than blood.

ELDERSIE TOFT

The tyenes would not move from the kitchen. He had a whole room upstairs and a list longer than his arm of things to do, and he felt that he needed to sit at Eldersie's table with his papers covering the entire surface. She should have had the space to knead dough for that day's bread, but Thomas Townsend thought that he knew better.

The morning had long been broken before his sister emerged. She wore clothes like her brother, brown trousers and a white jumper that was neither stained nor darned. She carried herself with far more grace than he did, however.

"Have you got any coffee kicking about this place?" Oriana asked, while sitting herself down.

Eldersie pointed to the ceramic jar on the shelf over the mantel, which had 'COFFEE' painted on the side in Eldersie's shaky hand. Oriana's gaze flicked to the pot and back to Eldersie. It was entirely possible that she had never been required to make it herself.

Eldersie took a mug down from the shelf and set it down next to Oriana.

"There's water in the kettle," she told her. Let the tyenes figure it out; Eldersie had too much work to do as it was.

She climbed the stairs. She stopped by her room to collect a pile of clothes she had folded, all of which were missing buttons, worn at the elbows, and with tears on the hems. She did not knock on her father's door. He had gotten used to her coming and going without permission. His room was as dark and musty as it always was.

"You should crack the window from time to time," she said, throwing back the curtains, causing puffs of dust to be caught in the light. Cold rays broke into the room, revealing her father hunched over his worktable, where a dozen new sketches were under his grubby hands.

"My candles have run low, Elsie," he proclaimed. He was indeed surrounded by the stubs of spent candles.

"You should not spend so much of the night working."

"How else would anything get done?"

Eldersie barely concealed a snort. She saw that there were cobwebs building above the window frame. There was no hope in asking her father to clean his own room.

"What venture is it now?" she asked. He took the deep breath that Eldersie knew was an overture to a well-rehearsed speech.

"Have you ever run out of milk, or bread, or eggs?"

"Not recently, Father," she said. Every day, she walked across the valley to get milk from their friend Almony. In the winter, when he was in residence, Jos did it for her. Martine Toft had not gone to fetch food since Eldersie had grown taller than his waist.

"Ah yes, these are essentials. You have to keep on top of those just to get by. But what sort of things do you run out of because you've forgotten about them?"

Eldersie pulled a cloth from the waistband of her apron and ran it along the foot of the bed. It was the finest piece of furniture in the house, but dust was always building in the scroll work.

"Eldersie? What do you run out of?" he pressed.

"Hmm?" She folded a corner into her cloth and cleaned the cherubic face in the centre of the bed's foot board. It belonged to Eldersie's grandparents, and they had given it to her mother when she married. It was made for a house with a flock of servants who would run their hands along it daily to remove the dust.

"Soap. I am always forgetting when to replace the soap bar."

"That is why I am always replacing it for you," replied Eldersie.

"Yes, that is why I thought that everyone needs someone to bring them their soap once they run out."

"Hmm." Eldersie wet the pad of her thumb with spit and rubbed it over the face of the cherub to shine it. "Or everyone could fetch their own soap."

"Why do that, when someone could do it for you?"

"What would you do, then? Bring people bars of soap every month?"

"No, no - it's a little more complex than that." He drew out a roll of paper with numbers scattered across it. Eldersie saw her own hand across the back and knew that her father had been re-purposing her shopping lists. "I have done the calculations," he continued. "I have been testing how long it takes for me to finish a bar of soap - it is longer than expected - and if we take down every customer's order, we should know exactly when they will finish their soap, even before they do."

He held his calculations under her nose while she dusted the headboard of the bed. Her father sat himself on one side of the bed, as he was wont to do. He had his tray on his lap, and the dirty sheets around him were layered in the papers he so prized. The other side of the bed was built up high with discarded cushions, dirty crockery and books that he had grown tired of.

"Eldersie? Eldersie, are you listening?"

"Of course, I've brought you some work, Father." She lifted the clothes that needed mending onto his lap, and his shoulders sagged.

"Busy work," he complained.

"They all need mending and I don't have the time."

"But I have work - real work - on my latest enterprise. This time I am sure of it."

"Get the sewing done first, and I'll help you with your enterprise," Eldersie lied. She walked to the door of the room, where her mother's miniature hung next to the door frame. Eldersie touched the glass with her index finger. It was the only thing in the room that was clean.

Eldersie thanked Solyon when she returned downstairs and found that Townsend had tidied away his work. His coat was missing from the hook, so she assumed he had departed her house. Oriana was nowhere in evidence, but she had left a used plate and empty coffee mug behind. Eldersie had to quell herself when she saw these. It would be easier to wash them than to find the tyenes and argue the issue, she cautioned herself, even as she knew her temper might not stand another slight of this nature.

She fetched water from the pail, and wiped the crockery clean with a cold cloth. She heard crunching footsteps outside. Jos must have returned. He should have brought the milk with him from Almony's. She dried her hands on her apron and opened the door, holding her hand out ready for the milk.

Only nothing met her palm. Eldersie looked around for him, and saw two shadows stretching across the path. Jos walked oddly. He had his arm around the clerk next to him. His face, normally pale, had gone paper white, and he held a bleeding hand close to his chest. Eldersie groaned. It seemed that the inevitable had occurred.

Without speaking, Eldersie ducked inside and opened a cupboard, pulling out clean cloths and gauze and bandages. Full of purpose, she set the kettle back on to boil. Jos squeezed himself through the door, dragging Ifry with him.

"What was it?" Eldersie asked.

"Gargin," Jos replied. "Four of them."

"And he didn't avoid them?"

"I didn't know what they were," insisted the clerk.

Jos helped him into a chair. He was a skinny thing really. His arms would probably break if one shut them in a door.

The kettle began to sing. Steam rose in tendrils, dampening her face as she filled a bowl. Jos grasped the wrist of Ifry's injured hand and eased it over the table; the clerk winced and shrunk away from Jos. He stared at Eldersie as she fished in a drawer for needle and thread. She found them, and used a match to sear them.

"Do you know what you're doing?" Ifry asked. Eldersie tutted in response.

"Eldersie learned to tend wounds at the temple. She's an acolyte there," Jos said.

"What has that got to do with anything?"

"The more I learn about you city folk, the less I enjoy." Eldersie perched on one of her dining chairs and reached for Ifry's hand. He gasped and tried to pull away, but she fastened her grip. She dipped the edge of a clean cloth into the water and dabbed at the cuts where the gargin's claws had rent his skin.

"What were you doing up there alone, anyway?" Jos asked.

"Working. Why were you there?" he replied.

Eldersie glanced up at Jos. She could guess the truth, but she doubted the tyenes could understand. She spoke for Jos.

"Jos is employed by the temple to keep the monsters back from the town." It wasn't a lie; it just wasn't what he had been doing. Jos nodded vigorously to confirm it. Ifry was not exactly satisfied.

"Just you?" he asked. Jos shrugged and nodded. "In every town I've been to, there are whole teams dedicated to finding monsters and their nests."

"There aren't enough people in Racken for all that," Eldersie said. She bit a piece of thread. There were only two deep cuts. He was lucky. The gargin had once gotten one of Almony's flock; the poor creature had only a torso left when she found it.

"Do you mind telling me what you're doing?" Ifry asked. He was curling his hand in fright. Eldersie had been holding a needle just above the skin. She shook herself. She was not being a good nurse.

"These two here are deep," she said, pointing at the cuts with the end of the needle. "I'm going to stitch them up to dress the wound."

"All right," Ifry said, though he continued to wince. She was about to pierce the skin with the needle when Jos interrupted.

"Shouldn't we get you a drink?"

"Oh no. I can't get drunk. I've still got work to do," protested Ifry.

"I'll get on, then." Eldersie pushed her needle through his skin. He gasped sharply.

"I've some brandy down here." Jos patted Ifry's shoulder and fetched three mugs from the shelf over the mantel. He delved into the nook where Eldersie let him keep his things and returned with a dusty bottle, which he uncorked. He poured a generous amount into his and Ifry's cups, but Eldersie removed hers from his path before he could fill it. Ifry chuckled.

"I would rather Miss Toft didn't drink, if I'm honest." He grabbed his cup and drank with all the fervour of a man in a desert finding a spring.

"Hold still now," she said.

She stitched his hand up relatively quickly. She had had worse patients.

"That's you done, then," she told him, tying the last knot in his bandages.

"Thank you."

"What about your back?" asked Jos.

"What has he done to his back?" Eldersie groaned. It was typical of Jos not to give her the full picture.

"He's bleeding and all."

"Why didn't you say anything?"

"I supposed we would get to it eventually."

"Get your shirt off," Eldersie ordered Ifry.

He froze. His eyes flicked to Jos and then Eldersie. "That really - that wouldn't be proper," he said.

"You should go bleed out, then. But make sure you go outside. I don't want to be cleaning any bloodstains off my sheets."

Ifry scowled. He played with the buttons on his jacket. He undid one, then stopped. Eldersie waited. Jos waited too, taking another sip of brandy.

"Must you both watch me undress?"

Eldersie raised her eyebrows and stifled a laugh. She turned in her chair, and heard Jos do the same.

"Anything to protect your modesty, sir." She waited a few moments, listening to Ifry's pained grunts as he removed his layers. She turned back and saw that he had shucked all his clothing, but he was clutching his jumper and shirt to the front of his chest. Jos turned too and frowned at this. He couldn't argue with it; the room was still chilly. Goosebumps decorated Ifry's skin.

Ifry was very pale. Mountain folk were supposed to be pale, or so people said, but they often weren't. Eldersie wasn't. Neither was Jos. No one in Racken was as colourless as Ifry Marheart. He shook as he had not when Eldersie had stitched his hand. His back was a mess of cuts and scrapes.

"Jos, I recommend you pour Mr Marheart some more brandy."

Jos accepted the task gravely, which involved pouring himself plenty more brandy too. Ifry repositioned his hands to keep the clothes clutched to his front, even as he drank. Eldersie began to clean his wounds. He shivered as her cloth touched his skin.

"Sorry," he said, "I just hate to be cold."

"You chose an odd place to come then." Jos laughed in the merry way that meant the drink was lifting his mood.

"I have to go where Mr Townsend goes."

"Why do you work for him then?"

"He's always happy to have me." Ifry offered no further explanation. He stiffened as Eldersie's needle pierced his back. His capacity to talk was lost as she sewed him up. He curled one hand into a fist, digging his fingernails into his palm.

When the time came to fasten the bandages, Ifry became panicky. He cringed away as Eldersie tried to pass them around his front. He doubled over, hugging his bloodstained clothes. Eldersie wiped her forehead with the back of her sleeve.

"Would it help if Jos left?" she asked.

Ifry spluttered in his drink.

"Why would that help?" Jos said, but Ifry was already nodding. Jos sighed but didn't protest, taking himself to the door. "I'll go get that milk now, Eldersie."

A cold waft of air hit them as he departed.

"Just hurry, all right?" Ifry said, his voice very small. "I'm so cold."

He was right next to the hearth, but she did not question it.

IFRY MARHEART

He had drunk too much brandy. He climbed the stairs wearing only bandages above the waist, which left him feeling terribly as if he had been dipped in ice water. Eldersie had pulled his clothes away from him and insisted on scrubbing them in her wash bucket, for which he supposed he should have been grateful. Inside his room, he fell on the wardrobe, pulling out a vest and a shirt, a jumper and a jacket. He wrapped himself up in them, still feeling as if the cold was trapped below his skin. He lay down on the bed, his back and hand throbbing, but shivering all the same.

He had been stupid. He had seen the janros on the railway line. He had stayed in over a dozen mountain towns. He should have known better than to go alone, and to approach unknown humps in the snow.

There was a knock at the door. Ifry groaned and pulled himself out of bed. Townsend had no doubt discovered that he was not busy at work.

He opened the door, but it was not Townsend filling the doorway; Townsend was not large enough to fill a doorway. Jos Nothernine stood there, holding his bottle.

"What did you go out there for?" he asked without preamble.

Ifry did not respond right away. They stood there in the weak light that filtered through Ifry's box window. "Can I–" Jos began, and moved as if he meant to step inside.

Ifry cut him off.

"I know I was stupid."

"What?"

"I know that I should not have been out there alone. What can I do for you?"

This made Jos frown. "He made you go alone?"

"He didn't think about it and neither did I," Ifry said, defensively.

An expression of disgust was forming over Jos' face. Ifry cut in before he could express his opinion. "No, he's not a bad man. He's not a bad employer. He's been exceptionally good to me. This was one mistake."

"Pretty fatal mistake, if you ask me."

"I'm not asking."

"All right then," Jos sighed. He held up his bottle. "Do you want another drink? You seem - and pardon me for this - a bit shaken up."

"I suppose I am. But this is nothing I cannot handle."

"You're not used to this kind of living."

Of course he was right, but something in Ifry's stomach quailed at the thought that Jos was concerned for him. He was not a man of great pride, but he could not tolerate being pitied so. He had to alleviate that. Turning Jos away would only increase his worry. He had to drink brandy and play it well. Then Nothernine would go away thinking he had done his good deed for the week.

"I'll take a little," he said. He held out his good hand, palm up, for Jos to place the bottle in. He took one swig and handed it back. "If you don't mind, I need to rest."

Jos nodded, but he didn't move. His eyes wandered, and Ifry could tell that his mind was elsewhere.

"Your boss is - well - how did you end up here?" Jos asked. Ifry could only imagine the words that he hadn't given voice to.

"He's not a bad man."

"So you said."

"He was an old family friend."

"Ah," Jos snorted.

"What does that mean?" Ifry guessed what he meant, but he thought he would have Jos explain, to remind him to be polite.

"Nepotism, is it?"

"Yes, but he was the only man in the city who would give me a job," admitted Ifry. "He made an investment with me."

"Are you cursed goods?"

"No - uh - my family. It's not important."

Jos did not reply to that. He took a swig from the brandy bottle instead.

"What's the matter?" Ifry asked.

Jos shook his head. "Naught. I should go."

Ifry found himself relieved that he did not need to ask. He began to close the door, but he heard a creak on the staircase as Oriana flew up the stairs. She pushed Jos out of the way as if his large form made no indent upon her.

"What on earth happened?" she asked. "I just saw Eldersie cleaning blood off your clothes." She glanced around the room, seeing Jos lingering on the landing behind her. "What are you doing in here?" she asked him with a sneer. Her eyes roved to the bottle he held. She breathed in, and Ifry knew she could smell the brandy.

"Ran afoul of some monster on the slopes," Ifry explained. "Eldersie kindly stitched me up. It's nothing to worry about." He tried to use his usual tone, but he could not disguise the breathlessness in his voice. Oriana closed the door, shutting Jos out, raising one hand to Ifry's face, but he flinched away.

"Stitched you up? How bad was it?"

"An afternoon of bedrest and I'll be fine," he claimed.

"Why didn't you invite me to join if you were drinking?"

"It was only for a spot of pain, Ori."

"He could have left the bottle behind," she complained. "My flask is empty."

"Ori, I need to rest."

"Why were you drinking with the natives then?"

"I was just trying to be polite. Get rid of him quickly."

"Lean back, let's see what's wrong with you." She put both hands on Ifry's shoulders and pushed him back. He relented, finding it easier than cringing away from her again. Oriana loved to touch people, and in the tight space there was no avoiding her. She grabbed his chin and turned his face from side to side. She frowned, finding no evidence of bruises.

"Stop that, Ori. It's my hand and my back."

"Your back? How bad is it?" She grabbed at Ifry's shirt and tried to lift it up.

He batted at her with his good hand. "Don't!" he snapped, too loudly. Oriana shrank back. He realised he had been too sudden. "Eldersie has already bandaged me up. There's nothing to look at."

She frowned and sat down on his bed, hand resting on his wrist, just below his bandages, skin on skin. Her fingertips were freezing cold. He shivered away from her touch.

"I worry about you."

"That's very kind of you, but I just need to rest. Don't trouble yourself." He smiled a little, knowing that had worked on Oriana in the past.

"Don't you dare go out alone again," she said, staring intently at him.

He pulled his wrist out from under her hand. "You have my word. I've no need to do that again. Where's Thomas, anyhow?"

She rolled her eyes. "Assessing the town or something. I asked him to find me the nearest drinking establishment."

"When he comes back, do you mind telling him what happened, and why I'm not at work?"

"I'll do that, and I'll bring you tea later, all right?"

Ifry nodded, wondering how well Oriana would survive in Eldersie's kitchen. "Thank you. I'm just – I'm so tired right now."

"Sweet dreams, then." She patted the side of his face and departed, leaving Ifry to ponder at the cold that still wracked him.

He found that he really was as tired as he had proclaimed. He could not bear the idea of baring his skin to the elements again, so he crept into his sheets fully clothed, reasoning that no one in Racken would bat an eye at creased trousers. Before he knew it, he was asleep.

Or he supposed he was, because when he regained a moment of thought, he found himself in a clearing. It was round, like a coin, and lined with fir trees that were all the same height. A blanket of snow was laid on the ground, yet it did not trouble him despite the afternoon's events. The light was greyish, not bright enough for him to see beyond the first layer of trees; The sky was a flat, blank white. There was nothing inside the clearing, except a boulder with a dish-shaped cavity in the centre, filled with water. A film of ice lay atop it.

He regarded the rock with some interest, and in a childish fashion, reached out with one hand to touch the ice, hoping that he could break it.

When his fingers touched the surface, it felt as smooth as glass, but stronger. He pressed against it, but the ice did not even shift. This was unexpected, as to the eye it appeared as thin as paper.

There was a blackness underneath. A void that he could not name, when he should have been able to see the bottom of the dish. It was coldly welcoming. He felt a dread so familiar that he had quite forgotten that it was part of him, lurking in the corners of his mind. He wanted to know what was beneath the ice.

"Interesting," he heard a voice say. It was clear and bright like crystal. He did not turn. He was too engrossed in the ice below his palm. His hand felt numb, like it wasn't his hand at all. He couldn't wrench it away, though the thought crossed his mind. "You aren't the sort of person I expected him to go for."

"What?" He turned, keeping his hand pressed to the surface of the ice.

She stood there. She was not tall. Her head came up to Ifry's shoulder. She wore a shapeless robe that was the colour of the sky above them. Her hair was bright, and her head was covered with a hood and cloak that were made from a blue velvet to which snowflakes clung like feathers. He knew her, and not just because there was a familiar echo to her face. He had seen her on the mountain, right when the gargin attacked. He had thought she had fallen. In the hours since returning, he'd assumed that she had been a figment of his panicking mind.

"I wouldn't worry. I am still only considering you."

"Considering me?"

"Solyon has picked a difficult one. He's big and strong. He has no parents. No siblings. Scarcely a friend, except for the Toft girl. Though it would be most unkind to pick her; I've taken too much from that family already."

She looked at Ifry's feet and slowly drew her eyes up to his face. Ifry could feel the chill of her gaze.

"Who are you?" he asked. His voice sounded weak, as if he was struck with influenza.

"Oh, that doesn't matter. I haven't decided on you yet. It was nothing. A flicker, I suppose. He will have to be more interested for my purposes. I need to think a little slant to finally beat that foul man. He always torments me so. Calls me tricksy. I am loath to choose anyone. But I cannot think of a way to force Solyon's hand..." Her voice trailed off. She turned and walked away.

"Wait," Ifry called, but his voice was faint. Mists were rising around the grove. The fir trees seemed to be fading in front of his eyes. The woman was gone.

The mist thickened at such a pace that he thought the air was freezing, or turning to water. He could feel droplets against his skin, the watery air in his throat. And then there was no air, no clearing, no light at all. He was in the water and he could not breathe. The numbness that he had felt in his hand, pressed against the ice, grew more intense, spreading up his limbs and filling his body, like he was hollow and the water was filling him up. He thought that he had forgotten the feeling of being submerged, but he recalled it thoroughly, like he had never left.

He woke gasping, as cold as he had been in the dream. He lay for a moment, feeling the air on his face and assuring himself that he could breathe, that he was not really under the water. He had thrown the blankets off during his sleep and the freezing air surrounded and bit at him. His breath clouded as it left his lips. He found he was lying on his back, and his wounds were screaming out. He retrieved his blankets and wrapped them securely about himself. It was merely an old nightmare, taken new form.

ORIANA TOWNSEND

She had woken with a half-seeded plan to go out to the slopes that was shot down before lunch. Not only had Thomas brought them to the dullest town in the mountains, he had taken them to a place where they were apparently under siege.

"You haven't seen my brother, have you?" she asked Eldersie.

The mountain woman was hunched over her washtub, which was right next to the table where she prepared food. It seemed Eldersie had no qualms about getting bloodied water over the table where she would soon prepare their lunch.

"Not since he retreated from my kitchen," Eldersie said.

"Well, let me know when he comes back."

"You can find him yourself," Eldersie replied, and turned back to her scrubbing. That was it, then. She was supposed to wait for Thomas to come back. She had spent a lot of her life doing that already.

"Eldersie? You couldn't point me to the nearest drinking house, could you?"

Eldersie stopped her scrubbing. She didn't speak, instead considering Oriana. Or judging her, more like. Her gaze was full of appraisal, like an auctioneer presented with poor goods. Finally, she clicked her tongue and said, "There's only one in Racken. The other end of the main street to the temple."

"Well, that seems appropriate." She pulled her arms through the sleeves of her coat. "Look out for Ifry, won't you?" she called to Eldersie, who tutted as she went through the front door.

The air outside was clean and fresh enough to make Oriana realise how badly Eldersie's house smelled. Snow lay in heavy drifts everywhere that she trod. On a day in the city like this, there would have been crews out since before dawn, salting and gritting and shovelling slush off the pavements. In Thomas' resorts, he employed people to do that sort of work. He didn't want the guests to get stuck in their motor cars.

Racken was missing any amenities of that sort. Spring could not come soon enough. She missed the lights of the city and its noise. Above one of her favourite bars, there was an old man who played the guitar on his balcony. It was mostly tuneless, but the sound was comforting to Oriana, like a siren that called her home.

Thomas had his work cut out trying to kick any life into Racken. There were few footprints along the main street, though there were furrows where a few carts had been wheeled down the way, and the deep bootprints of their owners. The only sound was the roar of the wind through the peaks.

She found the drinking house as Eldersie had said, at the other end of the street, at the place where the houses were sparser, and the road petered out into nothing. The drinking house itself looked much the same as Eldersie's townhouse; only a peeling sign out front indicated that they served drink at all. If she knew mountain towns - which, as an outside observer, she felt she could be fairly objective about - then the bar would be placed in the bottom of someone's house and livestock would mingle with the patrons. Beggars could not be choosers, as Ifry would say.

She pushed open the door and a brassy bell clanged over her head. A shower of dust landed on her forehead; more dust fell as the door closed behind her. It had to have gathered in the past few hours, because there was a contingent of drinkers inside. Either that, or they had been drinking long enough for the dust to accumulate.

It did look a great deal like Eldersie's house. The open hearth must have been made by the same mason. There was one round table with mismatched chairs, and a bench that looked like a pilfered pew against the wall. The bar was a tall workbench with bottles on the shelves. The place had never heard of electricity. The barkeep raised his eyes to her and squinted like he was staring at the side of a bright mountain. Oriana supposed that she must have been equally difficult to look at.

"You're serving, right?" she asked him.

"S'pose so."

"Any chance of an old fashioned?"

His eyebrows knotted together. Clearly cocktails were not an area of expertise. "Whisky then, if you've got it," she said.

He nodded and fetched a tin cup from a shelf behind him. From the stains on the inside of the rim, she presumed he had been using it for tea that morning. He splashed whisky into it, but added no ice. All the snow outside, and the bar could not even wrangle a bucket of ice cubes.

"One silver," he said. She fished the coin out of her pocket and tossed it onto the bar, where it bounced and spun before the barkeep slammed his hand on top of it. She took a perch on the pew, it being the only free spot in the room. As she did, she noticed the two drinkers at the table staring at her. She had not thought them interesting enough to warrant her notice at first. She supposed that even in her winter layers she cut a more glamorous figure than anyone in Racken was used to seeing.

She examined the other drinkers with the same intense gaze they were giving her. One was a weathered bald man, who was the sort that she considered set decoration in mountain towns. Opposite him was a young woman. She was slight, with long pale fingers and eyes that boasted heavy bags. Yet, for all their differences in appearance, both drinkers had the same practised sneer.

"Can I help you?" she asked them, knowing already that she couldn't.

"You're not a local," said the man.

"I would have thought that was obvious. Tyenes, as you would say." She winked at them. They flinched in return. "So, I return to the original question, can I help you?"

The woman clicked her tongue and turned back to her drink.

"Well, don't leave me wondering. I'm dying to know the mystery of it all," Oriana said.

"We heard Eldersie had guests," said the woman.

"And shouldn't she?"

"What might interest a tyenes in Racken?" the man asked.

"My brother wants to start a business here."

"There are plenty of other places to buy land."

"None with your mountains, alas," Oriana said. They must have heard of the other resorts. Thomas was not the only one buying up land, after all. "What are we celebrating?" Oriana stood up from her bench and took a seat at their table.

They leaned away so sharply that you might have thought that she was the one that reeked, not they.

"We aren't celebrating," the woman said.

"I can't think of any other reason for a couple of fine people such as yourselves to be drinking in the middle of the morning. Come on, you must have some good news to share."

The woman slammed her cup down so hard that a little of her drink sloshed onto the tabletop. The droplets shone there like coins.

"My nephew died a year ago today."

Oriana wished she were very small, so she could drown in the drops on the table.

"That - that would explain it." There was a long moment where all three of them drank rather than say anything. "Well, I am very sorry for your loss."

"People here don't generally drink in the morning for good reasons."

"My social circle must be cheerier," Oriana tried to explain. "What do you want to know, then?" she asked, considering that she may as well give them a little something for their time.

"What?"

"You must be curious. What is my brother doing? Who does he want to buy from? How can you run him out of town? That sort of thing."

"Fine," said the woman. "What's your name?"

"Oriana Townsend."

"Almony. And this is Stewart. What does he want, then?"

"Couldn't say for sure. But in his other resorts he bought all the land around the station. The railway is what makes this plan feasible. I might know more soon, but he almost got his clerk killed this morning."

"Ah. How?"

"Those beasties you have up the slopes."

"Seems like you might not need our help in being run out of town," said Almony.

"Oh, no. Eldersie patched him up. He'll be skiing again in no time."

"What will work on you, then?" Almony asked.

"On me?"

"Will a monster drive you out of town, or will we need more than that?" It had the cadence of a joke, but Almony's expression was far too sincere. It was disarming.

"I couldn't guess at your meaning."

"You promised us the works. How do we get rid of you?"

"You might start by asking."

"Can you leave us, or is that against your nature?"

There was another moment, but Oriana did not think she could wait this one out.

"I'll take my leave then." She still had most of her drink, but felt it prudent to abandon it. "Have a good afternoon."

"As it is the day that it is, I'm sure that I won't." Almony gave Oriana the most sickening smile.

She braced herself for the outdoors, but found that the chill out there was preferable than the one inside the bar.

She began walking back to Eldersie's house, having no particular plan for the afternoon. In any other town she would find entertainment on a stool next to a bar, but not here. Racken was exemplary in only one respect: its dullness.

She saw a figure standing in the road ahead. He was hunched, carrying two containers of milk, of the sort that she had only seen in picture books. His coat was a nauseating shade of yellow, and his hair was unfashionably long. It was Eldersie's other guest. Any company was better than none.

"Hello! Need a hand there?"

Nothernine glanced in her direction. "I can manage," he replied.

"Perhaps best. I only wanted to be polite." She laughed.

"You're full of pleasantries," he muttered, his tone far from civil.

"I don't know what you get taught in the mountains, but there's a great deal of value in pleasantries."

He huffed and did not say anything back, then picked up the pace.

"Listen here," she began, "I wanted to thank you for helping Ifry today."

"Only what needed to be done."

"Well, it was good of you. If we had all been listening to my damned brother, he would be dead."

"Your brother. He was foolish for suggesting that. So was his clerk for following through," Jos replied.

"I agree. Not a sound thought between them today. Ifry should not be going out alone."

"Are you not equipped to take him?"

"Sure, I've taken to the slopes myself. Haven't skied in a while. But I must admit I'm no match for any monsters that we might see out there. I'm usually more of a short ski and a long drink sort of person."

Jos snorted. "Both of you will end up dead," he said.

"Say - are you often out on the slopes in the morning?"

"I've to do my job, and check on my house."

"Do you think you could spare a minute to show Ifry the slopes?" She grinned at him. Flashing a smile usually worked on men. Of course, not much was normal in Racken.

They reached the door of Eldersie's house.

Nothernine set the milk down. "I'm too busy. Keep him out of trouble yourself."

"You are the only one capable of keeping him out of trouble."

"If that's the case, it's a wonder he isn't already dead." He absent-mindedly kicked a stray piece of snow off the path.

"You might say so, but he spends so much time getting me out of trouble that he's no time for himself."

"Oh."

"That was your opening to make some joke about how *I* should be dead by now."

He did crack a smile. It was a small one, but that was no hindrance to Oriana.

"Will you let Ifry come with you? Seeing as you'll be going already," she said.

"I would rather not."

She frowned. The man would not be charmed, it seemed. "I'll ask Thomas. Perhaps he can offer you an incentive."

She opened the door and gestured for Nothernine to enter. He grunted, ducked below the lintel, and walked inside.

The kitchen was somehow cold but full of steam. Eldersie had strung rope across the entire room. All of her laundry was hung on it, including Ifry's clothes from that morning. She had made no concession for residents to get through the kitchen.

"Careful now," called Thomas. "There are obstacles here today."

"If you knock something down, you have to clean it again," called Eldersie in response. Oriana ducked through a gap between two sheets and stumbled to the table. Thomas was set up there again, with his papers strewn about.

"It seems our host has no respect for public right of way," he said. There was a pair of socks dangling near his nose.

"Can't hang them outside; they'll freeze," Oriana pointed out.

"Must we hang them over my papers, though?"

Eldersie cracked a tea towel as she shook it out. Oriana was glad that there were two lines of laundry between her and Eldersie. A tea towel could be a fearsome weapon in the hands of a woman like her. Nothernine ducked under the edge of Ifry's hanging shirt.

"Milk's outside, Eldersie," he said, and she nodded back at him. He ducked under another line of laundry and stamped up the stairs.

Oriana glanced at Thomas' work. A damp circle marked the corner of one page, and the ink had run.

"Are you struggling without Ifry?" she asked.

"I might not be if he cared to show his face. I stepped out to take a look around the town and he vanished into his room."

Eldersie cracked another tea towel.

"You haven't seen him at all?" Oriana asked him.

"If I had, would I be doing all of his work?"

"You haven't seen what happened to him?"

"Obviously not, Ori."

"He got attacked by monsters after you made him climb the slopes alone. He's resting, and you shan't ask him to do any work today."

"Why didn't he just run away, if he saw monsters nearby?"

"As ever, Thomas, your compassion is astounding." Oriana shoved papers towards her brother, where they slid onto his lap and then fell on the floor.

"Charming." He leaned down to collect his paper from the damp floor.

"You need to make sure he doesn't go out alone. He can't handle himself against the monsters."

"He has done so in every other resort we have created."

Eldersie snorted, despite her pretending to be hard at work, and not eavesdropping.

"They weren't so provincial as this," Orianna said. "Convince Mr Nothernine to take him. Or find someone else."

She left the table, knowing it was prudent not to allow her brother to argue.

IFRY MARHEART

Ifry was confined to his bedroom for a few days, ordered back in every time he tried to leave. Eldersie even took the time to remind him that he had a perfectly good chamber pot, a statement that made his nose wrinkle. The evening prior, she had given him a look over and pronounced him well enough to ski again.

He woke before dawn, and set about making breakfast without Eldersie's judgemental eye upon him.

"Good morning," he said in a bright tone that was at odds with the darkness of the hour; he had heard Jos' moving about in the next door room and known he was awake.

"Eldersie is not even awake yet," Jos remarked, rubbing sleep out of his eye.

"Yes. Well, I didn't want to put you out of your routine," Ifry replied.

"I expected you to be up later."

"I didn't want to get in your way. I can't help but feel that you've been press-ganged into this." Ifry struck a match and a light was brought to life between his hands.

"Showing you around is a great deal less work than carrying you down the slopes again," Jos said in a gruff manner. If the words had come out of Oriana's mouth then they might have been a joke, but from Jos Nothernine they rang like criticism.

"When you put it like that, I do suppose it's only fair. I'll do my best to not impact your workload, and come out with you now, rather than making you take two trips," Ifry replied as he collected mugs from above the hearth. He turned his face away from Jos as he filled the kettle.

Jos made no attempts at conversation. He stepped outside. Ifry, wanting only to know what he was doing, glanced through the door and saw him setting out two pairs of skis. True to his word, he had retrieved Ifry's skis from the side of the mountain, because there they were, laid across the garden path. Ifry found himself stunned. He had not even asked Jos to do that for him. In a fit of gratitude, he cracked eggs and heated a pan on the stove.

"Usually I don't eat this early," said Jos.

Ifry dropped the wooden spoon. It bounced and landed in the embers of the fire. He gawked at Jos for a moment before snatching up the spoon and blowing on its blackened end.

"I– we don't have to eat."

"No, no. Don't want to waste anything." Jos sighed more than spoke. Ifry felt his cheeks redden, and could think of nothing to reply.

Jos did not sit, but spooned eggs into his mouth while packing a bag for the day. Ifry felt rather as if he was squandering Jos's time. He spooned eggs into his mouth as quickly as he could manage, and had to hide that he nearly choked.

"Come on, I need to get up there," Jos said as he tossed his plate into the pail next to the sink. He left the door open, inviting Ifry to follow. Ifry tried to ignore him, guessing that he was not a man used to being watched closely.

"Which slope are you headed up?" asked Ifry.

"Not the southern. Not after your last trip," Jos replied. Ifry looked at the ground, sheepish, thinking of the gargin.

"Too many monsters?" he asked.

"There's monsters everywhere."

"Oh."

"The northern side of the valley is not so steep," Jos said. He pointed at Ifry's skis laid out alongside his own. "There's yours."

"I - thank you."

"You going to try and tip me for it?"

"I - um - I - no."

Jos snorted as Ifry fumbled over his words.

"Your - uh - employer keeps trying to do it."

"I'll tell him not to," Ifry promised.

"Tell him to stop giving Eldersie orders. Or he might find himself out in the cold for the rest of his stay."

"I'll have words," Ifry assured him, though he wasn't certain that it would help. Thomas couldn't be convinced against giving orders to staff. One may as well have begged the sun not to rise.

"Come on, this way."

Jos led Ifry away from the house. He leaned his skis onto his shoulder and trudged through the drifts, with Ifry just behind him. They reached the railway. Jos stopped walking for a moment, apparently having sensed that Ifry was struggling to match his pace.

"Has it changed much around here?" Ifry asked, wanting to fill the silence with conversation, if only to make Jos less disapproving of his presence. He gestured down the line with one of his ski poles. It disappeared into the horizon, to some distant ending. "Every other town we went to had a new line and station. They're supposed to bring new industry."

"I guess we should be glad you've all turned up," said Jos, his voice loaded with disdain.

"I must admit that I don't know a great deal about Racken yet, but it might be a fine thing, to have new industry and all."

"Truth be told, the line hasn't brought much, except three tyenes," Jos said.

"Do I detect a little disappointment in your voice?"

"No– no. I wasn't looking for anything. No, it's just funny to me," Jos claimed.

"What is so entertaining?"

"It hasn't worked. It was sold to us as such a miracle. A poverty killer. And yet there's nothing here to show for it except the best part of land in the valley is never in use."

Ifry could feel the blood rushing to his face. "Well, perhaps it just needs some time to take," he said. He felt the need, after all, to defend himself.

"There might be new trade yet."

Jos grunted and stepped over the second rail. Ifry knew that his suit was lost, so he trudged along in Jos' footsteps. They walked past farms that had troughs that were iced over; the animals that drank from them were shut away somewhere warm. Jos hopped over fences and opened gates without worry for who owned them. Ifry couldn't imagine doing that in the city, where dropping an item over a garden fence meant you were liable to be chased away with a broomstick.

Jos led them to a shallow slope between two peaks. He seemed to walk, snow up to his knees, without tiring at all. Ifry struggled, though he bit back all of his complaints. Wordlessly, Jos set down his skis and buckled his feet into them. Ifry did the same, though he took longer, his fingers numb and useless. He managed one foot, but the second buckle kept slipping out from between his fingers. He nearly swore before he remembered to be polite. Before he knew it, Jos reached down and fastened his strap with one hand.

"Oh. Thank you," Ifry said, knowing he must seem deeply pathetic.

"Your bad hand."

"Of course. That was it," lied Ifry. "It's stiff," he claimed, though his injury was wreaking far less damage than the cold was.

They continued to climb until they came over a crest and saw the wastes beyond. Ifry was not used to seeing a view with no signs of humanity. With his back to Racken, there were no roads, no railway lines, no threads of smoke among the clouds. If there were houses, they were blended into the slopes like paint. Ifry was struck by the silence. No library, no exam hall, no crematorium could ever achieve such a silence as the mountains produced.

Jos was unaware of Ifry's wonder. He skied away, along a trail that he had no doubt followed before. Ifry, realising his mistake, hurried after him. He slid down the slope between some pine trees, being careful to avoid the roots that lurked beneath the snow. When he caught up, he saw that Jos had taken his gun off of his shoulder and held it at the ready.

"Is there something nearby?" asked Ifry.

"Shh," Jos hissed. He gestured with the barrel of the gun to markings in the snow. There were footprints that looked a little like the markings of a dog in the park. Ifry counted four paws, each as large as a dinner plate. Ifry's breath caught in his throat. "It's alone," said Jos. "Must be wounded."

"What is it?" Ifry whispered, but Jos did not reply. He straightened up, turning his head to catch a noise, like a dog who had caught a scent, then held out his hand to indicate that Ifry should stop.

"Shit." He glanced around them. "It's close. Follow me." He skied through the trees with definite haste, Ifry's stomach swooped as he tried to follow. He feared his ski catching on a root and being thrown into the air.

He kept on Jos' tail. The slope became steeper as Jos led him towards the husk of a fallen tree. The bark, mostly rotten, appeared black and mouldy. Jos skied behind it and crouched in the hollow left by the roots. He beckoned for Ifry to join him. In an ungainly fashion, Ifry slid alongside him, bashing his skis against Jos's, and crouched down. He felt the cold of the snow against his trouser legs; a small piece of snow crept inside his boot and his heart sank. There he was, being hunted by a monster he could not name, and he was worried about the cold once more. He shivered despite himself.

Jos kicked off his skis with apparently no trouble. Ifry could hear his breath, far too loud and rasping, and see it on the air. Jos, in comparison, showed no signs of being troubled by their circumstances. He turned around, brushing the snow off the log and using it to balance his gun. Ifry backed into the log, watching him, unable to look at anything else.

"What is it?" Ifry asked, still reeling from how quickly the mood had turned.

"Kuprum," muttered Jos. He settled the butt of the gun into his shoulder. Ifry followed the line of his gaze and peered over the log. There, at the edge of the trees, was a creature in the shape of a wolf. In fact, i looked like a wolf in the same way that the janros looked like a polar bear. It certainly had four legs, pointy ears, and a tail that brushed the snow. The resemblance ended there. It didn't have fur. It had overlapping scales that made a metallic noise as they moved against each other. It had long tusks that curled upwards from a jaw that seemed misshapen. There was nothing about it to indicate that it was related to the friendly canines to which Ifry was used. It turned, sniffing the air, and looked towards them.

"You have to get them in the eye," Jos muttered. He took a breath and squeezed the trigger.

The crack of the gun made Ifry jolt and squeeze his eyes shut. When he opened them, he saw that the kuprum had fallen. Blood, dark like wine, ebbed onto the snow.

Jos stood. He vaulted the log and rushed over to the creature. Ifry hung back, still fearing that it might leap up and bite him. A moment later, Jos beckoned. Ifry sidestepped up the slope until he reached the kuprum's body. The blood steamed in the cool air.

It had been shot through the left eye, which was now a bloodied crater. Ifry could see the bone of its eye socket.

"We're lucky that it was alone," said Jos. "Pack animals. Nasty creatures."

“Good thing you were here.” Ifry tried to compliment Jos, but he only shrugged.

“Now we wait for the others.”

“What?”

Jos trudged through the snow without looking back. Ifry thought he was about to faint. He couldn’t move. He stared at the kuprum’s empty eye socket, trying to imagine where the contents of its skull had ended up. He listened, though he was only surrounded by oppressive silence, with no warning of where the rest of the pack could be. He hoped for a howl, as in moving pictures, to indicate that wolves were nearby.

A hand closed around his elbow.

Ifry was so startled that he nearly fell. He turned and saw Jos standing behind him. He gripped Ifry by the elbow, though his touch was gentle.

“We need to hide,” he cautioned Ifry. He led gestured back to the log. Ifry nodded, steeled himself, and followed after him.

On the ground behind the log, Ifry felt the snow melting against his trousers. The cold hurt his lungs. He could not breathe for it. They were so exposed. Jos rested the gun on the log again, watching the body of the kuprum with more intensity than a sportsman at play. He didn’t notice how Ifry shook.

He should have refused Thomas. They should have known better than coming to a town infested with more beasts than people.

There was another crack and Ifry thought his heart stopped. Then Jos fired another without needing to take a moment to steady himself. The silence of the mountains settled back in. Ifry could only hear the crunch of Jos's knee against the snow as he turned. He could not feel his feet, nor his hands. When Jos spoke to him, he gave him a polite smile, as if all was well. "That's three," said Jos.

"Are there more?"

"Stewart told me about three. We should be fine." He reloaded his gun regardless.

Ifry thought he should get up, but he found his limbs were not working as they should. The quiet was rent by a high-pitched whine. It sounded like a beaten stray dog.

Jos sighed. "That's the young 'un, then."

"What?"

"Their litters are small. There should only be one."

Another gunshot cracked through the valley.

JOS NOTHERNINE

He didn't quite know why he had agreed to do it. He had enough to think about. Being chosen by a god had its own stresses. He hadn't slept well since Midwinter's Night. Solyon had an unfortunate habit of sending dreams around midnight that woke him whenever Solyon was done talking. Of late, he had not even had a lot of useful advice to give.

When it began, it had not been so hard. He told Eldersie. She praised Solyon's choice, and took him to the temple for a blessing. That day he was clapped on the back all the way down the street. Everyone he knew tipped their caps at him. It was an honour. Every year he had helped during the festivities: he had made garlands of golden paper suns to decorate the temple. He had baked sunburst shaped biscuits with Eldersie. He followed the procession down Main Street and sang old songs with the rest. He had done it alone, every year, since his mother had passed. He had been one of the many, and now he was the one. He was alone, and therefore strong. He was alone, and had no one to make him vulnerable.

They had done blessings, and he wore garlands in temple. He had accepted the salutes and the handshakes. He had touched children on their foreheads for luck. All the pageantry had gone away, or become tedium. In any other year they would have done the procession by now. Winter would have broken and he would be watching an early sunrise from his own house.

As it was, when he woke his breath misted before him. There was no chance of summer yet.

He waited for Ifry on the ridge, looking at the harsh line of the railway. Jos had once stood on that line and dreamed of where it might take him. Since then, the only passenger trains that had stopped in Racken were the one that took the railway workers away, and the one that brought Ifry to him. Otherwise the trains whistled through town, loaded with coal and rocks and making everyone cough their lungs out.

He had been shaken by their encounter with the kuprum, though he made pleasantries and pretended that it was all in a day's work. Though he had resented the clerk's presence, Jos found himself concerned about his welfare. One could only see a grown man shake for so long and not grow worried.

"I need to check on my house," Jos told Ifry as he caught up, breathless and pink in the face. "Should be less toil than this morning."

"You really live all the way up here?" Ifry asked, with laughter in his voice. Was he mocking Jos? Was he laughing at the idea that anyone would live like this?

"It's not so bad during the summer."

"Oh, I'm sure the views are marvellous, and it must pay to be so close to your hunting grounds."

Jos turned, surprised that he would appreciate the practicality of living so high on the slopes. Racken looked like a toy town below them.

"Yes, I could not live in town over summer," he told Ifry. "I only stay with Eldersie when the house is snowed under."

"It must be lonely, no?"

"Since my mother passed, yes."

"Oh. I am sorry for your loss."

"It's not an uncommon loss to have."

"You are right about that. I would know," Ifry said. Jos thought to ask when he had lost his parents, but he could not get the words out. It was too presumptuous to ask such a thing, he decided.

They reached the spot where Jos knew the path to his house lay under the drifts. He knew it by sight, sure, but also there was a feeling that made him recognise the pine trees that overlooked the path without needing to look at them.

"Would you make a piste past here?" Jos asked, suddenly concerned that tyenes would go past his door hourly.

Ifry was hesitant with his response.

"This area is so pleasant. I would not want to ruin it for you. But Townsend is hoping to encourage off-piste skiing in this area."

"What would he do that for?"

"He's trying to appeal to a different type of guest. You know, the drinking in the morning, looking for an adventure with friends in the afternoon. That sort of person."

"Now that truly is tomfoolery." Jos slid down the path and spotted the peak of his roof half-hidden, only found because he knew where it would be.

"What makes it so?"

"Look at you."

"What about me?"

Ifry followed Jos, but was too busy in expressing his outrage to steady himself properly. Jos felt Ifry hit against his back. He heard Ifry swear before he could turn around. Ifry slipped on the compacted snow that Jos had just skied over. He wobbled, stretched his arm out, and fell backwards. His skis got stuck under him and he ended up groaning on his back.

Jos could not help himself. He laughed.

"Stop that," Ifry said, but Jos laughed harder. Ifry tried to roll over, but couldn't, so he reached down and unbuckled one of his skis. He sat up and folded one knee under him, but stayed on the ground. "What were you saying about me?"

"You can hardly blame me for the criticism."

Ifry unbuckled his other ski and stood, brushing himself off. "Oh, I understand. I get into more scrapes than I should out here."

"You could say that," Jos said between laughs.

"I get it. I am of course the perfect advertisement for tyenes getting lost out here." The look on Ifry's face was so glum that it destroyed any of the humour of the situation.

"These mountains are crawling with creatures. You would need platoons of men to cull them," said Jos seriously.

"I suppose that's true, and here I am, empirical proof of the problem."

"I did not mean to mock you."

"It's fine. I have to admit that the situation has its humour." He forced a smile that did not calm Jos' nerves and collected his skis from the ground. "I hope your house is nearby."

"It is."

Jos led the way through the trees, which thinned as they reached the house. As expected, the snow was piled up to the eaves. You could not see the windows, nor the door. The sight of it clearly confused Ifry.

"This is where you live, correct?" To Ifry, no doubt the building looked like a one room shack. Jos was feeling along the eaves to find the door lintel. "How tall is it?" asked Ifry.

"There isn't a second storey under the snow, if that's what you were thinking."

"Nothing like a portal? Door to another place?" jested Ifry.

"No. Not here."

"That sounded sincere," Ifry teased. Jos had found the door and was clearing the snow with the end of his ski.

"No. I promise there's only a poor hunter's hut under here." He dug the end of the ski into the snow again, but felt movement in the snow behind him. There was a prickly sensation on the back of his shoulders, despite the layers he was wearing. Ifry placed a hand on the top of Jos' shoulders, and he found that he could not move for a second. He saw Ifry's hand wipe the snow away from the shape of his door knocker.

"A bumblebee," Ifry remarked. He crouched beside Jos, running his thumb along the edges of the bee. "It seems so out of place here. When there is a harsh winter, I forget that summer even touches places like this."

"How else would any of us get by?"

"How would I know? I'm a tyenes."

Jos found the door handle. He lifted it and pulled the top half of a stable door towards them.

Ifry ducked his head inside to look around. Jos reached to Ifry's shoulder to pull him back, but stopped short of touching him. He felt that he had to be careful with Ifry, like a porcelain tea cup.

Jos climbed inside, removing himself from the problem. He felt Ifry land on the flagstones behind him. He checked the house up and down, dusted, and removed some of the cobwebs. He looked under the cabinets for mouse droppings, but was rewarded with nothing of the sort. He shook out his blankets and found that there were no new holes.

"No hidden doorways to another land?" Ifry said.

"Ah. No," said Jos. "No mould either."

"It's lovely." Ifry looked over the house with an approving eye, though Jos would have thought the quarters were beneath him.

"Really?" Jos asked. "It's very small."

"Larger than my apartment."

"What?"

"Oh. I live in a shoebox over a locksmith." Ifry noted his mother's trunk and his father's prize cup on the windowsill. "Some heirlooms, I see?"

"Yes. He - uh - my father was proud of that." Jos pointed to the silver cup, which was tarnished enough to look like tin. Jos felt ashamed to be boasting about it. "His father owned it, or something. It's a bit old-fashioned."

"My father had one, from when he came of age. May I?"

"Sure."

Ifry picked it up and examined it. He looked at the bottom of the cup, where there was an insignia accompanied by a string of numbers. "It's good quality," he said. "This is the mark of a good silver worker. Not from Darrity, but Morinn. We passed through there on our way here." He passed it back to Jos. His words, though he could not know it, had banished that shameful feeling that Jos had been nurturing. His father had been right to be proud of this cup.

The house was shrouded in half-darkness, with the snow piled above the windows. When autumn passed, he'd hoped that he wouldn't be stuck in Eldersie's house for long, but winter hadn't broken, and there was no sign that Jos would be able to fix that soon.

"Is there supposed to be a scratching noise?" asked Ifry.

Jos paused. "No."

"I thought it might be a branch against the window."

"What branches?" Jos gestured at the windows, all protected by the ice piled against them.

"Oh. Well then, I don't know what it is."

Jos held a finger to his lips to hush him. Cowed, Ifry looked at the ground. Jos listened for the scratching and followed it to his cedarwood trunk. He crouched, moving as slowly as possible, and placed both hands on either side of the trunk. Ifry was frozen, though Jos could hear his breathing.

Jos grasped the trunk and pulled it back in a smooth motion. The trits shrieked. There were five, clustered in a ball, surrounded by shredded paper and droppings. They couldn't see him, but they panicked at the noise. He grasped at their skinny tails and only managed to catch one before the others scattered. It wriggled in his hand and squeaked, bending to try and bury its horn into the skin of his hand. It was as long as his forearm. He swung it by the tail against the bricks and it went still.

"Shit," he said. "A nest."

He inspected the detritus underneath the trunk. "The mother will be nearby."

"Can't you put poison down for them?" asked Ifry, holding a handkerchief over his nose.

"We will need a little something more for a trit mother," confirmed Jos. "I'm assuming you've never seen one."

"Only at the zoo," admitted Ifry.

"I need to get rid of it, or it'll breed right through to spring."

He got on his hands and knees, searching the floor for the black droppings. He found the babies and dispensed with them, ignoring the pained sounds Ifry made when he finished them off. He found no footprints in the dust that could belong to the mother.

"Say, can these things climb?" asked Ifry. He was looking at the ceiling beams over Jos' head.

"Not especially well."

"Not even if they were large?"

Jos stood up.

"They're not that clever," he told Ifry, whose eyes were still fixed on the ceiling.

Ifry inched towards the fireplace.

"You are being dramatic," said Jos.

Then the trit landed on his back. It was heavy. The shock of it made him stumble and land on his knees. He felt its claws even through the fur of his coat. Its tail fell across his shoulder. It wasn't skinny like its babies had been, it was wide, and fleshy. He felt its horn against the back of his neck.

Ifry cried out, and Jos thought he must have been cowering in the corner of the room. Then, he felt the trit thrown off his back. He looked up and saw the trit splayed across the flagstones. A moment later, the poker was driven through the spot where its eye would have been.

Ifry relinquished the poker. It wobbled as the trit kicked its last. Its tail thrashed, and then stilled.

"You have to get them through the eye, right?" asked Ifry.

Jos found himself feeling guilty. Ifry was so polite, but he was more capable than Jos had assumed. Jos took him to investigate the slopes, and didn't make any adverse remarks to his plans for pistes.

They returned down the slopes when Ifry's belly rumbled loud enough for Jos to hear. They walked back towards town with their skis on their shoulders. Jos walked ahead. He did not notice when Ifry fell behind. He turned to see Ifry standing in between the train tracks, staring back towards the city.

"Am I going to have to save you from a speeding train?" Jos asked.

"I think not. I just thought I might stand here. There's a certain thrill to standing on train tracks, and anywhere else that I should not be standing." He smiled at Jos.

"I suppose."

There had been a thrill when the train first came through Racken. The workers had leaned out of the windows and waved their hats. Jos had been tempted to run after the train as lovers are supposed to do, only he'd been trying to keep up appearances.

That day, Jos had caught his lover's eye through the train window. He'd stolen that moment, treasured it, even as the subject of his interest turned away out of embarrassment. Jos wanted some final sign, some proof that it had not been for nothing. That he had not shifted from the tracks of his life for no reason.

His name was Kristann. He had been a labourer, just another of the men that came to town to lay the tracks. Jos had said the name aloud as often as he could. He liked the harsh sound of it, and the softness that followed. He liked it more than his own name. He had never received a locket or trinket to clutch tightly under his pillow, like other lovers might. He held Kristann's name tight instead, and did not share it with anyone.

They met at night, and walked down the unfinished train tracks, just out of Racken where they might not be seen. Jos had alternately felt as if he walked on air, and as if he was drowning. Kristann's regard made him more valuable. When his moods soured and he ignored Jos, Jos could not be lifted from his bleak manner. He was filled with longing. He waited all the day, carrying rocks and receiving orders, to feel Kristann touch his skin again.

Kristann had climbed aboard that train and vanished down the tracks. He had not caught Jos's eye in front of the other workers.

It didn't matter anymore. Kristann was gone into that other world beyond the mountains that Jos could not name. He did not even know which town he had gone to. He could not catch a train to find him. Jos was just in Racken, waiting at the bottom of a well.

It had been summer then. Almony had stood by his side. She had been cheery to see them go.

"We'll never see them back," she proclaimed, with an energy that he did not feel.

"Perhaps we will, now that there are trains," he said.

"I would wager not." Almony picked up the handles of her barrow, which the tyenes had been using all summer. "Bloody hell, they've broken the wheel."

She went looking for tools to fix it, but Jos doubted that a single usable tool was left in the valley. With every step he had to watch out for rubble.

"When will you be moving down to Eldersie's?" Almony asked. She preferred when he stayed in town. It meant they could go out drinking in the evening.

"Don't much know. All of this has put paid to the year's schedule."

"That and more." Almony had her barrow upside down. She had removed the wheel to examine the bent axle.

"I have to ask Eldersie," Jos said. "Last I heard she was being eaten out of house and home. Three foremen to a room and all. She's been angry all summer."

"She's been angry all her life," Almony scoffed.

Jos kicked the wheel out of her hand. "Don't say that about her."

"I forget that you two are as good as engaged." She caught her wheel before it could roll away.

"That's not the case. She's just been through a lot."

"Nothing that everyone here hasn't seen, at some point or another." She dropped the wheel into the mud. "This isn't worth the repair."

"I'm not going to marry Eldersie, you know."

Almony was not listening; she was looking around for where she could deposit her broken barrow, but rubbish was all around them.

"I'm not going to marry Eldersie." Jos repeated. Almony let out one sharp laugh.

"I don't know why you're insisting, when we know how things work around here." Almony kicked the barrow wheel aside, and lacking anything else to do, abandoned the mess and crossed the train tracks. She stopped between the rails and turned back, pointing at Eldersie's house. "Go on then, it'll be your property soon."

She tried to step over the second rail, but Jos grabbed her by the belt. She stumbled, swore, and kicked the rocks that the railway men had worked so hard to place. She turned and slapped Jos' hand away. "What are you getting at?"

"Don't make fun, Almony."

She smirked. "I get it, she's your intended. You need to defend her honour."

"She is *not*."

"I would not have taken you for a romantic, Jos Nothernine."

"I'm not."

"I don't think Eldersie will like it. You know her. She's a practical soul. Get her a new pail instead of flowers." She winked.

"Almony, take me seriously."

"It's against my nature. I have never taken anything seriously." She batted Jos's hand away again and started along the well-beaten path to her family farm. "You want dinner?" she called back to him. "My sister's cooking."

"Praise Solyon. You can't cook yourself."

"Should have gotten betrothed to my sister, instead of Eldersie."

"NO ONE–" he said, too loud. He spotted Almony's dismay and altered his tone, trying to match her cheery manner. "No one's betrothed to Eldersie, and Helda's got a son already."

"That makes her less eligible than Eldersie, then?"

"Almony–"

"No, no, I understand. Eldersie's got a house and a business, and Helda's an unwed mother. Although Eldersie does have an invalid father, so surely that counts against her."

"He's pleasant enough."

"Of course you would say that. You secret romantic." She poked him in the belly as she did when she wanted to emphasise the joke she was making. He knew it was because she was hunting for a laugh, but he could not muster one.

As they walked to the farm, Almony switched to talking of the hearty lunch that would be prepared for them, and Jos could not help but glance down the railway tracks the way that the train had gone.

A hearty meal was indeed prepared at Almony's farm. Almony hid coins in the pockets of her nephew's coat. The sun was still shining. Solyon reigned, and Lady Winter was yet to torment them. It should have been idyllic. But Jos could not allow one thing to stand.

"I am not going to marry Eldersie, you know," he told Almony.

"What's got you caught on that?"

"I don't want everyone assuming it."

"Wait until you're older and you think it might be practical to set up a household." She stoked the fire, then glanced at her nephew. He was curled up in a chair, rolling the wheels of his toy train with one hand, and seeing how long they spun for. "I know I love mine."

As he stood on the train tracks with Ifry, he found himself missing that summer.

"Is winter usually this - uh - vicious? It begins to get milder in the city around this time," Ifry asked. He was watching his own breath mist in front of him. Jos' eyes had caught on an object discarded next to the line. Half buried in snow, he could see the frosted edge of Almony's barrow.

"This winter is longer than it should be," Jos replied.

"What an odd way of phrasing it," Ifry chuckled.

He overtook Jos, and for a moment put his hand on the small of Jos' back. It was only in passing, but Jos could not help focusing on it. Even after Ifry had overtaken him, the sensation of the touch lingered, despite Ifry's gloves. He was reminded of the burning image of Kristann's face at the train window, as he turned away. This had been the spot where he had stood. Jos turned and glanced east, as if he thought he might see a column of smoke heading his way.

Ifry stopped in the road and turned back to him. "You're the slow one now."

"Sorry. Let's go." Jos stepped over the tracks.

ELDERSIE TOFT

Almony stood outside, haggard, with her frayed hair falling about her face. She looked as if she had slept in her clothes, based on the wrinkles in her jacket. The collar stood up on one side, and she had made no attempt to fix it.

"Milk's in the usual place," she said.

"Jos not fetching it today?" Eldersie asked.

"I was coming across the river anyway," Almony admitted. Her dark eyes flicked into the kitchen.

"Did you want to come in?"

"I was looking for Jos."

"He'll be down soon," Eldersie assured her, guiding her indoors.

Almony wrung her hands and glanced into each dark corner of the room. She did not settle, but hovered until Eldersie pushed her into a chair.

"I have not seen you at the temple of late, Almony," Eldersie remarked, spiking bread over the fire for toasting; Almony grunted. "I have gotten used to not seeing you. It is odd, after all these years of working together there."

Almony slumped in her chair, as Eldersie set assorted crockery down with unwarranted ferocity. "Say, aren't you available for an hour or two now?" asked Eldersie.

"Uh, I wanted to speak to Jos."

"I was going to bring him to temple too," Eldersie said. He was the elect, chosen by holy Solyon. The temple was where he belonged.

"I–" Almony began, but she was interrupted by heavy footfall on the stairs.

Eldersie might admit that her house was old and full of aching bones, but they had never creaked so loud as when Oriana walked their floors. For a woman who was almost petite, she managed to announce her presence without saying a word.

"Is it not a little early for you?" Eldersie asked as Oriana arrived into the kitchen. The sun was only just beginning to wink above the mountains.

"My head aches," said Oriana. "You haven't got anything for that, have you?"

"Oh, I'll pop down to the apothecary, shall I?" Eldersie said. Oriana sat herself down next to Almony, rubbing her temples.

"That would be lovely, thank you," she answered sincerely, misunderstanding Eldersie's tone.

The kettle sang, and Eldersie set a mug down in front of Almony, taking the time to look at Oriana, but not to get her one.

"Lovely to see you again," Oriana said to Almony, in a perfect facsimile of Eldersie's own sarcasm.

"Looking for Jos," Almony muttered.

"I'm taking Almony and Jos to temple as soon as he's down." Eldersie set toasted bread and butter down just out of Oriana's reach.

"Oh. Wonderful." Oriana relented and fetched her own mug from above the hearth.

"I expect you don't spend a lot of time in temples in the city," Eldersie remarked.

"Not since my mother passed. She was a devoted follower of the wellspring gods."

"I don't know about them."

"Seems right. I don't know about yours either." Oriana stood, reached across Almony and snatched a piece of bread.

There was a soft creak on the stairs and Jos arrived, dressed in his yellow coat and cap. His hands were already mittened and he had a scarf wrapped around the bottom of his face.

"I am headed to temple, Jos."

"All right. I'll wait for Ifry." He made for the door, but Eldersie caught him by the coattails.

"You have been too distracted with Ifry of late. Winter only drags on. You need to show your face at temple to calm nerves."

"Calm nerves for what?" asked Oriana, crumbs falling out of her mouth.

"Almony, advise Jos. You know what he needs to do in this situation." Eldersie turned to Almony, whose face had gone pale. "For Solyon's sake, you were in Jos's position. Tell him what he must do, or must I fetch my father down here?"

The threat was empty, of course. She would rather have let Jos run around with the clerk for one more morning than involve her father in her concerns.

"Jos'll do what he thinks best," Almony said, with all the conviction of nougat.

"What are you wittering on about?" Oriana asked with laughter in her voice.

"It doesn't concern you," Eldersie said. "Jos, come now, we need to leave." She untied her apron from around her waist. "All the town will be there. I can't explain why you two are missing again."

It was with further grumbling that they left the house. Jos insisted on writing a note for Ifry to explain his absence, which Eldersie thought was unnecessary, as no doubt Townsend would keep his clerk busy. She shepherded Jos and Almony out, and to her surprise saw Oriana depart behind them.

"I thought that we were under a time limit," Oriana said. "Why are we standing around?"

"Why are *you* standing around? Why are you coming?" Eldersie asked her.

"Were you not just admonishing these two for not attending?"

"Yes, but–"

"Well, Eldersie, you have been criticising me for my city ways and my ignorance. This is the perfect opportunity to rectify that." Oriana gave Eldersie a smug smile that let her know that she did not intend to be demure during the service. There was little argument she could make to prevent it, however, as Oriana had not been incorrect in her statements. So it was with great regret that Eldersie led the way across the street to the temple. Folk stared as they passed, but Eldersie could not say whether they wanted to catch a glimpse of Jos, or sneer at Oriana.

Jos and Almony tried to sit at the back of the temple, in the pew nearest to the door.

"Get to the front. Almony, you should know better," Eldersie hissed, herding them to the front.

"Oh, figures of importance, are we?" Oriana laughed, lounging on the frontmost pew. She sat in the middle, so the rest of the group had to sit around her. Eldersie gave a slight snort as she realised that Almony and Jos were going to sit on Oriana's left hand side, marooning her on the right.

"This is lovely, isn't it?" Oriana said, pointing at the ceiling and the yellow garlands that hung from the rafters.

"They're offerings for mighty Solyon, to call the summer back in."

"Ah. I see. Are they working?"

Eldersie did not deign that with an answer.

The paper flowers were missing petals, which lay on the ground like rubbish. There was a silver cobweb threaded in between the nearest garland and the column.

Parson Tieron stepped up to the pulpit. His sun medallion gleamed, as if he had been polishing it in the cloisters not a moment ago. "Good morning all. Praise be to Solyon."

Eldersie parroted the phrase. Beside her, Oriana quashed a little laugh.

Parson Tieron began his sermon in a bellowing voice, and Eldersie used the noise to whisper to the interloper.

"Do you care to keep quiet?"

"I did not say anything."

"You laughed."

Tieron announced that it was time to sing. Eldersie shot to her feet. Oriana fussed, looking for something underneath her pew. Eldersie grabbed her elbow and pulled her up. The organ pipes sounded.

"Where are the song books?" Oriana whispered.

"There aren't any."

"What am I supposed to do?"

"Just be quiet," she hushed Oriana as the opening bars finished. She prided herself in singing as loud as she could in temple. Her mother had loved to sing; she knew old mountain songs and would hum them while she stirred soup or kneaded bread.

"What is that song about?" Eldersie had asked her when she was not yet tall enough to see over the kitchen table.

"The trolls," her mother had said. "They used to live in the hills over Racken, before they turned to stone."

Eldersie had frowned. She knew no songs other than the ones about

Solyon and Volana.

"Did they know the gods?" She knew that Solyon lived somewhere on the slopes behind their house. She dreamed of meeting him one day.

Her mother had made a tutting sound. "The trolls lived long before Solyon."

"But I thought that Solyon was born in the beginning of the very first summer." She'd heard Parson Tieron tell them so during their lessons.

Her mother had looked down at her. She'd had the serious face that she reserved for telling her husband when he was late for tea. "Eldersie, you must know that Solyon and Volana, well, they're no different from the janros and the gargins and the white garrotins. They're–"

Her father had come in. He'd been jolly, and raving about his newest business idea.

"A school to teach skiing! Think of that, Marjorie! We could get all sorts of people here."

Her mother had laughed. Of course he could not.

Oriana pretended to sing along for a moment, but her voice petered out. They sat and Tieron began speaking once more.

"Does this not get boring?" Oriana asked, far too loudly.

Eldersie refused to look at her as she responded. "Worshiping Solyon is important. It empowers him to choose his elect every year."

"And you truly believe that?"

"You're a fool not to."

She kept up with questions all through the service. Eldersie noticed that Tieron kept glancing their way every time Oriana clicked her tongue and opened her mouth. When Tieron dismissed the congregation, Oriana sighed louder than anyone's singing.

"That was long. And these benches are hard. How do you do this every week?" She tried to stand, but Eldersie grabbed her by the arm and pulled her back down. "What? Are we not done? How can there be more?"

Eldersie saw that Almony and Jos were both standing.

"Sit back down," she cautioned them.

"But the service is over."

"We've town hall," said Eldersie.

Almony's shoulders drooped. "What've we got to do that for?" she asked.

Eldersie's eyes flicked to Oriana. Almony slouched back into the pew.

"Must we discuss them?" Jos asked.

"We have to. Just like we did the railway," Eldersie replied, leaning over

Oriana.

"But there are only three of them. What can it amount to?" Jos leaned over too, so that Oriana was entirely trapped.

"What can it amount to? For Solyon's sake, Jos Nothernine, you spend all day with that clerk and you don't even know what they are planning."

"What are you planning?" Jos looked to Oriana.

"I think I know less than you," she said.

"Townsend has been buying up any land he can get his hands on," Eldersie informed them.

"If people aren't happy about it, why aren't they refusing to sell?" Jos asked.

"That's what we're here to agree on. But you know what people are like. They sniff money and they can't get enough. Townsend is preying on desperate people."

"He's not that sinister." Oriana laughed.

"Is he not? He has been asking me about everyone's finances. I would wager that he plans to buy from the poorest first, so the others are pressured to follow," Eldersie said.

Oriana shook her head. "He's really not that malicious. He's just a businessman."

"I don't know what you think that means." Eldersie sat back, shushing them. "Oriana, don't say anything unless you're spoken to."

"You're worse than my matron at boarding school," she hissed. She shut up though, so Eldersie did not take any offence.

The low hum of chattering voices had returned. Eldersie heard Jos' name being said over and over again, like the whistle of the wind.

Parson Tieron cleared his throat and waved his hands, calling for attention once more. "I'm sure you all know why we have called for a town hall today." Tieron glanced at Oriana. "The entrepreneur, Mr Thomas Townsend, has some grand plans for this town. We can't yet say where any of that will leave us. I open the floor for anyone to share their experiences with Mr Townsend."

"Does that include me?" Oriana said to Eldersie. "In Racken, or just in general?"

Eldersie tutted while Oriana laughed at her own joke. Behind them, Joan the baker stood up, wringing her apron between her hands.

"Mr Townsend came to call last week. He left us with an offer for our business, and the land that we own."

"Was it a good offer?" Oriana called out. Eldersie poked her in the belly.

"He said that he wanted to buy up all of Main Street," Joan continued.

"The bakery belonged to my father, and so forth. What sort of man is this, who wants to buy old family land?"

There was a general muttering of assent, and a few claps.

"Old family businesses sold for a good price! Sacrilege!" Oriana did a mock gasp and clutched her fist over her chest.

Ricklin Morney, the cobbler, stood next.

"Mr Townsend called around my house and my brother's. He wanted to turn our houses into a hotel."

There was a collective gasp at his words. Oriana looked around wildly.

"Why is that a scandal?" she asked. "He is just offering to buy houses. Why are we gasping?"

"Hush. This isn't about you," Eldersie told her.

"He's bought the field in between my plots," shouted Dafyd, a farmer. "Because stupid Maritt thought his money was worth more than our town. What am I to do now? Ask bloody Thomas Townsend if I can cross his field with my herd every morning?"

"You could make a written agreement. It's just a field," Oriana said.

"It is not just a field," Eldersie stood up. "It is my belief that all of this is just an overture. Thomas Townsend means to turn Racken into a resort for rich folk to come from the city and learn to ski. He's done this successfully in several other mountain towns."

"What's the matter with that? More folk for you to meet. Maybe a better bar around here," Oriana commented.

"And perhaps the end of our lives as we know them. I don't mean to turn the governance of our town over to Thomas Townsend," Eldersie said to her. Around her, the temple echoed with mild cheers.

Oriana stood up herself. "Now, I think you're taking this far too seriously. It's just a business. Just a spot of skiing. A holiday spot," She was met with ringing silence. "All this about your way of life coming to an end. That's - well - that's a bit of an overstatement."

"All right then, Miss Townsend. Enlighten us all. What are Mr Townsend's plans, exactly?" Parson Tieron asked.

Oriana gaped. She was a train with no further steam, having never expected there to be more track past her feet. "He - Well–well he wants a hotel."

Eldersie scoffed. "A hotel? Where?"

"Uh - I'm sure there's some room somewhere."

"Nowhere in town could he build a hotel without demolishing some of our houses."

"No one would have to sell if they didn't want to. Or so I suppose."

"As I suspected." Eldersie laughed now. "Townsend is going to prey on people here who have no other option. Can't you see that?"

"That still sounds a little extreme."

"Jos! Tell her that their presence here is unwelcome." Eldersie shook him by the shoulder.

Jos flinched as if burned. "Well - I - I'm sure if no one sells anything he'll just leave." He sounded a little crestfallen.

Eldersie tutted at him. "Jos, have you not–? We'll talk later." She thumped back into her seat.

Oriana hurried to sit down. Eldersie could feel her sigh of relief.

"Mr Nothernine's opinion notwithstanding," Tieron began in his sermon voice, "I think we are of an accord that we want Mr Townsend to leave Racken with as much haste as we can inspire in him."

There was another round of cheers. Oriana shrank in her seat.

The parson continued. "I believe that we should all take it upon ourselves to let Mr Townsend know that his business is not welcome here."

"Should I be finding somewhere else to rest my head?" Oriana asked once they were outside the temple.

"What?" Eldersie turned to her. She had not been listening. Jos had not spoken to her as they left; he had clapped Almony on the back and fallen in step with her, keeping his head down as he waded through the crowd. Eldersie wanted to call out to him. His name was forming in her mouth, but the thought of it died.

"If you are denying my brother all business, should I be looking for a barn to spend the night in, or something similar?" Oriana asked.

"I – no. I need the money."

"Isn't that always the case?"

"Let me think on it, all right? Don't go telling your brother anything." She took off back to her own house, letting Jos drift in another direction.

Oriana followed her. "I wouldn't tell me what to do. I don't think I learned that much at church," she said.

JOS NOTHERNINE

"Has she still not chosen?" he asked, though he expected the answer already.

"I haven't sensed it," replied Solyon. He examined his hand as if bored. "She might surrender, one never knows."

"She can surrender?" asked Jos, astonished.

Solyon's laugh was as bright as a bell. "She's far too selfish for that. Look around." He gestured at the grove, which was summer trapped in a jar. "If she had chosen, summer would already have returned."

"What can I do?" asked Jos. "Surely there is something."

Solyon shook his head. A butterfly, thriving on the perpetual summer of Solyon's grove, flew past; Solyon raised his hand and let it land upon his finger. It was black and amber, vividly painted like the windows in the temple. Solyon considered it, turning his hand over, lost in thought.

"You can practice patience," he said.

Jos and Ifry had settled into a routine. Ifry, even as he struggled to write with gloves on, made copious notes about their trips.

"Are most of the creatures here pack animals?" he asked. Racken was a distant thought, as they stood on the slopes of the highest peak in the region. Jos was on the trail of some capin.

"No," Jos replied. "Kuprum are, and the ankatze. Janros take care of their babies until they're juveniles, but then they're solitary creatures. If there were more pack animals, I would be useless, being alone and all."

Ifry nodded. Jos could feel his eyes on him as he found the capin's tracks along the ridge they were following.

"What are capin like?"

"Goats."

"Really?" asked Ifry in surprise. "Herds, then?"

"No. Solitary creatures. They only look like goats. Don't behave like them."

"I'm coming to learn that about mountain creatures. There must be a reason that none of them were tamed, nor kept in zoos in the city."

"Creatures here are vicious. Hardy," Jos replied, thinking that the same could be said for the local people.

Jos picked out a route down, and skied away. He stopped at the foot of the slope and looked back to check that Ifry was managing.

They followed the trail of the capin. Jos found drops of fresh blood alongside the footprints, and the indents where something had been dragged.

"Is it injured?" Ifry asked.

"No. It got one of the dogs from Aigner farm."

"How are we to get the dog back over these peaks?"

Jos laughed. "Oh, that dog is dead. I just can't let the capin run free, or it will come back."

Ifry had the grace to grimace at this news. "Carnivores, are they?"

"Yes. We're getting close, so be on your guard."

Ifry made a noise, perhaps out of fear, but didn't say anything more. They went uphill again, climbing alongside the face of the peak where grey rock showed through the snow, like holes in a woollen jumper.

Jos spotted the capin dragging the limp dog through the snow below them, unaware of their presence. The capin made the dog look small, like it was a miniature poodle that rich folk bought to sit on their laps during portrait sittings, though Jos knew it was fully as tall as his waist. He heard Ifry's low whistle as he noticed the creature.

"Hardly a goat, is it?" he whispered.

It would have been as tall as Eldersie's first floor. Its fur was so long that the shape of its body was indistinguishable. As a child, Jos had seen them from his window and wanted to touch them. His mother had warned him very sternly that while their fur was soft, it was certainly not worth it.

"How many of them are there? If you were to guess?" Ifry said.

Jos shrugged.

"At least a dozen. I never had time to make a survey."

Ifry made a note of his statement, though Jos felt that he hadn't given him anything worth writing down. The capin, unaware of their presence, settled into eating its kill with unappealing wet noises. Jos settled into place on the ridge. Ifry, who now acted like his shadow, knelt beside him and removed his skis.

Jos tried to ignore him as he took his gun off of his shoulder. He brushed powder aside and lay down, leaning on his elbows. Ifry followed suit, as if Jos were his teacher and he were attempting to perform well. Jos tried to keep his attention on the capin, but could not help but think about how Ifry was lying next to him. In the corner of his eye, he could see Ifry's misted breath.

He turned his attention back to the capin. Its shoulders moved as it ate, and its mouth was hidden in layers of fur, only made visible by the blood that ran down its chin. The corpse of the dog was missing its head, and intestines spilled from its stomach like ribbons from a sewing box.

"Be ready to run," Jos whispered.

"What?"

"If it scents us, it might charge."

Ifry's breath caught, but Jos ignored it. He peered down the barrel and squeezed the trigger. He felt Ifry jolt against his side at the noise and for a moment he lost all the attention he had been focusing on the capin.

The creature let out a low wail and let the body of the dog fall. Jos regathered his thoughts and fired again. He hit his mark and saw a spray of blood leap from the capin's hide.

It cried again and turned towards them. Jos couldn't see its eyes through the fur, but its attention was impossible to miss. It snorted, and the air froze in a way that looked like smoke. It reminded Jos of the demons that Parson Tieron spoke about in temple.

It lowered its head. Jos had a moment of knowing that it was about to charge. On another day, he would have run, leaving his skis behind. Instead, he looked to his left for Ifry, whose eyes met his. His face was contorted in such a look of fear that it struck Jos' heart, though he had been calm before.

He let go of the gun and grasped Ifry's arm. Ifry understood his meaning without needing to be told. He stood. Jos held his arm fast and drove through the snow, fleeing up the ridge. He felt the rumble of the capin's footsteps. He ran up the ridge, but Ifry's weight held him back. He wished that he were faster, that he could make Ifry move quickly.

Then, he felt Ifry claw against his hand.

"Wait." Jos reached for him, but Ifry got himself free. He was frozen for a moment, and he reached for Ifry's vanishing hand.

"Go," called Ifry, but he was already fleeing in the other direction. He swept up a handful of snow and threw it overhand at the capin, where it exploded and stuck to its fur.

"Ifry!" Jos shouted. He had never seen anyone do anything so foolish.

Ifry gestured for Jos to run again, which only cemented his foolhardiness in Jos's brain. His heart was thumping more violently than the capin's charging feet. He fumbled with the gun, retrieving ammunition from his pocket and loading it. Ifry was smaller than a toy soldier as he ran through the powder.

The capin had forgotten about Jos, and now tailed Ifry. It was faster. Jos knew that it would catch up within seconds.

He raised the gun again. He didn't allow himself another breath. He fired; the shot caught the creature's leg. It squealed, and realising the ruse, turned on its heel. Jos found himself counting its tusks again as it charged. He pointed his gun, not knowing what else he could do. The crack of the gun rent the air and the shot found its mark in the creature's left eye. It didn't stop as it died; its momentum kept it going. Its legs buckled and it slid through the snow, right up to Jos.

He didn't move fast enough. The creature hit against Jos' legs and he tumbled, dropping the gun as he fell. He landed, quite winded, with his head pointing down the slope, all of the blood rushing into it.

"Jos!" Ifry's cry was distant, though he was not far away. The wind seemed to have stolen his voice.

Jos groaned, feeling the weight of the capin's leg settle over him. Its fur was as soft as he had imagined.

"Gods," Ifry said. Jos heard the crunch of his footsteps on the snow. "Please be all right."

With what sounded like great effort, Ifry lifted the capin's leg off of Jos. His relieved sigh cut the silent air.

"Did you think I was dead?" asked Jos.

"Consider what it looked like from my end," replied Ifry with a laugh in his voice.

Jos crawled out from under the creature. He inspected the capin. There was a bloody mess around its left eye.

"The eye. Tried and tested," said Ifry.

He held out his hand to help Jos to his feet. Jos paused before taking his hand, though he couldn't tell why. He took it and stood.

"Why did you do that?" he asked.

"What else was there to do?" Ifry laughed. He clapped Jos on the back. "You are impressive, Mr Nothernine."

Jos felt the blood rush to his face.

IFRY MARHEART

The sky was weighing down on him like a blanket. There were no footsteps leading to where he stood and there was no snow in the air, so how had he arrived? He was on the tallest peak where the capin had so recently died. He thought that he had left with Jos, but perhaps he was stuck there.

"It grows late. I may have to choose you."

He shivered at her voice. It rang in the corners of his ears. She was just out of his sight, though he could feel her presence as one feels being watched across an empty street. When he turned and saw her, she was not as terrifying as her voice implied. Her face was soft, though plain. She had light, watery eyes, and skin that was dry between her eyebrows. Her head only came up to his chin.

"Who are you?" he asked, but he knew the question was useless. She would answer no more clearly than she ever had. He had dreamed her for weeks. She rarely spoke. Usually, she hovered out of sight, cementing his suspicion that she was a figment. That she was nothing but a phantom that his mind had conjured. Yet he had never known dreams where he was able to form words. He remembered every one of them upon waking, when usually his dreams faded like ink in water.

"Someone clinging to the edge of their time. Don't trouble yourself," she said in her crisp voice. "I should have been dead long ago, but here I still am. My hand is forced every year. Perhaps you can end it for me." Her words trailed off.

He turned back to the ledge and looked down. He paused when he saw the ribbon of the river and the long cut of the railway through Racken. There was Eldersie's house and the temple next to it. His eyes drifted to the point on the slope below him where he knew Jos' house was hidden.

"I think you will have to do," she whispered. "I see how he looks at you. He has looked at no one else with so much as interest. Did you see the way he paused before taking your hand? What else could cause him to hesitate? Some regard must be growing within him," she said.

He saw her shadow cross the snow. They stood, side by side, staring down at the town.

"Whom do you speak of?" Ifry asked, wanting to unpick her riddles.

She laughed. "You do not know? Oh, but surely you do. He is tall, and lonesome, and he revels in your company, though he cannot admit it."

He feared that he knew of whom she spoke. He closed his eyes, feeling dizzy from the height. A cold hand touched his face. He tried to flinch away, but his body was numb.

"I choose you, Ifry Marheart, as my elect," she said.

He did not dare look at her. He felt the sharp pinch of her fingernails and a freezing breath singed his cheek. He shook. She kissed his cheek and he could not tear himself away.

"I hope he is kind to you," she whispered in a hiss as harsh as an avalanche.

She relinquished him and he opened his eyes. Her hand hovered just above his face. Her fingers were as white as bone. She had a ring that glittered with a single paltry gem. The silver of it looked warm against the tone of her skin. Even her lips were blue.

"What do you want from me?" he asked.

"Very little. Only what you do anyway. Living. Breathing."

"You make it sound so very simple," he replied.

There was no fog in front of her mouth as she spoke, though he could feel his own breath like smoke between his lips.

"When I did it, it was," she smiled at him. Her face recalled his own. Was she a mirror that he had conjured? A reflection of his own self? "It was only my husband that made it difficult. He had that talent."

"I would not know."

"We were only in love for a spring, you understand. Wed too quickly. I think I fell in love with an idea of him. He presented himself very differently from how he perhaps was."

He took a look at the landscape. There were only the soft curves of drifts, with not even a tree branch above them.

"Why are you telling me this?" he asked.

"Look at me wittering on. He used to complain that I spoke too much. I suppose he might have had a point. I came here, I took the cloak from Lady Winter myself. But that was long ago."

"I suppose Racken looked a lot different."

"Not in a large way," she mused. "But that is not important. You have work to do. Now wake."

Ifry found that he had fallen asleep in his day clothes. His jacket was rumpled and his handkerchief had fallen out of his pocket; he had three pairs of socks on and an old jumper of Jos's that had holes in the sleeves. It was too large for him, but after noticing Ifry's constant shivers, Jos had pressed it into Ifry's hands. It was Jos' belief that the tyenes were under-prepared for the mountain weather. The truth was that it might have been nearing the end of winter, but Ifry felt colder than when it had began.

He crawled out of bed with all the energy he could muster, which was not a great deal. Whenever he dreamed of her - the woman, whoever she was - he woke more exhausted than when he'd drifted off. He searched around his room for another layer to put on, but found nothing clean, so wrapped a scarf about his neck. He supposed that he should dress properly, but he could not bear the idea of undressing and baring his skin to the cold.

He'd thought he had gotten used to it. A few winters in the mountains and he'd thought his aversion had passed. Once, he had not been able to step outside in winter without shaking, without fear filling his brain like water from a tap. Those days were past, though he could feel their claws picking at him. He could ski now, and go to the slopes with Jos, without fearing that his voice would crack whenever he spoke. Yet there he was, remembering the feeling of being in icy water as if he were still submerged. He thought that he had grown out of it, that it was a thing that belonged to his childhood.

He shuffled to the landing and onto the stairs. He glanced at the crack under Jos's door but saw no light flickering there. He was out, doing errands no doubt.

In the kitchen, a fire blazed and all the windows were shut tight; a knitted draught excluder was pressed up against the exterior door. Yet the cold lingered on his bones like burrs caught in sheep's wool. He drew himself close to the fire without checking for Eldersie's usual busy presence. In the moment he cared only for the fire. Looking into it stung, like he was looking at sunlight reflected off snow on the mountain.

"Marheart?" said a voice. Ifry looked up. Townsend was seated at the kitchen table. "Late start?" he asked.

"I don't know. What time is it?"

"I'm teasing, Marheart. But I've got work for you."

He sorted through his papers and extracted a list drawn up in fresh ink. He held it out for Ifry to take. Ifry did not want to stand to reach for it, as doing so would mean leaving the fireside. He waited for a moment, watching the paper held in Townsend's steady hand, before tearing himself away to receive it. He scurried back to the fireside like a vole returning to its burrow.

"Of course, who knows how much work we will be able to do today? Or for the rest of the season," Townsend said. He glanced across the room to where Eldersie stood over the sink. She set down the pot she held with an over vicious thump, causing soapy water to splash onto the flagstones.

"I have a right to deny you business, if I so choose." Her sleeves were rolled up to her elbows and steam rose in spirals around her. Framed there, with her red cloth tied over her hair and the suds in the sink, she looked like one of the paintings of peasants that hung in city galleries.

"You're denying us business?" Ifry asked her.

"She's been to some town hall where the locals have apparently rallied against us," Townsend remarked with more sneer than in his voice than Townsend generally used. He generally reserved all his disapproval for Oriana when she made some drunken error.

"What for?" Ifry asked. He inched closer to the fireside.

"Oh, the townsfolk are bemoaning my dastardly deeds, no doubt," Townsend replied.

"We have had pushback from the locals before," Ifry said, thinking it would be remiss for him not to mention it. Town halls had been called against them before, committees formed, business denied. It all turned out the same in the end. The lure of Townsend's money was too strong to deny.

"Miss Toft is considering going along with the town's plans, which she knows will be inconvenient for us." Townsend made a note with a harsh flourish that left an ink blot on the paper.

Eldersie dropped a cloth into her tub and splashed water down her apron. "It is my decision, which I will not make based on your convenience."

"You really have taken this to heart, haven't you? Here you go then - consider that a peace offering." He signed a scrap of paper with another flourish and threw it across the table towards Eldersie.

She dried her hands on her apron and picked it up. Ifry guessed how much the cheque was worth. It was probably more than Eldersie had ever seen in one place, judging by her expression. Whatever amount it was, by it she would be able to to judge how much Racken was worth to Thomas Townsend.

Townsend's hand was no doubt shifted by the lack of other accommodation. Ifry could not imagine, even if he tried, Townsend having to live anywhere that did not provide a feather bed for him. Ifry, on the other hand, had lived without such comforts before. He remembered, more vividly than yesterday, waking in his childhood home to find that there was a frost inside the windowpanes. Their supply of firewood had run so low that his father had taken to chopping the legs off their maids' old furniture and burning them. The good furniture from their parlour and dining room was loaded into the back of a truck and taken away to be sold. They kept only what they needed, and as time went by, they needed less and less. Ifry and his sister Minnie, then small children, slept side by side on the couch by the fire. Their small beds had been sold, mattresses, blankets and all. It was so odd to hear the wind whistling through that grand house. The windows were boarded over, or had newspaper tacked to the frames in lieu of curtains. In their old nursery, there was a crack between the glass and the frame. Snowflakes would drift in and collect like sawdust on the sill.

Ifry had woken, shivering, to hear the satisfying splinter of cut wood. He shuffled into the hall, wrapped in a blanket, and saw his father chopping at the banisters. That was the day, Ifry was fairly certain, that his parents had decided they weren't going to sell their house. They were going to take it apart, piece by piece, with all of them inside. Minnie did not remember a time when they had had servants, or velvet curtains, or candles in the chandelier that hung above their heads. She did not recognise the name of their housekeeper or their mother's ladies' maid, or the carriage driver that used to take their father to sup with the Townsends. Soon there was nothing but Ifry, Minnie, and the glow of the fire.

As he sat next to the fire, Ifry felt a hollow where Minnie should have been. Instead, Townsend was there.

"You cold, Marheart?"

"How is one supposed to be warm in this place?" Ifry was almost touching the flames.

"Winter should have ended by now," Eldersie remarked, in a heavy way that implied she had control over the winds and tides.

"Winter will end only when we finally leave the mountains," said Ifry. "Irony is often like that."

"Are you so desperate for our holiday to end?" asked Townsend.

"It's felt longer this year." Ifry might have said that he had not seen a worse winter, only he had.

"You are not wrong, Mr Marheart." Eldersie dropped her cloth back into the tub with a satisfying wet slap.

Ifry took a glance over his list that only made his heart grow heavier.

"Where is Mr Nothernine?" he asked. "I should begin with my tasks if I'm going to make any headway."

"What need have you of Nothernine? I could equip you with a rifle and you would be safe enough," Townsend scoffed.

"I would shoot myself by mistake the moment you handed it over, Thomas," Ifry laughed, but stopped as he saw Townsend's expression. "I only mean that I've no idea how to handle a firearm. And I do not have the aim required to manage those creatures."

"Perhaps before we return next year, I should send you to practise somewhere. I'm sure I have a contact or two who enjoys a hunt."

"If we make it to next year," Eldersie murmured.

"Where is he, then?" Ifry asked her, ignoring her dour statement.

"He went off with Almony. You might want to check her place. It's on the other side of the valley. Big place called Aigner Farm."

"Thank you," he said, and with immense regret, he drew away from the fire.

A fog had descended on the peak. Ifry could not see the top of the mountain, nor those that surrounded it. He shouldered a pair of skis and crossed the valley in search of Aigner Farm. There was a rickety bridge over the river. Two sets of footprints crossed it, which Ifry deduced to belong to Jos and Almony.

The farmhouse was of the traditional style common to the mountains. It had a wide roof with long eaves, and carved decorations on the sills and shutters. Townsend loved houses like this. Alongside hotels, they made perfect holiday houses once the smell of livestock had been expunged. Almony's farm was lacking the cheery paintings that sometimes adorned the front of these houses; the place was far more practical. Ifry could see dried mud splattered against the walls from last summer.

He deposited the skis against a trough, and raised his hand to knock, filled with a fervent wish that Almony kept her home warm. However, when she opened the door, she gave him a look that could have frozen his core.

"It's the tyenes," she called behind her. "Jos was just about to come find you," she told Ifry. She walked away from the door, which Ifry took as his signal to enter.

Almony's house was rather well-to-do. There was a hallway with thick rugs on the floor, and curtains that had lace on their edges, but the room was covered in a fine layer of dust that Ifry could not fail to notice. Almony vanished into the warren of rooms, and Ifry's hesitation meant that he lost sight of her. He wandered into the house without much thought as to what room he chose, except that he sought warmth. He could sense it like sailors knew the call of the sea. He found a sitting room where a fire was lit and raised his hands up to it, as if in worship.

"What's brought you here?" asked Jos' voice.

"I was looking for you, actually," Ifry said, though he did not turn away from the fire.

"I apologise. I had errands." He stood, holding his hat in his hands like he was standing before a lord.

"I would have waited for you, only Mr Townsend was cracking the whip."

"Were you not eager to get to work?"

"I can't say that I am," Ifry admitted.

Jos drew one of Almony's armchairs close to the fire and gestured for Ifry to sit in it. Gratefully, he clambered into it. Jos positioned a stool opposite him and crouched on it. Ifry suppressed a laugh upon seeing him like that. His knees were almost at his ears.

"Here," Ifry said, standing up, "you can't possibly sit on a seat so small."

"No, I don't mind." Jos stayed on his stool.

Ifry grabbed him by the coat sleeves and tried to draw him up. Of course he was far too heavy for Ifry to lift, so his effort had no effect.

"You are far too tall for that stool. You take mine." Ifry let go of Jos's wrists and held onto his hands to try and draw him up. As soon as their skin met, Jos leapt up from his stubborn little seat.

"Mighty Solyon, have you been rolling around in the snow?" He grasped Ifry's cold hands between his own, then blew on them. His breath was like the wave that comes out of an oven when it was opened.

"I only just stepped out from Eldersie's," Ifry admitted.

"Tyenes, you aren't half unprepared for this place."

"I have been in the mountains many times, I'll have you know."

"You wouldn't know by looking at you. You're as thin as a rake." Jos grasped Ifry's arm, just under the shoulder, as if to test how slender he was. He let it linger for the moment, then seemed to remember what he was doing and let his hand fall.

For a second, Ifry missed the weight of it. There was a creak on the floorboards and Jos' gaze snapped from Ifry to a spot over his shoulder. Almony stood in the doorway to the dining room. Ifry gathered himself.

"I do apologise, Almony. I have commandeered your fire for a moment." He stepped away from Jos.

"What brings you here, tyenes?"

"I only hoped to find Mr Nothernine here to get up the slopes. I am afraid that I have been shirking my work so far today."

"I would not be going up today. Have you not seen the cloud cover?"

"I could not see the peak as I came over," Ifry admitted.

"You would not be able to see anything. We know that you are prone to accidents," Almony said, not without venom.

She pushed past Ifry to add another log to the fire and attack it with the poker. Puffs of ash fell onto the hearth rug.

"I have been doing my best not to get into further danger," Ifry promised her.

"It's true," Jos confirmed. "He has not even fallen these past few weeks."

"Ah. Miracles must be prevalent then," Almony dropped the poker and the clatter made Ifry wince.

"Almony!" cried a voice from another room.

Almony pushed past Ifry as she hurried through the room. To his shame, he lost his balance for a moment.

"What was that?" He glanced to the doorway that Almony had just stormed through.

"Her sister," Jos muttered. "She isn't well."

"Oh. Is there anything I can do?"

"Not unless you know how to wake the dead."

Ifry coughed to mask his surprise.

"Whom did she lose?" he asked.

"Her son. Almony's nephew. This time last year. If I were you, I would not ask."

"Surely we should fetch tea, or at least leave them to their business." Ifry, like many, thought that tea was the most appropriate method of confronting grief.

"I was meaning to help Almony with a few things. Truth be told, I've no desire to return to Eldersie's at the minute," Jos confided.

Ifry laughed. "You and me both. I am afraid that a long winter with Mr Townsend and his sister is wearing my patience rather thin. What is Eldersie getting at you for?"

"I have not been as diligent about attending temple I should have been. The winter gets like that."

"Say, let us bid goodbye to Almony and be on our way. But not back to Eldersie's house. I think we can pass the rest of the morning without a scolding."

This plan cheered Jos a little. His face broke into a smile that warmed Ifry. "I know where we can go where the clouds won't bother us." He hurried along and beckoned for Ifry to follow him.

Jos knew his way through the warren well. Each room was chilly and echoed. Ifry could hear the sounds of his breath reflected back to him.

It was as if it had once been full of people who had suddenly left.

There was a basket of knitting with a half-finished mitten laid on top. A vase held drying flowers and rotting stems in the water. Enough coats for a large family hung in the hallway, ready to be taken out; a little boy's jacket was positioned at his height.

The kitchen was a room that by all rights should have been merry, but the gingham curtains were moth-eaten, and the cupboards, with their painted floral designs, were dry and flaking.

"Forgive me for asking, but is Almony quite well-to-do?" Ifry asked in a low voice.

"Her family own most of the land on this side of the river. Nearly half the town by my reckoning. You would know a rich person by looking, wouldn't you?"

"When you spend time with Mr Townsend, you learn the signs." Ifry picked up a porcelain ornament from the table. He turned it over to examine the maker's mark, which he knew to be an expensive firm.

"I - oh - I thought you might have been comfortable, I supposed," said Jos.

"Once. Maybe."

"Are you thieves?"

Ifry was so startled by the voice that he gripped Jos's hand tightly. He looked at the door, where a woman who looked much like Almony stood. She had the same mousy hair and long nose, but she lacked Almony's farmer woollens, dressed instead in a stained nightgown and housecoat.

"We were looking for Almony, Helda," said Jos.

She did not respond. She stood in sullen silence, until Almony dashed into the room behind her.

"They aren't thieves," she explained.

"He had better put that back, then." Helda's eyes landed on the ornament in Ifry's hand.

He put it down in a hurry.

"Ifry Marheart, if you please," he said "I didn't mean to startle you. I know this maker. I have walked past his shop many times in Darrity."

"What brings a tyenes to my house?" asked Helda.

"I only meant to steal Mr Nothernine from you."

Almony, swearing, fussed over the stove. She had gathered a tea set painted in matching pinks and blues.

"You'll have trouble tearing him away. Been here his whole life," Helda said. "He and Almony are old friends. Though he hasn't been here of late."

"I've been busy," protested Jos.

"You have been with Miss Toft. It was always her that caught his eye."

Half a smile crept to her face and she winked at Ifry.

"It was?" Ifry asked with genuine surprise. He had never sensed so much as a spark between the two of them. Jos did not even tease her, or argue when she gave him tasks.

"Oh yes. We always thought we would see the two of them down the aisle." Helda looked at Jos, but from his scowl, he didn't seem to share the joke.

"What are you muttering about?" he asked, making no attempt at light-heartedness.

"I was saying that you always had an eye for Miss Toft," Helda said.

"No, I didn't," he said. "I just stay with her over winter."

"There's plenty of room here, and we have offered."

It was almost indiscernible, but Ifry caught a look between Jos and Almony.

"I wouldn't want to be a drain in your time of need," replied Jos. "Now, Ifry and I should leave."

"Our time of need?" Helda snorted. Almony caught her by the elbow and guided her to the table, before setting tea in front of her.

"Drink," she ordered, but Helda wasn't distracted.

"You are as bad as everyone else in this damn town, Nothernine. You treat us as if we are diseased, because we have lost. Eldersie must be no stranger to that feeling, yet she can't do us the kindness of collecting her own milk."

"Miss Toft is kept rather busy by my companions and I," said Ifry, seeking only to free Jos from an awkward situation.

Helda tutted.

"Let him be," cautioned Almony. "You've got tea, and Jos has hunting to do."

"Aye, there are more of them about. Long winter," Jos confirmed.

"It wouldn't be so bad if you weren't cursing people and speaking foully," said Helda to her sister. "They are convinced that you are bringing bad fortune on them."

"Would that be so bad?" muttered Almony.

Ifry plucked at the sleeve of Jos's coat. He caught his eye, then looked to the door.

It was a relief to escape.

"I hope that I have not caused offence," Ifry said. "She seemed to think that I was going to pinch her best china."

"I wouldn't worry. Almony doesn't care about being rude. It's a family trait."

Ifry glanced up the slopes. The clouds had begun to clear, and he could see the peak like a shadow puppet behind them.

"What do you say? Up? Though you don't have your gun."

"I'll fetch it. I had a thought that we might go across the valley." Jos gestured south, behind Eldersie's house. Ifry paled.

"Is that not where the gargin roost?"

"Not since you encountered them last. There is a spot I want to show you."

JOS NOTHERNINE

"No one else really goes up here," Jos said. That was an understatement, as no one but the elect would have a cause to climb this slope. He did not want to admit the truth of it to Ifry; he was so proper that if he knew, he would insist that they turn back, lest he offend anyone. They had abandoned their skis, as the waterfall was far too steep and rocky.

"The view up here," Ifry said, "is astonishing."

"You should see it in the summer. The snow hides all the detail."

"I'll have to abandon Thomas and visit when it is warm," Ifry remarked.

"You would do that?"

"Yes. Well, I would like to. Mr Townsend has never given me holiday in the summer before. I have to keep working."

"What for?"

Ifry spluttered, then laughed. "Because I haven't any money."

"What?" Stunned, Jos almost lost his footing on the path, which was rather steep.

"What did you think? That I was a clerk just for the fun of it? I am up here with you, avoiding the work that I was supposed to be doing."

"I don't know. I suppose I thought you must be comfortable, being a tyenes and all."

"You really don't know much about the city."

"How should I? I've scarcely left this valley," said Jos. He reached out to help Ifry up the slope, though he suspected the action was mostly unnecessary. They had reached the fall.

Ifry approached the ice and held his hand out, as if in reverence to it. As much as Jos thought of it as a twisted, deformed thing, it seemed different with Ifry there. The wonder in his face made winter over anew.

"How does one climb it?" he asked.

Jos mumbled, not knowing how to explain it.

Ifry chuckled. "I've been told that I've been reckless of late, so I should at least be seen to be cautious. I seem to have gained an unfortunate reputation with the locals." Ever bashful, Ifry gave him a half-smile. It had been too long since he had felt hopeful like this.

The last time he had, the railway was freshly laid and Kristann was still in Racken.

"Does Eldersie suspect something?" Kristann had asked. Jos could feel the rumble of his voice in his chest. They were secreted in their usual haunt, the loft of Almony's barn, while the other workers took their luncheon.

"No. I'm sure of it." Jos had his ear pressed to Kristann's breastbone and felt the cocoon of his arms around him. "She's not used to keeping secrets. If she knew, she would confront me."

"This all happens under her own roof. I assume she must have an inkling," Kristann said.

"There are so many workers in her house, how is she supposed to keep up with them all?"

Kristann raised a hand to rest on Jos's crown, where he wrapped one of Jos's curls around his index finger.

"She must be run off her feet," he said.

"She always is."

They passed a few moments in silence, apart from the grumble of Almony's donkey below them. Then, Jos broke it with the question that refused to leave his mind.

"You'll leave soon, won't you?"

"When the railway's done, we'll move to the next stretch."

"How far is that? All the way to the city?"

"To lots of cities. All the way across the continent, I hope," Kristann said brazenly. Jos could not conceive of how large the continent was, and how long it would take to cross it.

"How many cities?" Jos demanded.

"I don't know. As many as the company has money for."

Jos did not like Kristann's talk of the company. He could not guess at how large the company was or how many people worked for it. Any time Kristann spoke about money, Jos became lost. He knew how much money he needed to last the winter, and how much he collected as his wage. Folk in Racken avoided coin when they could. It was easier to bypass the ordeal and swap for what you needed. If you wanted lace curtains or silk shirts, they would have to be purchased elsewhere. Jos possessed nothing like that. Almony did, but she had inherited it all. Eldersie had once had a trunk full of fabrics that had been her mother's dowry, but they were long sold.

"Will you come back?" Jos asked.

Kristann sighed so heavily that Jos felt his head sinking. "Why are you asking me?"

"I want to know if I can see you again."

"Jos, you knew what this was."

Jos was not sure that he did. Any time that he asked, Kristann laughed and said that he did not know where life would take him.

"I'll go where I am meant to," Kristann insisted.

Jos was not content to drift as he did. He did not know how one could. Racken was not a place that one could drift from.

"What if that changes? What if you were to come back one day?" Jos asked.

Kristann sat up, forcing Jos to move away from him. He reached for his shirt and trousers.

"Do you have to go back to work?" asked Jos.

"We shouldn't get caught," Kristann replied, pulling his clothes on and searching through the straw for his boots. He tossed Jos's clothes back to him. A boot landed on the small of Jos's back and bounced onto the hay-strewn floor.

"Why are you leaving so fast?"

"I don't know, Jos. Because you are being a barnacle on the hull of a ship."

"I don't know what that means."

"Of course you don't. You have never seen a ship, I bet." He shrugged his arms into his jacket. Jos sat there, naked. "What did you think? That we would get married? Raise a family? That is not how it works. You have to go off and marry Eldersie as you are supposed to. I will go off and see the world."

"Kristann–"

"You can't become too attached. You're already - well–"

"What?"

"Obsessed."

"I am not obsessed."

"Then never ask me again where I am going or when I will be back, because the answer will be not one that you care for."

Jos clutched his clothes to his chest. He wanted to sink into the straw and never emerge.

"Tyenes," muttered Jos. Kristann found the ladder and climbed down without speaking further.

When the train rolled out of Racken, Jos did not know where

Kristann was headed. He thought that he might clutch an address and send notes to the cities that Kristann visited. He thought he might get postcards back and tack them to the inside of his wardrobe door. Instead, Kristann had vanished as if they had never known each other.

"If you don't think that you can make it, we don't have to climb it," Jos told Ifry. Ifry took another measure of the frozen fall.

"Would you catch me if I slipped? I have been coming to rely on you, I admit. I hope that is not unwelcome."

Jos did not mind in the slightest.

"Are you going to leave on the train and not come back?" The words fell out of his mouth before he knew their meaning.

Ifry, startled, let out a chuckle. "What prompted this?"

"I just - I - it's happened before. People come and they leave."

"This is unexpected–"

"Sorry."

"And very flattering."

Blood rushed to Jos' face. "I - I don't want to be unwelcome."

"No. And I won't vanish into the aether once winter ends. If Mr Townsend is successful, then we will have every reason to return. We have visited Thomas's other resorts this winter already."

"Oh," said Jos, trying not to sound crestfallen.

"Though of course, if I could scrounge a holiday, I might choose to spend it here."

"You would?"

"I've grown quite fond of you, you know. Say, is the view up there worth seeing?"

"I'd say it is."

"Let's get up there then, before our responsibilities catch up to us," Ifry declared.

Jos did not imagine that Ifry would manage the climb well, but he clambered up without making a complaint. He did not even slip.

That honour fell to Jos. He was so distracted thinking about Kristann, and what Ifry had said, that he did not test one of his footholds before he put his weight on it. He slipped and flailed, wheeling his arms in the air. Before he could banish his panic, Ifry caught his wrist and steadied him.

"Careful now, Mr Nothernine." He laughed and clapped Jos on the back.

"I wish you would call me Jos instead."

"All right, Jos, but I would hurry and climb up before I fall too."

Jos was careful to take his advice, not wanting to disappoint him. He reached a hand down to help Ifry up the last few steps. He dared himself to hold onto Ifry's hand as they moved away from the cliff's edge. Jos longed to strip off his glove and peel off Ifry's along with it. Ifry did not loosen his grip, which Jos noted; he expected him to every moment.

"This way," Jos said, leading Ifry towards Solyon's clearing. With Solyon absent, they saw it in its wintry aspect, and there was no telling that there was anything godly about the place.

"Is this a special place?" Ifry asked, observing his surroundings with curiosity.

"It's sacred."

"Ah," Ifry tapped the side of his nose with his free hand. "I won't be telling Mr Townsend about it then."

"I hoped you wouldn't. I mean - I was going to ask - but I had trusted that you wouldn't."

Ifry had still not relinquished his hand. "I can't claim to know much about your faith, despite what Eldersie has attempted to teach me, but I would not dare to cause any disrespect."

"No, you wouldn't." Jos glanced down at their joined hands, then felt that he shouldn't have. He should not have drawn attention to that bond, or surely Ifry would feel the need to break it.

"It's beautiful," Ifry said, glancing around at the grove, "and secluded."

"You could say that."

Ifry had taken a step towards Jos, still clutching his hand. He was very close now. Jos could feel the edge of Ifry's breath as it clouded in front of his face. He had though that Ifry's eyes were brown, but in the clear winter light he saw that they were more of a hazel.

Ifry was not breaking his gaze.

Jos thought that he ought to say something, but in the moment he had no idea how to form words. He had forgotten entirely the nature of syllables and consonants and vowels.

It had not been like this, last time. He had gone drinking with the railway workers, and walked to the river to clear his spinning head. Kristann had caught up to him. He'd grabbed Jos and kissed him before Jos could consider what occurred. The details were fuzzy. They had been too urgent, too eager, and they had almost been caught as the other workers spilled into the road. There was no savouring of the moment, and Jos was surprised by how dull it had been. Kristann had left, not caring to comment, and returned to their fellows.

"Ifry?"

"Hmm?"

"Do you want me to kiss you?"

Ifry's brow furrowed. Jos could not blame him. It was an unexpected question. It was possible that Jos had misunderstood their situation.

Ifry let go of his hand, and Jos felt as if he should fall off the mountain face right then. He looked down, seeking to curtail his embarrassment.

Ifry's bare hand, cold as glass, pressed against the side of his face. Jos held in a gasp.

"You're cold." He peeled off his own glove and clutched Ifry's hand with his own.

"Yes," Ifry murmured. He moved his hand from under Jos's palm to rest on his neck. Jos forgot how cold the air was in his throat. He closed his eyes. He tasted Ifry's lips on his own.

The wind rose and Ifry shook. Jos broke the kiss.

"Are you always so freezing?" He wrapped his arms around Ifry's shoulders, and Ifry buried his face into Jos' neck. Ifry lifted his arms above Jos's shoulders and wound his ungloved hand into Jos's hair.

He breathed in the smell of Ifry's skin. "Are you all right?" he whispered.

"I'm perfect." Ifry leaned back and kissed him again.

Jos dropped his hands to Ifry's waist and wished that he had not brought Ifry to such a cold location. He should have found a warm spot for someone used to such sunny climes. Then he could have touched more of Ifry than just his face. Yet they were as far from Eldersie and Thomas Townsend as they could possibly be. Ifry put his hands inside the collar of Jos's shirt, perhaps to touch him, perhaps just to warm his extremities.

They returned to Eldersie's house well into the afternoon.

"Where's Mr Townsend?" asked Ifry, seeing that the table was vacated. Eldersie's sheets hung, dripping, over the kitchen while she kneaded dough.

"He's gone out," she said.

"Did he say where?"

"He does not care to keep me aware of his movements." She slammed the dough onto the counter.

"And Oriana?"

"I try to ignore her, if I am honest."

"I shall go up and change, I think," Ifry announced.

Jos moved to follow him upstairs, but he was caught by Eldersie.

"Jos, I need you to fetch some more logs. Then move my father's wastepaper basket to the kindling pile before he can root through it again."

Ifry paused on the stairs to smirk at Jos, but hurried away as soon as Eldersie glanced his way. Jos rushed through his tasks. He filled her basket with logs, then he stacked more inside the woodshed to dry them out. He tramped up and down the stairs with things for Martine Toft in the attic. Jos found him searching under his bed.

"She's taken my plans again, Jos," he complained. He wiped sweaty palms down the front of his night shirt, unfolding and smoothing out pieces of paper with copious, incomprehensible notes. Jos left him with few words, having learned not to get sucked into conversation with Martine; he had somewhere else he wanted to be.

When he descended the staircase, he clutched the basket of wastepaper that Eldersie had asked him to squirrel away. To his dismay, he found the kitchen noisy once more.

Townsend and his sister were seated at the table. Their arrival meant that Eldersie was kneading dough with unwarranted ferocity. Trapped at the table, with his fingers ink-stained and a scarf tied tightly about his throat, was Ifry. His brow was knotted and his shoulders taut, but when he looked at Jos, he softened.

Jos set the basket down next to the hearth, but Eldersie tugged it away from him, leaving flour on Jos' hands in her rush. She tore through the paper, balled it up, then tossed it overhand into the fire. She went to root around again.

"What are you doing?" he asked. She didn't answer him, but continued to destroy her father's work with the same ferocity she had applied to her kneading.

"Did you - If - Mr Marheart, did you need anything else from me?" Jos asked, fishing for a reason to steal him away.

"Marheart's got his plans full already," Townsend said. "Our acquisitions have finally started rolling in. There's more paper work than the government gets through in a year." He gestured to the mess he had made of Eldersie's table.

Jos lingered. He found the stale end of yesterday's bread and a small piece of cheese. There was no room left at the table, so he ate his lunch next to the sink, trying not to glance too often at the back of Ifry's head. Oriana walked over to him and he shrank back, unsure of her intentions.

She pushed past him and rooted through the cupboard to his left, then, failing to find what she searched for, decided to move on to the cupboard he stood in front of. She did not ask him to move, but tapped on his legs until he moved aside. She emerged from the cupboard, Eldersie's clay jar of biscuits in her arms. She leaned on the counter next to him, eating biscuits right out of the jar and letting the crumbs fall back in.

"Are you all out of tasks to do?" she asked between bites.

Jos glanced to the bin which Eldersie was tearing through. It was nearly empty. Soon she would have more instructions for him, or Parson Tieron would drop by with some elect duty for him to fulfil. Almony had been laden with them last year. She had been begged to bless every animal in Racken. Not that any of those animals were more fertile or in sounder health the next year, but people were prone to their superstitions. He had not been asked to do many blessings; he suspected that was Almony's influence. In the early days of spring she had run around, spitting curses on every animal she had once blessed.

Ifry was not left idle for the rest of the day, despite Jos's attempts to sneak a kiss in the stairwell.

Alas, Jos didn't have time to dwell on the matter. Mindri, the parson's youngest acolyte, appeared with word that another kuprum had been spotted nearby. He walked to the edge of town with Mindri, who was forced to jog to keep up with his strides.

"Joan spotted them just this afternoon," she said.

"Them?"

"Family of the beasts."

Jos steeled himself. Mothers were always more vicious, as one would expect.

"Go back to the temple," he advised Mindri. "Warn the parson."

He couldn't have a teenager on his tail as he hunted kuprum. The light was waning; she had vanished from his sight before a minute had passed. He climbed the slopes, finding Joan's tracks frozen into the snow, and found the kuprum with her cubs before long. The dusk had turned their flashing scales dull, so they looked like three shadows moving swiftly across the snow.

There was no good spot from which to fire on them, so he elected to scare them. They would flee, the mother seeking to protect her cubs. It was better than offing a whole family. He fired a shot past her ear.

Her head darted up. She didn't squeal, as he had seen kuprum do before. He might not have been able to see her eyes, but he knew she was staring at him. He crawled into a snow drift, fearing that she was about to find him.

She was. Lacking enough light to kill the mother and the cubs both, he fled to the trees. He heard the creatures' frantic breath as they pursued him. He was lucky it was such a short sprint.

He felt teeth tug on the cuff of his trouser leg as he leapt into the branches of a skinny pine. The trunk wavered as the kuprum leapt against it. He scrambled up, hearing the scratching of their claws against the bark. He hooked his arms over a thick branch and rested for a moment, feeling the burn in his muscles from the sprint.

A jaw locked around his ankle. He clutched onto the branch as he felt himself being dragged down. He glanced down and saw the white teeth of one of the cubs, stark against its black skin, locked around his boot. It was all he could do to hold onto the branch, though he could feel the harsh bark tearing at the skin on his palms. He might have tried to think of a way out of his situation, but unyielding panic filled his mind. The creatures growled wetly below him.

He was hit with the most astonishing luck. The tree trunk shook with the movement of the kuprum. Above him, weight shifted, and snow fell, heavy like a ghost, landing on the kuprum's face. It was young enough to be startled, and let go of Jos's leg. He allowed himself no moment of relief. He scrambled higher, ignoring the ache in his foot, and went as high as the branches could take him.

The harsh winter must have been getting to the kuprum, because they worried at the tree with their paws for longer than he expected them to.

Fog descended. He could only see Racken by the lights, then as the townsfolk went to bed, not at all. He held his arms tight across his front. He could feel the drip at the end of his nose freezing.

The fog turned to driving snow that caught inside his hood and filled his collar. He chanced a look at the ground, and found that he couldn't see the shape of the kuprum against the powder. He was finally alone. He began his descent, but his frozen fingers were not as helpful as they had been on the climb up. He lost his grip and scrambled, grasping onto a skinny branch to steady himself. It snapped and he plummeted. He hoped, in his moment of free fall, that the fresh snow might act as a cushion. He was not as lucky as that.

As he landed, his leg buckled under him. He fell onto his side, winded and with snow sticking to his face. He lay for a moment, commiserating at his own sour luck, then reached back to check that his gun was undamaged. He found it less worrying than checking his foot, which he already knew had not come out unscathed.

He took a look at it. It was not bent at an odd angle, but his boot could have been hiding the worst of the damage. He needed Eldersie.

The only thing he knew for certain was that it hurt. He tried to move it, and cried out. He might have been embarrassed by his momentary loss of dignity, but he was certain that there was no one nearby. He was certain in a crushing, deadening way.

He had a pair of skis to find, though he knew they would be obscured by snow. He tried to stand, but his shin bone screamed as soon as his foot met ground. He stayed on all fours and shuffled to where he imagined he had left his skis. The snow soaked through his trouser legs, and he felt its chill on his skin. His mittens, as thick as they were, were not warm enough to fight back the cold. In the dark, he could not tell which route he had taken to arrive; he only knew he should go downhill.

He could not guess how long he searched for. There was no good way to recognise time. He could not see the moon for the snow; he could not see the tree he had fallen from. He thought he was crying, but he wasn't sure whether his face was just wet with melted snow. He dragged his useless leg behind him. Home was still far, and the kuprum could still be nearby and hungry.

He had started the day well enough: fighting off giddiness when Ifry kissed him, hoping to sneak into Ifry's room whilst Eldersie and her father were asleep. Now he was alone, and half certain that no one would bother to look for him. When Solyon had chosen him, he had thought it might change things for him. He might have been loved, observed, noticed. Eldersie did turn a friendly eye on him again, but that didn't last. Her sour looks and words crept back in. He'd won some of Almony's sympathy from the depths from which she slumbered.

It was not enough. He was going to perish on the side of a mountain. Winter would cover the land.

"Mighty Solyon," he said aloud. "Help me now. Help your elect. I need to get home."

The prayer was unfamiliar on his tongue. He was not used to it. "Solyon?" he called. The wind moaned back to him. "What use is there in you?"

He had gone too far north. He should have stayed at the waterfall. He should have stayed with Ifry.

"What brings you here, summer's child?"

A hand touched his chin. Her fingers were cold, like the feeling of touching a windowpane. She tilted his face upwards. He could not quite hold her in his vision; it must have been the snow, or the faded light. She wore a hooded cloak, that, while it behaved like fabric, looked like it was made from blue ice.

"Who are you?"

"Winter's lady, you fool. Why are you here? Has my challenger relented so easily?"

"The kuprum. I was hunting the monsters."

She smiled.

"An accident, then. I could let you stay here. I would win the challenge, at last. That would show him."

"Please," he begged without pause. He must have been dreaming.

"That would hardly be fair of me. Solyon would call it cheating, and it would not suit my ends if you perished. No, I need you to confront my elect."

"I know I am supposed to."

"I have chosen now. I left it quite late this year. Last winter was so torturous, I was almost convinced that I had it. I suspect you will curse me when you find out."

"Who is it?"

She tapped a cold finger to the end of his nose.

"Now that would be telling."

"Please don't let it be her," he said, not quite knowing which of them he was thinking of.

"I cannot change my mind now. The game is at play, child. None of it matters, anyway. I hoped to lose, truth be told. I hoped that last year she wouldn't, but she did. I tried to tell her how to end it, but she couldn't hear me."

"End it?" he asked.

"End it all."

He thought of winter freezing the lakes and the rivers until no one remembered that they were ever there.

"I don't want it all to end."

"You misunderstand me. Get down the mountain and do your work." She stood and swept aside the snow with the edge of her cloak. As if she had conjured them, his skis and poles were uncovered. He fell on them like a janros on a fresh kill.

He shifted onto his rear and attempted to fix the skis onto his feet while seated. He pulled off his mittens with his teeth, but found that his hands were too frozen to be useful. He cursed until he got his buckles on correctly. He pulled himself up, leaning on his good leg.

"Solyon, don't let this hurt as much as I think it will."

In the distance, she laughed. "He would not help with that even if he could. He is not a kind man, and I would know."

He did not look at her. He lifted his foot and lowered it into the ski. Nothing but a few twinges bothered him. Perhaps he had been dramatic in his estimations of his injury. He uprighted his poles and leaned on them, pointing both skis downhill. Carefully, he shifted his weight onto his bad foot. He cried out and swore, then bit his lip in the hope that would distract him from the pain. It didn't work.

He waited. He could not do it, even on his skis. His hands were frozen. His mittens were wet inside. He had skis, but his straits were still as dire as they had been without them.

He steeled himself. There was every chance he would still die on the slope, but he might as well make it simpler for his body to be found. Pain be damned, or as damned as he could make it. He braced himself for the worst and leaned forward. He kept his weight on his good foot as much as he could, relying on the slope to take him down, without much thought for controlling his speed.

He couldn't turn on his left foot without collapsing, so he kept his skis as straight for as long as he could tolerate, though he feared going too fast. The fog and the darkness were so thick that he had no hope of seeing what lay ahead.

He went into a mogul and was tipped backwards. He landed face down, his legs tangled under him and one of his poles missing. His left ski was stuck upright in a drift. He had to move it, though he loathed the idea. He clambered up, screaming, and sat back on his skis. He groped around for the lost pole and realised that his mitten was also missing. His hand had been so cold anyway that he hadn't noticed.

Amongst the snow, there were amber lights glimmering. He dragged himself down the slope.

IFRY MARHEART

He dreamed of her again.

"She chose me too," she told him. "Lady Winter, and the lord chose my husband. Enmity ran deep between them, as it does between the two of us. They fought every year. I don't want to fight. I'm so tired."

Her hand was cold against his ear. She brushed his hair back.

"He's on his way," she whispered. "Watch the door."

Ifry did not register the foreboding. He did not care that the dream woman was back, even as he felt her touch. He was cold. He knew nothing else. He did not know where he was. The snow was swallowing him whole. It was in his mouth as he breathed and in his eyes as he opened them. He was under the water, clutching for the surface but he could not find it.

There was no air, and his skin was cold enough to feel burned.

He sank. He reached one arm out in hope. Perhaps he would find her down there, under the ice.

He woke with paper stuck to his face. His solitary candle was burnt low, with only a stub left, and Eldersie's roaring fire was reduced to embers. The biscuit jar was empty, with only a few crumbs that Oriana had left to mark her passing. Eldersie's sheets hung around him, their smell turned from fresh and floral to vaguely musty.

Ifry peeled the page from his cheek and set it back among the rest. Townsend had given him forms mixed with miscellaneous scraps that had fallen from the inside of his pocket book. Ifry was left to sort through what was official and what was not, and to total up the purchases that had been made.

Ifry tidied the pages for want of anything else to do. He leaned his chin onto one hand. He had not been using his time wisely; he had done far less work than he intended.

He could not keep his gaze from drifting to the door. He imagined the latch being lifted and Jos stepping through, stamping his boots on the mat and shaking the snow out of his long hair. But he was not there.

As they ate dinner, Ifry noticed his absence. Eldersie told him not to bother worrying. Jos was capable. Killing monsters was what he did all winter. Ifry could not help but be concerned that he had scared Jos away. He sat, pen hovering over the page, analysing his actions. Had he been too cold? Too stand offish? Had he come on too strong?

Jos could be avoiding Ifry. He could be hoping that Ifry would leave soon for the city, leaving Jos to go about his life as it was before. When they were stood above the waterfall, Ifry had been certain. Jos' words and his manner confirmed it. Yet his absence left a hollow note that made Ifry doubt it all.

He had been gone for hours. Ifry, though he knew he wasn't being reasonable, counted the hours as they passed by. It had been more than seven. He checked the clock again. It was closer to eight.

Jos wasn't a social man. He might have gotten injured. It was cloyingly dark. He could have fallen and broken his neck; he could be dead, his body freezing, and they would find him preserved only when the thaw came. Then they would have to take boiling water to free him from the mountainside, because the ice would be too thick to reach him.

He should sleep.

"Eldersie!"

The bellow came from outdoors. Ifry nearly knocked over his candle as he rushed to the door. He threw it open, but could not see for the snow that blew across the town.

"Jos?" he called. A half-formed groan replied. Through gusts of snow, Ifry could see the burnt yellow of Jos's coat. He was not moving as fast as he should. There was no rhythm to his gait. "Are you all right?"

He got no response. He rushed out in his shirtsleeves, feeling the bite of the snow against his arms. He could not judge how far it was with the snow, and stumbled into Jos. He was leaning on his skis, using them as a crutch.

"Lean on me." He looped Jos's free arm over his shoulder and nearly stumbled under the weight of him. He guided Jos to the door, fearing with every step that he would be forced to drag him.

By the grace of his gods, they made it inside. One pole hung from Jos's arm, and the other hand was ungloved and mottled purple. He tottered towards the hearth and collapsed there in Eldersie's chair. "What happened?" asked Ifry.

"I fell. My foot - can you–?"

"I'll fetch Eldersie."

Ifry thumped a fist on her door until she threw it open, red-eyed and fuming.

"Jos is hurt," he said before she could admonish him. She threw a wrapper over her nightgown and followed.

Jos sat by the fire. He had propped up his bad foot on a stool.

"What happened?" Eldersie asked.

"There was a kuprum and two cubs. They were hungry. I fell trying to get away. Messed up my leg."

Eldersie rushed to his foot, holding Ifry's candle aloft. Ifry hated to be a bystander. He marched to Jos's side. He picked up his arm and unhooked the pole from his wrist, then peeled the mitten from his hand.

"Gods, this is soaking," Ifry said as the mitten's lining dripped onto his hand. He tossed it to the floor, then pulled the hat off Jos's head.

"What are you doing?" demanded Eldersie.

"Look at him, he's soaked through. You get his boot off and I'll get him into some dry clothes."

She did not protest, which Ifry took as approval. He dashed up the stairs and into Jos's room. He gathered up a pair of blankets, a shirt, and a pair of trousers.

Back in the kitchen, Eldersie was hacking at Jos's bootlaces with a kitchen knife. They were apparently frozen together. Ifry went to Jos's side.

He found the buckle of his belt, then undid the duffels that fastened his coat. Jos grimaced. Eldersie was easing his boot off of his foot.

"I'll need to splint it," she said. "You haven't half done this at the wrong time."

"I thought I was supposed to be the one who got injured out there," Ifry joked, but no one laughed. He pulled back the coat from Jos's shoulders. "What did you do? Roll around in the snow?"

"I was crawling," Jos said.

"All the way down the mountain?"

"Most of it," he admitted.

"Gods, Jos. What could have happened if you died out there?" Eldersie wiped her brow with the back of her hand, perhaps more intent on criticising Jos than helping him.

"I was thinking of that the entire time, Eldersie."

Flush with an idea, Ifry touched Jos on the shoulder and dashed back up the stairs. Oriana was asleep, her mouth hanging open and her sheets tangled about her legs. She did not notice as he found her flask and ducked back out.

"Brandy," he said, passing it to Jos. He hoped that it would distract him as Ifry went to pull his damp jumper over his head. He took a swig and grimaced.

"Where does she get this stuff?" he said.

"I don't know." Ifry unbuttoned Jos's shirt, wishing that he was doing it under different circumstances. Eldersie, unabashed, reached up to untie his trousers and pulled them down. Ifry tried to give Jos a sympathetic look, but found that he couldn't communicate much. He was left in his long johns. "Take your underthings off and I can put this on you." Ifry held up the shirt he had retrieved.

Jos hesitated.

"If I had to strip in front of Eldersie, so do you," Ifry admonished him.

Jos slowly unbuttoned down his front and peeled his underclothes away. Ifry handed him a new shirt, but he struggled to fasten the front.

"My hands–" he said. Ifry clasped his fingers, which were colder than usual. It was so odd to find Jos so cold. He fastened the buttons for him, then wrapped a blanket around Jos's shoulders. Eldersie searched around for a splint to use, cutting a piece of kindling with a hatchet, and Ifry used her moment of distraction to clasp Jos's hands between his own and rub the life back into them.

"I think you've cracked your bone," Eldersie said.

"It's only my ankle," Jos insisted.

"The little bone in your shin." She indicated on her own leg. "You'll need to keep your weight off it for a few weeks."

"We don't have a few weeks."

"I know that."

"A few weeks for what?" Ifry asked.

Jos stiffened. "Oh. Just of the winter. I can't be chair-bound with kuprum coming down the hills. There will be more to the pack."

Eldersie picked a neat stick from the kindling pile. She measured it against Jos's shin, then used her knife to clean the edges.

"You're lucky it wasn't worse, if I'm honest," she proclaimed.

"I'm lucky I'm here at all." He gasped as she turned his leg. "Fuck, Eldersie. Could you warn me?"

"No. It'll hurt more if you know it's coming." She began to bind the splint to his leg.

Ifry let go of Jos's hands and went to the fire.

"Where–?" Jos reached for him.

"I've a hot water bottle." Ifry set the kettle over the fire. "We need to get you warm."

"There's a bed pan under my mattress," Eldersie said. "You can fetch that and put it in Jos's bed."

Ifry did just that and when he returned, Jos's leg was bound and Eldersie had fetched a pair of crutches. Ifry filled his hot water bottle, while Eldersie helped Jos climb the stairs. He groaned on every step.

"I'll check on you in the morning. I'll speak to Parson Tieron to see what we can do about this," Eldersie bade him goodnight.

Ifry caught her before she returned to her bedroom. "I can do some of Jos' tasks. I know you always keep him busy."

She frowned at that. "And Mr Townsend keeps you busy as it is."

"It might be high time for us to put Oriana to good use then," he said.

Eldersie laughed. He had never heard her laugh.

"That would be a fine thing to see."

"I know how to convince her," Ifry assured her. He shook the half-empty flask.

She nodded and departed. Ifry watched her go, and then he ducked into Jos's room.

"Are you all right?" he whispered to Jos.

"Truthfully?"

"Truthfully."

"No, though I can't tell Eldersie that."

"She isn't particularly filled with pity." Ifry picked up the corner of Jos' blanket. "I could sleep in here tonight if you wanted." He had been planning to ask this question anyway, though he wished the circumstances had been different.

"I need you to keep me warm." Jos still shivered, despite the bottle and the bedpan. Ifry, rather selfishly, longed to be warm himself.

Ifry kicked off his boots and crawled inside, guiding Jos's hands off the hot water bottle and wrapping them in his own.

"I was worried sick," he admitted. "Though I feared that I was the one who scared you off."

"Just the opposite," Jos murmured.

"Listen–" Ifry began.

"Sorry. Did that sound too sincere?"

Ifry ignored his question in favour of what he wanted to say. "You gave me some good advice a while ago."

"What was that?"

"You shouldn't go up the mountain alone."

Jos laughed at that. "Next time I go hunting you can come with me."

"I'll use your broken leg to guilt Thomas into letting me accompany you." Ifry leaned his forehead against Jos's cold one. He let go of Jos's hands and put his own on either side of Jos' neck. Jos had his eyes closed.

"I would like that," he said. "We could go to my house again."

"That was a cosy little place."

"It's my favourite place."

"In Racken?"

"In all the world."

Ifry had not been so certain about an idea like that since he was a child. He and Minnie used to play in the cupboard inside the wall of their attic. It was filled with blankets and teddy bears and faded picture books. He wondered whether anyone had found the time to clear it out, after she was gone.

"I don't have a favourite place," Ifry said.

"You can borrow mine."

"Right now, it's just here." Ifry pressed his lips to Jos's forehead.

ORIANA TOWNSEND

"He fell where?" she asked. The porridge fell off her spoon and landed with a wet splat.

"He didn't say, but he's broken his damn leg." Eldersie sliced through a carrot in a way that made Oriana think that she was wishing Jos's leg be parted from his body.

Ifry cleared his throat. "Which was why I was hoping that you might help Eldersie around the house a little."

Oriana gaped. That request, while it sounded mild, could mean any number of things. If Eldersie could put her to use, she might have Oriana scrubbing the floorboards like the youngest daughter in a fairytale.

"What do you want me to do exactly?" she asked.

"Anything that Jos might normally do."

"Should I be fetching his shotgun?"

Oriana looked at Ifry, hoping to communicate all her dismay in one expression. Usually he would have fended Eldersie off for her, yet he had the disapproving look that was usually worn by her brother.

"What's she getting you to do?" Oriana asked him.

"Nothing. But I can't help Eldersie and be a clerk for your brother. You don't have anything to do. You may as well help out a little bit."

"Why do I feel like I'm being scolded?"

"You aren't. It would just be very kind of you to do a few things for Eldersie." He stood up, and Oriana certainly felt like she had just been scolded. "I have to check in on Jos," he announced, and made for the stairs.

"What's got into him? Why has he decided he's Jos's keeper?" Oriana asked Eldersie, who snorted.

"I couldn't guess. Perhaps because he was awake at the right time."

Oriana stood, intending to escape while Eldersie was busy with her carrots.

"Not so fast," Eldersie said as Oriana's foot met the first step on the staircase. "I need you to fetch the milk from Almony's farm. Jos can't do it on crutches."

Eldersie had to explain the location of Almony's farm three times before Oriana understood. She arrived there to find Almony waiting with an expression sour enough to curdle the milk before Eldersie could get her hands on it.

"Where's Jos?" she demanded.

"He's broken his leg."

"He what?"

"He fell off a mountain and broke his leg."

"Is he all right?"

"I don't know. You can check for yourself. Eldersie's sent me here to get the milk."

Almony pointed Oriana towards a tin can with handles on the top of the sort that Oriana assumed only existed in picture books. "She can't expect me to lift that."

"There's no one else to lift it," Almony said. She let herself back indoors, leaving Oriana to have a staring match with a tin can.

She realised that she feared returning to Eldersie's house with nothing to show for her trip. She tried to heft the can over her shoulder, but she could barely get it an inch off the ground. She chose to shuffle it instead, turning it one way and then the other, like she was taking the damn thing for a walk. She left a trail in the snow like she was a slug, all the way from Almony's door, across the bridge and the railway, back to Eldersie's house.

"What did you stop for? A chat? Brunch?" Eldersie asked as Oriana shuffled the can through the door.

"How was I supposed to lift this thing?"

"You could try a little harder. Could you take this tray up to my father? I have to visit the parson."

"What for? What pressing religious issue could there be?"

"Just do it." Eldersie gestured to a lunch tray as she buttoned her coat. She let herself out, without giving time for Oriana to protest.

"I've become a maid, Mother," she said to the empty room. "You proud of me yet?"

The tray was made up nicely. Eldersie had set out toast and bacon and porridge. There was a mug of coffee with honey. She carried the damn thing all the way up to the attic.

"Mr Toft?" she called, after knocking on the door.

"Who's that?" he asked.

"Eldersie's gone to the temple. I've been turned into her errand girl."

"Where's Jos?"

"Broken his leg."

"That can't be right."

Oriana pushed past him into the room. It stank. It had the appearance of a bank that had been ransacked. Drawers were left half-open and the bed clothes were abandoned on the floor, which boasted upturned cups and saucers.

"Where do you want me to put this?" she asked, but Mr Toft was frozen, staring into the middle distance.

"Jos has broken his leg?" he repeated.

"That's what Eldersie said. I'll just put this down here." She shoved a pile of papers aside and slid the tray in their place.

"Can he walk?"

"He broke his leg, so I assume no."

Oriana was not desperate to wander back downstairs, fearing that Eldersie might have returned and would dispense more tasks to her. The room she was in chaotic enough to be intriguing. There was a carved bed that made her feel a little jealous. Strange that Eldersie had not claimed the best bed for herself.

"Why do you stay up here all day? By yourself?" she asked. Mr Toft apparently didn't even descend to use the outhouse.

"Eldersie doesn't like me to go out," he said.

He was a scruffy little man. He had not shaved in days, and his salt and pepper beard did not quite give him the dignified air that it might have given other men. He wore a dressing gown with a velvet trim that was faded with dust.

"What do you do up here all day?"

"I have business ideas. I want to come up with something for Eldersie, but she steals my plans. She thinks I'm crazy. You have to find them."

"Oh, that ship has sailed," Oriana said, taking a sip of her coffee. "That must have been what she was burning."

"Oh." He sounded devastated. "I will have to start again, then."

"Talk me through some of them. I can help you." She searched through the mess to procure a pen and paper. Eldersie had left a shopping list on one side of the page, but Oriana flipped it over to use the back.

"Oh, well, I had this idea for soap. A soap dispensary, in truth. The idea was that I would send out soap right at the moment someone finishes their last bar."

Oriana felt the tremors through the floor that indicated Eldersie's return. She reasoned that Eldersie would thank her for entertaining her idle father.

"I see why you stay up here. Tower full of secrets, this," she said.

He mistook her tone. "I'm glad you think so," he beamed. "I could use a bright girl like you. You're from the city – you know what businesses work."

"You'd have to talk to my brother about all that."

"It is nice to have someone who appreciates this sort of thing." He wiped his plate with the crust of his toast. "No one in Racken is very ambitious. They want to go on as they always have, to justify what they have already done." His voice was lowered, sincere, perhaps haunting.

"Is there a great moral weight to farming? Well – I suppose there has to be. To kill animals and all that."

"No."

"Killing animals is fine, then?" she asked.

"I'm talking about killing people," he said, with his brow furrowed in sincere confusion.

"What are you on about?"

"Do you not know? Has Eldersie not told you?"

"Told me what?"

"I assumed that she must have. It is that time of year, and she took you to temple."

"Not sure that I understood most of what was going on in there," she tried to assure him.

"Some things cannot pass you by. Not when they march the body of winter's elect through the valley to their pyre."

"You can't be serious." The old man did not seem to have much of a sense of humour, but Oriana hoped that this was just a poorly measured joke.

"They have to be killed to ensure the arrival of spring."

Oriana stood. "I know that this place is a little backward, but I don't think you would stoop to human sacrifice."

"I used to think that about myself. I used to think that I was a good father, a good husband."

"What do you mean?"

"When they lit her pyre it smelled like cooking meat. Did you know that happens?"

Oriana shook her head. She had buried her parents.

"She looked so cold," the old man continued. "Even as she was burning. She escaped the house in her nightgown. She lost her slippers in the snow."

"Who was this?"

"Marjorie. She was my wife. We used to sleep here, in this room, in this bed." He raised a hand to the bed knob. to a spot where the varnish had been rubbed away.

"Why was she escaping?" The image of a woman in a white dress was forming in her brain.

"She was running from me. She saw me - right there" - he pointed to his side of the bed - "holding a knife. I don't have the knife anymore. Eldersie took it." He looked at his butter knife as if more disappointed in its bluntness. "I was the elect that year. Solyon chose me to do his mighty work. I was stronger then. The strongest in all the town. They were all so proud of me, until I had to do the one thing that Solyon chose me to do."

Oriana thought of Eldersie's biscuits hissing and cracking in the fire.

"I tried to make it quiet," he continued. "Once I knew she had the dreams. And she was always cold. I could hold her in my arms and she would still shiver. She was sent visions by Lady Winter. I wanted her to go before she might know what had happened. I didn't want to disturb Elsie. But Marjorie woke, saw the knife."

"Any sane woman would flee."

"She knew what had to be done to save us. To save all of you, though you might not know it. Still she ran."

It should have been a story. A tale told around the campfire to admonish naughty children. Yet there was too much that made sense. The odd talk at the temple, and the energy with which Eldersie had destroyed her father's plans. She kept him locked away in the attic, with the best bed that she refused to sleep in.

"Why would you do that?"

"To make sure winter ended. To finish the ritual. It happens every year - you should really know."

"I think that I should go and help Eldersie." Lifting heavy buckets and scrubbing floors suddenly seemed very tempting.

"She puts too much on herself. She won't let me help her."

"Of course she doesn't." Oriana fled.

She tumbled all the way down the stairs. Eldersie was there, rolling dough with a pin that had seen better days.

"What in the name of fuck is going on in this town?" Oriana demanded.

Eldersie glanced up, with only the mild surprise of seeing a curtain blown open.

"I did not think that there was anything in this town that interested you," she said.

"I just had the most enlightening conversation with your father."

"I would have said that such a feat was impossible."

"You're intolerable. I need to find Ifry. Is he with Jos?" Oriana asked.

"He went out with Mr Townsend. I saw them crossing the river, in the direction of Almony's."

Oriana did not stay to hear what other jobs Eldersie had for her.

Racken presented her with another dull and foggy day that covered the rooftops of the higher houses. She spotted Thomas and Ifry crossing the bridge.

"Ifry! Thomas!" she called, waving her arms. They were stationary, mid-conversation, allowing Oriana time to catch up. "We have to leave Racken," she declared.

She had not considered what she wanted them to do before she arrived, but as the words tumbled out of her mouth she realised that it was the only option. They could not remain anywhere that encouraged husbands to kill their wives.

"Have you been at the bottle again?" asked her brother. His tone was colder than the climate.

"No, I've taken her bottle," Ifry said.

"What? Why did you do that?" asked Oriana.

"It doesn't matter. Why do we need to leave Racken?" Ifry glanced nervously at Thomas.

"I've been speaking to Eldersie's father," said Oriana.

"I thought he was a bit of an odd fellow," Thomas remarked. He tried to walk past, but she put her elbow out to stop him.

"He had a lot to say about this town's traditions."

"I'm sure they're a little dated, but that's nothing to get skittish about." Thomas tried to walk on and she stopped him again.

"What's troubling you, Ori?" asked Ifry.

"Eldersie's father killed his wife," she said in a hurry.

"What nonsense have you come up with now?" Thomas scoffed.

"He told me so!" She did not mean to raise her voice, but it happened regardless.

"Gods' sake, calm down." Thomas succeeded in pushing past her.

"I promise you I know what I'm saying. I was speaking to him just now. He said that there is a ritual at the end of every winter, where one person is chosen to kill another. Eldersie's father killed his wife. He chased her through the snow and he killed her."

Thomas laughed. "I know that you want to go home," he said.

"No, this isn't about that," she insisted.

"I will not abandon my business here because of your superstitions, Oriana."

"I am not lying. Ask him yourself."

"Thank you, but I have no need to waste my time talking to senile old men who live in attics."

"Ask Eldersie then. She will tell you about her mother."

"I thought that Mother taught you better manners. For what reason would I question our landlady on her dead relatives? Especially when she has already threatened to rescind her custom."

"Because there is a mystery to solve," she said. She had put the pieces together in her mind, and though she laid them out, her brother was refusing to see the picture.

"Ifry, make sure that my sister has a fresh supply of detective novels. Her energies need to be expended somewhere."

Knowing she was beaten, Oriana stayed back while Thomas continued on his merry way.

Ifry glanced between the two of them, concerned. Oriana put herself in his way.

"Ifry, you have to believe me. You know there is something odd about this place."

"I suppose." He tried to brush her hands away, but she grabbed him by the upper arms, pinning them to his sides.

"You have to help me prove this. He's not a senile old man. He's perfectly lucid."

"I do think that you are overreacting," he admitted.

"There isn't a measured way to react to this news."

"What proof do you have?"

"None, but I can get some," she assured him.

"How?"

"We ask Eldersie."

"That's such a poor idea." He tried to get free from her grip.

"I'm going to do it anyway." She let go of his arms and turned back to look at the townhouse. "If she wants to kick us out, that's all right. We won't have to stay in a house with a murderer in the attic."

"How? Have you seen a single train come through here since we arrived?"

She paused. She had not.

"We'll figure it out." She flashed him a smile. That usually worked.

"Give me half an hour, Ori. I can find out when the next train is. Then you can wage war to your heart's content."

"I don't see the need. Eldersie already disapproves of my every action."

"Do it anyway. Do it for me."

She considered. She needed Ifry to witness her questioning Eldersie. He would convince Thomas of her frame of mind. He always did.

IFRY MARHEART

Almony's telephone, from appearances, had been installed just after the invention of telephones.

"My father bought it five years ago," Almony told him.

"He bought it new?" asked Ifry in astonishment. The microphone was separate from the receiver. The whole thing was finished with tarnished brass. It looked like a prop from a motion picture.

"I don't know. He put it together himself. He liked electronics. He was an eccentric. No one else in town has so much as a working lightbulb."

Ifry picked up the receiver and punched in the number for the conductor at the next biggest town. Almony, morose as usual, slouched away. She had not taken Ifry's request to use the telephone as odd. As she possessed the only one in all of Racken, she had expected him to turn up sooner or later. There was a low beeping sound and a click as someone picked up on the other end.

"Hello, is this the conductor?"

"This is he," answered a voice that crackled.

"My name is Ifry Marheart. I am currently visiting Racken."

"What for?"

"Oh, it's my employer. He has a venture here."

"No one usually visits Racken," replied the conductor with indignation.

"Yes. Well. Do you have a schedule for the coming weeks? For trains heading to Darrity."

"Yes, but for Racken it won't be very long."

Ifry's pen hovered over his pocketbook. He had perhaps been overzealous in starting a fresh page for this information. "I understand. Go ahead."

"There is a train in two days at four o'clock. Wait, discount that. It's not scheduled to stop in Racken. The next train taking passengers will stop in Racken in just under a fortnight."

"Excellent. I cannot wait to be somewhere warmer."

"I wouldn't be so hopeful. It's still snowing here, and further down the line," the conductor admitted.

"Oh? I suppose it must be one of those years," Ifry responded.

"It must be. Good day, Mr Marheart."

Ifry heard the click again. He hung up the receiver, then made to leave, thinking to make a passing thanks to the residents of the house, but Almony was waiting by the door of the parlour for him.

"Is Jos really out of action?" she asked.

"Eldersie seems to think so. Though it could have been a great deal worse."

"That's good. That's all good then," she said, distracted.

"He's been confined to his bed all day," Ifry said, wanting to impress that little about the situation was good.

"How long will he be there for?"

"As long as Eldersie can keep him there, I suspect. Weeks, maybe."

"She had better keep him there. Wouldn't want him ruining the leg."

"I'll give him your regards."

"You do that," she said. She smiled briefly, as if she had been given good news. Ifry couldn't imagine for a reason for this break in her dour demeanour. He brushed it off.

"Than you again, for use of the telephone," He said, but suspected that she was no longer listening to him. The cold wracked him again, but he was getting less surprised by it. He hurried back across the bridge and the train tracks, praying to the gods of this old town that Oriana had the sense to keep her mouth shut.

"Where is she?" he asked as he stepped over the threshold. The kitchen was missing Eldersie's busy presence.

"I've been looking," Oriana said.

"Have you asked Jos?"

"No, why should I?"

"I'll ask him. Where's Thomas?"

"In his room," she said.

Ifry found Jos lying in his bed, struggling to get out of it. He had knocked his crutches onto the floor.

"Help me get my boot on, won't you?"

"I will not." Ifry wrested the boot from him and put it on top of the wardrobe.

"I can't stay in here. The kuprum were hungry. They will be back. The monsters are more vicious at the end of winter, and this winter has been harsher than most."

"And what are you going to do to them on one leg?"

"It's not that bad. I walked all the way back here last night," he claimed.

"You hobbled here. You can move about using your crutches, but I don't recommend it." Ifry leaned the crutches against the head of Jos' bed. "Now, did Eldersie say where she was going?"

"Gone to the woodshed, seeing as I can't do it today," Jos sighed, as if he were truly missing chopping and piling wood.

"I'll go find her there."

"Wait–"

"What?"

Jos reached for Ifry's hand and kissed the back of it.

"Ah. I see." Ifry leaned down and kissed him lightly. "You poor thing, stuck in this bed. Keep your leg up and I'll bring you a cold pack to reduce the swelling."

"It isn't that swollen."

"Whatever you say." He patted him on the cheek and stepped out.

"By the woodshed," he told Oriana, once he had returned to the kitchen.

"Where's that?"

"Good to know that you've been paying attention around here," he scoffed wrapping himself in a hat, scarf, coat, and mittens.

The woodshed, as Ifry had learned from watching Jos when he should have been doing other things, was situated behind the townhouse, halfway between it and the slopes. It was a sizeable shed, apparently servicing many residences.

"Look, there she is." Oriana hit his arm and pointed at Eldersie. She had a shawl tight across her shoulders and clutched an axe between her hands. She raised it and brought it down with a crack onto a log.

"Where have you been?" she called. "I needed you to chop wood for me."

"I thought I asked you to help out," Ifry whispered to Oriana.

"I did. It's impossible to keep up with all her demands."

"Eldersie, Oriana just became a little distracted. Can I help?" Ifry said in his best diplomatic tone.

Eldersie set her axe down next to her chopping block. She retrieved a basket that was half-filled with cut logs, then began to load up her freshest cut.

"Just these ones in half." She indicated the stacked logs inside the woodshed. Oriana, showing no sign of wanting to help, perched on the wall. Ifry held the axe in one hand and recalled the weight of it in his younger hand.

He had asked his father if he could help cutting down the banisters. The novelty of it all had surprised him, and he'd wanted to know what it was like. His father had been reluctant, but Ifry was insistent. His father's nerves were frayed right down to the bone. He'd let Ifry swing the axe, despite his youth.

The axe head had bitten less than an inch into the banister, but Ifry, not one to be dismayed, had swung it again. He'd sliced the banister through the middle, but was not satisfied. He'd hit it again. This time he had not thought of where he was swinging the blade. His father yelled as the axe head streaked across his chest.

Ifry did not care. He swung again. The axe had glanced off the edge of a step and gouged a splinter free. He could only been stopped when his father caught the handle of the axe and wrestled it out of his hand.

Now, he collected a log from inside the shed. He positioned it upright. He swung the axe over his shoulder and into the log. It split down the middle, revealing the pale, seamed insides. The axe had gone all the way through and bitten into the block below.

"Say, Eldersie," Oriana began. Ifry tried to give her a warning glance. "I was having a chat with your father earlier."

"Oh? Why?"

Ifry split another log. The halves fell away and toppled off the sides of the block.

"I thought the old man could use some company."

"If I thought he needed watching, I would have told you." Eldersie threw a pair of split logs into her basket. Shards and splinters bounced out, marring the snow.

"Well, anyway. He told me some interesting stories."

"Ori – don't. The next train isn't for a fortnight," Ifry cautioned her.

That made Eldersie stop her work.

"Are you leaving?"

"Yes, we are," declared Oriana.

At the same time, Ifry said, "Not quite yet."

"Surely we can hike down the river to the next town, and get a train from there," Oriana insisted.

Ifry ploughed through another log. "Since when will Thomas hike anywhere?"

"You would have to go more than one town along," Eldersie said. "It's further than that. You have to find where another train line meets this one."

"Exactly," said Ifry, hoping that this would calm Oriana.

"But–"

"Can't you just stay quiet?" he snapped.

Oriana's eyes were wide. Ifry supposed he should have felt regret about being rude to her, but he found that he did not. She never listened to anyone. Why should he expect that reason would hold any sway over her?

"Ifry - I–"

"Shut up. You're not doing anyone any good."

She pressed her mouth tight, a petulant child, and turned away from him.

"Eldersie, what happened to your mother?" she asked.

Ifry's stomach dropped. "Oriana, what is wrong with-"

"No, let her speak," Oriana insisted. "We have a right to know."

"No, we don't. And have you considered the consequences of–"

"I have considered the consequences," she said, cutting him off.

"Considered them and ignored them."

"You were talking to my father about my mother?" Eldersie interrupted their bickering. She had abandoned her work.

"Yes. He told me about your mother, but my brother and his bloody clerk don't believe me."

"Why don't you believe her?" Eldersie asked.

Ifry lowered his axe mid-swing, considering her question. He did not like how it sounded.

"I did not want to believe something so foul of you all, and Oriana is trying to get us to leave. She is bored and uncomfortable here."

"If what she said is true, that my father killed my mother, then you will leave?"

"I don't think, if any of that were true, we would be able to stay." He did not know for certain, but he presumed that even Thomas Townsend would not be able to stay in a house where a murderer lived in the attic.

"He did kill her," said Eldersie.

"What?"

"He killed her. He had to. Solyon instructed him to."

Oriana crowed. "See what I told you, Ifry."

"Ori, quiet." He buried the axe head in the block. "Eldersie, why would Solyon ask your father to kill his wife?" he asked.

Eldersie shrugged. "My father was Solyon's chosen. His elect."

"You told me about that the first night we met," Oriana said. "I thought it was just a ritual thing."

"A ritual with murder?" Ifry asked.

"Anything can be a ritual. My mother was chosen by Volana, Winter's Lady. Solyon's elect is fated to fight winter's chosen and win. Every year, to herald the coming of spring."

She was not upset, and she did not mince her words. He might have expected her to be reluctant in digging up a decades old secret. Eldersie expressed it all with the same tone that she used to instruct Jos on his tasks for the day.

"Every year? Someone is sacrificed every year?" Ifry asked.

Eldersie nodded. "Of course. How else would spring come?"

"Spring would come anyway."

Eldersie made a disappointed tutting noise. "I have no need to convince you of what is true," she said.

"For how long?"

"For as long as anyone remembers. For as long as people have lived. Every year. Last winter, it was Almony who was chosen."

Ifry thought of the little boy's coat by her door and a seed of dread grew in his stomach.

"You're just saying all of this to get rid of us."

"I am entirely serious," she smiled. She did not often smile. Ifry found that he did not like it.

"I need to speak to Mr Townsend. I'll sort all this out. Just leave it alone," he counselled Oriana, even as he knew that her fear would prove ill for them.

"We need to leave," she insisted.

"That would be well for us all," Eldersie said, collecting her basket.

Ifry turned, ready to seek out Thomas, but an odd noise distracted him. A huffing sound. It couldn't have been Eldersie or Oriana. The did not breathe nearly so loudly, or wetly. There was no rattle to their tones. He reached for the axe handle.

"What is it?" Oriana asked.

Eldersie shrieked. The wood basket tumbled. Behind her, a shadow rose. It was black and white and harsh against the snow.

It had raised its hackles; there were dappled markings along its back. It looked like a cat, but worse than any feral cat that Ifry had seen. It had one fang as long as his forearm. The other was chipped and was half as long. It did not have the soft, round ears that he had seen on lions at Darrity Zoo, but its head boasted a pair of curled horns, like a goat's.

Ifry was not at the zoo now, with an ice cream in hand and a set of iron bars between himself and the monster, and this was no tuxedo cat bearing down on Eldersie. He knew it from Jos's descriptions, if naught else.

It was a pack animal. An ankatze.

It raised one great paw and swiped at Eldersie's head. She dodged, just a moment too late, and its claws snagged on her ear. She fell to the ground and tried to crawl across her fallen logs.

Oriana swore and fled. She only stopped when she realised that Ifry was not with her. "Ifry, get out of there!" she cried.

Eldersie screamed.

Ifry weighed the axe in his hand. He knew it was unwise, but he was out of any wise options. He raised the axe and swung it at the creature. He missed.

The ankatze moved backwards with the casual demeanour of a tabby avoiding its owner's foot. Ifry stumbled on a fallen log, but he stopped himself from falling. Eldersie got to her feet. Blood ran in a line from her ear into her collar.

The creature leered over Ifry. He knew that he would not be able to run fast enough. The keeper at the zoo had assured the gathered crowd that the lion was a mighty predator, and no human could outrun one. This had been undercut by the laziness of the lion at hand, which only moved to swat flies with his tail.

This big cat was hungrier, larger, and Ifry did not doubt that it was therefore much faster.

Oriana called his name again. The only way for Ifry to escape was to abandon Eldersie to certain death.

He swung the axe at the ankatze again, but was just shy of its hide. It lost all interest in Eldersie. Ifry shut his mouth tight to keep from whimpering. He did not think that would be dignified. He didn't think he should have been worrying about being dignified at that moment, but he was anyway.

The ankatze coiled, and Ifry lost the capacity for rational thought. He plunged the axe into the side of the cat's neck. Blackish blood seeped out of the wound, but the cat tried to leap again. Ifry wrestled the axe free and swung once more. It landed between the ankatze's eyes.

The beast made a whining noise. Ifry swung again. The creature's skull was thick. He sliced through the cat's left eye. He chopped into its neck again. It was dead long before he realised. Eldersie touched his shoulder. She pulled him back and pushed his hand down until he ceased.

The ankatze was sprawled in the woodpile. Blood coated his hands. He wiped his face on his sleeve. There would be no saving his coat after this.

"Why is it here?" Eldersie asked. She eased the axe from his hands. "They have *never* come this close to the houses." She cast a worried look up the mountain.

"Jos said the kuprum were desperate," replied Ifry.

"If there's one ankatze, there will be more. Get inside. I need to tell the others."

Ifry could not tear his eyes away from the corpse. Eldersie pulled on his arm until he relented, and he followed her inside.

ORIANA TOWNSEND

The water was hot between her fingers. The steam rose in clear, well-drawn spirals, filling the hollow of Ifry's attic bedroom. The cloth Eldersie had allotted her was rough and full of holes; she suspected that Eldersie had cut it from the hem of an old dress. Oriana wished she had a proper handkerchief for cleaning Ifry's hands.

"Are you all right?" she asked him. He had been staring at nothing since they had got him inside. Eldersie had described him as 'shaken' and prescribed bed rest while she went to raise the alarm. He had made no attempt to clean off the blood himself, so Oriana appointed herself for the task. He hadn't wanted to surrender his bloodstained coat, complaining of the cold.

"I'm worried," he said, "that there might be more of them."

"You'll finish them off with your wood axe, no doubt."

He shivered. Oriana unbent his fingers on his left fist. He had dug his nails into his palm.

"It's all the more reason for us to leave," she said, "as soon as we can."

"Weren't you listening?" He wrenched his hands away from her. Drops of pinkish water landed on his bedsheets. "We can't. There are no trains. We are stuck here, in Racken, with all of these people."

"Thomas can get us a car. Or call us a new train."

"There are no motor cars. And if there were, where would they drive them? Through the snow drifts? There are no trains that Thomas can call. There is nothing that his money can buy."

Oriana threw the cloth into the bowl, spilling more stains onto the bed.

"You need to rest." She stood, nearly dashing her head on the low ceiling.

"No, I need to find Jos." He tried to stand, but she pushed him down.

"Have you forgotten that this town conducts ritual sacrifice? What makes you think Jos isn't part of that? Mr Toft killed his wife. Almony killed someone too. Who's to say it doesn't get worse? Jos might have killed his parents or his intended, or any other damn person he was told to."

"He needs to be warned about the ankatze. That's all. Is he in his room?"

Oriana hadn't checked next door to confirm whether Jos was there. Ifry stood, ready to do the deed himself, but Oriana put herself in his way.

"I will fetch Thomas. He will get us all out of here. He has to."

Ifry made a disgruntled sound and tried to push past her. She put her arm across his path, but her elbowed her in the stomach, an elder brother move if she had ever seen one. It startled her, and while she was smarting with the indignity of it all, he dashed into Jos's bedroom without knocking. Mercifully, it was empty.

There was a sour smell. She wrinkled her nose. It made her think of livestock.

"He's probably gone to help build the pyre," said Oriana.

"Pyre?"

"For the poor soul they intend to sacrifice." Oriana looked under the bed. Jos's boots were gone.

"Who is that, do you think?" Ifry asked. He picked something up from behind the door.

"Shit, put that back."

Ifry had found Jos's shotgun. He paid no mind to Oriana, instead opening a drawer in Jos's washstand and pocketing a case of ammunition.

"You can't be serious," she said. Ifry had insisted to Thomas that he had no idea how to handle a gun. She had no doubt that he was being truthful.

"You are certain that we are surrounded by murderers, and you don't want me to use a gun?"

"Do you even know how to use one?"

"I know enough," he declared. "Now, do you know who it is?"

"Who is what?"

"They aren't sacrificing people at random. Who is the chosen one? If it were up to them, they would have picked one of us. Tyenes, and all." Ifry went back to his room without waiting for Oriana to answer, and she was forced to hurry after him. She heard footsteps and closed the bedroom door, wanting to put at least another barrier between herself and Mr Toft's room.

"I don't know. Eldersie said something about there being two chosen. One who does the killing and one who gets killed."

"Mighty Solyon picks one and Lady Winter the other," Ifry said, confirming that he understood.

"That sounds about right. We don't know who is who."

"I think I've seen her."

"Who? Eldersie? We've all seen Eldersie," said Oriana.

"Lady Winter. On the mountain when I was injured. Then in dreams."

"You – in dreams?" She did not quite comprehend what he had said.

"I don't know who else it could have been. I thought I imagined her." He pulled on his bloodstained coat, getting ready as if he were not spouting half-thought sentences.

"Does that mean – does that mean that you're the one?"

"I don't know. I thought I was dreaming nonsense," he said, in his usual reasonable tone, but Oriana shivered.

"Mr Toft said that his wife couldn't get warm, even next to the fire."

Ifry stared at the ground. He often complained about the cold. Of late it had been worse, but she had attributed it to their stay in Racken.

"For fuck's sake, Ifry, could they be after you?"

"I have no idea. I only know that there are monsters coming to attack us, and that we have no way out. And now Eldersie expects us to leave. Thank you, Ori, for that."

"But you've considered it? You don't think it's a load of nonsense?"

He paused in tying a scarf around his neck. He didn't answer. If he had truly thought it to be baseless, he would have said so right away.

"I will get you out." She tried to put a comforting hand on his shoulder, but he shrugged her off.

"You won't," he said.

"What?"

"I don't need you to protect me. I certainly do not want it."

"What? Ifry, that's unfair."

"Is it?" He pulled the strap of the gun over his head. "I need to warn Jos about the ankatze. He'll be stuck out there, unable to run."

"Why do you care?" she asked. Jos was a stranger, as much an outsider to them as they were to him.

"Because, unlike you, I have the capacity to care about other people." He found his boots where Oriana had tidied them away. They were still muddied with the ankatze's innards.

"I care about you," she said. At home in the city, there would have been no point in saying it. They blustered through their lives. She distracted Ifry from his mounds of paperwork, taking him to dinner, or the theatre, or both. Every night, Thomas would appear to whisk Ifry off on some errand in his black motor car. Ifry had no social life and Oriana tried to remedy that for him. It had never quite worked, but she was sure he understood. She could rub off the sheen of the clerk, and help him remember who he could have been, had society not shunned him. But now, in long and empty

Racken, time was hollow, and there were only words she could say to him, and naught else to do.

When he responded, it was not with warm remembrances of nights in smokey clubs, or gilded dance halls.

"If only you acted like you cared."

"If only I acted? Of course I act like - I have spent so much time trying to take care of you," she insisted.

"Enlighten me."

He tried to push past her again, so she put both her hands square on his shoulders and pushed him back. She was taller, more athletic. She could keep him there.

"Let me out," he ordered her.

She put her back to the door and her arms against the walls, forming her own small barricade. "I got you to let off some steam. I saw that you were overworked and I made sure to get you away from Thomas some of the time."

"Overworked? Oriana, you *are* work."

Ifry had never been threatening. It was not in his nature. His stature and slight frame never made him appear frightening; he was softly spoken, and most often polite. Yet his words rang as cold and sharp as a knife blade.

"What?" she asked.

"Thomas paid me for all the time I spent with you. He wanted me to keep an eye on you, make sure you didn't get into any more trouble."

"Thomas wouldn't do that."

Ifry snorted. "Wouldn't he? After your father passed, he was so concerned. He was proven right, of course."

Oriana blanched with shame. She had overindulged at the wake, and was found passed out in the foyer of a bank, with no recollection of having arrived there. It was fodder for an exceptionally slow news day.

"Aren't we friends, Ifry?"

He opened his mouth and closed it again. The words got lost somewhere between his mind and his mouth. Instead he said:

"Let me out."

She shook her head. "We need to leave. We need to run, and we need to stay together."

"I need to find Jos," he insisted. "Leave me alone, Ori."

"I'll make sure that we get out. I can help."

"Your help has never been worth anything," he said. "I don't need you to keep me safe. I don't need you to get us out of Racken. I need you to let me help an actual friend."

"Actual friend?" she asked, holding in a laugh. "Thomas would have paid him to spend time with you too."

Ifry tried to get past her again. He drove his shoulder into her side, but she held her ground.

"Let me go, or I will lose any regard I have for you. You don't have to get in my way."

She let her hands fall from the walls. "Ifry, if you are the elect, you are in danger."

"There are monsters at the door, Oriana. We are all in danger."

He took two steps into the hallway and swore.

"Eldersie, my apologies, I didn't see you there." He attempted to plaster on politeness.

Eldersie was not half a step back from Ifry's door. Oriana met her eye, and Eldersie looked downward, bashful.

"Where are you going? Why do you have that?" Eldersie pointed at the gun.

"Where's Jos?"

"It's best you leave that gun to him and stay inside, Mr Marheart." She dashed to the stairs.

"Why were you up here?" Oriana asked her. Eldersie did not reply. Her patience worn to a thread, Oriana marched past her, overtaking her on the narrow staircase. She hurried down, taking three steps at a time, thinking only of finding Thomas.

JOS NOTHERNINE

Jos did not sincerely believe that Mr Thomas Townsend would bring anything of great value to Racken. However, at worst he could provide them with indoor plumbing. Eldersie had one tap in her kitchen, and that was often frozen over. Jos had considered that a luxury when he was small.

He wished Eldersie had an indoor toilet, soe wouldn't have to hobble out into the cold and peel off all his layers every time he needed to take a shit. On only one leg, he had lost the ability to empty his chamber pot, and it was stinking his room up. He had tried to call for Eldersie but got no answer. He had considered calling for Ifry, but he thought it was too embarrassing to ask his new beau to empty his chamber pot.

Business done, he limped out of the outhouse.

He hobbled along the packed snow path back to the house. Whoever had invented crutches had not foreseen how they might be used in the snow. He was so concentrated on the placement of his sticks, he almost didn't notice Parson Tieron waving him down. He stopped and waited for the parson to come to him.

"What's got you out?" Jos asked. The parson dashed to Jos with more energy than Jos thought warranted.

"Miss Toft has been raising the alarm. There has been an ankatze in town."

"What?" They were vicious things that Jos avoided. He tended to lure them into dens further away from the town using prime cuts traded from Almony. "Where is it? I'll get my gun."

"No need. I'm told one of the tyenes did it in. Nearly chopped its head off with a wood axe, if you can believe it."

"The tyenes? Which one?"

"I was as surprised as you are. The clerk, I believe. Hardly the sort to fend off monsters." He chuckled a little. "We are gathering a hunting party. Every able hand. We have to find the other cats. Then there's the matter of the elect, of course. If there are kuprum and ankatze threatening our borders, we need to take drastic action. It's been done before. We need to root out the elect from where they've been hiding, and bring them to you."

Jos had not thought that this was an option. He had put this particular duty out of his mind.

He did not want to do it.

He had not truly considered that notion, much less admitted it to himself. For a moment, he had enjoyed the status of the elect. For a flash in the pan, he had felt important. He had not thought about the deed itself. No one did. They could not speak about it. No one could make it through the day thinking about that sort of thing.

"What should I do?" he asked, though he knew that he would not like the answer.

"Whatever that leg of yours will allow. Though I agree that you will need your gun."

Jos turned back to the house, but saw Eldersie sprinting towards them. She had forgotten her coat and her scarf came loose as she ran. She did not stop to catch it. It fluttered to the ground, freeing her hair to the four winds. He saw that there was a bandage on her ear that had already been bled through.

"Wait," she called. "I know who it is." She stopped, sending a spray of snow over their feet. "I know who she chose." Her cheeks were flushed, and her eyes bright. She hardly seemed to know she was injured.

"Who? How?"

"The clerk. Mr Marheart. I overheard him talking with Miss Townsend. He has been having dreams of Volana. It's him."

A hollow feeling began in Jos's stomach.

"Are you certain? We have to be certain." He tried to sound as if he was not begging.

"If Eldersie says so, I believe her," declared the parson.

"But - if you only overheard them–"

"I know what I heard. They confirmed it," said Eldersie. "He is looking for you, Jos. He's upstairs." She reached into her apron pocket and took out one of her kitchen knives, then reached for him and tugged on the front of his coat. She unfastened it and tucked the knife inside. He was helpless to stop her; both of his hands held crutches. "Do it now, before he can run away."

She must have felt his heart pounding as she buttoned the coat over the knife.

"I'll just - I'll just do that, then."

Eldersie beamed at him.

Lady Winter had chosen Ifry. Just this past night he had been in Jos's bed. Jos had run his thumb over Ifry's cheekbone as he slept. He had watched the fluttering of his eyelids. Ifry had kissed the end of his nose in jest. As Jos dozed off, he had rolled onto his back, and Ifry had shifted over, resting his head on Jos's chest. Jos had spent what felt like hours staring at the top of Ifry's head. He'd lost himself in the colour of his hair. He had never met someone with such pale hair.

"Like sunlight over snow," he said.

"What was that?" Ifry had turned his head to look at him.

"The colour of your hair. It looks like sunlight over snow. At dawn, up in the peaks, the light plays tricks. The sky turns every colour. And the snow looks like your hair."

Ifry had smiled.

"I would like to see that, I think."

"When my leg is better, I can take you."

Ifry had leaned his head back onto Jos's chest, His hair tickling Jos's chin. He'd rested a hand over Jos's heart.

Now Jos was supposed to kill him with Eldersie's kitchen knife.

IFRY MARHEART

"Eldersie?"

Ifry heard a door creaking. Across the landing, the door was ajar. Mr Toft peered through the gap.

"She's gone downstairs," Ifry said. He had waited until she'd gone; he did not wish for her to see him leave. He did not want Oriana to know where he went either.

"Has she gone to find Jos?" the old man asked.

"I suppose she must have."

"You need to give him back his gun."

"For the ankatze, I know."

"Don't leave the house," he warned Ifry.

"I can handle myself against the ankatze."

He had proved that, though he did think that the cat had been starving. He took a step towards the stairs, but a hand grasped his arm. Mr Toft had fastened both hands around Ifry's wrist. His hands were lined and veined, but his grip was far from weak.

"You have to wait here for Eldersie to get back," he said. Ifry tried to peel his fingers back, but he gripped tight enough to bruise his arm.

"Get off!"

"You're the one." He grinned. "Lady Winter, you have made this too easy."

Ifry kicked at his shins. He left a smear of the ankatze's blood down Mr Toft's pyjama trousers. He yelped like a dog, but kept his grip tight.

"I'm not the one," he begged, but still the old man clawed at him. He stamped on his bare foot and Mr Toft shrieked. Mr Toft, limping, clutched at him again. Ifry got free, but the old man raised a palm and slapped Ifry across the face. It was not a clean hit. His hand glanced off of Ifry's ear, but Ifry was shocked by the strength of it. Mr Toft grabbed onto the back of his neck, like he was a cat being picked up by an indignant owner.

Ifry swung the shotgun off his shoulder. He jerked the butt back into Mr Toft's stomach, then turned and hit him across the face with the barrel.

Mr Toft clutched at his nose, and blood dripped from under his hand. Ifry did not stay to find out whether it was broken.

Coming down the stairs, he heard Thomas and Oriana's raised voices. Their argument lost all steam when Ifry tumbled down the stairs.

"Now, there's no need for that," Thomas said, holding his hands up in surrender, eyes on the gun. Ifry conceded to lowering it, but had no desire to put the thing down.

"Where's Eldersie?" Ifry demanded.

"She's gone out," Oriana said. "I've told Thomas everything."

"I don't know what on this good green earth she is on about," Thomas admitted.

In the past, Ifry might have paused to explain. He might have hoped that Thomas's shadow was long enough to hide Ifry, but Thomas had not just had to fight off an old man who had not left his bedroom for a decade.

"Don't tell them where I went," Ifry begged.

"Marheart, what are you on about?" asked Thomas. "Calm down and put that away." Ifry turned the gun on Thomas. He flinched and blinked, as if staring into a bright light.

"Tell them I'm still upstairs." He kept the barrel trained on them as he unlatched the front door.

"What do you think you're doing?"

"Running. Isn't it obvious?"

"Thomas, we are all in trouble. Didn't I tell you?" Oriana plucked at his sleeve, but he paid her no mind.

"Marheart, put that down this instant, or you will find yourself without a job."

"No." The door swung open and a sharp breeze met them. The cold pricked at his skin so badly that he considered running back up to his room. He forced himself outside before Thomas could express any further confusion.

"There he is." He looked to his right, where the temple lay. A man he recognised as the town butcher pointed at him. Ifry looked back the other way and saw a gaggle of townspeople in the road. They had sticks and forks and farming tools. Of course they did. How could they not? They had been looking for the ankatze, perhaps, and now they would hack at him like he had the ankatze.

He would not escape without a fight. Ifry chose the right flank. He ran towards the butcher, who squared up, revealing that he had a cleaver grasped in one hand. Ifry dug his heels into the snow, regretting his choice as he made it. He turned instead, choosing the alley that led back to the woodshed. There were dozens of footprints leading that way.

The ankatze's corpse languished where he had killed it. On a whim, he fetched the wood axe from where he had dropped it earlier. He slid it into his belt, not caring that more congealed blood was getting on his coat.

Another shout startled him. The butcher was on his tail. Ifry spotted Eldersie. Her hair hung in disordered strands about her face. She lacked the solemn demeanour that she usually possessed.

Ifry backed away around the woodpile. He did not know where to go. Behind him were the slopes that led to the waterfall, but there was no way that he could make that climb and not be caught by the hunting party. Even if he did make it, he would be trapped at the top of a nearly impassable slope.

He grasped the gun, and wondered if he had enough ammunition to scare them off. With the time it would take him to reload, he doubted it. He hadn't loaded it himself. He could only guess how it worked from watching Jos, and Jos made the whole process look easy.

"Look out," cried a voice.

Ifry assumed that they had seen the gun, but as he looked to the approaching townspeople, he saw that their attention had turned to something behind him. He turned to look and the knot in his chest tightened. Four more ankatze prowled towards him. They had sniffed out the remains of their dead friend, and he was now in the unfortunate position of being their nearest prey. They were in rough shape, much like the one he'd killed, but the lead cat looked about twice the size. Its horns were longer, and curled into a full spiral. They were untroubled by the deep snow; their wide paws allowed them not to sink, while Ifry was mired in ice up to his knees.

He didn't need to make an assessment of the situation. He knew that there was no good escape, so he pointed the gun at them. He closed one eye and looked down the barrel, his gaze catching on Jos's fingerprints on the metal. He spotted the safety and pulled it back with one thumb. Without taking another breath, he squeezed the trigger as tight as he dared. He fired two shots. The butt of the gun bruised the inside of his shoulder and he staggered. The noise made his head swim. Coupled with the glare off of the snow, he barely noticed where his shots landed.

An ankatze's step faltered. It did not stop, but flecks of blood marked the snow, a sort of blessing. The blood steamed and ran down the ankatze's front leg.

He steeled himself and ran towards it. It stilled and lowered its head in the familiar manner of a cat about to pounce. Ifry knew he had to use this moment to his advantage. He ran as fast as he could, but came face to face with the largest of the pack. Blood ran down its right foreleg. Ifry regretted firing those shots - he should have saved one of them for this moment - but he still had his axe.

He aimed for the ankatze's wounded leg and felt the sickening pressure of metal meeting flesh. The ankatze squealed in a tone too high-pitched for an animal of its size. He dodged its careening head and half fell into a snow drift. Snow crept inside his gloves and into his boots, which hurt worse than if the ankatze had injured him.

He crawled through the ice and made for the trees. The wooded area around the waterfall was the best place to hide, provided that the ankatze kept his hunters busy. He leapt behind the first tree that he found, though it was too skinny to hide him. He stole a look back at the crowd by the woodshed. They had scattered, driven away by the ankatze pack.

He took a few sharp breaths that were cold enough to burn his throat, shivering so hard that his muscles hurt. He could barely straighten out his thoughts. Slowly, he pieced together a plan, with a real place to hide. Yet a valley full of ankatze and murderous citizens stood between him and his destination.

He ascended into the wood, but did not go all the way to the waterfall.

He reloaded the gun while crouching in the roots of a pine tree. He waited there a while, listening to the roars of an ankatze in pain. He walked downriver and stumbled down the slope behind the temple. He could not see anyone, but he kept the gun in his hands, imagining that they lurked around every corner. He found his way, creeping along the edge of buildings, to the bridge that led to Almony's house. It was nearly clean of snow from all the feet that had passed over it. Ifry dashed through the slush and to the other bank. He shifted the gun against his shoulder, then looked up.

A figure stood on the ridge above him. He didn't know the face, but the broad shoulders and rough clothing made him think it was a farmer. He grasped a rifle of his own. Ifry's heart dropped to his feet as he saw a silver barrel pointed at him. Not knowing what else to do, Ifry reciprocated with his own weapon.

"The bridge!" shouted the man, looking to his right. Ifry followed the line of his gaze and saw a pack of townsfolk led by the parson. The parson clapped his hands in celebration and called out his thanks to Solyon. Ifry was stuck on the bridge, with no way forward and no way back.

There was one more alternative, though it sickened him. The days and nights had gotten so cold that the river had first moved sluggishly, then not at all. Ifry knew from experience how thick ice had to be to hold his weight. He knew to keep to the edges. He slid down the bank, then onto the ice. It did not crack. He nearly thanked Solyon for that. He felt the thumping of footsteps as he ducked under the bridge. Snow fell in clumps and landed inside his collar. He crouched underneath and shook.

"Where did he go?" the parson called.

Between the slats, Ifry saw a shadow fall, then another. Several people stood on the bridge above him.

"He can't have gone far."

There were shouts, but Ifry could not tell what they said. It was as if he was underwater. Was he drowning again? He couldn't tell. The tone of the voices above him changed.

"The ankatze!"

Someone fired a shot that made Ifry fear the ice was cracking. He shrank against the bank, shaking. He heard the growl of the ankatze, which was now unpleasantly familiar. He scrambled out from under the bridge and went up the bank on all fours. He looked up and caught his breath short. An ankatze had gotten past the townspeople and stood not six feet from him. Its horns were bloodied.

"It's only one, don't worry," said the parson, turning to the flock that stood behind him. Perhaps reassurance was all that he could offer them.

Ifry saw the skin ripple over the ankatze's prominent ribcage. It leapt and fastened its jaws around the parson's shoulder. Ifry offered a silent prayer to Solyon, though his guilt nearly outweighed his relief. He stood and ran.

He dashed up the slope to Almony's house. He hid behind the woodshed, hearing the shouts of the townsfolk behind him. He needed to climb the slope behind the house, but he knew that would make him visible to the townsfolk and the ankatze that pestered them. There was only one other hiding place in the vicinity.

He ducked out from behind the woodshed and made for Almony's front door. His prior visits had let him know that the house was a warren, with at least two other exits. He ran into the dining room as he heard someone cross the threshold.

"Show yourself," yelled a voice.

Ifry ducked into the parlour. He saw the telephone and resisted the temptation to call for help. It would take too long. They would catch him. He went back into the hallway. Their footsteps were still a shadow behind him. There were at least three. He could hear them speaking to one another, though he couldn't recognise the voices.

He made for the stairs. They were lined with a red carpet that needed a good beating. He approached the first door on the right and ducked inside, pushing the door closed as quietly as he could.

It was a porcelain bathroom. In the light from a half-curtained window, he saw a clawfoot tub with water up to the brim. No steam rose from the surface, and Ifry felt the chill in the room as if he were outdoors. He looked around wildly, fearing that the drawer of the bath would be nearby.

The beating of footsteps against the floor moved closer. The corners of the room were dark. The electric lights were dusty, and there were bulbs missing. He caught movement in the corner of his eye. Almony, wearing her overcoat, was crouched in the corner. She was shadowed. He could see her most clearly by the whites of her eyes. She raised a hand. He flinched, expecting her to reach for him. But she remained crouched against the wall like an animal. She put her finger to her lips. The footsteps went past the bathroom door. He waited, hearing them open another door and step inside. Almony looked him in the eye. They stared at each other. Ifry was unsure of what her intentions were. Her eyes flicked to the door.

"Go," she whispered.

He did not question the instruction. He shuffled out of the door, careful not to make too much sound on the old floorboards, and backed down the corridor, watching the walls for the shadows of his pursuers. Quickly, he found his way back to the stairs and crept down them.

He had to hold himself back from running. Once he returned to the kitchen, he drew back the gingham curtain that hung over the door. No one was visible out there, so he stepped outside, and tried to set the door back as if he had not gone through it.

It looked like a kitchen garden, though it was covered in snow. There was a deserted chicken coop, the residents shut away elsewhere for the winter. Ifry picked his way past. He did not want to leave tracks, but winter was against him; he could not travel through the powder without leaving instructions on where to find him.

The garden helped. He could crouch under the eaves of the coop where only a little snow had managed to fall. He could do the same next to the scattered pots and crates. But all of that would not get him far. He came face to face with the unblemished snow over the southern slope.

He allowed himself one moment of sorrow, tried to slow his breathing, though he felt as if he could not get enough air into his throat.

He looked up at the sky. For a moment, he thought the tears forming in his eyes were blurring his vision and blinked them away. The sky had gone cold. When he was under the bridge, or inside the house, the clouds had formed. Snow was falling. Lady Winter had blessed him. He started up the slope. Behind him, snowflakes filled his tracks.

JOS NOTHERNINE

They had decided to keep him at the temple. It seemed convenient, as that was where they would burn the body. They had not even found Ifry, but they were stacking logs in the yard.

He sat on the foremost pew. He had his leg raised on a stool that Eldersie had brought for him. Behind him, out of his sight, people bustled through, swapping stratagems and debating Ifry's whereabouts. He had the solace of knowing that Ifry had thus far evaded their best efforts to capture him, though it was scarcely a comfort. He was seated, but his heart raced, and he startled at every sound.

"Why do you tarry here?" Solyon's voice, soft like honey, buzzed in his ears.

Jos didn't turn to him, though he stood nearby. Warmth seeped off of him, and it made Jos sweaty and uncomfortable.

"Why are you tarrying here? Get outside. Volana's chosen has revealed himself at last." Solyon's voice was almost giddy.

Jos turned to look at him. Across the temple, Joan caught his eye and furrowed her brow. To her, it must have looked like he was staring intently at naught.

"Jos," Eldersie called from the doorway.

Jos flinched, but welcomed the distraction.

"Get gauze and water," she called.

Relief crept in, despite the situation. She would not want medical supplies for Ifry.

He got up, leaning on his crutches, and sought out Parson Tieron's supplies; he had a box of medical equipment stowed in his room. Jos emptied most of it into a satchel, which he slung over his head, then limped back to the temple proper. Eldersie had the parson laid up on a bench. He bleeding from a deep gash in his shoulder. His head sagged to one side, as if he lacked the strength to hold it up. Eldersie snatched the satchel from Jos.

"What happened?" he asked.

"The ankatze pack is out there," Eldersie said. "The clerk got away. Snow's come in."

"He did?" Jos tried not to sound too pleased.

"I've no idea how. Do you have any idea where he would go? Anywhere that you showed him when you were his guide?" She pressed gauze to the parson's wound.

Tieron hissed in pain, but Eldersie ignored him.

"No. It was just fine places to ski. Nowhere that he could hide, especially in the dark."

"We should ask the others," gasped the parson.

"What others?" asked Jos.

"The tyenes. Mr Townsend and his sister."

"They haven't left my house," said Eldersie.

"As far as you know." The parson cringed as Eldersie pulled back his robe to inspect the wound. "You saw it out there. Chaos. They could have slipped away."

Eldersie looked to Jos. "You need to find them. I am too busy here."

Blood was already seeping through the gauze she had applied.

"He's got your gun too," said Tieron.

"Shit," Jos groaned, though he found himself a little impressed. "How am I to get him? I'm not as fast as I usually am."

"Get faster," she said. "There will be more ankatze. There will be more kuprum. They are starving. There's no food left in the wild and no one hunting them. There will be more monsters coming for us until you get him."

He returned to Eldersie's house as fast as his crutches would allow. On his way, he passed Martine Toft, out of his dressing gown for the first time in years. He had armed himself with another of his daughter's kitchen knives.

"No luck?" he called as he saw Jos hobble past.

"No." Jos did not care to elaborate.

"We'll catch him, you'll see," he said, with excitement that rankled Jos. "We will be burning the pyre by dark."

Townsend awaited him indoors. From appearances, he had not registered the activity that had erupted. He was scribbling numbers in a list. Jos felt out of place, like he had walked straight from a hunt into a library.

"Mr Townsend?" Jos asked. He did not look up from his work. "I don't know if you've noticed what is happening out of doors, but–"

"Of course I have noticed. You have put my sister in a right dither and robbed me of my best clerk."

"Ah. Where is–" Jos began.

"Oriana? I suspect she is out chasing ankatze. She's quite worried that you're going to burn our Mr Marheart at the stake."

"Not the stake. But you know - you know that is what they intend to do."

Townsend crossed out a line of work harshly. His gold pen left an ink blot on the paper that grew and spread, marring the letters.

"I was quite aware of this town's traditions and predilections before I planned to come here. Yet I do not understand why they have to include us."

"Mr Townsend, we don't get to choose."

"No. You do." He matched Jos's eye. "You get to choose. Why did you have to choose him?"

Jos did not have an answer for that.

"Do you not have an idea of where he could be?" Jos begged.

"I'm afraid he explored Racken far better than I did," admitted Townsend.

"Yes, I suppose so."

"I'll be one to pay for his funeral, you know," said Townsend.

"It's not usual - not for the elect." There usually was no body to bury.

The parson never performed a service for them.

"His family lost their status rather suddenly. Poor investments, you know. My father thought gambling. They vanished from society for quite some time. They lost a daughter too. Very tragic. No one would hire Ifry. Not if they knew his father," waxed Townsend.

"What is the point? Why are you telling me?"

"I thought I would practice my speech for the funeral. How did it sound?"

"Don't get ahead of yourself."

"Why shouldn't I? If you are as dedicated to mighty Solyon as Miss Toft believes."

Jos left. He went to his room to fetch a bag, and paid no mind to Townsend as he raided the kitchen for any food that Oriana had not already eaten. He considered, then cut a portion of the fruitcake that Eldersie had been soaking to celebrate the end of winter.

He did not know where to find Ifry, but he knew a way to save him. If Jos wasn't in Racken, there would be no elect to kill him. Night was falling and snow had already made visibility poor. Few people would see him go. He folded a piece of cloth around the sides of the fruitcake.

Jos felt a wave of warmth and knew Solyon would appear a moment before he did.

"What are you planning?" asked Solyon; Thomas Townsend, unaware, kept his eyes trained on his work. "Do you know where he is?"

Jos did not reply to him. It would have caused alarm, and he had naught to say, and he had far to go. He knew the way to Berill, the next town along the river. It was a day's walk or so. Longer in the snow, and even longer on a bad leg.

When he was a child, he would walk down to Berill with the rest of them. There was less farm work over winter. If a family needed the money, they would send their children downriver and down the mountain where there would work on other farms, below the snow line. They left in a steady stream. There was no schedule, but the children waited for their friends to come out and join the parade. They walked over the landscape, which was greying with falling snow. They shared the food that their mothers packed for them and told stories that no adult could understand. Before they both turned nine, Eldersie and Jos walked together, hand in hand. She waited by the temple for him to come down the mountain. They walked and she passed on tales of monsters that her mother had told her.

"She said that Solyon and Volana are monsters of the mountain,"

Eldersie boasted.

"She did not! I don't think that's true."

Jos knew monsters better than Eldersie. He lived higher on the slopes than anyone else. His father went out with his gun every morning to hunt them.

"She did too, and she does not attend temple anymore." She swung his hand forward and back.

When they arrived in Berill, Jos claimed that he and Eldersie were siblings so they could stay together. The farmer's wife only laughed. She had noted Jos's dark skin and curly hair in contrast to Eldersie's paler skin and razor-straight hair. She was slender and he was broad. The woman accepted it without complaint. She let them work together.

After Eldersie's mother died, she did not walk with Jos again. Her father needed her in the house over winter. Even before she grew tall, Eldersie was stirring his soup and emptying his chamber pot. Jos walked alone. Almony never came. Her family were too rich to need to do that. She stayed warm by the fire all winter. Her nephew had too.

There was a second reason the children were sent away, a secret one. It was rumoured that it kept them safe from Volana's gaze.

There he was, reminiscing about a day long hike through rising autumn winds. He needed to go to Berill again to find a train. He could not ask for help. Some folk there would know his name, know he was the elect, and deliver him back home.

Would Ifry have gone that way? Was there truly nowhere else in Racken that he would hide? He could think of only one safe place that he had shown Ifry. There was a possibility, though small, that Ifry could have gone to his own house. It was out of the way; no one had mentioned scaling the mountain. Perhaps they did not think a tyenes would. They probably did not know, and had not guessed, how close Ifry and Jos had been. If they had, more folk would have asked him about it, more than just Thomas Townsend.

It wasn't such a foolish idea. He could return home, collect his father's old skis, and make his way to Berill as dawn broke. Travelling alone in the dark was not impossible, but it was not wise. More sensible to spend the night at home and set out at first light.

The street was empty. The hunting parties had retreated from the snow into the temple. He could see the blurred amber light through the windowpanes.

He was already tiring by the time he crossed the train tracks. Next to the bridge, he saw a pile of three ankatze corpses. The falling snow was already burying them, and had covered all signs of blood on the ground. He tried to lean on his bad leg as little as possible, but he struggled to remain vertical. As he reached the foot of the mountain, Solyon appeared again, and briefly Jos was pleased to see him as the warmth of summer washed through his bones.

"Where are you going? Do you know where he hides?" he asked, a hungry look in his eye.

Jos had not been quite aware of his decision until he saw the snow melting on Solyon's shoulders. He was joyful to the point of ecstasy. Jos's leg felt as if it were splitting in two, and the pain was making his own thoughts hard to follow.

Solyon smiled. "Do you have a weapon? How will you do it?"

Eldersie's knife burned in the front of his jacket, though Jos knew, suddenly and without doubt, that he would not need it. It was as if, for the first time, his life stretched out before him like fresh train tracks. He turned away from Solyon. He set foot on the slope, ignoring how his leg screamed out.

Solyon's voice appeared to become quieter, and more distant, though he was only a few steps away.

"Speak to me," he commanded, with all all the authority of summer. His voice rang like the temple's organ and shook Jos's core, but he continued on. He felt it, rather like a string behind him, his connection to Solyon. He had known it was there, but never named it. It stretched and frayed. Perhaps it was the driving snow, but he could hear Solyon less clearly. His voice was stolen, and it was much as if Jos was any other person in Racken, unable to see the face of their god.

In one journey he felt like an old man and a small child, as he crawled most of the way. Evening waned into full night as he forced his weary bones up the mountain. He bit back a prayer for help on his journey, as he didn't know to whom he would address it

He found the path to his house and nearly cried in relief. He crawled right to the door. Weary, working by memory, he opened the door and clambered inside. He landed face down on the flagstones.

"Don't move."

Jos heard the familiar clicking of a raised gun. He waited. A hunter's instinct overtook him and he stayed as still as he could, until curiosity overtook instinct and he had to look up.

"I thought you might be here," said Jos. He could not help but smile a little. Ifry was pointing his own gun at him. He knew the smile was at odds with the situation, but Ifry was there and unhurt.

"Jos. Ah. Forgive me." He lowered the gun. "I've been chased end to end of this town."

"I know." Jos shifted onto his elbows and pulled himself away from the door. Ifry set the gun down and closed the door up tight behind him. He knelt and set his hands on Jos's shoulders.

"How did you get yourself up here?"

"Crawling, mostly," Jos admitted. He got onto his knees, looking up at Ifry. "But don't worry about me, not when I've spent the whole day worrying about you. They said you killed an ankatze and I couldn't find you. Are you all right?" He grasped Ifry's hand.

"There's nothing to complain of," Ifry said. He looped one of Jos's arms over his shoulders. He helped him stagger into one of the armchairs by the fire. Ifry had built the fire as high as he could get it, and Jos became warmer than when Solyon stood nearby.

"They shouldn't guess where you are for a while yet. They're sheltering in the temple, but we should leave at first light. I know the way to the next town along. We can make our journey from there."

"It's 'we' now, then?" Ifry asked.

Jos realised his mistake. "I didn't mean to assume, but I meant to help you."

"I'm kidding with you. I wanted to look for you, but there was no time."

Jos began to unfasten the front of his coat. Ifry helped him shrug his arms out of the sleeves, and Jos was surprised at how normal he found the action. Ifry hung it up on a peg over the fire. He had found himself quite at home in Jos' house, not needing to ask where anything was.

Holding his leg straight, Jos began to shed his boots.

"Are you sure that you're all right?" he asked Ifry, watching him hang clothes in silence.

"Of course not. I am terribly afraid," Ifry told him honestly.

"I wish I could offer you some comfort."

"You have. Until now there was no one on my side."

"I suspect Mr Townsend is still, and Oriana."

"We had a fight, Oriana and I. And in any case, what use would she be?" he laughed coldly.

"What use am I going to be?" Jos asked.

"You've already proven your worth. You know the way to safety, and you found me when no one else managed to."

"I've got a bad leg. I had to crawl over the mountain for the second time in two days."

"All the more proof."

Jos swallowed the thought that he was not worthy of Ifry's regard. "I am just sorry that you were caught up in this at all."

He had considered Ifry to be separate from life in Racken, like he was floating over it while the rest of them were sunken. Spending time with him had felt like departing the life he had always known.

"It wasn't your fault," Ifry told him.

Jos wanted to refute Ifry's claim, but quashed the thought. "Ifry - I..." The words died on his lips.

Ifry stood by the fire, swathed in melancholy.

"What comfort can I give you, right now?" Jos asked.

Ifry turned and considered him. "You are kind, Jos."

"I – it's only what you deserve. Well, you deserve far more."

"That's very sweet. But don't cling to that sentiment. You'll regret it."

"It's a feeling. A true feeling." He felt that there was too much that he needed to convey.

"You do not get to decide what I deserve. And say no more things to disparage yourself."

"I'll do just that."

They stewed like that for a minute. Ifry inched closer to the fire.

"Are you cold?" Jos asked.

"Constantly."

"Lady Winter's gift. Come here." He meant to move aside and offer the chair to Ifry, but before he could get up, Ifry had climbed onto his lap. "I–" He could say no more. Ifry's head was already under his chin. The shock of it ebbed. He kissed the top of Ifry's hair. "For what it's worth, I am so sorry that this is happening to you, and I am going to get you out of it."

"Jos - how many people who were chosen in the past managed to escape?"

"I can't say for all time. I only know what I've witnessed."

"But how many? In all the time that you have seen?"

He could not lie, even to comfort him. "None of them. I haven't seen any."

"I'm doomed, then."

Jos moved his arms, held him tighter. "I can't believe that, and I won't allow you to believe it. If that's all I can do right now, then I'll do it."

Ifry's hand played on his chest. "You're warm," he said, rather bluntly.

"I don't feel warm. I'm still trying to shake the cold off."

Ifry moved his hand to rest on Jos's collar bone.

"Can I kiss you?" Ifry murmured.

"What?"

"You asked before. I thought it was only polite."

Jos struggled with his words before he realised that he did not need them. With one finger, he raised Ifry's chin so that he could kiss him. It started softly; Ifry was gentle. He rested his hand on Jos' cheek. Jos felt Ifry's breath, hot in his mouth. He did not know what to do with his hands. He put them on Ifry's waist, but slowly moved them lower. Ifry swung his leg over Jos so that he straddled him, wove his hands into Jos's hair. Jos crossed his arms behind Ifry's back and pulled him as close as he could.

"Oh shit," he said against Ifry's mouth.

"What?" Ifry pulled back, suddenly concerned. "Is this all right?"

"I was going to do something impressive. I was going to pick you up and go over there." He nodded his head towards the box bed. "But I've got this stupid leg."

Ifry laughed. If only he could bottle that sound. "You could have just asked."

He stood up from Jos's lap. He ran his hand from Jos's cheek down his neck and arm, then clasped his hand tight. He pulled him up steadily. He moved towards the bed. Jos leaned on the back of the armchair, then Ifry's shoulder until he stood next to the bed. Jos sat on the bed first, easing his bad leg in. He knew that he had exerted it too much already, but he was unwilling to cease the moment's activities.

"It's a bit cramped," Ifry observed.

"I hope it's all right. It's warm," Jos said.

Ifry shrugged off his layers and let them fall to the floor. He was far too slow. The wait was agonising. Jos felt him climb into the box bed. He was right. It was cramped. He could feel Ifry's whole body against his back. He reached across and found that Ifry had shed all of his layers.

IFRY MARHEART

The curtains over the bed were embroidered with suns and spirals. A loving hand had stitched those patterns; Ifry found joy in imagining Jos's mother sat by the fire, stitching with yellow thread to brighten her little house.

Jos moved against his back, still dozing. His skin was like a summer's day. Ifry allowed himself a smile. If only there had not been so much threat to his life, he might have been pleased they came to Racken. He would have been happy to invite Jos to the city. They could get pastries from his favourite bakery and cook together in Ifry's flat.

That was perhaps too fanciful. Ifry had never had anyone who cared to stick around to eat with him. There was he was fantasising about dinner dates while he was still in the direst straits he had ever known. It was too hard not to feel comfortable when Jos was sleeping with his arm around him.

Jos moved, kissing the back of his neck. "Still night?" he asked.

"Very much so." The sliver of sky he could see between the curtains was as dark as a crow's eye.

"Where are we going when we get out of Racken?"

"We should start in the city. I can show you where I used to live with my parents. It's a big house with a large garden. A little way out of the city proper."

"I'd like that."

"Then we should probably vanish for a while. I can hand in my notice to Thomas's office and empty all my savings. We could travel south. Somewhere warm."

"I could sell to Thomas," Jos said.

"What?"

"You told me that in other resorts Townsend needed to build avalanche defences. I own land above where he wanted a piste. If Townsend owned it, he could build all the defences he liked."

"You would do that?" Ifry thought of the curtains, and the happy hours spent in this little house.

"If I am going to flee my life, I think I should draw a line under it. Make it proper."

"Won't you miss it?"

Ifry felt Jos' sigh.

"I don't doubt that I will. I don't think I'll be suited to city life, but I have always wondered what it would be like. I've wanted to go elsewhere for a long time. But I always stayed." He stroked Ifry's ear with the pad of his thumb. "When it no longer matters, and the gods have shrunk away, who knows what I'll be."

"What will Racken be like without them?"

"I don't think it will have changed much. It never does."

"Thomas has already decided where he will build his hotel and who he wants to manage it. He had the money to start right away. Next summer, this place will be on its way to being a resort."

"I hadn't thought about that."

No one ever did. The other resorts had been hesitant too, but they had relented. What no one realised was that the resort made it inhospitable for anyone else.

"Should we get moving?" Ifry asked, despite all his desires to stay in bed.

"I wish we could stay." Jos turned Ifry over and kissed his nose. "But you are right. We should get dressed."

"Just one minute." Ifry kissed him again.

"Don't let that be the last one," Jos begged.

Ifry pulled away from Jos and felt a shiver wrack him. Jos noticed and drew him close again.

"What was that?" he asked.

"It's just cold."

"But the fire's been roaring for hours."

"I just need to get dressed, I think."

He tried to sit up and shivered again.

Jos sat up like a bolt and gave Ifry the most concerned look. "You are going to freeze to death out there like this."

"It must be Lady Winter, like you said. It's not real."

"It's real enough." He climbed out of the bed, wrapping his blanket around Ifry as he went. "You should wear my coat, it's warmer than yours."

"What will you wear? Mine's too small for you." It was encrusted with bloodstains, too, though Ifry didn't feel the need to add this detail.

"I'll be fine." He bent over a cedar chest. From its depths, he retrieved a mauve coat and shook it out. It was fur-lined, just like his yellow one. Ifry, trying to hide his shivering, watched him with fascination. His skin was the colour of firelight.

"Where did that come from?" Ifry asked.

"My father. I haven't had the heart to use any of their things." He collected his yellow coat from the line over the fire. Ifry made to get up. "No, you stay right there," he said. He picked up Ifry's clothes from where they had been tossed about the room and limped back to him. As Jos handed him the clothes, Ifry felt a rush of warmth from the brush of his fingertips, but it was too fleeting. Ifry clutched the blanket tight around his shoulders, and allowed himself to watch Jos getting dressed; he held his bad leg up where he could, and leaned on the furniture. He was strong, he had to be, to come all that way on that leg. Ifry put the fur lining of the coat to his face and breathed in. He thought it would be musty, but it just smelled like Jos.

Jos began unwrapping a pair of old and heavy skis, which no doubt were also family heirlooms.

"What I haven't put together is that there's someone slated to kill me," Ifry mused aloud.

"Yes," Jos replied, producing a pair of poles and dark glasses.

"The elect."

"Yes."

"Who are they? Then I would know who to avoid."

"You should avoid them all," Jos said, checking the straps on the skis.

"Who would it be? Someone strong? Fast? Almony has both of those qualities, I expect. Eldersie's father. I don't know what he was like as a young man." Ifry said his thoughts aloud in the vain hope that would help him sort them.

"You don't know all the people in Racken." There was a tremor in his voice.

Ifry was deep in thought. "The real thing that links them is the relationship. It had to have been hard for them to kill their target. But that doesn't make a great deal of sense, as there aren't many people in this town who would hesitate to kill me. Even Thomas Townsend might consider it, though I can't see him leading the mob." Ifry chuckled to himself at the idea of it.

Jos fastened a belt outside of his coat. He set a pack by the door and briefly checked the supplies he had inside. He set it and the gun near Ifry.

"You might have to carry those," he said. "I'll take it easy, but as soon as we see a monster, you hand it to me, all right?"

Ifry nodded, though he was still lost in thought. "I don't need to fire that again, thank you. But I do wonder - no one would hesitate. They have proven that, with their pitchforks. Why wouldn't the elect show themselves?"

He had talked himself into a circle. He should hurry and dress. It was not yet light, but they should start out before the townsfolk had a chance to rouse. With haste, he stepped out from the blankets and collected his layers from where they had been scattered around the room. He pulled on his own bloodstained coat, then put Jos's yellow coat over it.

"Jos? We should go."

Jos nodded, but he avoided Ifry's eye. He looked at the ground so mournfully that it made Ifry concerned. Ifry moved to fasten the coat, but something weighed down the front. He reached inside and found a pocket. Inside he felt something cool. He drew out a knife. He recognised it. He had seen it in a matching set hanging on Eldersie's kitchen wall.

"Jos? Why do you have Eldersie's knife in your coat?"

Jos opened his mouth, but he found no words. He was looking at Ifry like he was already dead. Ifry realised something he should have assumed before.

"You–"

"Ifry, I–"

"Oh, fuck."

He was standing in the way. This was a small house in a cold clime. Of course there was only one exit.

"I never – I never meant to hurt you," said Jos.

"Then get out of the way."

"You can't go out there alone. They'll catch you."

"*You* are the one that is supposed to catch me. Please, get out of my way," begged Ifry.

"No."

Jos had come here, not with the goal of helping Ifry, but getting him somewhere quiet. He was right, Ifry would not last long alone in the mountains. He must have praised Solyon for his stroke of good luck when he found Ifry in his own house. He had slept with Ifry, made one last overture of love while knowing he was chosen to kill him. He had pretended all would be well, just as a spider weaves its web.

Ifry reached for the gun and raised it. Jos put up his hand, palm forward, in the manner that one would use to calm a wild animal.

"Get out of my way," Ifry said.

"Ifry, please, I promise I won't hurt you."

"Unless Solyon tells you to. Jos, please, I won't ask again." He tried to steady the quiver in his voice. He did not want to face his death with watery eyes and a runny nose. "Please let me run. Let me try. I need to try."

Jos shook his head. "They'll kill you."

"No, they won't. They'll capture me and they'll bring me to you."

"Ifry, I–"

"Get out of my way!" He raised his voice without meaning to. He realised that he was truly crying. In a wild moment of idiocy, he nearly reached into his pocket for his handkerchief.

Jos put both of his hands in the air. He backed away from the door. Ifry pulled the pack onto his shoulder. He kept the barrel of the gun trained on him as he approached the exit. With one hand he grasped for the skis and poles that Jos had prepared. He took his pair, then tucked the second pair of skis under his arm. If he was sensible, he could stall Jos's pursuit.

He fell outside and crawled upon the snow. The cold was painful and his tears burned his face. He hurried into the trees, listening for Jos behind him. Sunlight had not reached over the mountains, but the grey pallor of the snow made him think that it soon would.

Under the trees, he found a moment to strap the skis to his feet. He kept the gun in one hand in case Jos chose to emerge. He stood up, ready to go, only he was not sure where he should head. Without Jos, he would surely get lost trying to follow the valley, and lose his life in the cold. There was another way out, if he was fool enough to try it. His call to the conductor had informed him that a train was soon to pass through Racken.

He turned aside and skied downhill, back the way that he had come. Back to Almony's farm and Eldersie's house and the temple full of people who hunted him.

"Lady Winter protect me," he prayed, "and keep Jos from knowing where I have gone."

Snow still fell, and he hoped it would fill his path behind him.

ORIANA TOWNSEND

The temple was so full of incense that Oriana couldn't breathe. This was one of the things that she could not tolerate about religion: the pageantry. Oriana liked pageantry as much as the next person. She liked the expensive clothes that she bought at the beginning of every season; she liked the rituals of getting ready for an evening. The primping and the pressing. Trying on earrings three times over. Asking others about the look for pandered approval. That was pageantry, but it was pageantry about enjoyment. It was built to make people feel good about themselves.

Religious pageantry, that was more likely to remind people of their own misery. That was what the incense was for. There could not be just enough to make the temple smell pleasant. No, it had to be so thick in the atmosphere that she choked on it.

All the people of Racken, as far as she could guess, were crammed inside the temple. Eldersie tended to the wounded that had traipsed in through the door. The priest was laid up on a bench with bandages built up around his shoulder. Oriana had been given the option to return to Eldersie's house to sit with her brother many times, but she had to be a witness to whatever atrocities they had planned.

She was sat against the pulpit, which was the best vantage point in the temple. She kept her eye on Eldersie, who marched about, barking orders to her peers as if she was the new leader of the town. Oriana found herself concerned, even as she admonished herself for such a feeling. There was something about the way Eldersie's eyes darted around the room that struck Oriana with a sense of foreboding.

"What makes you watch Eldersie so?" said a voice from behind her.

Oriana turned. A middle-aged man was seated below the pulpit. She had not seen him before, but she was also realising quite how many people there were in Racken. She had imagined that it was no more than a hamlet, yet they had crammed the temple nearly to the rafters.

"Is she a second to the parson, or something?" Oriana asked.

"She is an acolyte. Nothing official, but she does the most work for the parson. She's been offered a higher position, but she turned it down. Still, there is no one else below the parson."

"I would have thought she might relish that kind of thing," Oriana said. "She always struck me as a rather bossy soul."

"I don't know about that," said the man. He had a warm look to him, mostly in the calm demeanour that only came from basking in the sunlight. Oriana took a raking glance over his clothes, his buttons, the shine of his shoes, the cuffs of his shirt. She could not tell much by them. His buttons were gold but tarnished. His shoes were the beaten leather boots that were favoured by mountaineers. His cuffs were folded back, so she could not tell if he had cufflinks.

"Have we had any word of how the search is going?" she asked, hoping this man was part of the town's inner circle.

"The search has been called off. Visibility is too poor. He can't be comfortable, wherever he is."

She had not thought of that. Ifry might already be frozen to the hillside, dying.

"It has to be dawn soon, right? The storm will break then, surely."

"Maybe. But we have another problem. My elect has gone missing," he said. "Even I cannot find him."

"*Your* elect?"

"The elect? Has Eldersie not explained it to you? The elect is chosen to bring back summer," he said, in the patronising manner that Thomas was so fond of.

Eldersie had explained it to Oriana on her first night in Racken. It was just the murder that she had left out.

"I must have misheard you. I know what the elect is. Though not who it is, I admit."

"Ah, that will be Jos Nothernine."

"What?" The broad gunslinger who lived in the attic. If he was in a fight with Ifry, the latter would not stand a chance.

"Only the best fighters of Racken are chosen to be the elect." The man smiled in a self-satisfied manner.

"So, Jos has gone missing too?"

"Eldersie cannot find him. He is not here in the temple. I have been searching for him." He gestured to the room with open palms to demonstrate the lack of Jos Nothernine.

"He can't have gone far," Oriana muttered.

"Why not? Jos Nothernine is a most adept mountaineer. He had been all over these slopes and the clerk has not. I have faith that he will find him."

"I don't think so. Not on only one good leg." Oriana could not see anyone being able to get up a mountain on crutches. She would have bet that he was tucked up in bed, waiting for Ifry to be brought to him.

"What has happened to his leg?" the man asked, full of concern.

"He's only gone and broken it, and on the eve of his coronation, no less," she laughed. The dread that filled her after she heard Nothernine's name dissipated.

"That can't be right," said the man. "He is the chosen one. He should have known not to get in such trouble."

"I don't think he fell off the side of a mountain on purpose. I'm not even sure he did it out of stupidity. I think it's just a risk of living in a place so hazardous. Why do you even live here? Why does anyone? Think of it, living somewhere that doesn't have avalanches. Imagine going outside and not nearly freezing your balls off. Gods fuck, I cannot wait to get out of this place. Even the shittiest tenements in Darrity have indoor plumbing." She heaved out a breath.

The man, though concerned, could not let her tirade stand.

"Why not stay in the place that you are born?" he asked. "What greater good is there, than serving your community?"

"Spoken like a true peasant," Oriana said. She was growing bored of him now.

"Tyenes," he muttered. It was so predictable that Oriana mouthed the word along with him. "Of course you would not understand. This community has been united, year on year, against *her*. What else could bring people together like this? This town is a great one, and a noble one–"

She interrupted him.

"That's enough of that," she said, loud enough to cover the speech he was no doubt about to give.

"Are you pleased with yourself?" Eldersie's voice was tired.

Oriana looked up, not having realised that she was nearby. Her apron was marked with browning bloodstains. Her hair made dark lines around her face.

"What business is it of yours?" Oriana asked.

"You are yelling. Can you keep your conversations with yourself down?"

"I'm not talking to myself, I'm talking to–" She turned to get the name of the man, yet he was not there. "I was speaking to someone."

"No, you weren't."

"But - he was right here." Oriana looked at the groups nearby, but he was not among them. He couldn't have left the temple in the time she took to glance to Eldersie.

"Dawn is breaking. Folk are wondering what you're doing."

"I am just sitting here," she stated.

"Exactly. We need to go out soon. We cannot leave you here and we cannot take you with us. I need to fetch some things, so I need to take you back to your brother," Eldersie told her.

"I don't want to sit with my brother."

"I hope you enjoy being locked in the temple cellar then."

Oriana slid off the pulpit. At least her brother's eyes were less watchful than Eldersie's.

"What part am I supposed to play in all of this?" she asked.

"An audience member, preferably. Or perhaps better, the wise soul who knew to leave at the interval."

"Eldersie, I'm impressed. I did not know you were so cultured."

Eldersie gave no response. Instead, she led Oriana through the temple and the forest of watchful eyes. They stepped out into the blistering air.

"I think the interval might have passed us by," said Oriana as she felt the chill.

She had not listened to Ifry as closely as she should have. There really was no train coming for them.

ELDERSIE TOFT

Townsend had let the fire die. The last flame struggled against the ashes that nearly engulfed it. He did not ask for news as they entered but continued to scratch away at his lists and his papers.

Eldersie sought out the dresser next to the hearth and opened the topmost drawer. She grasped for the iron door key, which she transferred to her pocket without her guests' notice. Oriana rushed to the stairs, driven by unusual purpose; Townsend barely glanced at her passing.

"Stay indoors," Eldersie advised him. A watery light leaked through the kitchen window. Dawn had broken, but the weather was still foul.

"I assure you, I've no desire to be out at a time like this."

She was not sure if he referred to the situation or the weather.

"Good. It won't be safe for you, or your sister." She smoothed the front of her apron. A thought buzzed in her ear that it was useless to keep up appearances when she had come inside disheveled and bloodstained.

"I suppose there has been no sign of Mr Marheart?" he asked. His tone was tight, but still as casual as if he were ordering the morning paper.

"No. When there is, you will know."

"I thought as much."

"I expect you will be leaving on the next train." Eldersie hoped that a way to be rid of him sooner might arrive, but she had not seen Townsend so much as strap on skis.

"My investments have not yet paid off," he said. "I will leave only when my work is done and not before."

She gritted her teeth. "How fast can that be arranged?"

"Oh. Well. There is a little something you could help me with. In my other resorts I have often employed locals. I find it far more expedient than the alternative. Local people know what the climate demands. You mountain folk are quite right that tyenes can be foolish when it comes to such matters."

"That is more insight than I might have expected."

"I have done this several times. I know what works and what is unwise. I have been observing the people of Racken for potential candidates. I haven't made a long list, but I have been impressed."

"I think you won't find anyone for your purposes."

"Quite the contrary. I have been impressed by you."

"Me?" She stopped her work. He was lying. He was trying to bribe her.

"Yes. Your work ethic. You run this house with surprising efficiency, given how the deck is stacked against you."

It was flattery. She was not so stupid to fall for it.

"How the - what do you mean?"

"Well, a lack of funds, an ailing father, no staff, no plumbing. You have plenty working against you. Yet this house is clean. It has kept us well. I would offer you a job. I need someone to run the hotel, once I get it off the ground. It will start small, but it will grow. It would be like running a house, only you would have far more people to order around."

His bid was higher than she expected. He was a rich man. He would build a hotel with brass doorknobs and silk wall coverings. He would have telephones, plural, one in each room. There would be stained glass lampshades and brass light switches. She would walk across soft carpet every morning. She could imagine it, the slight give on the plush surface beneath her toes, the warm feel of it even on a wintry morning. She could hear the faint buzz of the lightbulbs above her head.

"Of course there would be some sacrifices," he continued. "You might have to find someone to care for your father, but you would have access to the funds for outside help. You would have to give up your business at the temple."

Temple. The soft sound of the word hurled her back to life. She was in her kitchen with the rough flagstones and the smoke stains on the ceiling. There was no hotel with fitted carpets and electricity even in the service quarters.

"I'm afraid that I don't think that life's mine," she said.

"Don't give me your answer just now. I know it's a lot to consider, but you have to wonder, what will help you move on with your future? Have you had the thought? I know you can't have. I cared for my father too before he passed. It's hard to consider, at such a time, how the future will turn out. As far as they are concerned, there is no future. Not for you. The older you get, the smaller your world becomes. By the time my father passed, his world was just his room, his nurse and me. He had even squeezed Oriana out of it. Terribly sad, but when he passed, the future opened back up again. I left his funeral and there it was. All of a sudden, I had so much more to do. Forgive me for being morbid, but when he isn't here, how much will you care about your temple and your mountain gods?"

He put down his pen and shuffled his papers into a pile. He ran his thumb down the edge to check that it was aligned. "I have been blunt, but you understand that this is a pivotal moment. I know that a lot is being asked of you. I wanted to present another option for what the future might hold." He stood. "If you'll allow me your kettle, I am going to make some tea." He got out from behind the table.

There was a thumping on the stairs. Oriana tumbled back into the room.

"Drat," she said.

"What is it?" Townsend asked her.

"Nothernine isn't in his room."

"Of course he isn't. He's far too busy," said Eldersie.

"I thought he might have sneaked back to rest his leg."

"No. I would have seen him," insisted Townsend.

"Where is he then?" asked Oriana.

Eldersie opened her mouth to question why Oriana cared about Jos's whereabouts, but, she realised that she did not even know the answer to Oriana's question. He had left the temple and not come back. He had a broken leg and there had been a storm raging all night.

"He'll be back," she declared, though even she noted the quaver in her voice.

"I need to find him," announced Oriana.

She was getting ideas.

Eldersie walked to the door without another word. She closed it behind her and fixed the key into the lock. She turned it, hoping that Townsend and his sister had already sprung into an argument that would keep them occupied. Eldersie pushed down the last thought of plush carpets and electric lighting and turned to the temple.

IFRY MARHEART

Every whistle of the wind, every rustle of the trees sounded to Ifry like Jos's uneven step. He tried to calm the staccato beat of his heart, but nothing worked. He saw that the doors to the temple swung open, like the maw of one of the mountain creatures, spilling townsfolk into the street. He spotted Eldersie pacing the temple steps.

Ifry crouched behind a fallen log that had its height doubled by a cap of snow. He glanced to the horizon and pushed back his sleeve to check his watch.

He had Jos's coat, so at least he would not look like himself when he stepped out. It still smelled like Jos. He berated himself for being comforted by the scent.

Ifry shifted his position to the woodshed behind Almony's house, which was a decent spot for him to watch the movements of the valley folk. They had piled the bodies of the ankatze next to the railway line. He could see their mottled pelts, even partially masked by snowfall.

The winds were rising. The snow fell thicker and faster. Instead of moving away, the storm lingered on Racken like it had been summoned there.

He crept out from behind the woodshed, tiptoeing around Almony's house and down the path to the bridge. His stomach turned as he approached the ice underneath the bridge. He tried to reassure himself that he had already crawled on this ice and not gone through. He settled into a crawl, reasoning that it would be harder to fall that way. He had left dignity behind.

He felt a shift under his palm; felt as if he had heard a crack, as if it had shot through the shards of his soul. He scrambled, only realising that there was no crack once he was clutching the frozen rocks of the other bank. He kept on his belly as he moved up the bank, feeling the ground leach his warmth away.

The bed of the railway was raised enough to keep Ifry hidden from the eyes on the other side of the valley, but this was not reassuring. If anyone chose to walk up to the tracks, they would see him.

The ankatze were piled about ten feet away. The cold kept them from smelling and prevented flies from finding them. He could thank Lady Winter for that. He scuttled across the tracks like he was a stray dog. He glanced in the direction of Eldersie's house.

He could see no one. In the snow, the roofs of the houses were murky, like he was viewing the town through a grubby lens. He drew hope from that. If he couldn't see anyone, they could not see him.

He climbed out of the snow drift that was forming around him and dashed to where the ankatze lay. He wrapped his mittened hands around an ankatze's back leg and tugged. It moved. He gasped out a quick prayer to Lady Winter that it was not as heavy as he had feared.

He dragged, taking the corpse away from the pile and leaving it splayed across the tracks, with its head resting on an iron rail. It looked much more like a cat now that it was no longer leering over him; it had the same furry underbelly that house cats showed when they were inviting their owners into a trap. Ifry stood back, allowing himself this moment of success. Looking up, he saw that the townhouses were clearer to his eyes. He had a wild moment of thinking that he was just getting used to looking through a blizzard, but he realised that the storm was moving on. The air already felt lighter.

"Fuck," he muttered.

He dove back to the ankatze and grabbed another. This one was larger. It must have been older and better fed than the first, as Ifry struggled to shift it. He ground his teeth as he pulled on the animal's leg. He had to walk in painfully short steps, his back bent and aching. He shifted the corpse onto the line. The sky was clearing for certain. He checked his watch again and glanced down the line to end of the valley. There was a line there, like a pencil dragged lazily across paper. A thin column of smoke was approaching.

Trains had to stop for leaves. The ankatze would be enough. He dashed along the line in search of a hiding place. He found one in a spot that would have been obvious in any other town, but he doubted would be checked in Racken: under the bench inside the platform shelter. The last time he had been here, he had carried their luggage with Jos at his side.

Even as he thought this, the snow ceased its falling. He was curled inside the shelter, hidden only by the lip of the bench. If he moved so much as an inch, he would be seen. He froze right down to his bones as, through the gap in the boards, he saw Eldersie's father stalking the far side of the river, poring over the ground with all the concentration of a hunter on the trail of a rabbit. He seemed sharper than before, and that only daunted Ifry, who curled as close to the splintery wall as he dared.

Mr Toft's eyes roved over the river and the railway line, and up to the platform. Ifry thought he could feel his heart pounding through both of the coats he wore. Mr Toft looked away. Ifry felt the rumble, then heard the shriek. A train, a great lumbering beast, was pulling into Racken. Ifry watched the wheels, so intricate with their spokes and bars, halt in front of him. He saw the rust-red siding of the carriages and the peeling paint of the company name. It was not a passenger train. There were no clean windows or plush seats. There was certainly no dining car.

Ifry thought of it as something holy. Not a moment after it stopped, workmen in overalls hopped down and ran along the line to investigate. He knew that he did not have long. He had moved the ankatze in a matter of minutes, but the stronger train workers would get rid of them in a quarter of that. They mightn't even stay to find someone to pay the fine.

He dashed across the platform and fell upon the side of the carriage. It was not as easy as pulling open the door and diving in. There was a heavy sliding door with a stiff handle. It was agonising, the time that it took to open it. It screeched worse than the gargins had when they attacked him.

When he was successful, it was like the relief of finding a loved one safe at home. He placed both palms on the floor of the carriage and pulled himself up. The carriage was filled with sacks. A lone potato rolled between them. He turned, ready to close the door, and saw the black mark of Eldersie's hair against the snow.

She cried for him to stop, then dashed towards him. Ifry braced himself and slammed the door shut in half the time he had taken to open it. She beat a single fist against the outside. There was only time for one thump before the floor shook under him. The potatoes rolled and smacked against his feet. Ifry heard the hiss and the shuffle of the train's movement, like the laboured breathing of a dying janros.

He sagged against the door, leaning his forehead on the rusted metal. The carriage lurched and he stumbled. He sunk to his knees. Caught in near darkness, unable to see to the end of the carriage, he laid on his back and let the potatoes roll against his sides. He was leaving Racken.

JOS NOTHERNINE

The train left a smudge on the horizon long after it had snaked away. Jos watched it with a great deal of satisfaction. He stared through one of the windows of Almony's house. The bedroom was abandoned. It was damp. The mattress had been removed from the bed.

"He called the conductor from Almony's own phone," Eldersie said. She had paced a line into the carpet. "How could we have been so stupid?"

"Don't worry about that, Elsie," said Martine Toft, who sat in a half-collapsed armchair. "You did not know he was the chosen."

"We should have guessed," Eldersie said.

"I wonder how you could have." Martine had gained a comforting tone to his voice that Jos had not heard since he and Eldersie were nine.

"I suppose." Eldersie stopped her pacing. "None of us guessed. The clerk does not follow the usual pattern." She gave Jos a look that he hated more than he hated Lady Winter.

"She must be trying to trick us by choosing unexpected people," said Martine, in the manner of a detective from a motion picture.

"Father? Can I have a minute to speak with Jos?" asked Eldersie.

He glanced between the pair of them in the hesitant, drawn way that people had always used back in the days when Almony had teased Jos for his connection to Eldersie.

"I suppose so." He stood and shuffled to the door, giving one last worried look to his daughter as he went.

"Why did Volana choose the clerk?" Eldersie asked as the door closed on him.

Jos didn't answer her. If she wanted to know, she could guess. She sighed and came to sit on the low sofa beside him. He shifted his bad leg away from her.

"I know that it can't be random. That is not easy to believe," she said.

"I don't know what you want to hear," he muttered.

"I want you to tell me that you love him."

He felt sick. Eldersie was bunching her apron in her fist, her knuckles turned white. He shook his head.

"What does that mean? You don't love him?"

"I don't want to talk about this with you." He shrank back into the window, as if he could flee through it.

"I wish that this could remain your business, but your feelings are all of our concern now. All of Racken, and everywhere else too. Every soul will freeze to death under her hands."

The words were dusty. The meaning had been wrung out of them by years seated in temple.

"You can't help me, Eldersie."

"I didn't expect you to want my help." She made a short, sharp laugh that revealed the extent of her good humour.

"What do you want from me?" he asked.

"I don't know. Perhaps you could rouse yourself and plan what to do. You're the elect. You were chosen by a god. Why are you holed up here?"

He shrugged. The townsfolk had gathered in Almony's house while the temple housed the wounded. He had slipped in without offering explanation for his absence.

"I hoped that you were out there dealing with him. Last night," finished Eldersie in a small voice.

He revolted at the idea that Ifry could simply be *dealt with,* like the creatures he dispatched.

"Is that how your father described it when he strangled your mother in the woods?" he asked her.

She hit him. She aimed for the soft part of his belly with her knuckles, and it hurt more than he thought it would. He had not reckoned that all her days of scrubbing and sweeping and wringing had made her strong. And she didn't leave it at one - she tried to swing at his face. He caught her by the wrist and shoved her away from him. She nearly fell off the seat, but caught herself.

"You are not allowed to talk about my mother."

"Why shouldn't I? Because you will never stop hurting about her? I know. I don't want to be like you." It was a thought that he had long nurtured but never given voice.

"You would rather be a dead man, then, with the rest of us frozen with you?" She pulled herself back onto the sofa and continued her assault of him. He could hardly blame her. He knew he was being cruel.

He cringed away from her attempt to kick him, but her boot grazed his bad leg and he yelled. She let both her feet fall to the floor.

"I forgot," she said in a hurry. She stopped her attempts to attack him and sat there, breathing just a touch too hard for someone seated.

"For fuck's sake." He clutched his leg, though nothing eased it. "I don't know what to do, Eldersie. He's gone. I can't walk. I don't know how to make it better."

"Are you not our link to Solyon?"

He laughed. "He's no help." He had not even dreamed him of late. "He's gone somewhere." He neglected to mention how he had pushed Solyon away.

She frowned. "He's the god of all summer. He should help us," she mumbled, like she was a child struggling with a brand-new thought.

"Have you actually met him?"

She shook her head.

He laughed. "I had an idea that you had. Somehow. You are the best of his acolytes and all."

"Why do you want to keep the clerk alive?"

He willed himself to shrug and shake his head. He wanted something to tidy all of it away so that he would not have to tell her the truth, but he could not summon anything. He stayed silent, scalding tears welling in his eyes.

"Oh. So you do love him," she said.

"Don't do that."

"What?"

"Don't tell me how I feel."

"I have to guess. I always have to guess. You are not an easy book to read. I have known you my whole life and you have never trusted me with a damn thing." She was crying.

"Why would I need to? Why do you care?"

He fumbled around for his crutches, intending to find his way out of the room at any cost. He would rather be rinsed out by Parson Tieron than by Eldersie.

She snatched one of his crutches away from him. "I want to sort all of this. I want winter to end and - Solyon help me - he's chosen you to do it."

He turned away from her. The smoke was disappearing from the horizon.

"I don't want to kill him, Eldersie. I don't know how."

"*I* certainly don't," she said, as if she was above it all.

"You build the pyre every year. You cannot wash your hands of this."

"That is not the same," she insisted.

"You play your part, Eldersie."

"You are not - this is not hard for you. You have it so much better than anyone else." She pointed at him with the end of the crutch.

"There's no need to compare."

"You are not killing your wife. You are not killing a child. You are killing a stranger. A tyenes." She added venom to that final word, but he had the sense she was convincing herself as much as she was convincing him.

"Do you really think it's that easy?"

"You have it so easy, Jos. You have no one to care about. Your parents are dead. You have no partner. No children. No nieces or nephews. Neither does he. When he goes, who would care?"

"I–" He stopped himself. He did not want Eldersie to know. She would only mock him or chastise him. She was so practical. She would never understand something that had no purpose, only feeling. He changed the subject. "Would you not care if I died?"

She frowned, then turned her eyes up to the ceiling. "I suppose," she said. "But I don't think we've cared about each other all that well for a year now."

That was more specific than he would have guessed. He would have said longer.

"A year?"

"Do you remember, a year ago, the summertime?" she asked.

"I recall it, yes."

"You vanished during all of the warm months."

"I was working on the railway like every other damn person in this town."

He had worked, bent over, the sun burning the skin on his back. The grass had turned yellow. He remembered the way that the heat had smelled. The heavy dust in the air from shifted earth. The sweat of the men who tramped past him, tugging crates filled with rock. The sharp smell of Kristann's skin.

"If it was just that, I wouldn't have said anything," she said. "I meant that even when I was speaking to you, your mind was somewhere else. That had never happened before. It's never come back."

He stared at her. She was complaining about all these nothings while the town was clamouring for Ifry's head.

"Eldersie, I don't know what you want from me."

"I want to know what changed."

"Nothing changed," he lied.

"You changed your mind."

"My mind? About what?"

"About me." Her eyes were as shiny as marbles.

"I didn't – I don't know what you mean," he said.

But he did. He remembered the end of last summer. Kristann had just left and his absence left an ache that Jos could not describe. Their relationship had been secret. Not a soul knew why Almony's jokes failed to cheer him, or the slightest remark would send him into spirals of melancholy. The frost had set the slopes, and the peaks wore their white cloaks again. Eldersie was often found in the temple, readying paper garlands to celebrate the elect when they arrived. Jos had returned to his old life and found it curiously wanting. He had never considered before the sheer length of his life. Then he'd found himself wrangling with the entirety of it as he attempted to do ordinary tasks. He'd been filling a pail of water from the river when he was struck with the drudgery of it. He would do this every day for the rest of his life. Twice a day in the winter. There was something horrific and unyielding in the idea that he would never stop doing this.

He'd felt the same thing when he walked the path up to his house. Only his own feet had trodden this path in years; the path from Almony's garden to his front door was worn clear of grass and only his boots were responsible. He could not exist here, with only his footprints leading to his front door.

Summer was dying when Eldersie had come to his door. It had occurred to him that Eldersie had not been in his house since it had become just his.

"I want to start a family. I want to get married," she had said. He'd known that she meant with him, but he played at ignorance. "I never understood why you didn't ask me," she'd finished.

"Just because we're close doesn't mean I'm going to marry you," he'd said, in a tone more forceful than was warranted. "You don't really want to marry me, Eldersie. You just don't want to be happy."

She had left without dignifying him with a response. He hadn't seen her for a week or so. They never spoke of marriage again. Jos had returned to her house when the first snows fell, back into the drudging routine which had settled over his life. She wanted help over winter, and he wanted bed and board. They needed one another.

"Did you really want to marry me?" he asked her now, more than a year later, as they sat on the collapsed sofa in Almony's house.

"I wanted to be married. I didn't want to be alone all my life."

He shook his head. "But I was just there, I was just nearby. You don't love me."

She tutted again. “Marriage isn't all about love.”

“It is.”

“No. That's a fanciful thought. That you could be in love with someone for that long. It's more sensible to find someone you can get on with. That you work well with.”

“You can't actually believe that,” Jos said.

“You can't possibly believe the alternative.” She tutted again.

“Why shouldn't I? My parents were in love. Unlike yours.” He wasn't sure of the declaration until he said it. As the words left his mouth he became certain of them. If he had loved her, he wouldn't have killed her.

Eldersie raised her hand, as if to slap him. He saw her palm stretch out, open towards him, but she lowered her arm.

“You don't mean that,” she whispered.

“Why shouldn't I? Think of what you are asking me to do.”

“You are only supposed to do what every elect has done before you.”

He ignored her. He had found a line of his own and intended to follow it.

“Is that it? Do you fear loving people, Eldersie? Because the people who love you are supposed to hurt you. And you them.”

“You are being childish,” she accused him, just as she had done a thousand times before.

"No. I'm right."

"So it's true, you love him?" Her voice was cold, and just as disapproving as a well-disciplined teacher.

His tongue went heavy in his mouth. "I always wanted to be in love, in a way I don't think you cared about."

"That doesn't matter now."

"Eldersie..."

"I know now why you refused to kill a tyenes. You picked up a foolish crush. That can be cured." She dashed from the room and closed the door with a snap.

He pulled himself up, leaning on one crutch, and tried to turn the doorknob, but it stayed firm. He shook the door. It was locked. She must have had the key in her pocket before she arrived. For about twenty minutes, he beat the door and called her name. He could hear the murmur of the hubbub below him. He slouched back into his seat and closed his eyes. He must have drifted off.

He woke in the dark, shocked by how deep a sleep he had fallen into. His head was heavy.

"Eldersie?" he mumbled. His voice was scratchy.

"No," said Almony. "Though she did send me here." He felt the seat depress as she sat down next to him.

"What did she do that for?" he asked.

"Something about coaxing you into doing your proper duty. I'm supposed to set a good example," she laughed. "I don't think Eldersie has been that aware of me of late."

"You and me both."

"It's either that, or she's more desperate than I imagined."

"What are they talking about down there?" He could still hear the chatter of all of his neighbours.

"There are big plans for how to find him, but no one knows where he could have gone. The Townsends are no help either. The woman keeps giving fake addresses and telling the parson to go fuck himself."

"I never much liked her, but I do appreciate that."

They lapsed into silence. Almony hunched her back, half-curled into a ball like a snail.

"Did Parson Tieron give you the talk about being the elect? The one that sounds as if he's rehearsed it?" she asked.

"I suppose so," he said.

He could not quite remember the contents of it. He had been

thinking about his tasks for the afternoon when the parson had started speaking.

"He gave me the same one when he thought that I had gotten cold feet. He told me that summer's elect and winter's elect were called the same name because they were the same. Wrought of the same stuff. That two people being picked as the elect was proof that they loved each other."

"Is that your tactic too? Convince me that I have to do this out of love?"

"No. I want you to tell me he was full of shit." She put her forehead on her knees. For a moment, he didn't register what she had said. His brain was tangled in knots for a moment, before all was undone.

Almony continued speaking. "The only proof of love you need is inside your head." She tapped her temple with two fingers.

"Almony - I–"

"They want me to tell you that it will be over soon. But it will linger. Anything that reminds you of him will make you want to vomit. And it will not be over quickly. Did I tell you how Peter died?"

He shook his head. He felt guilty. He had avoided Almony ever since it happened. He had not known what to say.

"I haven't told anyone," she said. "No one asks me. I wish they would. I might have felt like it was as normal as everyone said it was going to be. Instead, they all clamoured at my door for me to kill him, and when the deed was done they didn't want to hear a word. Afterward it was my secret, and it was shameful. As if it was something that I should not have done. There's no calm way to kill someone. There's no going quietly. I drowned him. Took ages."

Jos remembered the parade, and seeing Almony leave her house with a bundle in her arms. He'd averted his eyes from Almony as she walked past, knowing that he did not want to look. It was much like finding carrion left over by janros on the slopes: too foul to look at.

"If you want to convince me to kill Ifry, you've chosen a strange way of going about it."

"Don't do it," she said. The words tumbled from her mouth at speed, like she had been longing to say them.

"What?"

"This town gets by on the idea that all of this is necessary. I still think that it is. But it wasn't worth it. I wish that I hadn't done it. I wish that we were buried under ten feet of snow and my Peter were still here." She let a sob creep from her chest but, well-practised, she fought it back while it was still nascent.

"I – thank you, Al. I didn't think I had any friends left here."

"Oh, this will do that. Even Helda hates me."

"But she's so devout."

"Faith can't cover all things. She's going to hate me more when she finds out what I've done."

A knot of fear twisted in Jos' stomach. "What did you do?"

"I've sold the place to Townsend. He got a bargain, I think. He was very polite about the whole thing. He offered to have movers come from the city and collect our things. I told him no. I'm going with what I can carry. Then Townsend will own half the town." She delivered it without any majesty, as if she had not just changed the lives of everyone she knew. With a brusque motion, she stood. "My skis are outside the front door. There's a pack with supplies."

"You're – what are you going to do?"

"I'm going to give you time to escape."

"I'm not going to make it far on this leg," he admitted.

"Then by all means, stay here."

He got up, leaning on his crutches as much as he could.

Almony threw the bedroom door open and marched through it. She stopped at the top of the stairs. Jos could hear the conversation below them like the buzzing of the bees. "Don't take this the wrong way, Joseph, but I hope that I don't see you again."

He allowed himself one bright moment of hope.

"Maybe you'll see us one day in the city."

"We can nod at each other across the street," she responded. She descended the rest of the stairs without a second glance back at him. He waited.

He heard her footsteps as she walked into her parlour. She clapped her hands and the hum of conversation died.

There was hardly a moment of anticipation before Almony cut right to the chase. "You're going to have to clear out. Thomas Townsend owns this place now."

The uproar was such that Jos flinched away from the noise. He could hear Helda's angered shouts but did not pause to discern what she said. He limped to the kitchen, glad that Almony's revelation had covered the noise of his crutches scraping against the flagstones. He hobbled out into the cold.

Almony's skis were right where she had said they would be, along with the bag she had packed for him. He strapped the skis to his back, deciding to take advantage of Almony's distraction and use his crutches for as long as he could. He kept to the railway line, remembering the route they had taken as children. Once he had walked this way in the line of children leaving Racken, Eldersie at his side. She had shared buns from a package wrapped by her mother. Her hand had been sticky in his.

ORIANA TOWNSEND

She was as clear-headed as she had been in years. It was not going to be an easy trip. She dressed up in all her best gear, which had languished at the bottom of her trunk from her competitive skiing days.

She had never really skied from one location to another. She was used to taking a chair lift, gripping tight to the bars, and taking a gambol down the slope before going for a drink. She didn't know how long it would take to get to the next town down the line. She didn't know what she should take with her. Would she need food? A tent? An avalanche kit? It could not be that hard. She had skied while blind drunk, after all.

The day was bright. The air was clear. She had taken all the portable food from Eldersie's kitchen. She had a bottle of water and matches to start a fire in an emergency. She should leave. Ifry was already far away and she needed to catch up with him, but she was reluctant. Eldersie's house was not comfortable, but compared to the icy wilderness it might as well have been a city hotel. She hovered in the kitchen while her brother worked.

"You going somewhere?" he asked, noting her winter gear and dark glasses.

"How are you still working?" She did not think he had paused to sleep since Ifry had gone missing.

"Business does not stop because of personal matters," he said.

"I think it would only stop if an avalanche landed on your head."

"I'm sure that would not keep him from working for long," Eldersie sniggered, stepping into the room with her sewing basket under one arm. "He has to keep on top of his arrangements. The faster he works, the less likely he is to be run out of town. You going somewhere?" Her eyes roved over Oriana's clothes.

"Why is he being run out of town?" Oriana asked, avoiding Eldersie's question.

"He's bought Almony out," said Eldersie.

"It's not just Almony," said Thomas.

"Who else is it?" Eldersie demanded. She dropped her basket on top of

Thomas's paperwork. She flipped the lid so it landed on his fingers; surprisingly, he didn't complain. Eldersie rifled around inside, spilling thread and fabric quarters and ribbons over Thomas's work.

"My matters are confidential," he replied.

"You have been sneaking around town, convincing people to pawn off their family homes." Eldersie swept his papers aside.

Thomas, in a manner most unlike himself, quietly tidied the mess and continued working.

"If people didn't want to sell, they wouldn't," Oriana defended him.

"He knows what he's doing," muttered Eldersie.

"I'm not intending to divest Racken of all its locals, as you well know, Miss Toft," he said.

"News to me. Again, where are you going?" she snapped at Oriana.

"Thought I might take to the slopes," replied Oriana, in the best casual voice that she could feign.

Eldersie laughed. "I have never heard anything so unwise. There's ankatze in their droves out there and every other monster that you cannot name."

Oriana had not considered that. The slopes she usually entertained herself on were kept clear of monsters, but Racken's only defence system had vanished on borrowed skis with a broken leg.

"Where's your gun then?" Oriana asked.

"We no longer have one, after your clerk took off with it."

"Anyone would be given to violence," Thomas said, "if they were pursued by ankatze and angry townsfolk."

Eldersie flicked the fabric she grasped with such force that the gust she generated sent Thomas's papers flying into his lap.

"If anyone requires me, I shall be upstairs," he said and left.

"I do not know why anyone would require him," Eldersie muttered. Oriana scoffed in return. "It's just his way. That's what he says when he goes to his office." He'd added some variation, of course, but they might as well have been in the drawing room of their town house, having yet another conversation in which he decided that he was tired of talking to her and stormed out.

"You won't make it far out of Racken. You don't know the way," said Eldersie. She had clearly seen through Oriana's lie about her wardrobe.

"Who said that I don't?"

"Logic, Miss Townsend." She gave Oriana a smug look with which Oriana was eminently familiar; she was used to giving that expression to Thomas every time she had a point over him.

"I can't stay here and not go look for him," Oriana said, relenting.

"You could. Though I admit, someone needs to look for him. We are all sitting ducks here, hoping that winter might end."

"Because winter never ends by itself."

"I need you to show me around the city," said Eldersie, choosing not to rise to Oriana's bait.

"What?"

"We can make a deal. An exchange. I'm going to look for him, but I can't make head nor tail of that place. I can get you there. I need you to help me with where Ifry might be." She sounded so reasonable, even when discussing attempted murder.

"As if I would sell him out like that."

"How else are you going to get to the city and help him?" She tucked her sewing kit back into the basket. "But that's up to you, of course."

"You're having me on."

"I'm not. I can go without you. It might all take longer without your help, but I can still make it," Eldersie proclaimed.

"You aren't dressed to go," Oriana said. She knew when she was made a good offer, and she wasn't willing to wait. "I don't care to dawdle. The weather is good just now. I know the mountains well enough to understand the grace period never lasts long."

"There's wisdom to that," Eldersie admitted, with surprise.

"Get on, then. Don't delay us any further." She snapped her fingers until Eldersie removed her apron and walked to the stairs. She had such a look of surprise, like a rabbit faced with a loud noise, it was almost adorable. Hell, if she wasn't so provincial, she might even be pretty. Of course, to really manage that, she would have to abandon the handkerchief she tied on her head and the series of threadbare skirts that were entirely identical.

Oriana penned a quick note to her brother while Eldersie changed. She kept it brief. He would not approve no matter what arguments she made.

Eldersie returned to the kitchen. She wore different clothes which, by Oriana's reckoning, was the first time in years that she'd abandoned her skirt and wool tights. Now she sported a pair of cream trousers and a short, fur-lined jacket.

Oriana had to admit that she looked better this way. She was not hiding her legs under all those layers. She had even abandoned the red handkerchief that made her look like a peasant in an oil painting.

Eldersie took Oriana's pack from her and repacked it, fitting another tin of biscuits and a package of bandages inside. Without words, Eldersie indicated that they should leave, and Oriana made no complaint.

They took a brisk walk to the edge of the town. The silence allowed Oriana time to think. She was bringing a murderous heretic closer to Ifry, but that fate could apparently not be avoided. Eldersie had promised to journey to Darrity regardless. Oriana could abandon her guide as soon as they reached the city. Or better yet, keep her distracted until spring had well and truly broken.

They passed a pile of dead ankatze next to the railway line. Eldersie stopped and let her skis fall to the ground, sending up puffs of snow. Oriana drew alongside her and bent to fix Ifry's skis to her own feet. She took care to do it faster and more cleanly than Eldersie. There was a great deal of satisfaction in outperforming her. Oriana had long sensed a smug sort of pleasure in Eldersie, that she was better than the tyenes, but Oriana was sure she could not be better at skiing. Oriana had lessons with champion slalom skiers, after all.

"We'll follow the line," Eldersie announced. "It's the most direct route."

"Or else the makers would not have built it there."

Eldersie did not respond to the comment, which Oriana took to mean that it was correct. Eldersie led the way. At the start, Oriana made a great show of overtaking Eldersie and waiting for her to catch up. It did not last. Oriana found herself tiring, while Eldersie seemed to trundle on as if the journey did not weary her at all.

"I need a break," she called.

Eldersie was far ahead. She stopped where she was and waited for Oriana to catch up.

"How much further?" she asked.

Eldersie shrugged. "It's been a long time since I've gone this way," she admitted.

"If you get us lost in the mountains–"

"Do you think that I would be so foolish?"

"I would not rule it out."

Eldersie snorted. "The line won't lead us wrong. It has to arrive in the next town."

Oriana had to admit that she was right, though she did not give voice to the thought, and instead fished her dark glasses from her pocket to cover her eyes.

Oriana took comfort in rolling her eyes without Eldersie being able to notice. She found a way to keep pace, remaining just behind Eldersie. They stopped again to share a lunch of bread and cheese while standing, as they were both reluctant to unbuckle their skis. Quiet settled over them.

In the early afternoon, they found a place where the tracks bent to the left, and crossed them to reach flatter ground. They moved along a ridge with a tree-lined slope to the left and a sharp drop to the right. There was a breathless view. Oriana could see peaks that were soft like meringues, inky trees, and the shape of a frozen river. There were no other buildings, yet she judged the distance to be the width of Darrity.

"You are truly alone," she said to Eldersie, who had not been paying attention.

Eldersie looked back, quizzical. She opened her mouth, ready to say something, but her eyes fixed instead on something behind Oriana. Her face was wrought with horror.

"What is it?" Oriana asked.

Eldersie gaped, apparently too in shock to speak. Oriana turned to look behind her.

Between the trees, she could see the shining eyes of a creature. It had teeth that protruded from its bottom jaw, rising above its lips. Its fur was white, and its shoulders were as wide as a motor car. Oriana could see its claws marking the snow, long like a bear's.

"Janros," whispered Eldersie.

Oriana had only seen the ankatze up close, and at that moment they seemed rather puny in size. The janros was twice her height. It had to weigh as much as an elephant.

Instinct overtook her. Her eyes tracked the slope past the janros. It was steep, but not impossible.

"Be quick," she told Eldersie, hoping that she would catch her meaning.

Oriana skied towards the janros and Eldersie shouted in dismay. She took a sharp left turn and slid down the slope. She glanced back to see that Eldersie, no doubt against her better judgement, was following her. Behind her, Oriana saw the janros kicking up snow as it galloped after them.

Oriana's muscles settled back into a rhythm that she thought she had forgotten. She could feel the texture of the slope better than she could read books.

"Follow my tracks," she shouted to Eldersie, as she turned to avoid a mogul.

She could hear Eldersie making panicked noises as the janros kicked snow against their backs. Oriana kept her path, knowing the slope would give them more speed than anything else could. She bent down, tucking her arms into her sides so her poles stuck out behind her like the antenna of an insect. She only hoped that Eldersie knew a little technique.

They hurtled down the slope towards the river. Oriana could see the dull grey stripe of it, and hoped that it was solid enough.

"Do not slow down," she warned Eldersie.

The slope evened out. Oriana kept her arms tucked in, and kept her speed up even as her skis shuddered on uneven ground. There was a thin crust of snow on the river; she could see the vague movement of water below the ice as she slid across the river in a straight line. Relief washed over her as she reached the other side intact. She cut her skis into the ground as she turned, sending up a spray of snow.

Eldersie rushed into her. She flailed, unable to control her speed. Oriana, sure on her skis, caught her by the arms and held her upright.

"What in the name of Solyon are you doing?" Eldersie asked. "Now we're stuck."

The janros still pelted behind them, and they had run out of slope to ski down.

"Can they swim? I've gambled this on them not being able to swim well."

"What?"

She felt the beat of the janros' footsteps. It approached the river at haunting speed, but when it set its foot on the ice, a crack echoed through the valley. It didn't pause, but pressed on until all four feet were on the ice. Cracks shot out from its paws like cobwebs. For a moment, Oriana and

Eldersie stood on the other bank, both shuddering, and then the ice swallowed the janros whole.

Eldersie let out a heavy breath. "That was clever," she said.

Oriana gasped. "You gave me a compliment."

"We need to go. We can't risk it getting out," said Eldersie.

The janros, far from finished, struggled in the water, trying to pull itself back onto the ice.

They skied along the river and crossed back as soon as they could, finding the ridge once more, and rejoining the railway line. They did not hear the janros behind them again.

The sky was darkening by the time they saw another building. They walked into the middle of Berill, which, like Racken, lacked paved streets. Oriana spotted a bare station platform and veered towards it. Eldersie caught her by the elbow.

"There's no train," she said.

"But there's a platform."

"This is the same line as Racken. If there wasn't a train there, there won't be one here."

Oriana's heart sank. She was already bone tired. Eldersie had no friends in that town, so she took them to a paltry inn that had only one room available. Eldersie began to count coins from her belt purse, but Oriana fetched her own wallet. She flashed the notes to the landlady and handed over a generous payment before Eldersie could. Oriana received an odd look, but didn't think much of it. She knew how Eldersie lived. She had no business making her pay for things.

When she saw their room for the night however, she regretted handing over so much for it. Naively, she had not realised that there would only be a single bed.

Eldersie made a dissatisfied noise, but began to undress without making a complaint. Oriana found herself staring, and had to mentally reprimand herself. Oriana turned and removed her outer layers. She hung them on the pegs that were the room's only decoration. Eldersie did the same, taking care to push Oriana's hand aside so that she could not use all of the hooks. For a moment, Oriana considered batting her hand back, or better, beginning some playful banter. She was getting too *used* to being around Eldersie.

She forced herself away and went to the inn's common room, a place that was a step up on the ladder of civility from Racken. A place that was high enough to possess a reasonable bar. They only served ale, a local kind that Oriana could not recommend, but she had not had a drink in so long that it tasted like liquid gold. She finished the cup and ordered another.

"You come from Racken?" asked the barkeep. Oriana nodded and held out her hand for the drink to be pressed back into it. "Say - are they doing anything about this winter?"

"What?"

"Are they not working on changing the season? What's keeping them?" the barkeep asked. She was cleaning a tankard with a rag in the manner of barkeeps everywhere, so it was almost as if she was not asking Oriana about the whims of the gods.

"You know about all that?"

"Why shouldn't we? What is keeping them?"

"I don't know. I'm just a tyenes. I'm going home," she said.

"I suppose things like this can't be rushed."

She let Oriana drink in silence.

Eldersie only came to the common room to eat a bowl of stew at a separate table. Oriana continued to drink. She found herself a little offended that Eldersie had chosen not to sit with her. She continued to glance at Eldersie as she ate, hoping that she might realise her mistake and welcome Oriana over.

Oriana could not stand to be alone. She did not understand why Eldersie might prefer to eat facing the ugly wall of the tavern than sit in companionable silence; Oriana needed to be in a place with bars, dancing and good-humoured folk soon, or she might truly go mad. She watched Eldersie leave the common room without even a word to the other guests. Oriana had never walked into a room without speaking to the people in it, yet Eldersie did not even look back.

Oriana climbed up to the room without getting a real buzz. Eldersie was already in bed with her blankets drawn up to her chin. She had kindly left a candle lit, though she was pretending to be asleep. Oriana pulled off her boots and stripped down to her long johns and shirt. She had had the forethought to wrap her hair before stepping out, so did not even need to fix her silk scarf before getting into bed. She had a feeling that it might have cost more than all of Eldersie's wardrobe.

She crawled into the bed, facing away from Eldersie but still feeling her heat under the sheets.

"Wake me up when you wake," she said.

"I'm not your alarm clock."

"I apologise. I didn't pack my alarm clock in my essentials."

"Fine."

Oriana sank her head into her pillow, but her mind was full. She watched the back of Eldersie's head on the other pillow.

"How do the people here know about your sacrifice?" she asked. It buzzed in her mind like a gnat.

"They know what we do. They know Racken is special," said Eldersie.

"Why don't more people live there, then?"

"They're scared."

"Of the sacrifice? How could I forget?"

"I'm not sure. I don't know how many people know about our home," Eldersie admitted. She turned over so that she faced Oriana. She had her hands clasped under her chin. Her fingers were long and blistered, and the bed was so narrow that her hands almost touched Oriana's face. She looked so much younger with her hair loose, and in her nightclothes. There was a pink ribbon tying the front of her nightgown.

"How far have you travelled?" asked Oriana.

"No further than here."

Oriana let out a laugh, then stifled it. "Sorry, but that's so ridiculous. You've never seen outside of these two villages."

"Don't mock me."

"I'm not. But I can't imagine the kind of life you lead." She realised quite how close they were. She had not shared a bed with someone since summer had died. It was just typical of her recent luck, that she had to find herself in a bed with Eldersie Toft, rather than anyone who would actually be interested in her.

The morning brought only further misery. Eldersie roused her before dawn had broken, then dressed at speed. She had the right idea. Oriana dressed fast to avoid as much of the cold as possible.

She might have hoped that her money could have bought them some warmth, but it was endangered in these parts. They went to the common room, where they shared a pot of weak tea and burnt toast. Oriana found herself holding up a one-sided conversation. Eldersie never felt the need to make small talk, but apparently that preference extended to a lot of other talk too.

They set out for the slopes while the light was still grey, and followed the railway on. Eldersie was more uncertain of their path. She kept as close to the rails as she could. Knowing her limits better, Oriana did not try to overtake her again, instead keeping close to her tail.

They passed two more nondescript farming towns before they reached the next station that could take them back to Darrity. There was a squat kiosk on the platform with a foul-tempered man who sold tickets through a grimy window. Oriana bought them two singles to Darrity. She did not bother getting them first class, knowing the train would be short and cheap regardless. They were two of half a dozen passengers.

"You've never been on board one of these," she guessed, seeing Eldersie looking more apprehensive than ever. "You can hold my hand if you get nervous."

Eldersie tutted. As if to prove herself, she climbed aboard the train before Oriana could. She found them a pair of seats facing each other. They lacked even the threadbare cushions that had decorated their arrival train; instead, they sat on wooden slats that had long scratches in the varnish.

"How fast do these things truly go?" Eldersie asked. The question betrayed her naivete. She could not behave sternly here. The wrinkles in her forehead were smoothed out now that her fear was overriding her judgement. Divested of her sour demeanour, Oriana remembered how pretty Eldersie could be.

"You ever ridden a horse?" asked Oriana.

"No."

"Well, faster than that."

Eldersie's back was straight and she tightened her fingernails into her fists.

"Look at you, you're nervous!" Oriana could not stop herself from smiling. It was the first time that Eldersie had been charming.

"No."

"You're afraid of the train," she cackled. Even as she said this, the train rumbled and Eldersie gasped a little. "Mighty Solyon's most trusted servant, and you're afraid of train travel."

"I never claimed to be his greatest servant," she snapped.

"Maybe just his most available one."

Eldersie didn't refute that remark. Oriana settled and realised how weary the slog from Racken had left her.

"Make sure that you wake me once we hit the outskirts," she told Eldersie. She put her feet up on the opposite seat, forcing Eldersie to shuffle to one side.

"Once again, I am not your alarm clock."

"Oh, but you are far more reliable."

It was far from comfortable, but she was tired enough to fall asleep regardless. She was looking forward to the rainy climes of the city. She had seen far too much of snow.

She woke when Eldersie shook her by the shoulders.

"We're nearly there," she said.

Oriana opened her eyes and was blinded by blank white light beyond the window.

"We must still be in the mountains," she said. "It's bloody snowing."

The train pulled to a shuddering halt.

"No. I think we've arrived."

"That can't be right." Oriana peered out of the window. Through the fog of falling snow, she could make out the strong lines of the Darrity station building and its familiar clock tower. "How is it snowing here?"

She had only ever known it to snow in Darrity for a couple of days over midwinter. Even then, it barely stacked up to an inch of snow. The motor cars turned it into a muddy slush within seconds. But now, the snow had fallen pristine on the city. It was waist deep where paths had not been cleared.

A conductor with a scarf tied over his nose opened the carriage door. The air that blasted them was as cold as wind through the mountains. Eldersie shoved Oriana's bag into her hands, and they hurried across the platform and into the station building. Eldersie pressed close to Oriana's side as they moved through the press of people.

Oriana had feared she would be frowned at for wearing her sweaty mountain clothes in the city. On most days, she would never be caught dead wearing boots where a pair of court shoes might be more elegant. Yet it seemed as if every tyenes had dug out their most practical boots to face the day. They passed a newsboy hawking papers that told of the sudden cold snap.

"This doesn't make any sense," she said. "It should not be this cold at this time of year."

"Of course it should not. Jos should have done the deed already." Eldersie clutched her bag to her front in the manner of a tourist who had just learned of the existence of pickpockets.

"I'll order us a cab," Oriana said, still uneasy.

"I don't know why you are so concerned. We already know why the winter is enduring."

"I've seen no proof of that."

She grasped Eldersie's arm and led her out of the crowded station building. There were droves of people headed towards what Oriana thought of as the holiday platforms, the ones which serviced trains that went south to the coast.

When they wove outdoors, where a row of black motor cars should have been waiting, they found only an unswept pile of snow.

"Gods, we'll have to walk all the way there."

As Oriana stepped out onto the pavement, her foot crunched on the grit. It seemed that the salt was not working, as snow continued to fall atop it. The roads were empty of the expensive vehicles that trundled down them. The snow made the city quiet.

She guided Eldersie through the streets she knew well, but found that they were all unfamiliar, masked with snow on the ground and in the air. Eldersie jumped every time someone passed them on the pavement. She nodded at every stranger that passed them and was surprised when they did not greet her back.

Oriana and Thomas lived in a fashionable townhouse in one of the old money districts. There was a park with a gate that was locked at night, that Thomas paid a maintenance fee for. That fee was doing no good now, as the whole place was groaning under snow and the gate could not even be closed, let alone locked.

Unfortunately, some guilty soul had decided a year ago to turn one of the houses that overlooked the park into a boarding house for the less fortunate; Oriana knew to walk a little faster past this house and to hold one's coat a little tighter. She grabbed Eldersie's arm in anticipation. One glance at the boarding house windows told her that it was packed to the rafters, owing to the inclement weather. The glass was opaque with steam and handfuls of poor souls loitered on the steps, sharing cigarettes. Eldersie needed no encouragement to walk quickly past the establishment. She picked up the pace and crossed her arms across her front tightly.

Oriana spared one guilty glance at the wretched lot. Thomas always used to ask Oriana to rank the quality of the doorstep crowd; it was his method of judging how the business was faring. He had had a campaign to oust the business from the square.

To her dismay, she recognised one of the hollow faces staring back at her. For a moment, she thought it was a horrible coincidence that he had found his way to their square. But of course, their address might not have been common knowledge, but it would be easy enough to find by asking around.

Eldersie stopped as she saw him, and Oriana lost any hope that she might have shepherded her away.

"Joseph Nothernine!" she shouted.

JOS NOTHERNINE

His arrival to the city had not enlightened Jos about why people chose to live there. The snow fell in handfuls, but it could not cover the dirt and the trash on the pavements. Every smell refused to be fresh. Everywhere he went, there were people crouching amongst the muck.

The first person like this that he saw he thought was unfortunate, but there were more around every corner. Then, in the first park he found himself in, he found a poor woman lying on a bench. Snow had collected on her face. She had fallen asleep in the cold and would no longer wake. Jos informed a pair of constables, but they were worryingly unsurprised about the whole affair.

Not a soul in the city seemed prepared for the snow. There were folk spending their days outside without even a pair of gloves to their name. Jos had never thought of himself as well off - he did not have much - but in Darrity, wearing his father's good coat, he felt as if he was doing well for himself.

He knew the rough location of Townsend's office from Ifry. It was near a famous statue where Ifry often ate his lunch. He asked a few of the workers where Ifry lived, but no one knew. They could tell him where to find Thomas Townsend's house, with the note that sometimes Ifry slept there while working late. Jos did not have a great hope that Ifry would be there, but he had nowhere else to start.

He saw only a handful of servants leaving and entering the Townsend house. The butler took deliveries at the front door and smoked cigarettes at the back door. There was a gaggle of maids. When they threw open windows to air the rooms they cleaned, Jos could hear them giggling and gossiping. He saw no sign of Ifry. Jos stayed in the boarding house, finding only a spot on the floor to sleep on and feeling his leg ache with the cold. In the daytime he stood on the front steps and watched, as if Ifry was likely to walk around the corner.

Oriana and Eldersie did instead.

He considered running, but Eldersie shouted his name and marched up to him before he could so much as right his crutches. The people who stood near to him on the steps knew how to avoid trouble and departed.

"You had better tell me that you are here to hunt him down," said Eldersie.

"I don't know what you want me to say," he replied.

"I think I've made that pretty clear."

"Could we perhaps do this inside? Somewhere without snow up to my knees?" Oriana interrupted them. She grasped Eldersie by the arm again and led her away. "Come along, Mr Nothernine, or I shall have you arrested as a vagrant."

Feeling that she had him there, Jos limped after them. Oriana knocked on the townhouse door and was let in by the snobbish butler who had turned his nose up at Jos.

"These are my new – ah – friends," Oriana explained. "Mr Townsend's acquaintances from the mountains."

"Very well, Miss Townsend," he said, sounding as if everything was very much not well. Jos crossed the threshold and felt decidedly unwelcome. He had been in high class houses before; he had spent a good part of his childhood in and out of Almony's house, chased by her mother's reminders not to spill on the lace tablecloths. But Thomas Townsend's house was another world. There were fresh flowers on a table in the hall, though the owners were not in residence. Jos could have fitted his entire home in the hall alone, and this was a city house. They were supposed to be smaller. All of the walls were a fresh, light blue, and decorated with mirrors so clear that Jos might have mistaken them for windows.

Jos stayed on the doormat, fearing that he would ruin whatever he touched. Oriana seemed not to care. She kicked the snow off her boots and let it melt into the carpet.

"Will you be taking tea, Miss Townsend?" asked the butler, ignoring the guests. "When will your brother be joining us?"

"He's still in the mountains. This was an unexpected early return. We will take tea, thank you." She disappeared into one of the rooms, beckoning for Jos and Eldersie to follow.

Jos peeled off his boots and set them alongside Oriana's abandoned footwear. The butler observed him with scorn. He leaned on his crutch and tried to ignore him.

A blessed fire lit the parlour. Without thinking to ask permission, Jos went straight to the armchair nearest the fire and eased his bad leg onto a velvet footstool. The boarding house, crammed as it was, had lacked any good places to sit. Oriana gestured for Eldersie to take a seat on a lilac chaise longue, while she herself stood next to the grate, warming her hands.

"I assume, Mr Nothernine, that you were hoping Ifry would be here," she said.

Jos considered how to phrase his response. He knew that Eldersie was not about to help him. Oriana, however, had a connection to Ifry. She liked him, apparently, and was a tyenes who must think herself more civilised than mountain folk. She had naught to gain from killing Ifry.

"I was looking for Ifry," he confirmed, "but only to make sure he's safe."

Eldersie snorted.

"Exactly," Oriana began, "though I can't say that I trust you with Ifry's well-being."

Eldersie caught back cold laughter.

"What's got her like that?" Oriana asked, gesturing at Eldersie with one thumb.

"She knows the truth and she's laughing at you for it," said Jos.

"She's nearly always laughing at me. Out with it." She snapped her fingers in Eldersie's face.

Eldersie was momentarily affronted and batted Oriana's hand away. Contrary to Jos's expectations, Oriana reacted to the gesture with a smile.

"We were all set to help Jos with Solyon's challenge when Almony distracted us and he fled town," Eldersie explained.

"What was it? Performance anxiety?"

"No." Jos understood her playful tone, but he did not care for it.

"He's run off to the city on some foolish romantic quest, as if we would not come here to stop him," Eldersie said.

"Gods above, you can't be serious." Oriana tried to laugh, but found that the situation was devoid of humour. "You've come here to find Ifry, because you love him?"

He found himself nodding.

Oriana looked between Eldersie and Jos. "What a fine pair you two are. Promise that you won't get blood on the carpet trying to kill each other."

"I don't want to kill Eldersie. I don't want to kill anyone."

"Finally. A reasonable person." She looked him up and down and despite her words, seemed to find him lacking. "What am I to do with the pair of you?"

"You could tell us where to find Ifry," Eldersie suggested.

"I'm not telling you. Who do you think I am?" Oriana stepped away from the fireplace. "I'm going to get our tea. Eldersie, you can wash up in the upstairs bathroom. The spare bedroom is to the left of it."

"What?"

"We've been on a train all day. You don't want to use the bathroom?"

"I – I suppose so."

"Get on, then. You'll both know where Ifry might be when I decide what to do with that whole mess."

She left. Eldersie, unwilling to stay alone in a room with Jos, followed her and he heard the creak of the stair. Jos sank into his armchair. He hadn't been this warm in days, but he was not comfortable. He was waiting for the house to spit him out. It had tasted him and knew that he was not right.

"Number seventeen, Oskirk Street."

He turned to the doorway.

Oriana stood there. She repeated the address. "Do you need me to write it down?"

"No, but I might need directions. Where are you sending me?"

"It's where he'll be," she promised him. She opened a writing bureau that was laden with unopened envelopes. She scribbled a few lines with a fountain pen and handed him the paper before the ink had time to dry.

"Why are you telling me this?"

Oriana snapped the bureau shut. "I need him safe. I can't leave Eldersie alone. She'll either find him or she'll end up dead in the park." She shrugged, and Jos recalled the image of what he now assumed was a common occurrence.

"I'll tell him that you helped me," he promised.

"I would appreciate that. I'd let you have more time to rest your leg, but she'll try to follow you if she sees you again."

He leaned on his crutch and tried to ignore the pain that shot up his shin. Oriana vanished up the stairs before Jos could make his steady way to the door.

ORIANA TOWNSEND

She could not stuff her bed with enough bedpans. She could not wear enough layers. She could not get close enough to the parlour fireplace. Oriana felt as if the temperature was dropping by the hour.

"It's never this cold," she told Eldersie. "The newspapers say it's a new record."

"Why do they know? Why do they keep track of such things?"

Eldersie shunned the paper. She did not care for any of the headlines, not knowing what they referenced. If Thomas were there, he would have been waxing lyrical about the latest turnovers in parliament, then musing about how he wanted to get on the benches one day. The papers left most of that out. They only cared for the ever falling snow.

"It's unnatural. All of it," Oriana proclaimed.

She knew that Eldersie would scoff even before all the words left her mouth. She had decided that she liked it when Eldersie scoffed. There was something deeply entertaining about this girl being so angry at the world. She had to put effort into creating frown lines. It must take effort to project such disdain at the world. Oriana was even a little impressed.

"We shouldn't stay inside. I can't stand staying in," she said. Eldersie scoffed again. It would do Eldersie good to see more of the world. Oriana asked a maid to fetch her a coat, hat, and boots. She was not in the mountains anymore; there were places to go if she was bored. She snapped her fingers at Eldersie, who was dawdling.

"Why do I have to come with you?" she complained.

"I have to keep an eye on you. I promised to show you the city, after all."

"You know that is not what I meant."

Oriana grinned and tweaked her nose. They stepped into the breach. On another day, she would have taken a cab, but the street was frustratingly empty of vehicles. She decided that it was not worth going to one of her favoured bars, but the nearest one.

It was a middling establishment. They had electric lights in the common room, but could not always afford to replace the bulbs, so made up the difference with long wax candles that they did not trim neatly enough. At least it was good and dark. No one wanted to be caught drinking in clear light. Eldersie let out a little snort as they stepped inside.

"There's no need to be so rude. This is hardly my regular spot."

"I'm more disappointed that you have a regular spot," Eldersie replied.

"Oh? So I have it in me to let you down? I did not know that you had such faith in me."

Eldersie snorted, but Oriana caught half a smile on her face.

Oriana bypassed the booths and found them two seats at the bar. The barkeep was the only person in evidence.

"What's got you out?" he asked. He had shirked his usual uniform in favour of a pair of woollen peacoats and a moth-eaten scarf.

"Nothing to keep me in," Oriana replied. "Business is slow then, Terrence?"

He considered her, then his face melted as he recognised her. "Miss Townsend, we haven't seen you here in months."

"I've been stuck in the bloody mountains. I was keen to get home, only it seems that I've brought the mountains with me."

"It's been like this for nearly a month, though it's gotten worse of late.

It was warming up, as usual, then this cold snap."

"Perhaps it got worse around the time that Volana chose her elect," Eldersie hissed.

"What's she talking about?" asked Terrence.

"Ignore her. She's just rural. Let's have two beers here, all right?"

Terrence shrugged off the comment in favour of getting paid.

"You can't deny that the timing matches," Eldersie said. "Whenever Lady Winter chose the clerk is when the cold snap began."

"It's a coincidence," hissed Oriana in return.

"Say, Terrence–" Eldersie raised her hand to catch his attention. He returned with their drinks and greeted her with an expectant look. "Is it only this region having this awful weather?"

"It's nearly the whole country, and more besides," said Terrence. "I read in the paper that even Lenkia are freezing their arses off and they're across a whole sea."

"You hear that, Oriana? Even in Lenkia."

"This proves nothing. My friend here isn't very worldly, Terrence."

"She has a point," Terrence replied. "The river's frozen. That hasn't happened in a century."

She could not just take his word for it. She finished her drink and then

Eldersie's for good measure, and rushed them both back into the cold.

"It just doesn't make any sense." Oriana said, fumbling to fasten her coat.

She knew the way to the river, though she had never been one to take pleasant walks along the embankment. The road, which might normally have been busied by couples leaning on each other's arms, ladies with parasols, and children with hoops and sticks, was instead as blank as paper. She pushed through the snow and stopped in front of the stone wall that kept pedestrians apart from the river.

Only there was no river to speak of. The river, which had churned grey green through Oriana's life, had been stilled in its path. City folk, as industrious as they always were, were making profit from the situation. Muddied tents and haphazard stalls had been erected by entrepreneurs hoping that the novelty would enhance the sales of their mediocre wares.

"This has never happened," she told Eldersie.

"Oh, I believe you. We have never been this late in making the sacrifice before."

"Oh, please. Can you even speak about anything else?" Oriana pushed her aside. She had been struck by the urge to climb down and stand upon the ice.

It was slippery. She felt the ice slide under her boot, but she steadied herself by grabbing onto Eldersie's arm.

"We don't have time to shop for fancies," said Eldersie.

"How many times do you get to walk on a river?" Oriana replied, grasping her gloved hand.

"Every year, back home. We skied over one on the way here."

"Don't be smart with me." She dragged Eldersie along.

The fair had sprung up in open defiance of the weather, with a kind of stubbornness that only struck city folk when it came to commerce. A child with a tray offered them roasted chestnuts and rattled a tin can with a few coins in the bottom. There was a man with holes in his gloves selling squashed pork pies. There were representatives from half a dozen public houses, offering tankards and promising a warm spot by the fire if passersby returned to their establishments. In any other situation it might have been fun, but the ice was frustratingly solid under her feet. This was not the natural way of things.

Winter the year prior had been no better or worse than any other year in the city. Oriana had feigned illness and begged an early return from Thomas's resort. She had bade Ifry goodbye from the platform outside Thomas's hotel. It had still been chilly when she got back to Darrity, but it was nothing a bedpan could not fix.

"This can't be so," she muttered again. "Last winter was mild. Why would this happen now?"

"You know the reason already."

"You've only one answer to everything. Gods. You should pray to them to make yourself less irritating."

She relinquished Eldersie's hand and strode away from her. She believed in meeting words with actions, and felt that Eldersie might only understand her own shortcomings if Oriana displayed a dislike so strong she could not stand near her. It was a statement, rather than a real desire to get away from her.

Oriana stepped between two flapping tent sides, but found that Eldersie had not followed her. She glanced around the tent, a temporary establishment selling chestnuts that looked as if they had been roasted in dirt. She turned her nose up.

"Can I offer you some refreshment, Miss Townsend?" She heard a voice at her elbow. There was a familiar tenor to it.

"No, thank you," she replied. She turned to see a middle-aged man she recognised from the temple in Racken. "How have you gotten here?"

"An illusion, I grant you. Caught somewhere between your iris and your pupil. I can never leave Racken - that would be impossible." He winked.

"Do not lecture me on what is and isn't impossible."

"Because you are no longer certain yourself?"

"I don't need lectures from provincial folk." She turned to go, but found that he had gotten in front of her in a movement smoother than light.

She could tell that he was not there. He did not have the presence that people had. There was no scent to him. Even in the cold, Oriana could smell the rancid scents of unwashed city dwellers and rotting food. This man was standing close, but she could not feel his breath on her face. When she exhaled, there was a cloud of cold smoke in the air. It was as if he was living in the balm of summer, while all around were trapped in winter.

"Miss Townsend, I did not imagine that you were so rude," he said.

"Then you do not know my reputation at all. Who are you?"

"We met in the temple, remember?"

"I do," she confirmed.

"You were not so hard to find once I had already met you. I have the power sometimes to appear to those I have met, even when they are far away."

She was already cold, but the thought that this man had followed her on the train from Racken, through the city, and to her home, chilled her even more.

"I don't know what you intend, but if you continue to follow Eldersie and I, there are police in the city who frown on that sort of thing."

"I don't understand why you might claim ownership of Eldersie now," he said, mocking.

"What do you want?"

"I want you to get out of my way. Who are you to stand in the way of mighty Solyon?"

She had been preparing a witty retort, but all the words fell from her head once she heard his name. Clearly the man was deluded.

"Do you think you are the idol they all pray to?" She laughed and turned to go. She stepped out onto the river, where the first few flakes of a blizzard were falling.

"There you are," called Eldersie. She grasped Oriana's arm. "You can't leave me alone in a place such as this."

"Let's get back before the snow buries all of these poor souls." She tried to lead Eldersie on, but she caught sight of the man standing in the hollow of the tent.

"What are you looking at?" Eldersie asked.

"That damned mountain man," she explained, nodding in his direction. Eldersie glanced at the tent.

"There's no one there."

"No, I met him in the temple in Racken. He's only gone and followed us here."

"There's no one from Racken here."

"No, he's right here." He hadn't even moved.

"If there was someone from home here, I would know. I could do with a familiar face right now."

Oriana was caught in disbelief; he was standing two steps away. "What? Are you saying that you can't see him?"

Eldersie shook her head.

Oriana pushed her aside. The man was walking behind the tent he had just left. She ignored Eldersie's dismayed shout and skidded across the ice to catch up to him. "Who are you?" she shouted.

"I am Solyon. I have been Solyon for a century or more," he said, as if it was as obvious as daylight.

"Why would Solyon want to speak to me?"

"My elect has gone against my will. He can't hear me anymore."

"And what do I have to do with any of it?"

"I have lost sight of Winter's elect. You know where to find him."

"I shan't tell you."

"You doubt me?" he asked.

"Who wouldn't?"

"I'm the lord of summer, you petty mortal. You will rue this."

As he approached, his shadow was cut clean across the ice and snow. When the sunlight shone on him, the edges of him became blurry. He was just a little less than opaque, yet when he placed his forefinger between Oriana's eyes, his touch was hotter than coals.

She lost sight of the cold glass river. Warm breath beat through her veins. She could smell daisies and cut grass. She heard the distant clip-clop of horseshoes, and the creaking wheels of the carriages they pulled. She opened her eyes and saw a scene so riotous and vivid that it should have been a painting, but she remembered it. This was Montgomery Park in the height of summer.

She was seated on a gingham blanket. A fly buzzed past her ear, but she was not bothered by it. In front of her was a picnic of sausage rolls and prawns and cucumber slices on porcelain crockery. She could taste lemonade in her mouth. In the grass ahead of her, she saw her father dressed in cricket whites, and her mother in a floral dress and sun hat. Their laughter was like birdsong. They played catch with a soft leather ball. Between them ran Thomas, only waist high, leaping to catch the ball and failing. This was a memory.

It faded as soon as it arrived. She was left on the membrane of the river. Cold washed over her like water over a broken dam.

"Do not doubt me again. Winter's elect must die, or summer never returns." Then he was gone, without footprints in the snow to say that he had been there.

IFRY MARHEART

Snowflakes fell in lazy circles from the hole in the roof. Ifry trained his eye on one of them, reminded of when he would sit next to the window as a child during the rain and watch the raindrops slide in tandem down the glass. He sat by the deadened hearth. The house had gone grey in his absence. The wallpaper had faded to the colour of unpainted plaster. The floors, once a rich brown parquet, had gained a dressing of dust and leaves. There was no furniture. It had long been sold to pay for his father's debts, and before that, used as firewood. He ran his hand up the ruined banisters and imagined them there like missing limbs.

By rights the house should not have been there, or at least, it should have been empty. It had been sold and churned through multiple hands since Ifry had lived there.

A family had owned it right after the Marhearts. They were up-and-coming sorts; they had owned stock in the railway and had aspirations of holding elite gatherings in Ifry's front room, but they sank too much money into renovations and had to give up.

The next owner was a bachelor who wanted a gambling house. Predictably, he had lost all his money before he could move in. Next was a newlywed couple. They both had rich parents who bought the house, but the idyll didn't last. They moved to warmer climes and lived in separate houses.

Ifry, despite his better intentions, had kept a weary eye on them all. As Townsend's clerk he had requested the sale records from the city library. Finally, the property had gone to a developer. A man with a lot of money and little time. He had never gotten around to renovating the house. He had been too caught up being a landlord to other people. He did not lock the doors. He did not check on his property. Ifry was left well alone.

He knew that it was safer that way, but a hollow feeling was building inside him. He wished that Jos were there. He knew that he shouldn't, but the cold bit into him and he longed for Jos's warm touch and steady voice. He had been happy believing, even for the shortest while, that he and Jos might have fled the mountains and gone to a sunny coastline together. He knew it was hopeless, but as he crouched under the scratchy blanket, he allowed himself to believe it. In the hours between waking and sleeping, he let his mind float until he arrived at some coastal town. He wore a wide-brimmed hat and a light-coloured suit. Jos strode by his side. His eyes were bursting with sunlight. He drank everything in: the turquoise port, the chalk-painted houses, the lobster cages, and the barnacle-dusted fishing boats. They slept in a rented room above a cafe and threw the shutters open at night to tempt a fresh breeze to caress their skin.

He knew that he indulged. It made him heartsick, but he could not relinquish it. He was a foolish, doomed man, and he allowed himself the only comfort he could manage.

He dozed, wishing that he had thought to acquire firewood before going into hiding. He had used the very last of his coin to buy tinned food in a shop where no one was likely to recognise him. Otherwise, all he had to his name was Jos's gun and the golden coat that still held his scent in the seams.

When he heard the shuffling of the door, it felt like a dream. No one had tried to enter since Ifry had arrived. He could not think of a reason that anyone would, unless they were looking for him. His heart shuddered and kicked into gear. He went to the stairs. He remembered hiding in the crook of the staircase with his sister; it was much easier to hang his head over the steps now that the banisters were destroyed. He crouched there and watched the door tremble.

He heard the uneven step and the dragging of a stick across the front doorstep.

Two instincts fought within Ifry. He wanted to run down the stairs and into Jos's arms. But even as that dream caught root within him, fear grew stronger. Even injured, Jos was stronger and heavier than Ifry.

"Ifry?" Jos called to the empty house.

Ifry fled. Light as a bird, he felt the stairs vanish under him. He had one advantage: he knew this house, even with the furniture torn out and the people gone. The best hiding place was still there. He went to the attic.

He had not been here since Minnie was alive. They had toys aplenty, but there was nothing more intriguing than the mysterious detritus in the attic. It was a world waiting to be uncovered. There had been furniture piled to the rafters, which had belonged to their grandparents and their great-grandparents and ancestors they had never heard tell of. They crawled under dust sheets and watched the motes dance in the air. Ifry had once told Minnie that dust motes were fairies in disguise.

Only the spiders remained.

He felt the thump of Jos's footsteps through the house and fell to his knees. It was as natural to crawl here, in this room, as it was unnatural to crawl anywhere else. He went to the wall, where the scratched panelling grew mould. There was the panel there, the one that was set just a little deeper than the others. He placed his palm on the wood and pushed. It swung open easily.

No one had cleaned it out. Ifry hadn't entered the attic after Minnie was gone, and perhaps their parents never knew about their hidey hole. There was a teddy bear and a picture book. There was a biscuit tin where she had kept seashells and painted pebbles. All of it made him pause. She might as well have been there, behind him.

He fought off his reluctance and crawled inside. He had never seen her grave. He did not even know where it was. Crawling into the cupboard felt like he was visiting her tomb. He prayed to all the gods he didn't worship that Jos would not look inside, and closed the door behind him.

He did not quite fit anymore. As roomy as it had once seemed, he now had to crouch with his knees drawn to his chest and his head bowed low. He curled in on himself, not wanting to touch any of her belongings. It was dark. He could only see by the light that crept through the gaps around the door, like bright pencil lines. He felt the fur of the teddy bear brushing against the back of his hand and snatched his hand away as if he was burned. The sense of her was trapped in the cupboard with him, and rotting. He tried to shake the image of her from his mind, but her face appeared to him, clearer than it had been since he had lost her.

He began to shiver. The air around him was not cold, but the ice felt trapped inside his bones. He shook so hard it hurt. She hovered in his mind, a phantom, playing with the buttons she collected in her coin purse. He could hear her laugh, like the sleigh bells that decorated the ponies and traps in the park. Breathing hurt, like the icy air in Racken. It became effort. He dragged in cold, painful breaths, but none of them seemed to fill his lungs. A pain grew in his chest. He thought that he could ignore it and it would go away, but it did not. It felt akin to the cold ache in one's fingertips after a day skiing, but transported to the centre of his being. He clutched one hand to his chest, though it did not help. The action made him brush against the books that she had left behind, which only made it harder to breathe.

He was going to die in that cupboard. He could not breathe. There was no other choice he could make. He could die hiding, or he could take his chances with Jos Nothernine.

He flailed, battering his fists against the cupboard door until he found the handle. He cringed against the wall as he pulled it inward and tumbled out face first. He dragged himself by his elbows across the attic floor.

It did not help. It was not like surfacing out of the water. He knew that feeling well. He was still trapped below the ice, where every movement was painful. He had always thought that he would go back. The memory followed him like a bad penny, catching up with his thoughts when he was least expecting it. He would feel like he was drowning, like he was freezing, like everything was turning blue and dark. He could not escape the memory. He considered it a prophecy. He was wrought in the ice.

"Ifry?"

He heard Jos's voice as if from under the water. But, even as he knew what he should have been feeling, he was relieved to hear him. He felt Jos's fingers, light against his shoulder.

"What's happened?"

At that moment, the threat of embarrassment became more overwhelming than the fear of death. He could not explain himself, having neither words nor breath to do so. He managed to get himself onto his knees, though he still dedicated most of his energy to trying to breathe.

"What's going on? I came to help you." Jos's hands rested on both of his shoulders. He leaned his forehead against Ifry's own. "Breathe with me," he said. "In and out, count with me, one, two, three."

Ifry followed his instruction. He might have done anything he asked in that moment, the lord Solyon be damned.

"What happened?" Jos asked.

Hesitantly, Ifry placed a palm over Jos's cheek and shook his head, trying not to think about how much calmer he was with Jos there.

Jos let go of Ifry and peered into the cupboard, as if checking for attackers. Ifry supposed that he was used to monsters showing up wherever there was trouble. Finding nothing but a hidey hole filled with children's toys, he lapsed into confused silence.

Ifry waited until he felt calmer and sat back on his heels. He did not turn, choosing not to look at Jos as he spoke.

"Are you taking me back to the mountains?" He noticed that Jos's crutches were abandoned on the floor. If he wanted to run, he could probably still make it.

"No."

"You would say that."

"No, Ifry, I swear." Jos knelt down in front of Ifry, who saw that he held his bad leg straight. He knelt anyway. "I am not going to take you back. I will not let anyone take you back. I came here to help you."

"Why would you do that?"

"There was never any other option."

"You're the elect," Ifry said.

"It all changed. I met you." Jos tried to smile. "Where are we?" he asked.

"How did you find me, if you don't know?"

Jos reached into the pocket of his father's coat and pulled out a crumpled piece of paper. Ifry recognised his own address in Oriana's handwriting.

"She told you?" She must not have grasped what was going on.

"She - uh - she vetted me first. She stayed back to make sure that Eldersie didn't do anything. Where did she send me?"

"I used to live here when I was small."

"Why were you in the cupboard?"

"I was hiding from you."

"Oh. Well. I wouldn't have found you, if you didn't come out," Jos admitted.

"I might have survived longer if not for...well..."

"You are going to survive. I'm not going to kill you."

Ifry found himself believing him, perhaps because he already wanted to.

Jos kindled a real fire in the parlour. He did not ask for an explanation of what the attic meant, or why Ifry had reacted as he did. Ifry knew that he would not have been able to say, even if he had asked. They heated soup over the embers and ate it from the tin.

"This reminds me of when I was in the scouts," Ifry said.

"What does that mean?" asked Jos. Ifry regaled him with tales of boyhood adventure, while Jos mocked the idea of city boys paying to sleep in the open.

Jos asked him questions about his parents. Ifry answered them all but avoided talk of Minnie. There were gaps in some of his stories where she should have been. Jos filled them with tales of his own, or kisses on the back of Ifry's hand, then his mouth, and his neck. They slept, curled together, in the glow of the fire, relishing the last taste of safety they would no doubt have. They would need money to travel south, and neither had it. But for the moment, Racken was far away, and Eldersie was in hand, and they were together.

It was such a shame that Ifry had to dream again. He found himself aware that he stood on the ridge overlooking Racken, in the brightness of the day, though he knew it to be night.

"This is so very tiring," he said. The more he dreamed of her, the more used to the sensations he became, and the more he was in control of his faculties.

"I only meant to congratulate you," she said. She stood next to him, blue hood drawn over her face. "No other champion of mine has lived for this long."

"I do hope that is not meant to cheer me," he replied. He looked down to Racken, but found that it was not a familiar view. There was no railway like a fold in the valley. There were fewer houses. He looked for Almony's, but found it missing. Eldersie's house, too, was not there. The temple still cast a shadow over the main street, though he would have guessed that its spire was shorter than the one he knew.

"Where am I?" he asked.

"Racken."

"This is not Racken."

"Not as you know it," she said. "Forgive me, I am feeling nostalgic." She smiled, though he noted that no joy reached her eyes. "Though I cannot say why. It is not as if Racken was a comfortable place to live when I did live there." She raised her arm and pointed a pale finger down the valley. "Look, there, I am standing in the main street."

They were high up, so Ifry could not expect to make anything out. Yet he did notice a figure, smaller than an ant, walking up the main street. It was a woman, perhaps Volana, though she wore no cloak. Beside her, arm in hers, was a taller man wearing gold, like Jos.

"Who is that?" he asked.

"My husband," she whispered. "He was chosen by the lord of summer, whose name wasn't Solyon then. It was something else. Perhaps Aurion. And I was chosen by Lady Winter." A wind whipped through them, flapping her cloak so it glanced off Ifry's legs. "I was sure he would spare me. I don't know why."

Ifry had his eyes trained on the couple, trying to see the resemblance. They stood now, facing each other, hands clasped as if in a wedding ceremony. Then, the woman crumpled. She fell, face first into the snow. Her husband steadied her, then pulled a knife from inside her belly.

"He was kind, I suppose, though far from thorough," she said.

The husband almost fell as he backed away. He could not stay by her side as she died. He dropped the knife, then staggered into one of the buildings and closed the door. She was alone.

"He missed anything vital. I was still alive."

Ifry watched her struggle to her feet, clutching at the wound in her belly.

"I did not want to die there, alone in the street. I wanted to find my patron, and let her know what she had done."

She walked, leaving blood drops like jewels in the snow. With every step, Ifry thought she would be finished, but some unnatural power kept her going. She was coming towards them. As she approached, he recognised her face. It had looked familiar to him the moment that he had met her, though he would have said it was by chance, rather than design. She was Volana, dressed in peasant skirts like Eldersie, and climbing to meet them. Blood ran through her fingertips, but still she climbed, and in her other hand she clutched the knife.

Ifry looked to his right, wondering where the other Volana had gone. He looked behind him and thought he saw her for a second, blue cloak against the blue sky. Yet this cloak-wearer had dark hair that streamed from under her hood, and a sharp jaw that he did not recognise. She had her back half-turned, her attention trained on something else.

Volana staggered up to her, unable to see Ifry. She wasted no time, and plunged the knife into Lady Winter's back. The snow swirled, and for a moment both were invisible. Then, when it cleared, Volana was stood again beside him, wearing the cloak with which he associated her.

"I had my vengeance," she said. "But not upon him. He took his place as Aurion's heir once he realised what I had done. I have sent champion after champion against him, and none have been as successful as you."

Ifry looked at the blood in the snow. "Why not give up the fight?" he asked.

"I have already done so," she replied. "Don't you understand?"

"I am not certain that I do," he said.

The snow gathered in the air. She became hidden from his view.

ELDERSIE TOFT

The bath in the Townsend house ran hot water within five minutes of turning on the tap. Eldersie watched the mirror over the sink fog up with steam with no small amount of satisfaction. She had taken a bath every day since arriving to the city. Hot baths, in a porcelain tub that she could stretch out in. She dried herself with towels that were softer than any other fabric she had touched. The comfort fought off the guilt that gnawed at her.

She dressed in her nightgown and a heavy brocade dressing gown that Oriana had lent her. She padded down the hallway to her bedroom. She heard a creak, and spotted Oriana stood outside her own door. They both waited for a second. Eldersie knew, in her stomach, that she should be pressing Oriana more for where Ifry was. She should be unkind. She should make threats. Yet there were more excuses than she could name. If she harmed Oriana, they were surrounded by people who would have her arrested. Oriana could well lie, leading Eldersie to get into trouble elsewhere in the city - and she would no longer have access to the luxuries of Oriana's house.

"What are you doing?" Oriana asked.

"Going to bed."

"It isn't late. Get dressed."

"What? Why?" The snow had not relented. There could not be a good reason to go outside.

"We are going dancing," she said.

Eldersie should have guessed it would be something so trivial. She tried to protest, but Oriana soon appeared at her door with a velvet dress and a mink coat over her arm.

"I'm tired of dressing inelegantly and huddling around the fire," she proclaimed. "Miss Emma said that there's a dance hall still open. I'm going to enjoy being in the city."

Eldersie fought her for a moment or two longer, but the dress she had picked did look tempting. If she humoured Oriana, she might get more out of her. This would help Solyon, in a roundabout way.

Oriana pinned her hair up in a way that was apparently fashionable, but Eldersie did not love.

"I like the curls," she told Oriana, who admittedly had pleasantly curled hair.

"We would have to wet your hair, and truly there is not enough time for that. You look wonderful," she said, looking over Eldersie's shoulder in the mirror. Eldersie agreed, but did not say so aloud. It would sound silly, coming out of her mouth.

There were no operational motor cars, but Oriana ordered them a pony and trap that had a cover over the seats. They crammed in alongside each other, and Oriana wove her arm through Eldersie's. Eldersie supposed that it was a natural gesture for Oriana. She had people who she could walk with, and dance with, and touch in casual moments. For Eldersie, it was deeply diverting. People did not often touch her.

They were driven for a few streets until they came to an evenly paved square. Oriana grasped her by the hand and led her to the only establishment where lights still danced in the windows.

"What are we doing here?" she asked. She knew, but the endeavour was seeming rather silly now that she was faced with it.

"I'm showing you what the city is really like." She dragged Eldersie inside. It was warm, almost humid. They were in the foyer of what looked like another bar. It opened up further back, and Eldersie saw a golden hall with high ceilings. There was a band in tailcoats playing music Parson Tieron would describe as frivolous, with lots of trumpets and cymbals. Oriana shrugged off her fur coat and handed it to a serving man who had appeared, as if from nowhere. She smirked at Eldersie, as was now normal.

"Shut your mouth, Eldersie, you'll catch flies."

"I wasn't gaping," she insisted. She shrugged off her own coat and held it over her front.

"Whatever you say." Oriana unfolded Eldersie's arms to free the coat, which she held out to the serving man.

"Won't he take that?" Eldersie asked. It seemed far too easy to run away with a pair of rich coats like that.

"This place is far too well-to-do," Oriana said, which Eldersie did not remotely understand. Thieves could be anywhere. Eldersie thought they were more likely to frequent a rich establishment, there being more to steal. She was diverted, however, as Oriana linked their arms again and steered Eldersie into the dance hall.

"It's emptier than usual, though I suppose that is to be expected," she said.

Eldersie did not know what she was on about. There were more people in that one room than lived in Racken. It was twice the size of the temple and three times as busy. A man in a tailored suit brushed past them, close enough to touch, and Eldersie shrank into Oriana's side.

Oriana laughed. "I think we need a drink, no?"

She ordered them a pair of cocktails that looked like water but reeked of spirits. They sat together at a small table in the corner, where Oriana watched the dancers with an appraising eye. She pointed out which were more adept, though Eldersie had no way to tell the difference. Oriana's tongue was looser, Eldersie supposed, and she felt the need to fill every silence with words; the lower the surface of her drink became, the more words she crammed into her sentences. Eldersie supposed this was no bad thing. She was losing her defences. There was perhaps no better way to get the clerk's location from her.

While she might acknowledge the seed of guilt, she did not want to go back, or go to bed. She might not know how to dance like these people did, but she was entranced by them. The music gave her a giddy feeling that she could not fight. She even polished off her drink. A gentleman asked Oriana to dance.

"Is that all right?" she asked Eldersie, who found herself surprised.

"When have you needed my permission for anything?" she asked.

"Oh, I don't know."

"Go on, I'll be right here."

Oriana danced with the gentleman, who even Eldersie could see was as stiff as a board. When the number ended, Oriana excused herself before a conversation could develop.

"I think I'll be limping home," she complained. "Trod on my feet with every step, and he still thought he would be seeing another dance."

Eldersie smirked at the cheek of it.

"He wasn't even particularly handsome," she replied.

Oriana raised her eyebrows. "I never thought you would notice."

"Oh, I notice. I suppose I just don't usually care."

"Which gentleman in here might be considered handsome, then?" She gestured her hand at the crowd.

Eldersie took a cursory glance, but knew already that she found none of them to be of any particular interest. They were all men with strong jaws and slicked back hair and dark suits. There was nothing interesting about any one of them.

"I don't think any of them are worth the energy," she said. "Is this really all the city has to offer?"

Oriana laughed so suddenly that it was almost a cackle. "As if Racken is full of eligible bachelors–"

"I would wager they are better dancers."

"Are you mad? Did you have secret dancing lessons in the temple?"

"I don't need any," she claimed, though she knew very well that she had no idea how to dance, though she found herself longing to do so. "I know how not to look down my nose, like these city folk."

"*You?* Really?"

"What?"

"You look down your nose more than anyone I've ever known," claimed Oriana.

"If that's true, it's only because so many people are not worth my approval."

"I did not know you were the arbiter of the universe, though–" She was interrupted when another suited gentleman arrived to ask her to dance. "No, can't you see that I'm busy?" she asked, and laughed him away. She waved to a waiter, and ordered more drinks.

Eldersie did not remember how many drinks. Oriana knew how to order with just a gesture and a look. Eldersie had not been drunk often. There had been no cause. She had not ever gone drinking with Jos or Almony, or anyone else for that matter. But she was in the city, and Oriana would pay for everything.

In the end, she did dance, though not well. She trod on her partner's feet so much that he bowed out before the song ended, claiming he needed to get some fresh air, despite the blizzard that raged outdoors. Oriana claimed that she fell off her chair laughing. It sounded hyperbolic, but Oriana was drunk enough that she might have fallen off of anything.

When the cab dropped them on the pavement outside the Townsend house, the driver gave them no farewells. He could not get away fast enough, though Eldersie suspected it was more to do with their giggling than the inclement weather.

They toppled in through the front door. Oriana collapsed on the staircase, laughing for no apparent reason. Eldersie realised that her hair had come down on one side. She turned to one of the hallway's mirrors and tried to fix it, but her hair got stuck to her fingers, and she only made it worse.

The butler appeared.

"Miss Townsend, I do hope you enjoyed your evening," he said, though it sounded very much as if he meant the opposite. "Can I get you some water? Your rooms are prepared."

"Don't need water," Oriana said between gasps of laughter. "Eldersie! Come on, let's get a nightcap."

"I can bring you some tea," said the butler.

"I've got brandy in my room," insisted Oriana. She held out her hand. Eldersie removed her hand from her mess of hair and took it.

They went to Oriana's bedroom, which could easily be described as sumptuous. Eldersie slumped onto her bed, looking up at the lilac hangings above her. There were lace curtains, like clouds. Oriana dove under the bed. Eldersie rolled over and saw her legs kicking. She emerged, a smear of dust across one cheek, but empty-handed.

"Damn. He must have gotten to it."

Eldersie could not tell whether she meant her brother or her butler, but she supposed it didn't matter. Oriana lay face down on the bed next to Eldersie. Compared to the din of the dancing, the bedroom was unnervingly quiet. Oriana's voice too, was quietened for the first time in the night. Eldersie could only hear the ticking of Oriana's silver clock. Snow lashed against the windowpanes.

"It's stupid cold," muttered Oriana. She shuffled closer to Eldersie on the bed.

Eldersie heard two thumps as Oriana's boots landed on the carpet.

"You know how to end that," replied Eldersie, without thought.

"You're so stupid," groaned Oriana. She propped herself up on her elbows to look at Eldersie. "Do you know what life is like outside of your damn gods and your temple?"

"Is it like your life? Where nothing's important except yourself?" she replied. She sat up and climbed off the bed. There were still touches of dizziness, though she felt far more sober than when they had left the dance hall. She steadied herself on one of the bedposts.

Oriana too rolled off the bed and stood.

"So what?"

"You're letting winter go on forever."

"I know." Oriana stood at the end of the bed, very close to Eldersie. Her own hair was messy, and her lipstick smudged. "You're so exhausting."

"And you aren't?" Eldersie leaned close to Oriana, so close that she could see her own reflection in Oriana's pupils. Gods, she enraged Eldersie.

"Please shut up." Oriana looked as if she was about to shove Eldersie or order her out of the room. But her breath became uneven, like Oriana had forgotten how it worked.

Eldersie did not think. She put her hands about Oriana's neck and pressed her lips to hers. She felt Oriana's half-laugh before she reciprocated.

Oriana grabbed the cloth on either side of Eldersie's waist and balled it in her fists. Eldersie felt her skirt lifted slightly. Oriana eased Eldersie back towards the bed and she felt the silk sheets against the back of her legs. She leaned back into the mattress. She grasped Oriana's collar and pulled her down with her.

ORIANA TOWNSEND

Oriana wasn't prone to dreaming. When she did, it was usually in odd notions of colour and mood. When she found herself dreaming vividly, it was quite the surprise.

She smelled grass and heard the hum of insects. She was in a clearing that was as round as a coin. There were pine trees that were bright in the sunlight. Oriana squinted. She held her hand up to shadow her face and saw something in the clearing's centre. It was a log, and atop it was a man she recognised.

"Do you believe me now?" he asked, with a smile upon his face.

Oriana laughed. "Are dreams often considered proof? If that was the case, I would be a terrible runner and I would have no teeth."

She was distracted by a sapphire-coloured butterfly that flapped around Solyon's head. She held her finger up for it to land on, but it glanced against her and flew away. "That's the colour of the sky, do you see that?" she said.

"Yes, it's delightful," he said in a gruff voice. He jumped up and marched past Oriana. "Follow me."

"Oh, so polite," Oriana replied. She followed him anyway; the logic of dreams demanded it. Tree branches brushed against her head and shoulders as they walked. As they emerged from the clearing, cold air hit Oriana like an avalanche. She clutched her stomach, feeling her lungs burn as they filled with freezing air.

Solyon seemed not to feel the cold. He wore no coat, but he did not even shiver.

A cliff opened out before them. Oriana, who had been secure in the grove, felt a swoop in her stomach as she realised how high they were. Below them was a valley laden with snow. There was a temple with a sharp steeple and a row of townhouses, and farmhouses dotted over the slopes. She knew it was Racken.

"I knew this would turn into a nightmare eventually," she said. Solyon stopped short at the edge of the slope, where there was a chunk of ice.

Oriana looked down and saw the jagged edges of a frozen waterfall. "Why else would I be back in this place?"

"I wanted to show you what is happening to it."

"Haven't you tormented me enough?" She could feel the give of the snow beneath her feet so clearly that her certainty in the dreamscape was ebbing away. She could hear the peal of the wind through the valley and see the condensation of her breath. She had never dreamed so vividly. She had never seen phantom gods before either, but there was a first time for everything.

"The creatures that haunt these hills have run out of prey. Winter has killed most of what remained. They're desperate enough to come down the mountain."

He raised one arm and pointed down the valley, where Oriana could see the trails of animals in the snow. Two large creatures – goat-like and hairy, with horns that reached their feet – galloped down the main street. They scattered the townsfolk gathered there, and despite the distance, Oriana could hear the screams. The people fell against the walls of the buildings and ducked inside. There was one poor man, whom Oriana could not have recognised if she tried, who had the bright idea to run towards the temple. He wasn't faster than the creatures, and by the time he realised this, there was nowhere else for him to go. The creatures caught up to him, and one opened a maw that was unfeasibly wide. Within moments, the man was missing an arm and blood was spurting onto the snow.

"Can't you do something?" Oriana asked. "You're their god. Can't you help them?"

"I am helping them."

"You're asking me to do a lot, you know. Most people aren't happy about colluding in murder."

"I'm not asking more of you than I have of anyone else," he said, with all the normality of a conductor collecting train tickets.

"Why is the weight of the world on my shoulders all of a sudden?"

"The honest truth of it all is that you are close to winter's elect, and my own elect has abandoned me. I hoped that you might be able to find him." He shrugged and smiled. "You were merely nearby."

"Is that all it takes?" she asked.

"It's all it took for me to be chosen," replied Solyon. He gazed back down at the town, where another pack of ankatze were prowling across the railway line. "Look there – they must have smelled the blood. There will be more of them by dusk, no doubt."

Oriana averted her eyes. She had no stomach for watching people's limbs get eaten off their bodies.

"Must we see this?"

"What's the use in averting your eyes? You had better understand, Oriana, that this is the way of things. When the monsters are finished with Racken and they move down the mountain, who else do you think they will come after?"

"What if this is nothing but a dream?" she asked. "I can hardly have room for doubt."

Solyon sighed. "It hasn't been this hard since I began," he said.

"Began what?"

"Oh, began choosing."

"When did... You mean it has not always been this way?"

"How much concern do you have with the way of the world? You know so little of the changing of the seasons, except to know what shoes to wear," he scoffed. "Don't doubt me again."

The snow whirled around him, though Oriana could not feel the wind picking up. Within moments, he was gone entirely. Oriana waited, half expecting to be woken, yet nothing came. She called Eldersie's name in the vain hope that her sleeping self might shout too, but nothing came of it. She tried to walk back to the grove, but she found the last traces of summer were gone. The circular clearing was still there, but it was muffled by a thick layer of snow. Oriana hugged her arms around her, but couldn't find any warmth. She shook. She could feel the snow melting against the hem of her pyjama trousers.

She heard a rumble which was now crushingly familiar. She knew that sound, and she knew this time not to mistake it for an avalanche. The paw of a janros landed on the pure snow. Oriana backed away as she saw the janros push through the trees, breaking the branches of the pines with ease.

She ran, but the snow was too deep to run properly. The janros galloped behind her, snorting. She escaped from the trees but skidded right to the edge of the waterfall. Her stomach dropped.

There was a way down, but she wore only slippers, and every surface was laden with sparkling ice. She stopped on the edge, heart hammering, and saw the janros prowling towards her. It slowed down, sickeningly certain that it would catch its prey. Oriana saw her own reflection in its eyes. It raised one paw and slashed. Oriana gasped, though it was a moment before the pain set in. She saw the gash down her thigh, but was too shocked to touch it. She clenched her jaw so tightly that it hurt. The janros opened its own jaw. It was so close to her face that she could smell its rancid breath.

She was without options. Her leg throbbed, and she had no desire to get injured again. She leaned backwards and fell into the dark.

When she woke, her sweat was cold against her skin. The sheets were tangled around her ankles. Eldersie lay on the bed next to her. Sleep had removed the worry from her face; one hand was drawn up to her chin, and her lips moved slightly.

Oriana had one moment of blessed relief. Then she tried to turn over and put her arm around Eldersie, and pain jolted through her leg. She gasped and clutched at the bedsheets, ripping them back. Eldersie was shaken awake.

"What is it?" she asked, looking around, as if a monster had burst into the room. She looked over Oriana, and her eyes landed on her leg. "How did you get that?"

Oriana peeled her hand back. It was bloodied, like an actor in a tragedy. Around her leg, the silk sheets were ruined with wine-dark blood.

"I don't understand," she said. "I thought it was a dream."

It was a nasty gash, but Eldersie was practised at sewing people shut. She tied her scarf back over her hair, which was a small sadness to Oriana.

"I like your hair," she muttered.

"Shush," Eldersie replied as she pushed the needle back into her skin again.

Oriana took her advice. She leaned back into the armchair and let herself get lost in thought.

In the morning, she caught Eldersie in the kitchen, taking solace in preparing breakfast. She was brewing coffee, taking time to admire the stove and the shiny copper pans that hung over it. Oriana accepted a cup of coffee, but they stood in silence, not meeting each other's gaze. Eldersie no longer quite knew how to speak to her.

Oriana broke the silence first. "Get your coat," she said.

"What? Don't you want breakfast?"

"We can eat. I just feel a little like I might throw up." She mimed retching.

"Oh. Regrets from last night?"

"Yes. Well. I - I mean no. And yes. The leg doesn't help."

It smarted, though it was not nearly as bad as it looked. She was not in need of crutches yet. Eldersie ignored her request and instead picked up the bread knife and sawed into the stale loaf.

"That's beside the point," Oriana said. "Get your coat. I'm taking you to Ifry."

Eldersie dropped the knife. It landed near Oriana's feet and she swore.

"You're not lying?" Eldersie asked.

"What? No, I wouldn't. Not to - well. I'm just saying that I believe you. I have been pestered by Solyon enough. The river's frozen through. Let's go get him."

IFRY MARHEART

"Where are we going then?" Jos asked.

They were watching the fire in the parlour grate, and the light brought out the warm tones in his face.

"I hoped somewhere warm," said Ifry.

"No, I was thinking of heading right to the pole. I haven't had enough of ice and snow for my whole life," Jos jested as he shrugged off his father's coat.

"We could go to the sea. Live on a boat." As a child he had been enamoured with the idea of living on a boat, but that was before Minnie drowned. Perhaps that dream could be unearthed.

"I don't know how to sail a boat. I don't even know how to swim."

Ifry laughed. "Neither. Maybe we should stay on land. It seems as if that plan is a disaster waiting to happen."

There were no soft furnishings left in the house, so they leaned on each other while seated on the floor.

"How are we going to get there?" Jos asked. He stroked the top of Ifry's head.

"There's a train."

"Have you got any money?"

"Not enough. But we could visit Townsend's office. He owes me wages. I can forge his signature."

"Is he the sort of man who won't notice a large sum of money?"

"Yes," Ifry answered, which made Jos snort.

"I can't imagine anyone being like that."

"Are you certain?" Ifry asked, not having paid much attention to what Jos was saying.

"What?"

"Are you certain about going away with me? You're giving up everything you've ever known."

Jos considered it. "I'll miss it. But I think that it's been gone for a long time. Almony is different. Eldersie, well, I always think about the person she could have been, if none of this had ever happened."

Ifry had been caught in that circle before. He wanted to know what sort of person he would have been. If his father had not lost his money and tried to hold onto the house until the last minute. If they had not lived next to a pond that had frozen over. He was certain that he would not have been chosen by Volana. He would not have been working for Thomas Townsend.

"The hometown I used to have isn't there anymore," Jos said. "Townsend has nothing to do with it." There was something resigned in his voice that made Ifry unconvinced.

"Have you ever seen the sea?" Ifry asked, not wanting to dwell on melancholy things.

"No."

"That's what we'll do, then. We will go to the first place we can see the sea and we will cross it," Ifry suggested.

"I suppose it depends on how far they hunt us."

"How far do you think they will?" he asked, wishing for a certain answer.

"How cold do you think it will get?"

"Point taken."

He curled into Jos's side, felt Jos' arm encircle him and pull him tighter. Ifry stared into the fire, where the last few banisters cracked in the flames. He slipped into hazy dreams.

He thought that he was asleep next to the fire in the parlour, but his sister was next to him.

"Still here, I see," said a voice. He had never heard her speak in this house, but she belonged there somehow. It was as if he had always known her. Lady Winter had a face he had never quite recognised, but she had Minnie's blonde curls and her grey eyes. She looked like his sister, if she had ever been allowed to grow old. She placed her hand on his cheek. "Stay alive, Ifry Marheart. Leave him behind. Don't you worry that he will kill you while you are sleeping? That he will love you less than he loves summer?"

Ifry wanted to wake but found that something weighed his limbs down. He could not raise his head from the floor.

She continued. "I thought that my lover would not betray me either, but he did. He tried to kill me, and now he sends champions year on year to attack me. He always chooses first, you know? I would not do it unless he threw the first stone. Why do you imagine this only happens once a year, instead of twice?"

Ifry thought that was a poor excuse, but he could not say so. His mouth was full of water. It was freezing around him, inside his throat and in his lungs. He was under the ice again. He had stopped reaching for her. His sister's hand had slipped from his own. He did not search for her but wasted his energy hitting the ice above him.

He woke gasping. Jos was shaking him by the shoulders. He dragged in air, but it still felt like water. Jos's face hovered over his own.

"What were you dreaming of?" he demanded.

"The last time I was here. It's nothing," Ifry tried to brush him off, but Jos was stubbornly concerned.

"It's giving you nightmares."

"She, my sister, died here. She drowned during the winter. We were playing on the pond after it had frozen. Stupid, really. We had seen people skating on a frozen lake in a picture book."

"Oh, Ifry, I'm so sorry."

"It's such a tyenes thing to do, I know." He imagined that the children in Racken were well versed with the dangers of snow and ice.

"You'd be surprised," said Jos.

"Really? You grew up in a place where the river freezes over every year."

"Therefore it's much more of a problem."

"I can't sleep without her voice in my head." He grimaced and saw the concern in Jos's face intensify. He ducked out from between his arms. "Does Solyon not lurk inside your head?"

Jos frowned. "Not anymore," he admitted.

"Does he ever speak of Lady Winter?"

"Only as his enemy."

"I think they knew each other. In a human way." He remembered the vision that Volana had shown him. He had seen Solyon, but only as a distant figure.

"What do you mean?"

"I don't know. But gods should not speak as they do."

"How many gods do you know?"

"Maybe none," Ifry replied.

They waited several more hours. They had made plans for the future, but neither knew how to begin. There was the problem of money, and also of Jos's leg. He claimed that it was not so bad, but Ifry could tell otherwise.

Ifry wandered through the house, looking for things to pack, although he knew it was empty. He associated leaving with packing too strongly to not do it. He wandered to the attic window. The pane trembled inside the frame from the wind that roared outside. Looking out, he saw that the snow had abated for a moment, leaving only a few lonely flakes to fall on the street where he had grown up. The trees that lined the road were aching underneath the weight of their load. Their limbs, black and spider-like, were plain where they should have sprouted spring buds.

The snow had turned the city into a story book. The scene was blank, with black lines inked in. There were the watercolour edges of buildings and the downward strokes of lampposts. In the street, he saw the footprints of brave pedestrians. Two newcomers stood there with their hoods drawn against the wind. They had come to a halt outside Ifry's front door, seemingly ignorant of the buildings on either side. The house had failed to draw interest for decades, so it was odd that they noticed it now. His thoughts were sluggish, and he did not quite realise that his presence had changed the house irrevocably.

One of the newcomers turned her face up to the sky, and it took him a moment too long to recognise Eldersie. In that moment, her eyes met his through the iris of the attic window. She raised her arm and pointed, like the icons that decorated his childhood church. He flinched backwards as if cursed by the gods for a second time.

He staggered.

"Jos!" he cried, feeling his fright echo around the house and back into him.

"What is it?" Jos limped up the stairs. They stumbled into each other.

"They've found us. Eldersie is outside."

"Alone?"

"No. Another woman."

"Oriana," said Jos.

"Would she do that?"

"You know her better than I."

Jos grasped Ifry's hand and moved as fast as he could. The only staircase led past the front door. Jos did not hesitate. He did not consider hiding. He gripped Ifry's hand tighter and hurried them past the front door as it shook on its hinges. Ifry heard Oriana shout his name as they flew past. Jos got hold of his crutches, while Ifry fetched the gun.

"Follow me," he said to Jos. He might be the one they hunted, but this was his house. For the first time since he was ten years old, he breached the garden. The snow did not make it unfamiliar; it was exactly as it always had been. He had been holding her hand, the way that he held Jos's hand now. They had been sent out of the house while their parents met with the banker again. Ifry had been instructed to keep her distracted, and he was good to his parents, so he agreed. They'd built a snowman with a wide smile and twigs for arms, but her eyes kept drifting back to the house.

"Let's go further," he'd said. He'd taken them to the tree line. They'd played swords with sticks but she'd got bored and announced she was heading back inside.

"What if we went skating?" he'd suggested.

"We don't have any skates," she'd pointed out.

"I bet that the ice will still be fun." He'd approached the pond. Minnie had been fascinated by it, and by the idea that creatures could live under the ice and survive until the thaw. She'd agreed. Ifry had gone out first, unsure of the strength of the ice, but when it held, he'd pushed forward.

Ifry and Jos cut a path down to the trees. The world was full of the quiet that snow brings, broken only by the thunder of their pursuers' footsteps through the house. Jos left a line with his crutch like a furrow in spring soil. He leaned on Ifry's arm more than he perhaps meant to.

Minnie had done the same. She had almost fallen when she took her first step on the ice. She'd laughed anyway, even as she clung to him.

Jos did not pause as she had. He was born and raised in winter. He knew that the ice would hold his weight. Minnie had not known any of that, and her winter had not been as fierce as this one.

"Ifry!" Jos called.

He had walked on, not knowing that Ifry had stopped at the pond's edge. It was hidden under the snow, but he knew exactly where it was. He sensed it like the border of the underworld. Jos was already three paces onto the ice.

Back then, he had heard the first crack and thought nothing of it. He had thought the wind was picking up beyond the trees. There might have been a branch breaking. He was foolhardy, back then. Now, the cracking of the ice was as much a part of him as his legs or arms. He would never divest himself of that sound.

"Ifry, they're coming!" Jos yelled.

Ifry glanced back. Oriana and Eldersie had found their way into the garden. Both of them held long, metal implements. Fireplace pokers, perhaps. They hadn't come to talk. He knew that he needed to take the next step. He needed to cross the pond.

It had happened so suddenly, back then. There'd been another crack and the world had given way. He'd reached for Minnie in pure instinct. He'd wanted to grasp at the nearest solid thing, and there she was. He was sure that she had been standing straight and solid before he had taken her under with him. He could not describe how painful it had been. He had not thought that the cold would scald him so.

The black water had taken him, pressed him against the ice ceiling. He'd beaten his fists and his knees against it, but he had not even made a dent. He'd felt a hand close around his ankle. as his father dragged him up and out of the water. He hadn't found Minnie. Ifry had lain on his back in the snow while he searched and called her name. His vision had darkened.

It had been this very spot. He had been lying here dying. His father had made his choice. His hands, hot as irons, picked Ifry up. He ran as fast as his legs would allow, to get Ifry to the fire. He let Minnie languish under the water. They had not found her body until spring and the smell of her filled the street.

Ifry should have died. His head should have lain under where his feet now pressed and the snow should have covered him like eiderdown.

"Please," Jos cried. He was halfway across the pond. "What are you doing?"

Ifry's legs felt weak. He couldn't step onto the ice.

He turned, and with a painful shock, realised how close his pursuers were. The strap of the shotgun weighed on his shoulder. He fumbled with it, not knowing whether it was loaded or not. The gun fell, and he barely caught it with his stiff fingers. With a sinking heart, he remembered that the ammunition remained indoors, hidden under a floorboard.

"Ifry!" He heard the shuffle and the scrape as Jos tried to come back to him. There was a strangled nature to his voice that made Ifry feel sick.

"You don't want to do this, Ifry." Oriana stopped short and held up a gloved hand in a signal of surrender. In her other hand, she held a brass-ended poker. Ifry pointed the gun at her. Eldersie was behind Oriana.

"Get back," he warned, though he knew that he did not sound threatening.

"Please just come with us. This doesn't have to be hard."

"Dying is never easy, Ori."

"We need to call back spring."

"You sound just like her." He nodded to Eldersie, who was suspiciously silent.

"No!" cried Jos from behind him.

"I get it. You'd rather let the world freeze. I'm not you," said Oriana. She stepped closer. "Shoot if you're going to. We have a train to catch and we would rather get this over and done with." She shrugged as if this was all mere inconvenience.

"I don't want to," he admitted. He felt tears scalding his cheeks and hoped she wouldn't notice. He did not have the choice to make. He had left the ammunition indoors. He lowered the gun.

Jos screamed.

Oriana's shoulders slackened. "Eldersie," she said, softly.

Ifry felt Eldersie's hand grasp his hair and pull. The shock of it made him drop the gun. He didn't have any time to scramble for it. He felt the harsh cloth against his face, and aether filled his lungs.

ELDERSIE TOFT

Oriana was surprisingly adept at getting unconscious people onto trains. Her arrival dragging Jos and Ifry was not considered unusual by the station master, who had apparently seen her doing something similar before. She booked them a private compartment, so that no one might question as to why their guests had their hands tied. Finding that the gun was unloaded, Oriana had decided to dispense with that weight. Once Eldersie had managed to silence Jos, Oriana had picked up his crutch and thrown it away.

"No sense in making it easier for him to escape," she'd said.

Eldersie had to admit that there was some sense there, but the sight of Jos sprawled unconscious on the ice made her stomach turn.

The compartment was tainted with the old smell of cigar smoke and whisky. A tartan fabric covered the seats, and was not even worn on the edges. Oriana set her feet on the fine fabric, paying little attention to Ifry, who was slumped at the end of the seat. She massaged her injured leg and rested the back of her head against the fogged window. It was a blank white rectangle.

"What will happen when we get them there?" she asked.

"If Parson Tieron is recovered, he will take over."

"And if he hasn't?"

"I suppose I will be in charge," Eldersie said, though she was not champing at the bit to do so. She hadn't quite imagined the life where she became the next parson. She had not considered much of her life beyond what next winter might bring.

"What will they do to him?" Oriana asked, her voice suddenly low.

Eldersie had seen the ceremony every year since she turned ten, yet she found herself thinking about them rarely. Those memories lived in the shadowed part of her mind, along with the shape of her mother against the kitchen window, and her tales of how the gods were trolls that lived in caves and hated humans.

"There's a ceremony, but it doesn't really matter. We burn the body of winter's elect, just to make sure that Lady Winter has no further hold over them. It doesn't matter how they die, except that Solyon's elect kills them."

Oriana nodded to Jos. "Or we would not be lugging this weight around."

Eldersie nodded. "There are words we say. I've practised them. We wait until the fire burns low, then everyone goes home, really."

"What? That's it?"

"More or less."

"Pardon me, but I did think that there would be a little more majesty. Don't you at least stay up to see the thaw?"

"What fun is there in watching snow melt?" Eldersie asked.

"I suppose. But no songs? No solemn chants?"

"That's not how it is."

"I always thought that church should have a little more splendour."

"I disagree."

"As we do on most things." Oriana settled her back against the window. A few minutes lapsed in silence, and a few miles passed between them, before Oriana felt the need to speak again.

"This is going to weigh on me forever, isn't it?"

Eldersie thought of her father, trapped in his attic. "Yes."

Oriana pulled her feet away from Ifry. His head lolled with the rocking of the train. She moved to sit alongside Eldersie. There was still something unspoken between them, like the air had solidified. Eldersie had the feeling that she had whenever she saw the brown leaves of autumn appear in the air. She was hovering at the edge of something that was ending. Oriana would leave. She would return to the city and have no gods to worry her again. It was the way of things. Eldersie knew she should draw back, make the break cleaner, but she let Oriana sit alongside her. She wanted that last taste of her.

They watched Ifry's head fall to one side.

"It will never be fine," Eldersie said. She did not remember her mother's words of comfort, and her father had never offered any, but she had found her own sort of comfort. "But sometimes, in summer, you'll see wildflowers, or bumblebees, or a brook, and you'll know what you bought."

"What if you're wrong?" Oriana asked, in as small a voice as Eldersie had ever heard her use.

"I'm not wrong."

"Have you ever wondered?"

"That is a privilege I can't afford," Eldersie admitted. There was no alternative, or she had lost a mother for nothing. She had lost her mother for summer's great rays. There was no other way.

Oriana curled up against her side. Eldersie did not understand it. To her, the tyenes had always seemed cold, aloof, better than her. She did not know why Oriana had wanted her, even for a moment. It would die like summer always did.

They slept and woke alternately. Oriana was quick to the call and knocked their companions out when they woke, before they could shout or scream. She caught Jos while he was trying to reach for Ifry across the compartment. She kicked his bad leg and held her cloth to his face until his eyes rolled.

In Racken, they found the townsfolk waiting for them. Eldersie hung back as strong hands lifted Ifry and Jos from where they slumbered. They stood in an anxious parade, carrying farming tools or guns. Their eyes were shadowed and every one of them had purpling bruises.

"What happened here?" asked Eldersie. In the main street, she saw a smear of blood in the snow.

"Get inside, quickly," ordered Joan, without elaborating. The explanation became unnecessary as Eldersie heard the not-so-distant roar of a creature. It was a janros, and a large one based on the pitch of the sound.

It was accompanied by the cackle of gargins.

"Gods, they've invaded." They ran to the temple.

The temple was packed wall to wall. They barred the heavy doors to make sure that no monsters could breach the sanctum. The wounded and the ailing hovered by the walls. Racken's children were there too, clustered in corners, shielded from the proceedings by their parents.

Night had fallen, and they had lit all of the hearth places to keep Volana's breath at bay. Parson Tieron did not emerge. He was doped up, they said. He had been drinking to help with the pain. Eldersie's father stood by her left hand side. Oriana lingered at the edge of the circle, unsure of her place in it. Eldersie kept reminding herself not to look at her, as if she would be able to help.

"You remember the rites, don't you?" Martine asked. She nodded. "If you forget, then I could take over. I know how. I know all the words."

"No. I know what I am doing," she lied.

She felt weary. Her time in the city had drained her. The temple was loud with the collected voices of everyone she knew. They had Ifry on the altar where Parson Tieron performed services. He was on his side, cheek against the stone. He looked almost comfortable. Jos lay below him on the ground, his bad leg bent underneath him. Eldersie only knew the medicine that Parson Tieron had taught her, but she would have guessed that Jos would no longer go running up and down the valley.

He had always run the furthest and the fastest. He and Almony had raced each other down the slopes and Jos had always won. Almony, half-joking, would accuse him of cheating. She boasted that she was the second fastest, anyway. She was quicker than Jos in most instances. When they played cards, she always beat him because she read the game faster than he could.

Eldersie never played. She watched them race down the northern slopes from her doorstep as she hung sheets in front of her house.

Oriana spoke in her ear. Eldersie had been too lost in her thoughts to realise that Oriana had moved.

"How does it start?" she whispered.

"Jos needs to be awake."

"Do I need to fetch something to rouse him?"

Oriana had never offered to fetch something before. Where would she even look?

"No. He's coming to. Look." His eyelids were fluttering and his lips moved. He tried to move his hands but they were tied. Others in the temple noticed him move. A hush fell over the crowd. She heard her father's breathing hitch and then quicken. She pushed him away and knelt in front of Jos. Oriana stayed back, arms folded over her chest.

He didn't rouse calmly. His eyes were bloodshot. He jolted back from Eldersie and collided with the altar. He winced as he tried to move his bad leg.

"It's all right," she said, unconvincingly.

He shook his head. "Where's Ifry?"

Eldersie glanced above him to where Ifry slumbered. Jos tried to pull himself up. It took him a good three tries to get up on one leg. He bent over Ifry and pressed two fingers to his throat.

"He's alive," she tried to assure him.

"He would be. It wouldn't work otherwise."

"You haven't forgotten it all, then?" she asked.

"How could I forget?"

"This doesn't have to be painful."

He turned his head to face her, even as he kept his hands on Ifry's pulse. The look in his eyes was one of undiluted fury.

"Is that what he said?" he asked, voice low, even as Eldersie was certain he should have raised it.

"What who said?"

Jos's eyes flicked past Eldersie and to her left shoulder. She turned and saw her father watching Jos with hungry eyes.

"We shouldn't let him talk this much, Elsie," he said, using her old nickname. "He'll only protest."

"Isn't that what you did?" Jos asked him. "Or were you all too happy to see her go?"

"Don't you dare talk about her." Martine started forward, leering over Jos in a manner that would have been threatening, only Jos didn't seem to care.

"Or what? You'll kill me?" Jos smiled. "That would make all of this so much easier."

"Elsie, you have to convince him."

Jos turned his eyes to Eldersie. His look stung her.

"What is she going to tell me? Perhaps that being the elect is a sign of love, because why else would she have chosen him?" He reached with both hands to stroke Ifry's face. "But I don't think that's true. If he loved her, how could he have killed her?" He looked at Martine again.

"Jos, *please*." She stepped in front of her father, pushing him back. "Everything will freeze over if you don't do this. It all ends."

"Then it ends."

Her father touched her arm. She pushed him away.

"What would it take, Jos?" she asked.

He didn't answer. He couldn't have.

"Eldersie, we need to finish this." Her father fastened his fist around her arm.

She tried to pull away, but he forced an object into her palm. It was one of her kitchen knives. She had given this one to Jos earlier. Now she wouldn't have a full set.

"Put it into his hand. If he can't be convinced, he can be forced."

Eldersie was ready to protest. Jos was too strong, even on one leg, but her father moved forward, two other men on his tail. Jos cringed away, but he could not get far. Martine grabbed one of his arms. Another man took his left, while the third held Jos's head by his hair.

"Elsie, the knife!"

Eldersie realised that she was standing too still; Oriana was ushering her back into the action. The crowd swelled and pressed, drawing towards Jos and Ifry. Oriana pulled Eldersie through the press until she hit her knees against the altar. She almost dropped the knife.

Jos struggled. He wrestled against his captors. He was strong, the strongest man in Racken, and he almost got free. Martine saw this and stamped on his leg. Jos screamed loud enough to drown out the clamour of the crowd.

Oriana turned to Eldersie. "I can – I can help you, if that's what you need."

"What?" Eldersie's gaze snapped to her.

Oriana looked sickened. "I don't know what to do. Tell me what I can do."

"Jos has to kill him," Eldersie tried to insist, but the certainty was missing from her voice.

"Does he look like he is killing anyone?"

Jos was crying. He crumpled, forcing his captors to prop him up. Below him, Ifry stirred.

"The knife! Elsie! Damn." Martine relinquished Jos and pinched Eldersie's arm, pulling her close. He directed her hand to Jos's bound fists, which were locked tight.

No one had needed to force her father's hand. Here he was forcing Jos. He had tried to kill her alone in their bed. She had run out into the snow and he had chased her. For how long had he raged against Solyon? Jos had gone further, tried harder. He had gone to the city, where Martine Toft had never set foot. He had found Ifry and he had tried to keep running. How far might he have gone, if Oriana had not changed her mind?

Eldersie's mother had wanted to travel.

"My little girl," she would say, "the world is larger than this valley."

"I know it is, silly."

"But it is so much stranger. There are places out there without janros and gargin and all number of trolls bearing down on you." She'd tweaked Eldersie's nose and shown her the illustrations she had in her picture book. There were blue canals and sultry rose gardens and tall, timbered buildings. Her father had burned that book after she had gone.

Her father pinned Jos's hand under his own. He clawed at Jos's fingers and forced them to unclench.

Under his palm, Ifry's eyes opened. He didn't shake or struggle as Jos had. He seemed curiously unsurprised at the tableau above him. Eldersie realised that she had forgotten to put a gag in his mouth.

He looked at Jos. Perhaps that was why he was not scared. Eldersie could not imagine feeling that safe because of one person.

Jos sobbed. Her father forced Jos's hand open.

"Please," Jos begged. "Please don't."

There was nothing more important than mighty Solyon.

"Elsie, the knife!"

She felt hands push her in the back. She fell onto the altar and caught herself on Ifry's side.

"The knife," demanded Martine. She had not seen him so animated in years. This had been her mother's kitchen knife. Which had he used to kill her? It could have been this one.

"For pity's sake." He grabbed Eldersie's wrist with his free hand. What would he do, if she refused? "Hand it over!"

She reached forward. She intended to pass it at first. She brought the blade down on her father's wrist. Red as poppies, blood welled from the cut. He cried out, as surprised as he was hurt, then let go of Jos and pressed his hand to the cut; took a moment, then staggered. Eldersie felt the knife handle fall from her grip and onto the altar.

"You idiot," her father cried. Then he fell. She had cut him worse than she'd thought. There were plenty of people around to catch him before he hit the floor. Jos fell forwards, nearly crushing Ifry, who had used the moment's distraction to sit upright.

Eldersie backed away from the scene as if she was not part of it. She heard Oriana speaking to her but did not care to recall what she said. Her hand was sticky. She wiped it on her apron, leaving a red smear. She felt the cold air touch her as she stepped out of the press of the crowd. She began walking, without thinking of where she would go, but still knowing where she would arrive.

She heard her father calling her, but she had already left. She followed her feet.

She stepped into the warmth of her own kitchen. She turned and pulled the bolt across the door.

"Are we expecting intruders?"

His voice was as clean and clipped as glass. Thomas Townsend used her kitchen table as a desk again. The night's events were not enough to keep him from work.

"Don't open the door. For anyone," she instructed him. His expression soured as he took in her appearance, his eyes lingering on the bloodstain on her apron.

"My sister–"

"She's the only one. Only her."

A fist landed on the door, making the bolt rattle.

"Is that her?" Townsend asked.

"Eldersie, open this door," demanded Martine from outside.

"Is that your father?"

"Don't let him in," she told Townsend firmly.

"Why is he outside?"

"Leave him there." She halted on the bottom step of the stairs. "Is that offer still open, Mr Townsend?"

"I would be a poor businessman if I went back on my word."

"I'll do it. I'll run your hotel." She climbed the stairs, leaving Townsend to listen to her father's pleas at the door.

She went to her room. It all seemed so dowdy and pathetic after seeing Oriana's bedroom. She had a quilt that she prized, but the fabrics were faded, and none of the colours matched. She sank onto it and curled into the shape of a shell. She could still smell the blood on her hands. She cried.

She did not know how much time passed. She did not think that she slept, but it seemed to her as if she lay there for hours. There was a knock at the door, soft and hesitant, and a voice that was even more so.

"Eldersie? It's Ori. Can I come in?"

Eldersie took a moment, trying to compose herself, but remembered the blood and decided it was useless.

"Come in." She sat up on the bed as Oriana came through the door and closed it behind her. "Is it over, then?"

"Oh, I've no idea."

"Haven't they done it?"

"I left right after you did. Had to fight my way out of the crowd a bit." She shrugged.

"Was it a bit too gory for you?" Eldersie wanted to pull off her bloodied apron, but the strings were too tight. She fussed at them but was too frustrated to undo the knot. She felt the mattress depress next to her as Oriana sat down.

"No, I just - you weren't there, so I followed you," said Oriana, as if it were the simplest thing in the world.

IFRY MARHEART

He knew that parts of him hurt. He had been pushed about, maybe, but he thought about it as if it had happened to someone else. This was such a surreal situation that it could not be happening. He could not be lying on an altar, surrounded by fraught faces. The voices, the clamour, were such that he could not parse it all out. He took stock of his own form, as it he was outside of it. They had not thought to gag him, or tie him by the ankles.

Jos was above him. Ifry could feel his presence like the sun through a clean window. He was crying.

Eldersie's hair, dark like a crow, cut a shadow over him. She had a knife in her hand. It had to be the end. She would drive that kitchen knife into his belly.

He turned away, trying to find Jos's eyes. He didn't want to look upon his own destruction.

It did not come. He heard the knife fall, ringing against the stone altar, then the shouts and the screaming. The handle knocked against his knee and whatever acceptance had filled him was drained with a breath. He understood where he was, the stakes that were laid against him. He sat up and clutched the knife handle between his bound hands.

Blood had sprayed across the front of Jos's coat, which Ifry still wore. Eldersie's father wailed, clutching his wrist. Ifry did not consider what had happened to him, he only noted the gap that was left as Martine backed away from the altar. He scrambled and swung his legs onto the floor. His knees nearly buckled, but he caught himself.

Jos was nearby, but he was being restrained. There would be no help there.

He spotted another gap. He did not hesitate. He ran through the temple, out of the cloying crowd and towards the fresh air. The townsfolk stood too close, and he had the knife in his hands, so he swung to get them back.

He got out into the cold. An urgency was alive in him, though he did not know what to do. There was no safe place in Racken. Barricading himself inside one of the buildings would only delay the inevitable. He had only one instinct. The snow was building in the air. He turned towards the northern slopes, towards Almony's house, towards Jos's home, and ran.

He looked for the black line of the river, but found it missing. Of course, the river was frozen in the city - why would it be different in Racken? He did not hesitate this time. He ran onto the ice.

He could not keep going once he stood on it; he stopped, remembering the sensations, fearing the noise of it breaking. He turned the knife upside down and used the blade to scrape at the ropes that kept his hands together, sawing, feeling the blade nick his wrist. The ropes fell away and landed, like a lock of hair, on the ice.

He knew of only one way forward. The person that he was, that he had become, had been made under the ice. He had been born there. It would not be so wrong now, to go back whence he came.

He raised the knife. It was a good one, with a serrated blade. He would crack the ice, and Volana could take him, once and for all. She had always had her claws in him. He raised the blade further, above his head, but his will faltered. He did not even touch the metal to the ice. He could not let himself go under.

He was still pursued. The wind was swallowing their voices, but he could hear them, perhaps half an echo. There was only one other place that he could go to. She had shown him for a reason; perhaps she was tired, and she wanted to end it. He still had two good legs, though he might have asked for a pair of skis. The mountain loomed above him, steeper and more insurmountable than the walls of the temple.

He began to climb. The more snow that covered him, the more his skin burned. But it felt like a salvation. If he still felt cold, he still felt alive.

He found himself up the mountain before he could consider what he was doing. The wind and snow might freeze him solid, but that was quickly becoming the most preferable of his options.

"Lady Winter," he cried. "Where are you?"

He never knew where she lingered, but he had met her here. She seemed to exist here, in this space, somewhere above Jos's house. This was the clearing where she had found him in dreams. It was clear and perfectly circular.

"Volana!" he demanded. He was her champion, and he would have an audience.

"Why do you call for me?" She came from nowhere. He heard no footsteps, but she appeared behind him, blue-robed and chilling.

"I need to speak with you," he told her.

They stood on the ridge over Racken, where he had so often dreamed her.

"No champion of mine has ever demanded my attention," she claimed. "Speak, then, out of curiosity, if nothing else."

"I suppose."

"What is the point?" Ifry asked.

"Of what?"

"Of any of this." He gestured at the wind, the snow, himself. "Why do you battle Solyon every year? What need is there for it?"

"To decide who wins, of course."

"But you always lose."

"I have not lost yet." She smiled at him and his insides turned over.

"You will," he assured her. "There is nowhere to run. They will find me here and they will kill me."

He had only gotten a small head start. They were already ascending the mountain.

"Not if you kill the other."

"What?"

"Kill summer's elect and you win. Winter falls," she said.

"No." He did not even consider it.

"You have the opportunity that others have not had. You can try," she warned him.

"No," he begged her. "Why must this be the choice that I make?"

"I cannot let Solyon win without a fight."

"Did you ever fight him yourself?" he asked.

"When we were mortals," she said, in a small voice. She looked tired.

"Why do it at all? Not every fight has to be undertaken. I could walk down this mountain and I would not fight them. I would lose. I would just go."

"He would not agree. He bruises myself better than any other person ever could - it comes when a person knows you so well. He loved me once, but he no longer does." She touched a point on her stomach, where he knew that a knife had pierced her.

"I would surrender," Ifry said. He was willing to, for Jos.

"I surrender too," she said, "but not to him."

He understood what she had been trying to tell him. He glanced downward and saw the line of townsfolk was getting closer. The wind rose and snowflakes danced in front of his eyes. She was standing close to him.

He was holding a knife. He thought about it for one moment, but it was like when he had faced the ankatze; his instinct rose within him.

He drove the knife into her belly, not imagining that it would work.

Volana's eyes widened. Her breath hitched, then came in ragged gasps. Ifry felt something scald his hand. There was steam in the air. She sagged away from him and blood fell once more onto the snow.

"I'm sorry," he whispered.

She fell onto her knees. Steam rose as her blood fell onto the snow. She had been alive, though soon she wouldn't be. She leaned on his arm, clutching at his sleeve.

"I didn't mean this," he told her. He suspected that she did not care.

He stepped back and let her collapse into the snow. Her breath rattled in her throat. She had an empty gaze, as if she no longer knew he was there. Her blood was pooling under her.

She died.

He let the knife fall. It broke through the powder and was buried. Volana, Lady Winter, was being covered by snowfall. Her cloak fell from her shoulders and cascaded like water around her. Even as she expired, he feared that it was a trick. It could not be finished.

The world swayed under him. He felt himself sink into the powder alongside her. There was a pain in his chest. The bright snow turned dark.

He existed between waking and dreaming. He was under the water, but he was not trapped; he belonged there. Volana's face swam in his mind, like a reflection on the surface of the water. He was cloaked in cold winds and crowned with icy shards. He might have been confused, if he had a voice to express confusion.

When he came to, he was standing on the ledge above Racken. There were no pursuers on the path below him. The town was unmarred by clouds. A purple dawn was breaking. The only lights in the town were at the temple. In one inexplicable moment of loneliness, he wished that he were down there, among them. He wanted to tell Jos that he was all right, unless of course he wasn't.

He took stock of himself. He was not hurt, but he did not feel right. He felt as if he was floating, yet sickened at the same time. He felt as if he was on a rattling train, and his stomach was being turned with every lurch of the carriage.

He did not feel cold. That was the strangest part. But he was not warm either. The sun winked at him from over the peaks. He looked to the spot where he knew the frozen waterfall lay. He sighed.

There was no blood on his front. Jos's coat was unmarked. Volana's blood had run hot over his wrists, but they were clean. He pressed his palms to his stomach. He was fine. Yet something weighed on his shoulders and his arms as he moved them. He felt fabric under his fingers, velvet, but cold.

He pulled it in front of him, and noticed how it swathed his shoulders and neck. He wore Volana's cloak. Had he pilfered it from her body? He could not have done. He did not remember coming here. He looked around. There were no footprints. There was no blood.

He staggered back from the cliff's edge. He needed help, no matter the danger that it posed. Something was wrong with him. He found his way down the mountainside, wishing again for a good pair of skis. He trudged through snows as high as his waist, but found that they did not trouble him.

He walked past Almony's house, then crossed the bridge over the frozen water. The town was empty. Snow had fallen over all of their footprints, to soften their passing.

He walked to Eldersie's house, but found the door locked, so he went next to the temple. The voices still hummed inside like a disturbed hive. He half-wished that he still had the kitchen knife. At the very least he could have earned a little goodwill from Eldersie by ensuring that she had a full set. He hovered by the door, considering whether he should knock.

It opened by itself and Ifry's breath was stolen from his lungs. Helda emerged. Ifry, in a foolish moment, thought to hide, though there was nothing nearby that would cover him. But Helda did not even glance his way. She walked past him as if he was not there at all.

He began to understand.

He walked into the temple, unafraid. The townsfolk did not turn his way. In the dawn light, he did not cast a shadow onto the floor. Jos remained by the altar. He had tried to crawl away, but the pain in his leg had finally gotten to him. Still he tried to haul his body weight across the floor, but he moved by inches only. Ifry knelt in front of Jos.

Almony hovered nearby. "We should get you inside," she said.

"Have they found him?" he gasped.

She shook her head.

"They'll struggle with the snowfall." Jos rested his forehead onto the ground. "It's not over, is it?"

"I'm afraid it is," Ifry told him. He thought that Jos heard, because he raised his head a little.

"What if he's already gone?" Jos asked.

"Then you've been spared," replied Almony, though she did not sound convinced.

"It can be over," Ifry said. He touched Jos's face. "You can win, Jos. Solyon can win. I surrender."

Across the valley, water dropped down the icicles in the waterfall. The drops gathered into rivulets. Pressure built, and the ice burst.

JOS NOTHERNINE

The trains through the mountains were infrequent, but regular. Jos travelled in a modicum of comfort in second class but kept wondering what the first-class carriage looked like. The white slopes passed by him, as fast as a flooding river. It was midwinter again, and the familiar trepidation that he associated with the holiday had returned. Tyenes did not mark it, so he had found himself almost forgetting that the auspicious day was approaching. He had only been reminded when he passed a newspaper stand and saw that 'midwinter' had been used in some half-witty headline about shipping reports.

He feared what he would find back in Racken. Would the town be decked in Solyon's golden garlands again? He scratched an itch along his jaw. He shaved daily now, and he wore his hair short. His face and neck were already rebelling against the cold, dry winds in the city, and he was in no doubt that the mountain chill would torment him yet further. He had never looked so neat and tidy in his life. He resented it, but it was the only way to be taken seriously in the city.

The conductor walked down the carriage, announcing that Racken would be the next stop. The tension in Jos only built. He took a look at his fellow passengers. He had been surprised to find so many of them. They were service folk, maids and footmen and chefs and servers. There was not a farmhand among them.

A girl in her twenties, wearing a functional dress, leaned over to speak to him.

"Do you know what to expect when we arrive? I've heard it's quite the hub for the season."

Jos found himself affronted. "I've been to Racken before. I know it quite well."

"Oh, what are you going for? I was in service in the city, but you know how it is these days. The old families can't afford to keep people on like they used to."

"I'm going to sell off some old land. The papers have already gone through, but I've to pack up some personal items."

The girl shrank back, realising that she was not speaking to a peer. She frowned, as if she could not imagine why a property owner would be travelling second class. They lapsed the train's arrival into the station in silence.

The station was not as he anticipated. He had expected to see the roof of Almony's house, but a haughty station building with a clock tower blocked it from view. A station master in a smart green suit blew on a whistle and gestured to the train driver.

Jos gathered his bag and cane and descended to the platform with the rest of them. He halted, observing the edifice, as people streamed around him.

"Sir, the hotel is across the platform bridge," the station master yelled at him, and he was taken aback.

"I'm going that way." He pointed up the slope towards his own house. The station master shrugged, confused, but not willing to press the matter any further. Jos troubled himself with how best to leave the station. Tall iron fences had been erected, and he could not spot the gate.

"Do you need help?" the station master asked him.

"Why have they turned this into such a maze?"

"The hotel is that way." He pointed again. The train was pulling away, giving Jos a view of the town.

Or what was left of it. The main street was towered over by a new building. It looked like an edifice from the city, with a pointed iron roof and gilded spandrels. In shining letters down the front was written 'HOTEL'.

He was diverted. He followed the stream of tyenes onto the bridge over the railway. It was apparently no longer acceptable to walk over the tracks. He tried to guess which buildings had been flattened by the hotel's construction. Most of the main street appeared to be there. Upon the crest of the bridge, he realised that the temple was gone. The steeple had once been the highest structure in Racken, and now there was no sign of it.

He trudged across the railway bridge, and over a well-groomed path free of snow. It led right to the hotel door and nowhere else. The other passengers from second class were ushered by a uniformed worker to a back entrance. Jos peeled away from them, choosing instead the glazed front doors, which were marked with Townsend's name in golden lettering.

He regretted his choice as he crossed the threshold. The soft carpets hushed his footsteps and wall-length mirrors reflected his image back at him. He caught one glance at the other guests and knew that his tyenes clothes would not be good enough.

He attracted a few glares from fur-lined, pearled, and tweeded guests.

He picked up his pace as well as he could manage with his cane and found the front desk. The bespectacled man behind it made a quick assessment of Jos and asked in a clipped tone:

"What can I do for you, sir?"

"I - uh..." He realised that he did not know what she did here. "Is Eldersie in?"

"Excuse me?"

"Is Eldersie here? Eldersie Toft?"

"Who should I say is calling?"

"Joseph Nothernine."

"Sent from whom?"

"No one. She isn't expecting me."

"If you don't have an appointment, I'm afraid you will struggle to see her."

"I can wait. I'm not on a schedule. Can you just tell her that I'm here?"

"I'll see what I can do, Mr Nothernine," he said, in a manner that made Jos believe that he had sorted it to the bottom of his priorities. He gestured for Jos to move away from the desk.

Feeling like a recalcitrant child, he found a lonely armchair in a corner. He sat down with his suitcase set across his knees.

As he waited, no other guests came to sit by him. He watched them descend a wide staircase and relax with newspapers or cigarettes, but they did not invite him into conversation. None of the staff stopped by to offer him a drink. He was half grateful.

The day waned. He gazed about the foyer. There were multiple chandeliers. He had never imagined that he would be in a room with more than one chandelier. They were not even dusty. He looked and looked for a single silken cobweb, but there were none.

The sun began to go down. He thought he might hear the raised voices of the midwinter ceremony, but he heard only the records chosen by the Eldersie's guests. He leaned his head on his hand.

"Sir, we are going to have to ask you to leave."

He hadn't meant to fall asleep. There were two men standing over him, both wearing embossed tie pins.

"I haven't seen Eldersie yet."

"I suggest you call back and make an appointment. She's a very busy woman."

"I'm not here for very long," he protested. "I can't come through without saying hello."

"You can leave her a message," suggested one of them. "Unless you want to book a room."

"No. I can't afford a room. I have a house here."

"Surely you can leave Miss Toft your address."

"There is no address, but she knows where it is."

"You could write that in your message."

"No. I'm sure she wouldn't come," he admitted. The rift had grown too wide between them.

The hotel workers frowned at each other.

"Sir, you really do have to leave."

Knowing when he was beaten, he fixed his cane into his hand and made to stand.

"Jos Nothernine, as I live and breathe."

The workers stepped back in surprise. Behind them, dressed in a white snow suit and dark goggles, was Oriana Townsend. She had evidently just been on the piste, as snowflakes still clung to her hair.

She approached him with energy that he felt was entirely misplaced in his arrival. She waited patiently for him to struggle to his feet, leaning heavily on his cane.

"Jos is an old friend of Elsie's," she explained. "I'll take you through for tea. Have you been waiting here long?"

"No." He lied.

She beckoned for him to follow her. The staff fell away with a sort of deference he might ascribe to a benevolent king. He limped alongside her to a lift with marble-effect sides and a man inside to operate it.

"Elsie lives on floor five," Oriana told him.

"Elsie?"

"Oh, I've gotten so used to it. I forget sometimes that it's not proper."

The lift operator keyed on the fifth floor without being asked.

"What brings you back to Racken?"

"I'm making good on that promise to your brother."

"Ah. His avalanche defences. He'll be able to use that piste finally. It's the best way to get down from those slopes."

"He's sworn to demolish my house, so I've come to clear it out."

"Oh," she sounded solemn. "You grew up there, isn't that right? Elsie told me so."

"I did."

"Must be hard." She let that thought linger. The lift halted and the operator pulled the door back. Oriana led him into a corridor with pinstripe carpets and mahogany panelling. "Elsie," she called. "Look who crawled out of the woodwork."

Eldersie was halfway down the corridor, in conversation with another blazered employee. If Oriana had not called her by name, he would not have recognised her. Her hair was short, set in fashionable curls that he knew would have taken her a great effort. She wore cosmetics like the stars of the silver screen. She had a velvet dress that was wine red and without even a spot of lint marring it. There was not a blemish or a torn seam on it. She wore dark stockings that had no ladders. She was not Eldersie as he had known her.

"I'll pick this up later," she told her companion. "I've more important things to attend to." The man left obediently, as Eldersie assessed Jos's appearance. "Jos, I almost didn't recognise you."

"You're one to talk."

She blushed.

"Let's get the kettle on, all right?" said Oriana. She moved towards a bright door.

Eldersie's apartment, such as she called it, was larger than Oriana's four floor townhouse had once been. She had wide windows that looked over the southern slopes and a balcony that was shut up for winter. She had heavy curtains with golden cords, and a kitchen that was so clean he was sure that she did no cooking inside of it.

Oriana made them tea, which he found odd, but Eldersie made no comment on it. They sat in her parlour, and Jos tried to avoid touching the uncreased fabric of his armchair as much as he could.

"You've done well," he said, a little bluntly.

"I wrung Townsend for all he was worth," replied Eldersie.

Oriana chuckled, as she returned and set down the tea tray. "That you did. He didn't half send me a lot of letters about it."

"I think I proved my worth to him," Eldersie said, proudly.

"She got the locals on side," boasted Oriana.

"What's left of them," Jos muttered. There was a moment of silence.

"You're right. Some have left. Others have adapted. Don't mourn what we lost, Jos."

"How can *you* say that?" he asked.

"I had a change of heart."

"You chose a fine moment to do that. You could not have done so a second before?"

"Don't speak to her like that," said Oriana.

"No. He's right, Ori. I chose the wrong moment to help Ifry. He's allowed to be upset about that."

He would rather that she wasn't so reasonable. He would rather that he was able to scream and shout at her. He stood.

"Jos, where are you going?"

"I need some water."

"I can get it for you," Eldersie insisted.

"No." He was already halfway to the kitchen. "I'm not helpless."

She organised it much the same as she always had. He found the mugs easily. There was running water now, though this convenience was of no comfort to him.

Her knife set was hung on the wall. They had belonged to her mother, he knew. She had placed one inside his coat. She had failed to place one in his hand. The full set was hung on the wall.

He hobbled back to the parlour without his water.

"Where did you find the knife?"

It was a testament to how long they had known each other that she knew what he meant without clarification.

"We found it on a cliff. Above your house. There was a lot of blood."

"And there–" His voice broke. "There was no other sign of him?"

He dropped into one of her chairs. He hadn't wanted to cry in front of her, but it was becoming an inevitability.

"I wanted to keep looking for him. But my leg–"

"As soon as the thaw came, the urgency just died," Eldersie confirmed. "I'm so sorry, Jos."

"I know you are."

"Ori, can you give us a second?"

Oriana left without complaint, explaining that she had to return to her ski school.

"What are you doing now?" Eldersie asked him.

"If I was a fitter man, I might have joined the railway crews. I'm doing what he used to. I was never that good at my letters but I've got to do something that keeps me off my feet."

"I'm glad you've found purpose."

"It's a living, not a purpose," he spat.

"I suppose that's why you came back."

"I came to get my mother's curtains and my father's cup."

"Don't mourn the world we lost, Jos. I don't. I'm going to become the person I choose, rather than what I had to be."

"That's a luxury, isn't it? I do mourn them. I got lost coming here - I shouldn't get lost in my hometown. This place spat me out. Our whole way of life, gone. We could have done without the gods, but what else? Did we have to lose it all?"

Her look softened. "Stay here tonight. Tomorrow, I'll show you something important."

He agreed. His leg pained him too much to climb to his house. She showed him to a bedroom that was smaller than her own. He recognised the bedstead.

"This was your parents'." It had once been relegated to the attic of her house, and now it was relegated to her guest room. "Where is your father?"

"I have no idea." She did not seem troubled.

Like the rest of her new belongings, Eldersie's skis were expensive. They were varnished to a shine, and had clean leather straps. He had never found the need to keep skis looking that fine. One might as well polish a rake.

She had a suit much like Oriana's for the outing, too. He guessed that they bought them at the same time, Oriana in white and Eldersie in red.

She led him, with a contingent of early bird guests, to a chairlift built where Almony's barn had been. From this angle, he could see her house still standing further down the valley. It looked much the same as it had, but Townsend had added bright floral murals and window boxes. They were what tyenes wanted to think of peasants.

"Mr Townsend rents it out," Eldersie explained as she saw him looking at it. "Rich parties who want a little independence. It's popular. He wants to buy up more of the farmhouses for the same."

Jos snorted to express his disapproval. "The house where Peter lived, and now rich folk swan about in it."

Eldersie ignored this statement. "How is Almony?" she asked.

He took his time thinking over an answer. Almony worked at the train station in the city, selling tickets from a hole in the wall. When he passed by her kiosk, he always stepped in to say hello. Sometimes he caught her smiling and chatting with her customers. However, when she saw him, she returned to an expression of well-practised sadness.

"She's fine," he said.

They arrived to the front of the chair lift queue.

"Must we?" he asked Eldersie. "Can we not just walk all the way up?"

"Is your leg suddenly better?" she sniped at him.

He took her point and went quiet.

The chairlift picked them up by their behinds. The cables groaned, and he could see all the chairs rocking in the wind.

"Don't people fall out of these?"

"They know that skiing has risks."

"Townsend must have a robust insurance policy."

He felt his stomach drop as they shuddered along the cable.

"What is your plan here?" he asked. "I've not been able to ski since I did my leg in."

"I thought you would need to see this."

"I've seen this view a thousand times and more. I preferred it when there were fewer of these beetles scurrying about," he said, referring to how he saw the rich folk on the pistes below.

The cold stiffened his bad leg. He should not have let Eldersie talk him into anything. The piste below led to his house. He had marked it with Ifry. A red string was staked across trees by the entrance, presumably because Townsend did not have insurance to cover avalanches.

The chairlift made its ponderous ascent up the mountain and Jos sank into the seat. Eldersie pinched him, and he batted her hand away.

"Look there," she pointed to a spot below them. She indicated a place between two rocks. He saw nothing amiss. She hit him again. "He's there."

He saw a flash of blue. Something was behind the rocks.

"A monster?"

"No." She pointed again. He looked, craning his head to watch the spot that was quickly shrinking. He saw the head and shoulders of a person, who raised an arm in greeting.

"One of your guests get lost?"

"No, it's him. It's Ifry."

"You've lost your mind."

"Look again."

Despite himself, he turned back, but the figure was already lost to sight.

"Eldersie, please don't do this."

"Don't do what?"

"Don't show me visions. Don't try to give me comfort. It doesn't help me."

They were approaching their final destination. The seat in front of them tipped its passengers out onto the slope.

"I am not fooling you," Eldersie insisted, "and lean on your good leg. We'll go down the easy run."

He followed her instructions, though he hadn't needed them. The chairlift deposited him on the side of the slope, and he nearly tumbled on his bad leg.

Eldersie guided him to the edge of the piste. The couple who had been behind them set off down the slope with giddy shouts.

"I think I'll go to mine," he told her.

"You aren't supposed to go that way."

"I risked avalanches every day. This is still my land." He tried to storm away, but he couldn't move as fast as he once could.

"I can't let you go alone."

"These mountains haven't changed."

"You have. Look at you. You aren't the man who used to hunt janros over these peaks."

"I need to be alone."

"I wasn't lying to you," she said, "about Ifry. People have seen him. Usually around here." She caught the chairlift operator by the arm. "Tell him about the ghost."

The operator seemed prepared rather than perturbed for this kind of question. "Strange fellow. You know he's a ghost because he doesn't leave footprints."

"What does he look like?"

"Young-ish. Blonde hair. Blue cloak."

"Yellow coat?" Jos asked.

"Yes."

Eldersie gave Jos a knowing look. He began to make his way towards his home. She followed.

"I've got to do this one alone, all right?" he asked.

"I don't think I should leave you."

"If I fall, I'll just crawl down the mountain again. Didn't bother me before."

She frowned, as if to confirm that it had bothered him and she knew it.

He pulled away. She caught his arm.

"It might not help you, seeing him again," she said.

"Why do you still have your mother's kitchen knives?"

She paused to think about it.

"This isn't an accusation," he clarified. "Why do you keep them, if not to have that last piece of her?"

She ignored the question. "I'll see you back at the hotel."

He nodded, though he didn't intend to return.

He swore all the way down to his house, and he did not see Ifry once. He was convinced that Eldersie had been peddling false promises. Like every winter, the house was buried up to the eaves with snow. He dug out the smallest amount of snow needed to crawl inside, then collapsed over the threshold and curled up on the floor.

He lay there for quite some time. It was cold. No one had visited since he had been there with Ifry. The cup he had used still sat on the sideboard. The bedclothes were still rumpled, as if he had just left them.

Jos hobbled around his house, wishing that he had brought his cane with him. He made good on the promises he had made to himself. He took down the curtains from inside the box bed. He found the goblet that his father had inherited. It had once been inscribed with something, but the words had long been rubbed away. He packed up the crockery and the cutlery. He found all of the handkerchiefs that his mother had embroidered with her initials. There was not much left of her dowry, nor did he know what he would use it for, but he could not bear to imagine his mother's linens being thrown away with the rubbish. When he had finished packing, it all fit in one sack that he could fix to his back.

He waited in the house for most of the day. He ate the food he had brought in his pockets, little that it was. He wanted to savour the house, though he realised that it was a rather stupid activity. He was sitting in an empty house, with nothing to do. He left home, knowing it was the last time, while the sun gilded the sky. He had wasted the day on longing.

He did not attempt to ski back. He cursed himself for having missed the afternoon train. Now he would have to return to the hotel and beg a bed for another night.

The powder was deep. The other slopes were slippery, cut with the lines of the skiers who had already gone past. Here, on this slope, he was alone. If he had his gun on his back, and no pain in his leg, he might have been about to go on a hunt.

Yet as he passed through the trees, he saw the cables of a gondola. It looked like a postcard.

He allowed himself one last moment to wallow. He was going to start his new life. With Townsend's money, he could travel. He did not know where yet, but he thought he might start at the coast. He allowed himself one last look at the mountains that had raised him. He knew he was being foolish.

Movement caught his eye. He expected gargin lurking under the snow and feared that he would be attacked without a shotgun to protect himself. Yet a man stood there, head and shoulders above the snow, partially concealed between two rocks. No tracks led to that spot.

"Hello?" Jos called.

He was sure that the man heard, because he raised his hand. Jos had seen him before, as he rode the chairlift. He wore a cloak, blue as summer skies. He had a yellow coat that Jos knew well.

"Ifry," he called. He tried to run towards him, but his leg would not allow it. Jos struggled through the drifts towards him, but Ifry seemed to become no closer. "It's me, come here."

Ifry did not move. He lowered his hand.

He was not there. Jos halted. The sun's rays shone through Ifry's form, like stained glass. Not knowing what else to do, Jos waved back. The sun descended, and all sight of him was gone.

The doors of the hotel were locked by the time he stumbled back there. He beat the door with his fist while he shivered. He hadn't been forced to crawl, but he'd stopped and leaned on trees more than he liked. Eventually, a steward with a sour expression opened the door.

"Sir? Can I call someone for you?"

Jos pushed past him.

"Eldersie is expecting me," he proclaimed. "Fifth floor, I know where it is."

Eldersie welcomed him into her home with neither surprise nor resentment. In silence, she indicated her guest room, then turned back to her bedroom, where Oriana waited in the doorway.

When Jos woke again, he felt hungover, though he hadn't had a drop of liquor.

"You look dire," said Oriana with half a smile upon her face. She poured him coffee without being asked. He accepted it. "What happened to you yesterday? Eldersie was up half the night."

He grunted. "You've seen the ghost on the mountain?"

"Unfortunately, yes." She raised her hand towards him, as if she was thinking of giving him a comforting pat on the shoulder but thought better of it. "Well, this place has opened my mind to things outside of the ordinary. Ifry's still out there."

"I can't help him, can I?"

Oriana chewed over the next moment.

"Have you not thought about how he ended up there? And how winter ended at all?" she asked.

"Wouldn't you say that it ended on its own?"

She shook her head. "What happened to believing in mighty Solyon? You have met him, Jos. So have I." Her certainty surprised him. "He's been seen since but Lady Winter has not shown her face."

Jos did not think that unusual. She was no doubt dithering once more.

"Don't do this to him," said Eldersie. She stood in the doorway to her bedroom. Her hair was set again. Her lipstick was exact, as were the lines of her stockings down the front of her legs. Jos felt underdressed.

"Don't do what?"

"Peddle your theories."

Oriana sipped her coffee in lieu of a reply.

"What do you mean?" asked Jos. The idea of it was half-formed inside his head. He knew it was desperate.

"Don't say anything more, Ori," warned Eldersie. "Jos, when are you going back to the city?"

Her question made him remember his flat in the city with the mouldy ceiling, his single dining chair, and the stained mattress he'd inherited from the previous owner.

"The next train is at ten o'clock," finished Eldersie.

"I won't impose much longer," he promised her.

"Good. I wouldn't want you to lose time in the city."

She departed into her bedroom, leaving Jos alone with Oriana once more. Jos glanced out of the suite's impressive windows, where the mountains seemed like a distant painting.

"Ifry had a knife on him. We found blood, and we found a body in the snow," she said.

"Eldersie said you didn't find him."

"We didn't find him, did we? There was someone else on the mountain."

Jos considered saying farewell to Eldersie. He saw her speaking closely with a steward in a velvet coat. It wasn't an ideal time to interrupt her. She would understand later when she found her kitchen knife missing once again.

He attracted many eyes as he crossed town. He had swapped his stuffy city clothes for his father's old coat, and he knew he was presenting a rustic image to the prim visitors he passed. His cane added to the effect, perhaps making him appear to be a wizened local. Regardless, he found himself more comfortable than he had been in a year.

The path to the waterfall was arduous. His bad leg was useless, and he tired far too easily. He pressed on. Wind ripped through the valley, freezing his fingers to the rock as he climbed. When he reached the top, he rolled onto his side and rested. He turned to his head to one side to see his hometown below him. The shape of it was the same, but the details were different. The street was clear of snow, even in the height of winter. The cables of chairlifts were strung over the slopes like cobwebs.

He staggered to the clearing. It was snowy and untouched even by wildlife. He sat down on the log at the centre and let his cane fall into the snow. He waited.

"I didn't think you would return," said Solyon. His voice sounded distant, as if he was at the end of a tunnel. Jos concentrated on it, and tried to remember what it was to be connected to the god.

He came into view as if he stepped through a blizzard, though the air was free of snow. For the first time, Jos considered what Solyon might have been like as a person. He wasn't as tall as Jos, nor as broad, though he held himself as if he were. He had a strong widow's peak and a front tooth that was crooked.

"I didn't intend to," admitted Jos. "But some callings cannot be left behind."

Solyon nodded. "It's only fair, though I thought you were lost forever. I can't quite say that I'm glad to see you here. I have a new elect, and soon summer will be won."

"Do you know what happened to Volana?" Jos asked.

An odd expression flashed over Solyon's face, though it was only for a moment.

"What could have happened to Lady Winter? What concern is it of mortals?"

"I suppose none, but I wondered if you were aware. I know what happened to her." He felt around inside of his coat and found the handle of Eldersie's knife. "I know what will happen to you," he promised.

He plunged the knife into Solyon's side. Solyon wheezed and was too surprised to say anything more.

Jos found himself uninterested in the last thoughts of the man who had shaped their lives so. For a moment, Jos felt the hot sting of Solyon's blood against his hand, then darkness overtook him.

Thaw came to Racken slowly. The tyenes used the pistes until mud showed through the snow. Eldersie waved them onto the train with good humour, though she welcomed a summer of fewer guests and more rest. Drops from melting snow fell from trees like rain. The brook below the waterfall flowed neatly and watered the livestock who roamed the grassy slopes. In summer, Racken was quiet, the chairlifts obsolete. The town half-remembered that it was a place where people farmed and knew all their neighbours.

The god of summer failed to show his face. He wandered, dreamlike, through the hills where he was now trapped, calling a familiar name. The people of Racken, so used to the whims of their gods, half-expected Solyon to return, though they dared not speak his name. Summer parted with muted fanfare, turning into a rainy autumn. The god of summer felt the return of the cold and remembered a little of himself. He crossed the valley and the railway line that had altered his life, and climbed the slopes. He found a house he remembered, though it was buried in snow. Behind the windows, he saw the flickering of a fire, and the outline of a face he knew well.

The elect became forgotten, like a soap bubble in water. In time, the gods of summer and winter lost their names, and were remembered only in moments, like the feeling of being warm by a fire, or the look of sunlight over snow.

THE END

ACKNOWLEDGEMENTS

We always think that writing a book is a solo effort. Every day of me sitting alone on my laptop comes with someone else reading, editing, offering advice, or just being patient with my nonsense.

I'd love to thank my wonderful editor Adie Hart for all her work, advice, and support.

Many thanks to writing friends and critique partners: Charlie, Fox, Oliver, and Leo; as well as beta readers: Kat, Olivia, and Valentine.

I would also like to give my most effusive thanks to the stone of destiny, and pray that one day in future I will get to tumble it.

ABOUT THE AUTHOR

Ash Parker was put on this earth to do two things: make mischief and write stories. Fortunately, they're not out of stories yet.

When they're not writing, they spend all their time taking up new crafts, playing the sims, and visiting niche museums.

WS - #0160 - 030924 - C0 - 203/127/26 - PB - 9781068754111 - Matt Lamination